ABOUT THE AUTHOR

Nancy Carson lives in Staffordshire and is a keen student of local history. All her novels are based around real events, and focus on the lives and loves of the people of the Black Country.

By the same author:

Poppy's Dilemma
The Railway Girl
The Dressmaker's Daughter
The Factory Girl
A Family Affair
Daisy's Betrayal
Rags to Riches

NANCY CARSON

A Country Girl

avon.

AVON

A division of HarperCollins*Publishers*
1 London Bridge Street,
London SE1 9GF

www.harpercollins.co.uk

HarperCollins*Publishers* 2017
Copyright © Nancy Carson 2017

1

Nancy Carson asserts the moral right to
be identified as the author of this work

A catalogue record for this book is
available from the British Library

ISBN-13: 978-0-00-817354-8

Typeset in Minion by Palimpsest Book Production Ltd, Falkirk, Stirlingshire

Printed and bound in Great Britain by CPI Group (UK) Ltd, Croydon, CR0 4YY

MIX
Paper from
responsible sources
FSC™ FSC® C007454
www.fsc.org

FSC™ is a non-profit international organisation established to promote
the responsible management of the world's forests. Products carrying the
FSC label are independently certified to assure consumers that they come
from forests that are managed to meet the social, economic and ecological
needs of present and future generations, and other controlled sources.

Find out more about HarperCollins and the environment at
www.harpercollins.co.uk/green.

A COUNTRY GIRL

Chapter 1

'Aye up, the Binghams are coming through the lock,' Kate Stokes cried provocatively, knowing it would rouse Algernon, her brother, from his sun-induced reverie.

As soon as she'd heard the clip-clop of a horse's hoofs and attendant voices, Kate had rushed to peer over the garden fence to see who was on the towpath of the canal which ran alongside. There was some personal motive in this, too – it could have been Reggie Hodgetts. Till that moment, she had been stooping down to tend their father's vegetable patch, creating the illusion that she was a homely girl, which she patently was not. She was, however, extraordinarily pretty but with a tongue like a whip, and her relationship with Algernon was, at best, thorny.

Algernon had seemed unflappable as he leant against the back door of the lock-keeper's cottage where the siblings lived with their mother and father. His face was sedately and serenely turned upward to receive the warmth of the spring sun. But, on hearing the news that the Binghams were coming through the lock, his heart missed a beat and he was at once stirred into a renewed vigour. The Binghams, you see, had a particularly lovely daughter, and he duly rushed to the fence to join Kate to gain sight of her. Sure enough, he spotted Seth Bingham leading his strong little horse as it pulled their pair of narrowboats towards the lock gates.

1

Kate flashed a knowing look at her brother. 'I thought that might get you going.'

'Why should the Binghams get me going?' he protested, feigning indifference. 'You were pretty quick off the mark yourself . . . to see if it was the Hodgettses, I reckon.'

'The Hodgettses ain't due past here till Tuesday.'

'No, but you sprang up quick enough, just in case it was that scruff Reggie,' Algernon countered. 'So you'll just have to wait till Tuesday, won't you, before you can go gallivanting off with him?' He glanced at his sister disdainfully. 'Reggie Hodgetts ain't much of a catch, is he?'

'Mind your own business,' Kate replied, at once rallying. 'You're interested enough in Marigold Bingham, the daughter of a scruffy boatman. I've seen you. Every time she comes a-nigh you're up, ogling after her. You can't keep your eyes off her.'

Algernon – who answered more readily to Algie – replied calmly, 'She's different. She looks nice. She's got something about her. I'd like to see her without her working clothes on.'

'Pooh, I bet you would, you dirty sod—'

'I didn't mean *that*. I mean I'd like to see her in her Sunday best—'

'Huh!' Kate exclaimed suspiciously. '*I* know what *you* mean. And you'm already a-courting Harriet Meese . . . You ought to be ashamed.'

'Ashamed?' he protested defensively. 'Why should I be ashamed? I ain't promised to Harriet Meese.'

'You could do worse.'

'And you could do better,' Algie replied, as he scanned the towpath opposite for sight of Marigold.

'Oh, well,' remarked Kate loftily, 'We all know Harriet's face ain't up to much.'

'Neither is yours,' Algie responded with brotherly disparagement. He would never let Kate believe he considered her nice-looking.

Kate reacted by bobbing her tongue at Algie, but he ignored her and watched the progress of the Binghams. Hannah Bingham, Seth's wife, was at the tiller, steering the horse boat, the leading one of the pair which they used for their work. Hannah, he perceived, was not like the usual boatwomen. For a start, he had an inkling that she was not narrowboat born and bred. She did not wear the traditional bonnet of the boatwomen, which fell in folds over their shoulders and back, like a ruched coal sack, and which was about as appealing. She had large, soulful dark eyes, and was blessed with high cheekbones; a handsome woman still, who must have been a rare beauty in her youth. The Binghams seemed a cut above many of the boat families. Their boats were spruce and shining, and always looked freshly painted with the colourful decorations that were traditional among their kind. They obviously took care. They stood out.

A child was crawling at Hannah's feet, tethered with a piece of string to prevent him falling into the canal. Various other sons and daughters, all youngsters, watched the proceedings, scattered randomly aboard the second narrowboat which they towed, known as the butty. A lark hopped about in a bamboo cage, set between tubs of plants which stood like sentries on top of the cabin.

'I can't see Marigold,' Algie complained. 'Is she there?'

'There . . .' Kate pointed impatiently. 'Opening the sluice. Hidden by the hoss . . .'

He shifted along the fence and caught sight of Marigold Bingham bending over the mechanism, a windlass in her hand as she deftly opened the sluice that let water into the lock. Her dark, shining hair was pinned up, giving an elegant set to her neck. Algie was glad she never seemed to wear those hideous bonnets either. He waited, his eyes never leaving her until he was blessed with a rewarding glimpse of her lovely face. She walked jauntily back towards the boat swinging her windlass, the breeze pressing her thin dress against her body, outlining her youthful figure and slender legs. She patted the horse as she went, and Algie basked in the sunshine of the smile that was intended for her father.

'How do, Mr Bingham!' Algie called amiably, rather to draw Marigold's attention than Seth's. 'And you, Mrs Bingham.' He touched the peak of an imaginary cap as a mark of respect.

Seth Bingham turned around and addressed himself to Algie, whose face was bearing a matey grin as he peered over the lock-keeper's garden fence. 'How do, young Algie. It's a fine day for it and no mistake.'

'Mooring up here for the night, Mr Bingham?'

'Soon as we'm through the lock, if there's e'er a mooring free,' the boatman replied. 'It is Sunday, lad, after all's said and done.'

'God's day of rest, they say.'

Seth scoffed at the notion. 'For some, mebbe.'

To Algie's delight, Marigold flashed him a shy smile of acknowledgement. He saw a hint of her mother in her lovely face.

'How do, Marigold.'

'Hello, Algie.' She answered coyly, avoiding his eyes further as she stepped onto the butty.

Their strong little horse took the strain, stamping on the hard surface of the towpath to gain some purchase as it hauled the first narrowboat, the horse boat, slowly into the lock. Steadily, surely, the narrowboat, lying low in the water under the burden of its cargo, began to inch forward away from the side of the canal. Marigold had nimbly jumped aboard and was at the tiller of the butty now, waiting for her turn to enter the lock.

Algie watched, unable to take his eyes off her. She was as statuesque as the figurehead of some naval flagship, but infinitely more lovely. Her back was elegantly erect, her head, which he beheld in profile now, was held high, showing her exquisite nose to wonderful advantage. He reckoned Marigold was about eighteen, though he did not know it for certain. For years he'd kept an assessing, admiring eye on her, catching occasional glimpses as she passed the lock-keeper's cottage. In the last three years he'd noticed how her looks and demeanour had really blossomed. It was as if he'd been patiently watching the petals of a slow-blooming rose unfurl into flawless beauty. She stood out from the other boatmen's daughters; always had. In fact, she stood out from all the other daughters of men, boatmen's or not. She was endowed with a natural grace where others seemed ungainly. If girls like Marigold, who lived and worked on the canals, hadn't escaped to work in the factories by the time they were eighteen, it was generally because they were wed to a boatman, some by the time they were sixteen. Yet there was never anything or anybody to suggest that Marigold was spoken for. Maybe Seth was too protective of her, realising her worth, saving her for somebody with finer prospects. It would not surprise him.

'You look a picture today, Marigold,' Algie called, giving her a wink. 'In your Sunday best, are you?'

She smiled shyly and shook her head as the butty slid forward. 'Just me ornery working clothes, Algie,' she answered in a small but very appealing voice.

'Then I'd like to see you in your Sunday best. I was just saying to our Kate—'

'Algie! Kate!' Clara Stokes, their mother, was calling from the back door. 'Your dinners are on the table. Come on, afore they get cold.'

Algie rolled his eyes in frustration that his attempt to get acquainted with the girl, his intention to flatter her a little, was being thwarted at such a critical moment. 'I gotta go, Marigold. Me dinner's ready. See you soon, eh?'

'I expect so.'

He hesitated, aware that Kate was already making her way across the garden to the cottage. 'Are you due down this cut next Sunday, Marigold?' he asked when Kate was out of earshot, endeavouring to sound casual.

'Most likely Tuesday, on the way back from Kidderminster.'

'That's a pity. I'll be at work Tuesday. I shan't see you.'

Marigold smiled dismissively. It was hardly of grave concern to her. Yet she wondered if his questioning her thus meant he was interested in her. The thought at once ignited her interest in him and she looked at him with increasing curiosity through large blue eyes, hooded by long dark lashes.

'So when shall you pass this way again on the way to Kiddy?' he persisted.

'Dunno,' she replied, and he noticed that she blushed. 'We might not be going to Kiddy for a while. We might be going up again' Nantwich or Coventry. It depends what work me dad picks up.'

'Course . . .' He sighed resignedly. Yet her blush somehow uplifted him, and he wallowed in the wondrous thought that he might appeal to her too. But he had to go. His dinner was on the table. 'Ta-ra, then, Marigold. See you sometime, eh?'

She smiled modestly and nodded, and Algie strolled indoors for his Sunday dinner, disappointed.

'Our Algernon's keen on that Marigold Bingham, our Mom,' Kate said over the dinner table.

'You mean Hannah Bingham's eldest?'

Kate nodded, unable to speak further yet because of a mouthful of cabbage. She chewed vigorously and swallowed. 'Fancies her, he does.'

6

'He'd be best advised to keep away from boat girls,' Clara commented with a warning glance at her only son. 'Anyroad, what's up with Harriet Meese?'

'Nothing's up with Harriet Meese as I know of,' Algie protested. 'I just think as Marigold Bingham's got more about her than the usual boat girls.'

'Fancies her rotten, he does,' Kate repeated, with her typical sisterly mischief.

'So what?' he said, irritated by her meaningless judgement of him and of his taste in girls. 'There's nothing up with fancying a girl, is there, Dad? It ain't as if I'm about to do anything wrong.'

'Just so long as you don't.'

'Chance would be a fine thing,' Algie muttered inaudibly under his breath.

Will Stokes was, for the moment, more concerned with cutting a tough piece of gristle off his meat than heeding the goading remarks of his daughter. 'Oh, she's comely enough, I grant yer,' Will remarked, looking up from his plate, the gristle duly severed. 'But looks ain't everything. Tek my advice and stick with young Harriet. Harriet's a fine, respectable lass. She'll do for thee. Her father's in the money an' all, just remember that.'

'Money that'll never amount to much if she's got to share it with six sisters, come the day,' Clara commented, as a downside.

'Well, our Kate can talk, going on about me and Marigold Bingham,' Algie said, aiming to turn attention from himself. 'She often wanders off with that Reggie Hodgetts off the narrowboats . . .'

Kate gasped with indignation and blushed vividly at what her brother was tactlessly revealing. She gave Algie a kick in the shins under the table.

7

Noticing her blushes, Will eyed his daughter with suspicion. ''Tis to be hoped you behave yourself, young lady, else there'll be hell to pay – for the pair o' yer.'

'Course I behave meself,' she protested, glancing indignantly at Algie. 'You don't think as I'd do anything amiss, do you, Dad?'

'I should hope as you got more sense.' He wagged his knife at her across the table in admonishment. 'Else I'll be having a word with young Reggie Hodgetts. You've been brought up decent and respectable, our Kate. Tek a leaf out o' your mother's book, that's my advice. There was never a more untarnished woman anywhere than your mother. That's true, ain't it, Clara?'

'I had to be,' Clara replied, conscientiously trimming the rim of fat off the only slice of roast pork she'd allowed herself. 'Else me father would've killed me.'

Algie pondered his mother, trying to imagine her as a young woman being courted by his father. She had been a fine-looking young girl then, he knew it for a fact. For a woman of forty-two, she still held on to her looks and figure remarkably well. It was obvious from whom Kate had inherited her looks and figure, which the local lads found so beguiling.

He finished his dinner quietly, deeming it politic to add nothing more to that mealtime conversation. His thoughts were still focused on young Marigold Bingham. He'd noticed her blushes as she'd spoken to him and he wondered . . . Algie was in no way conceited, and he rejoiced in the thought that maybe he had aroused her interest. If so, it was the greatest event of his life so far. Damn his dinner being ready at exactly the moment when he was about to get to know her a little better. Right now she and the rest of the Binghams would be moored in the basin outside. So frustratingly close . . .

So conveniently close . . .

There was a knock on the door. One of Seth Bingham's

younger children had come to pay the toll for passing through the locks. Algie waited. His mother moved to clear away the gravy-smeared plates, cutlery, pots and pans, which she stacked in an enamelled bowl. When she and Kate were in the scullery washing them, and his father was sitting contentedly in front of the parlour fire with his feet up and his eyes shut, attempting his Sunday afternoon nap, Algie silently and surreptitiously made his exit . . .

Although Algernon Stokes was twenty-two and a man, yet still he was a boy. Or, more correctly, a lad. His view of the world had not yet been tainted by its artificiality and pretence, so he lived life, and looked forward to what it offered, with a naïve enthusiasm that emanates only from youth. He was largely content. His upbringing had been conscientiously accomplished by a strict yet fair father's influence, endorsed and abetted by his mother, although she still followed him around the house dutifully tidying up behind him. His sister Kate was tiresome, though, a bit of an enigma to Algie, and a nuisance to boot. Algie was utterly fascinated with girls in general, yet absolutely not with Kate in particular.

He had drifted into a sort of half-hearted courtship with a girl called Harriet Meese, only because she had shown an interest in him in the first place, an interest which flattered him enormously. She was not his ideal, however, hence his half-heartedness. His ideal girl was beautiful of face and figure, utterly desirable and unresisting, even prepared to risk ruin by submitting to his sexual endeavours; qualities he believed he might find in Marigold Bingham. Many young men his own age were married, some had even fathered children already, and Algie envied their access to the sensual pleasures they must all enjoy in their marital beds, for such pleasures had always been denied Algie. The thought of spending the rest of his life in celibacy horrified him, but from his point of view, it looked as if he was destined to, unless he could nurture some girl who appealed to him physically, and who would be unreservedly willing. Thus, he had become preoccupied with finding a solution. It boiled down to this: he was twenty-two already, but he hadn't lived. Therefore, he might as well still be seven.

Marriage would have offered a solution, but not marriage to Harriet. Oh, most certainly not to Harriet. He would not rule marriage out completely, though, if the right girl came along. On the other hand, why not simply bypass the institution of marriage altogether? The world offered too many pretty girls to have to settle for just one, especially one whose face was particularly uninspiring, as Harriet's was. He knew from hearsay that there were plenty of girls willing enough to partake of those delectable stolen pleasures for which he yearned, if only such girls were not so damned elusive. He was thus inclined to believe they all inhabited another planet. They never seemed to pass his way at any rate. Even if they did, he would hardly be able to recognise such qualities in them as he was seeking, and why would they look at him twice anyway? He was nothing special, or so he thought. He did not like his own face, he did not like his dark, curly hair, nor his tallness, nor the shape of his nose either. How could he possibly appeal to women? Especially the sort of women that would interest him, who just had to be pretty, with appealing, youthful figures. Otherwise there was no point to it.

That same spring Sunday afternoon in 1890 was one of those delightful, lengthening days which herald the approach of summer. Soft sunlight caressed distant hills, and already the air, bearing the sweet smell of greenness, had a mollifying summer mildness about it. A warm breeze gently flurried the fresh crop of young leaves that bedecked the trees after their long winter nakedness. A flock of pigeons flapped in unison overhead, wheeling gleefully across the blue sky in celebration of their Sunday release into glorious sunshine.

The lock-keeper's cottage was situated alongside the Stourbridge Canal at an area called Buckpool, set between the township of Brierley Hill and the village of Wordsley, yet no great distance from either. The warmth of the spring day cosseted Algie as he stepped out into it. He stopped to appreciate it, closing his eyes, wallowing in the sensual touch of sunlight, a touch too long denied him. For a fleeting moment, he allowed himself the luxury of a sensual thought; that of spooning in the long grass of some secluded meadow with Marigold Bingham. He'd had his eye on her for so much longer than he would care to admit.

Hannah, Marigold's mother, saw him and waved amiably.

'Still having your dinners?' Algie called, disappointed that he'd mistimed his appearance and they hadn't finished.

'You gotta eat sometime,' Hannah called back. 'Even on this job.'

'I'm just on me way to the public.' He felt it necessary to explain his presence, even though the explanation was an instantly conjured lie, in case Marigold, who could be listening, might rightly presume that he was seeking her and decide to avoid him. 'I just fancy a pint after me dinner.'

'You'll very likely see Seth in there.'

'That's what I was wondering,' he fibbed.

'He always likes a pint or two *afore* he has his Sunday dinner.' She said the word *afore* as if she considered it strange that Algie should want to drink beer after his dinner. 'I don't mind keeping it warm in the stove till he gets back. He likes the beer at the Bottle and Glass, you know. It's why we moor up here when we'm this way.'

'I might see him inside then.' Algie smiled openly, hiding the disappointment at his inability to speak to Marigold without making his intentions obvious to her mother, and continued on the route to which he'd unthinkingly committed himself.

He walked the few yards to the next lock, which lay beneath the road bridge. There, he left the canal, crossed the road to the public house and entered the public bar. Inside, he leaned against the varnished wooden counter and greeted the publican, Thomas Simpson, familiarly. He ordered a tankard of India pale, peering for a sight of Seth Bingham through the haze of tobacco smoke. Seth was sitting on a wooden settle that echoed the shape of the bowed window, in conversation with two other men whom Algie recognised as boatmen also. They acknowledged him, but he thought better of getting drawn into their company, for it was likely to cost him the price of three extra tankards. He decided to give himself fifteen minutes to finish his beer, by which time he imagined Marigold would have finished her dinner. Then he would try again to catch her while her father was still supping and, perhaps, her mother's back might be turned.

The huge clock that adorned one wall had a tick that sounded more like a clunk, even above the buzz of conversation, and Algie watched its hands slowly traverse its discoloured face. He drank his beer, trying to appear casual and unhurried, as if he was really enjoying it. He dropped the occasional greeting to various men who approached the bar for their refills, and took a casual, benign interest in a game of bagatelle other men were playing.

Eventually, he stepped outside once more into the unseasonably warm sunshine of the late April afternoon. At the bridge he hesitated and, for a brief second, watched the sun-flecked sparkle of the water as it lapped softly against the walls of the canal, plucking up the courage to approach Marigold again. He looked for the *Sultan* – the name given to Seth Bingham's horse boat – and saw Marigold conscientiously wiping down the vivid paintwork of its cabin with a cloth. It was now or never, he thought as he rushed onto the towpath and approached.

'Busy?' he asked, beaming when he reached her.

She looked up, momentarily startled, evidently not expecting to see him, and smiled when she realised it was Algie Stokes again. 'It has to be done regular, this cleaning,' she replied pleasantly.

Up close – and this was as close as he'd ever been to Marigold – she was even more lovely. Her skin was as smooth and translucent as finest bone china. Her eyes seemed bluer, clearer, and wider; her dark eyelashes so unbelievably long. Her lips were upturned at the corners into a deliciously friendly smile, and he longed to kiss her. The very thought set his heart pounding.

'Your two boats always look sparkling,' he remarked with complete sincerity. 'I've noticed that many a time.'

Marigold smiled proudly. 'It's 'cause me mom's so fussy. She don't want us to be mistook for one o' them rodneys what keep their boats all scruffy. And I agree with her.'

'Oh, I agree with her, as well. Where's the sense in keeping your boat all scruffy when you have to live in it?'

'And while we'm moored up, what better time to clean the outside?' she said with all the practicality of a seasoned boat-woman. 'We'm carrying coal this trip and the dust gets everywhere.' She rolled her eyes, so appealingly. 'You can taste it in your mouth and feel it in your tubes. It gets in your pores and in your clothes. It's the devil's own game trying to keep anything clean when you'm a-carrying coal.'

'I can only begin to imagine,' he replied earnestly, truly sympathetic to the problem. 'I know what it's like in our coal cellar. It must be ten times worse on a narrowboat. So you're bound for Kidderminster, you reckon?'

13

'Tomorrow. We'll be on our way at first light.'

'What time d'you expect to get there?'

Marigold shrugged. 'It's about dinner time as a rule. Then it depends if we can get offloaded quick. Some o' them carpet factories am a bit half-soaked when it comes to offloading the boats, 'specially if you catch 'em at dinner time. Me dad likes to wind round and get back. He gets paid by the load, see? Me, I don't mind if we get stuck there till night time. We do as a rule.'

'Got much more cleaning to do?'

'Only a bit. We've all got our jobs, but I've nearly finished mine for today.'

'Fancy a walk then?' Algie enquired boldly, seizing the moment.

'A walk?'

He nodded. 'I could take you a walk over the fields or up the lanes, if you like. You must be sick o' looking at the cut all the time.'

She instantly flushed. 'I'll have to ask me mom.'

'Ask her then.' Algie's heart skipped a beat. Marigold had agreed in principle. This was significant progress. All that stood in the way now was perhaps her mother.

Marigold smiled with blushing pleasure, and nipped inside the cabin.

Algie could no more help flirting with a pretty girl than some people can help stammering, but he had not the least intention of breaking anybody's heart. For a start, he did not take himself seriously enough, he was not good-looking enough to succeed. The desire to elicit a smile from a pretty face was strong within him, however.

Hannah Bingham nipped out, holding a limp dishcloth. 'You want to take our Marigold a walk?' she asked, not unpleasantly.

14

'If you've got no objection, Mrs Bingham,' he answered with an apologetic but appealing smile. 'She says she's finished her jobs.'

'I got no objection, young Algie, as long as she's back well afore sundown.'

'Oh, she'll be back well before then, Mrs Bingham, I promise.'

'Then you'll have to give her a minute to spruce herself up if she's going a walk.' She turned and spoke to her daughter in the cabin. 'Our Marigold, change into another frock if you'm going a walk with young Algie.' She turned back to Algie and smiled. 'Why don't you come back in ten minutes when she's ready, eh?'

Algie grinned with delight. 'All right, I will, Mrs Bingham.'

He could hardly believe his luck. Marigold had agreed to accompany him on a walk, and her mother had sanctioned it. The prospect of getting the girl alone had, till that moment, seemed an improbable dream, but a dream he'd diligently clung to. He sauntered back to the lock-keeper's cottage, thrilled. Maybe he had a way with women after all. Maybe he did possess some fascination or irresistible power over girls, despite his doubts. For so long he'd thought it unlikely. There was a suspicion meandering through his head – he knew not from where it came – that, in any case, a handsome face was not the be-all and end-all for women, but he just didn't have the experience to know if it was true. For the time being, it was enough that some young women blushed when he spoke or smiled at them; and he made a point of smiling at all those girls who were pretty, whatever their station in life, rich or poor. If they thought he was ugly or uninteresting they could always turn their heads and ignore him. Yet they seldom did. Only the very stuck-up ones, and stuck-up girls he could not be doing with anyway.

He returned home to wait. Over the fireplace in the parlour was a mirror. He stood in front of it and looked at himself, but was not impressed. He straightened his necktie and tried unsuccessfully to smooth his unruly curls with the flat of his hand.

'Oh, there you are,' his mother said, suddenly appearing from the brewhouse outside. 'Fetch some coal up from the cellar for me, our Algernon. There's scarcely any left in the scuttle.'

'Can't our Kate do it?' he complained. 'I'll get all mucked up and I'm going out in less than ten minutes.'

'Our Kate's busy changing beds ready for washing day tomorrow,' Kate herself chimed in, opening the stairs door as she descended with a bundle of sheets and pillowcases in her arms. 'You wouldn't be very pleased if your bed was black as the devil from the coal in the cellar, would you? Anyroad, where are you off to of a Sunday afternoon?'

'Mind your own business.'

'I'll mind me business if you'll fetch the coal up.'

'Oh, all right,' Algie muttered reluctantly, knowing it to be futile attempting refusal to these two women, ranged against him with a singular will. He opened the door to the coal cellar and disappeared with the scuttle.

His task completed, he went to the brewhouse and washed his hands. Behind him, his mother complained that he had left damp coal dust on the scullery floor, which he'd brought up from the cellar on the soles of his boots.

'Our Kate should have gone down,' he called back. 'She's got smaller feet than me. She wouldn't have made so much mess.' Then, before he could be asked to perform any more disagreeable chores, he dashed outside and returned to the Bingham's butty, waiting for Marigold to appear.

From where the Stokes's cottage stood, the canal descended

by a series of locks and basins towards Wordsley. You could see, beyond the massive cone of the Red House Glassworks, green valleys swooping between wooded hills and leafy glades. Towered and spired churches clad in the ivy of centuries dotted the landscape, as well as cosy homesteads, farmhouses and stately old manor houses. Nibbled pastures, where sheep and cattle grazed, receded into the hazy green distance. It was a sight that cheered Algie's heart.

Over the hill in the opposite direction lay, incongruously, a black industrial wilderness of slag heaps, mines, glassworks, and forges. Foundries and ironworks belched forth acrid brown smoke from great chimney stacks, and red flames from open hearth furnaces, even on this warm spring Sunday. Humble little red-brick houses shared this desolate eastward outlook, sparsely dotted with clumps of coarse grass, railways, viaducts and bridges as well as the interlinking canals with their locks, basins and wharfs. This was the astonishing land-scape of the Black Country, that broad tract of man-made bleakness that lay roughly between the opposing boundaries of Wolverhampton to the west and Birmingham to the east. Yet it held as much diversity as you could reasonably assim-ilate in a month of Sundays if you cared to look. Prosperity lived symbiotically with hardship, as did culture with ignor-ance, good taste with bad, virtue with wantonness, respectability with indelicacy, and hard work with idleness. Significantly, the Black Country, for all its limited size, gener-ated a disproportionate amount of the enormous wealth that enabled Britain to wield such undeniable power in the world.

Marigold popped her head round the cabin door.

'Oh, you're back then.'

'Yes, I'm back. Are you ready yet?'

She nodded and stepped out onto the gunwale, then onto the towpath. 'I just wanted to change me frock, wash me face

17

and tidy me hair up a bit. Me mom don't like me venturing away from the cut in me working frock. She says it's common to do that.'

He smiled his response, looking her up and down. The frock was plainly cut in muslin and well-washed, the floral pattern almost faded from enthusiastic and frequent laundering, but she looked divine, and there was no shame in cleanliness. It fitted her perfectly, enhancing her slender figure. Her dark hair had been hurriedly brushed and re-pinned, and it was tidier now.

'You look ever so nice,' he said sincerely.

'Thank you. So do you in your Sunday best suit. Where you taking me?'

'There's a path over the fields to Kingswinford. I bet you've never been there?'

She shook her head. 'Not if there ain't a cut what goes there. Is it far?'

'A mile, a mile and a half, maybe – nothing really. But it's a fine afternoon for a stroll.'

'What is there at Kingswinford? Anything special?'

He shrugged. 'Nothing special. It's just a nice walk over fields.'

He led her back to the bridge he'd just come from and onto the lane that led first to Wordsley.

'I'm thinking of getting meself a bike,' he announced, in a manner calculated to impress.

'A bike? Blimey.' Marigold sounded duly impressed. 'I wish I could have a bike. I could ride to the locks ahead of our narrowboats and open 'em ready. It wouldn't half save us some time.'

'Suggest it to your dad. Mebbe he'll buy one.'

'I doubt whether he could afford one. How much do they cost?'

'About twelve pounds with pneumatic tyres. Pneumatic tyres are best. You don't want solid tyres.'

'Twelve pounds?' Marigold queried with disbelief. 'That's a fortune. Me dad would never spend that much, even if he'd got it to spend.'

'I've been saving up for ages.'

'Where would you moor it?'

'In our shed.'

'What d'you do for a living, Algie, if you can afford to buy a bike?'

'I make brass bedsteads at Sampson's up at Queen's Cross in Dudley. A bike will be handy for getting to work and back.'

'Don't you fancy being a lock-keeper, like your dad?'

'Me? Nah. It don't pay enough wages. You get your coal for free, granted, and a house to live in as part of the job, but I wouldn't be a lock-keeper. Me dad gets called out all hours. I wouldn't want that. I like peace and quiet. How about you, anyway? D'you intend to spend the rest of your life on the narrowboats?'

'Depends,' she said with a shrug.

'On what?'

'On whether I marry a boatman – a number one, f'rinstance.'

'A number one? You mean a chap who owns his own boats?'

'Yes.'

'Got your eye on anybody?' he asked, dreading her answer, but grinning all the same.

She shrugged again. 'Dunno. Nobody on the boats at any rate.' She gave him a sideways glance to assess his reaction.

'Who then?'

'I ain't telling *you*.'

So there was some chap in her life. Damn and blast. It was naïve of him to think otherwise, a girl like Marigold.

'Go on, you can tell me.'

'There is a chap I like,' she admitted. 'He ain't a boatman. He works at one of the carpet factories in Kiddy. He's one that generally helps offload us.'

'Oh, I see . . . So the crafty monkey sees to it as you don't get offloaded on the same day as you arrive. That way, you have to stop over till next day, eh? Then you can meet him at night. Is that it?'

Marigold blushed, smiling in acknowledgement of the truth of Algie's astute assessment.

'So you'll be doing a spot of courting tomorrow night, then?'

'I suppose. It depends.'

'What's his name?'

'Jack.'

'Shall you tell him about me?'

'What is there to tell?' She glanced at him again.

'Well . . . you could tell him that you went a walk with another chap.' He regarded her intently, and caught a look of unease in her clear blue eyes at the idea.

'So, what about you?' she asked, intent on diverting the focus from herself. 'Do you have a regular sweetheart?'

'Me? Not really.'

'Not really? You either do or you don't.'

'There's this girl I'm sort of friendly with . . . But it ain't as if we're proper sweethearts . . . I mean we ain't about to get wed or anything like that.'

'And shall you tell her you been a walk wi' me this afternoon?'

'Like you say, there's nothing to tell, is there?'

'Not really . . .' She smiled at his turning the tables back on her. 'What's her name?'

'Harriet.'

'That's a nice name.'

'Maybe we should get Harriet and your Jack together, eh?'

She laughed at that. 'Is she pretty, this Harriet?'

'Nowhere near as pretty as you. Jack would fancy you more than Harriet, for certain. I do at any rate . . . I've been noticing you for a long time . . . seeing you come past our house from time to time. I've often thought how much I'd like to get you on your own and get to know you.'

'Have you, Algie? Honest?' She laughed self-consciously.

'Yes, honest.'

'That's nice . . . I'm surprised, though.'

'Don't be surprised. Next time you come through the lock and pay your penny let *me* know you're there, eh? 'Specially if it's of a Sunday, or if you're mooring up for the night close by. We could go for walks again then. I mean to say, the summer's only just around the corner.'

'And you wouldn't mind me asking for you?'

'Course not. I'd like you to. I'm inviting you to.'

She looked him squarely in the eye, with an open, candid smile. 'I just might then . . . And your mother wouldn't mind?'

'Why should she mind?'

She shrugged girlishly. 'Dunno . . . What if she don't like me?'

'Oh, she doesn't dislike you, Marigold. She knows your family. Lord, you've been coming through our stretch of the cut long enough.'

'How old is your mom, Algie?'

'Two-and-forty.'

'She don't look it, does she? She looks about thirty. I mean she ain't got stout or anything.'

'No, she doesn't look her age, I grant you. She looks well. We got a photo of her when she was about your age – what is your age, Marigold, by the way?'

21

'Eighteen. I'll be nineteen in July.'

'Anyway – this photo of me mom – she was really pretty when she was about eighteen. There must've been one or two chaps after her, according to the things I've heard said . . .'

'But your dad got her.'

'Yes, me dad got her. Just think, if he hadn't got her, I'd have been somebody else.'

'No, Algie,' she chuckled deliciously. 'If he hadn't got her, you wouldn't have been born. It's obvious.'

'Course I would. But I'd have been somebody else, like I say.'

She smiled, mystified and amused by his quaint logic.

'Your mom's nice-looking for her age as well, ain't she?' Algie said easily. 'It's easy to see who you get your pretty face from.'

'So how old are you, Algie?' Marigold asked, not wishing to pursue that line.

'Two-and-twenty. I'll be three-and-twenty in September.'

'So how old was your mom when she had you?'

'Can't you work it out?'

'I can't do sums like that, Algie. I ain't had no schooling like you.'

'Oh, I see.' He smiled sympathetically. It was difficult to imagine what it must be like for somebody who couldn't read, something he took for granted. 'Well, she must've been about one-and-twenty,' he said, answering her question. 'Something like that. What about your mom?'

'My mom was nineteen when she had me.'

'Nearly your own age,' he remarked.

'I reckon so,' Marigold admitted. 'She must have bin carrying me at my age.'

'So how old is your dad? He looks older.'

'He's nearly fifty.'

'Quite a bit older, then?'

'I suppose,' she mused. 'It's summat as I never thought about. Anyway, I don't see as how it matters that much.'

'Nor do I,' he agreed.

They left the lane and ambled on towards Kingswinford over fields of sheep-cropped turf, tunnelled by rabbits and sprinkled with glowing spring flowers. Young pheasants, silvery brown, fed near a stile, hardly bothered at all by the couple's approach.

'It's lovely here,' she commented. 'Maybe we should stop here a bit.'

So they sat down and talked for ages, never quite reaching Kingswinford, never stumped once for conversation. When it was time to go they returned by the high road, passing the Union workhouse which provided yet another topic of conversation. Marigold decided she liked Algie. He was easy to talk to and she felt at ease with his unassuming manner. She enjoyed being with him. He was handsome, too, and his obvious admiration of her made her feel good about herself.

'It's a pity I can't see you tonight,' he said, about to leave her at the pair of moored narrowboats, 'but I go to church of a Sunday night.'

'With your family?'

'No, with Harriet.'

'Oh . . . with Harriet . . .'

'Well, she's always been brought up to go to church.'

'I bet she's been learnt to read and write proper as well, eh?'

'What difference does that make?' he said kindly, so that she should not feel inferior to Harriet. 'Anyway, don't forget to ask for me when you're next passing, eh, Marigold?'

She shrugged. 'I might . . .'

Chapter 2

The sinking sun cast a long, animated shadow of Algie Stokes as he ambled that evening along the rutted road known as Moor Lane on his way to see Harriet Meese. To his right lay a rambling Georgian mansion, an island of prosperity set in a sea of stubble fields. The grand, symmetrical house seemed entirely at odds with the tile works, the slag heaps and the worked-out mines which it overlooked. No doubt it had existed long before its sooty neighbours had been dreamed of; a rural haven, set in bowers of peace and tranquillity. But no more. Yet it never occurred to Algie what the well-to-do occupants might think of the black, encroaching gloom of industry. He never noticed any of it, taking for granted these immovable, and probably eternal, man-made elements of the unromantic landscape.

The crimson glow from the sun at his back was augmenting the ruddiness of the red-brick terraced houses he was passing. He bid a polite good evening to a passer-by, and his thoughts returned to the golden sunshine of Marigold Bingham's natural loveliness. Yet, strangely, he was finding that he could not ponder Marigold without Harriet Meese also trespassing unwanted into his thoughts. Mental comparison was therefore becoming inevitable. Maybe it was a guilty conscience playing tricks.

Harriet was twenty years old, the second of seven daughters belonging to Mary and Eli Meese. Eli was a respectable trader who described his business as 'a drapery, mourning and mantles shop', situated in Brierley Hill's High Street, where the family also lived above the shop. Four of the seven daughters were sixteen or over – of marriageable age – but Harriet was blessed with the most beguiling figure of them all, wondrously endowed with feminine curves. She was slender and long-legged, her curves and bulges were in the appropriate places, and as delightful in proportion as Algie had ever had the pleasure to behold in or around Brierley Hill. However, to his eternal frustration he had never been privileged to know Harriet's sublime body intimately. Nor was such a privilege likely as long as they remained unmarried. Chastity had been instilled into Harriet from an early age, both at home and at church. So, despite Algie's most earnest endeavours, he had never so much as managed to unfasten one button of her blouse, nor lifted her skirt more than eight inches above her ankle without a vehement protest and an indignant thump. It was, of course, her figure which was the sole attraction, since her face was her least alluring feature.

After a twenty minute walk, Algie strolled up the entry that lay between Eli Meese's drapery shop and his neighbour, and tapped on the door. Priscilla, Harriet's older sister, a school teacher who was manifestly destined for eternal spinsterdom, answered it. Facially, she was unfortunate enough to resemble Harriet but, even more regrettably, not in figure. Her crooked lips stretched into a thin smile, yet her eyes, the most attractive feature in her face, creased into a welcoming warmth as she led him into the parlour.

'Looking forward to church tonight, Priss?' Algie enquired familiarly.

'I always do,' she responded. 'But sometimes, you know,

after I've sat and listened to the sermon, I wish I hadn't bothered. Sometimes, if it's a good sermon, I get a thrill up and down my spine, and for three or four days after I'm inspired. Once, I remember, after the vicar had preached about generosity, I took it all to heart and took a bag of bonbons to share amongst the children in my class for a few days . . . until after that they expected it every day. But on another Sunday he preached against vanity and the love of nice dresses . . . Well, I was livid. I love nice dresses, as you know, Algie.'

'Is Harriet ready, or am I in for a long wait?'

'I should sit down if I were you. She's been around the house again checking whether there's enough coal in the scuttles and on the fires, rather than leaving it to the maid. I wouldn't mind, but she always waits till it's time to get ready to go out. Besides, it's pandemonium upstairs right now, with everybody vying for space to get ready. I got ready early, you know, Algie. You've no idea what it's like, all seven of us sisters trying to get in front of the mirror at the same time, not to mention Mother, and when Mother gets there there's no room for anybody else anyway. Father got tired of waiting. He's already gone . . . How is *your* mother, Algie, by the way?'

'In good fettle last time I noticed, thanks.'

'Does she manage to get out these days?'

'Only in daylight. She won't go out at night after what happened . . .'

Priss nodded her sympathetic understanding. 'I know. Such a pity . . . But how's your father?'

'Oh, he's well.'

'What about Kate?'

'Oh, she's fit enough, the sharp-tongued little harridan.'

'Sharp-tongued?' Priss uttered a little gurgle of amusement. 'Are you joking? I've never thought of your Kate as sharp-tongued. She always seems so cheerful and pleasant, whenever I meet her.'

'Oh, she's always cheerful and pleasant to folk she doesn't know very well. You should try living in the same house.'

'But she's such a pretty girl, your Kate. I'd give anything for her looks.'

'But you wouldn't want her character or demeanour, Priss.'

'Oh, I don't know . . . People seem to like you more if you're pretty than if you're plain. Mind you, I always think that if you go to church regularly and do your duty by your neighbour, you'll find plenty of people ready to like you . . . so long as you carry yourself well and don't stoop,' she added as an afterthought. 'Anyway, I'm sure Kate's nowhere near as black as you paint her . . . Which reminds me, Algie – will you do me a favour?'

'What?'

'Would you mind asking her if she wants tickets to see the plays? It only wants a fortnight.'

'I daresay Harriet will remind me . . .'

Harriet appeared at that precise moment, wearing a white skirt printed in a delicate, blue floral design, and blouse to match. The ensemble did full justice to her figure. Because of the family's business, the Meese girls were able to indulge themselves in the latest materials and designs, and several dressmakers too were always keen to run things up for them, for the recommendations they customarily received from the family.

Harriet greeted Algie with a smile as she put on a short jacket, also white. 'I'm ready,' she announced. 'Are you ready, Priss?'

'I've been ready ages.'

'But you haven't got your hat on,' Harriet reminded her.

'Oh, but I'm not going to wear a hat, our Harriet.'

'Not wear a hat?'

'According to the journals I've been reading, London girls are no longer wearing hats. They regard them as old-fashioned, and I'm inclined to agree. Anyway, does my hair look such a mess that I should cover it with a hat?'

'Your hair looks very becoming, our Priss. I teased it for you myself. But you really ought to wear a hat. Don't you think so, Algie?'

Algie duly pondered a moment, stumped for an opinion, not really bothered one way or the other. 'Not if she doesn't want to, Harriet. Let her go to church without a hat if she wants. Who's it going to hurt?'

'But it *is* Sunday. All the ladies will be tutting.'

'Let 'em tut,' Priss said defiantly. 'I don't care.'

Harriet shrugged resignedly. 'Once she's made her mind up there's no persuading her, is there? Shall we go, Algie?'

He nodded. 'Yes, come on, then. See you there, eh, Priss? Unless you want to walk with us . . .'

'No, I don't want to play gooseberry. I'll be along with the others.'

Algie led Harriet down the cobbled entry. As they walked along High Street facing the low setting sun, he thrust his hand into his jacket pocket and Harriet linked her arm through his familiarly.

'Priss asked me to ask our Kate if she wanted a ticket to see the plays,' he said conversationally.

'Oh, yes, the plays. It's only a fortnight away and we've sold plenty of tickets already. I need to know so's I can get her one. I know how she likes to see our plays.'

'I'll ask her.'

'What about your mother and father? D'you think they'd like to come? They're ever so comical.'

'My mother can be comical,' Algie quipped. 'I'm not so sure about my father, though.'

She landed him a playful thump. 'I mean the plays, you goose. One's a farce, the other's a comedy.'

'Sounds like our house two nights running. But you know my mother never goes out of a night.'

'Oh, I forgot. What a shame that fear of a bolting horse can stop you going out of a night. It'd be a change for her, though, to go out with your father.'

'I know it would, and you know it, but she won't budge. Not at night.'

'As a matter of fact, there's something else I'm supposed to ask your Kate, Algie.'

'What?'

'Well, she's quite a pretty girl, isn't she?' Harriet admitted grudgingly, 'and Mr Osborne wants to recruit some "pretty girls" into the Little Theatre, to use *his* words. I must say, though, I was a trifle narked when I heard him say it, so was our Priss. I mean, how demeaning to *us*. Not everybody can be pretty, can they? It would be a boring old world if they were. Priss told him so as well. Well, you know our Priss . . . But you know what men are like. Anyway, he mentioned your sister by name and I said I would enquire after her. Mr Osborne would like her to come along one rehearsal night so he can assess her ability to act.'

'I'll ask her then, shall I? I reckon she'll jump at the chance to show herself off. You know how vain she is.'

'But, in the long run, it all depends whether she can act,' Harriet affirmed. 'Not how pretty she is.'

'It might divert her from that ne'er-do-well Reggie Hodgetts she seems so fond of.'

'Reggie Hodgetts?'

'The son of a boatman,' Algie explained disdainfully. 'A proper rodney. Plies the cut regular in that filthy wreck of a narrowboat his family own.'

Harriet gasped in horror. 'Oh, goodness, a boatman? I hope she's not thinking of throwing her life away on a mere boatman. A rodney at that.'

'It's coming into contact with 'em like she does,' Algie responded defensively. 'Being a lock-keeper's daughter and all that, I reckon. Mind you, some of the boat families are all right. I see a family called the Binghams occasionally. They're decent folk. Most of them are.'

'You must make Kate see sense, Algie.'

'She won't take any notice of me. You know what it's like between brothers and sisters.'

'Then I'll have a word with her when I see her – discreetly, of course.'

He considered Marigold and how Kate might reveal his secret desire for the girl, a mere boatman's daughter, if she thought Harriet was poking her nose into her liaison with Reggie Hodgetts. 'No, don't,' he blurted earnestly. 'It wouldn't do any good. Our Kate's too headstrong to take any notice of *anybody*. She'd only resent you for it. She'd think you were meddling.'

'All right, if that's what you think, Algie.'

They arrived at the door of the old red-brick hulk of St Michael's Church which stood loftily at Brierley Hill's highest point, sensing at once the cool reverential ambience as they entered. Harriet bid a pleasant good evening to the sidesman who handed her a hymn book, and made her way to the family's regular pew on tiptoe, so that her heels did not echo off the cold hard floor. Algie followed in her wake.

When the service finished the congregation gathered outside by the light of a solitary gas lamp installed above the main door; a collection of nodding bonnets, top hats and fawning smiles, all content in their self-righteousness. Some merely drifted away into the night in a random procession while others tarried, determined to elicit recognition from or conversation with the vicar, or even the curate. By now there was a chill in the air as the Meese women and Algie lingered outside waiting for the head of the family. When Eli Meese rejoined them he announced that he was going to the Bell Hotel for his customary two pints of ale, which would give him an appetite for his supper. He would be about an hour.

'I take it as you'll see me girls and me wife home safe and sound, young Algie?' Eli said patronisingly as he parted.

'Course I will, Mr Meese.'

Actually, it had occurred to Algie to leave the company of Harriet and the rest of the Meeses as soon as the service was over, with the idea of seeking Marigold again; her father was likely to be in the Bottle and Glass for the evening getting pie-eyed, so why not take advantage? But to make an unusually early departure, on whatever flimsy excuse he could quickly invent, would only draw comment and speculation after he had gone, especially when he had given Eli his undertaking to see the family home safely. So, as they ambled down the path through the churchyard to the road, he decided to exercise discretion, to remain patient and wait till Marigold's next passage through the lock at Buckpool.

While the others walked on ahead, Priss attached herself to Algie and Harriet.

'I thought the sermon tonight was a bit of an unwarranted rebuke to us all,' she commented airily. 'The vicar's wrong about God being just, you know. I hardly think He's just at all, not all the time anyway. I've come to the conclusion that He is often unjust. Look how so many good and kind people suffer, while too many evil rogues prosper. What did *you* think of the sermon, Algie?'

'Me? I didn't listen to it.'

31

'Algie was daydreaming as usual, Priss,' Harriet said with measured scorn.

'I was contemplating more earthly things,' he replied.

'Oh, but you shouldn't of a Sunday,' she reproached. 'Anyway, what earthly things?'

Actually, he'd been contemplating Marigold Bingham; her smooth skin, her fine complexion, her beautiful face and her delicious figure. She'd been the cause of a troublesome disturbance in his trousers during the sermon as he'd allowed himself to imagine her lying warm and playful with him in some soft feather bed. He could hardly admit as much to Priss or Harriet, though.

'I was thinking about the bike I'm going to buy,' he fibbed judiciously.

'Can you *afford* a bike?' Priss queried, sincerely doubting it. 'Surely they cost a fortune?'

'I've been saving up for months. Now I've got enough money to buy one.'

'But a *bike*? Couldn't your money be more wisely spent?'

'On what?'

'Well, you're two-and-twenty now. The same as me. And our Harriet is only two years younger. Have you not considered the future?'

'Priss!' Harriet hissed indignantly, digging her sister in the ribs with her elbow as they walked.

'Don't prod me, Harriet . . . I only mean to say that if you are contemplating marriage, then it would be far more sensible to save your money, rather than buy a bike.'

'Who says we're contemplating marriage?' Algie remarked clumsily. 'We've never discussed marriage, have we Harriet?'

'*You've* never discussed it with *me*.' There was a catch in her voice, which suggested antagonism at the lack of any such conversation.

'I just assumed . . .'

'Assume nothing, Priss,' Harriet said with resignation. 'Algie obviously has other priorities . . . and so have I, come to that.'

Eli Meese, Harriet's father, having risen from humble beginnings as the son of a house servant, had embarked on his road to fortune buying bolts of cloth and selling them in lengths to whoever would buy. He viewed this as a means of escaping the pits and the ironworks. His first enterprise involved the purchase of two thousand yards of flannelettes at tuppence ha'penny a yard, which he sold at fourpence ha'penny a yard from market stalls in several of the local towns. Business prospered and he rented a shop in Brierley Hill as a permanent base. Soon afterwards, he met and married Mary, from whom his daughters inherited their uninspiring faces and would, in time, also manifest her stoutness. When their first child, Priscilla, was born he bought the building which was still home and workplace to him and his family. Eli was proud of being a self-made man. He had raised himself from obscurity to his present position, one of considerable standing in the community. He had made money a-plenty and, as money always commands influence, so Eli grew to be a man of some consequence in Brierley Hill, being not only churchwarden at St Michael's but Guardian and Justice of the Peace as well. In his social elevation he sought to do his best for his daughters, and ensured that each received as decent an education as he could reasonably afford at the Dudley Proprietary School for Girls, to and from which they took the tramcar every day.

Eli was not entirely comfortable with the thought that his second daughter, easily the most appealing of those of marriageable age, could feasibly end up with the inconsequential son of a lock-keeper. He had hoped she would have set her sights higher, but was wily enough to realise that to forbid the liaison would only serve to launch it into more perilous waters, the consequences of which could be devastating and too painful to contemplate. In time, Harriet's superior education would reveal itself to both of them, and Algernon Stokes would come to recognise his social and mental inferiority – and so would she. Meanwhile, he tolerated Algernon without actually encouraging him at all. Besides, Algernon's father, Will, used to be Eli's regular playmate in those far off days of mutual impoverishment. The lad's mother, Clara, too . . . Indeed, when Clara was a young filly and Eli was a young buck with a weather eye for a potential mate, she had been a feast to the eye and a definite target. The trouble was, she was too preoccupied with his rivals and would have nothing to do with him. So he had to content himself eventually with Mary, who he'd put in the family way. Mary would never fetch any ducks off water. Her plainness, though, had proved an advantage in one respect, Eli pondered; she was never attractive enough to appeal to anybody else, which ensured her fidelity. On reflection, perhaps he had been too hasty in agreeing to marry her. The acquisition of wealth had made him much more appealing to other women – better-looking women – he'd noticed over the years.

Such were the ruminations, contemporary and nostalgic, of Eli Meese as he supped alone in the saloon of the Bell Hotel sucking at his clay pipe, his head enveloped in an aromatic cloud of blue smoke. Because he was an important citizen and a Justice of the Peace, few of the lesser locals these days considered themselves socially fit to sup in the same room with him. One man, however, walked into the hotel some little time after Eli, greeted him as an equal, and asked if he would allow him to buy him a drink.

Eli grinned in acknowledgement. 'A pint of India pale, please, Murdoch.'

Murdoch Jeroboam Osborne paid for the drinks and took them over to the table where Eli was sitting. 'You was deep in thought when I walked in, ha, Eli? Summat up?'

Eli swigged the last inch of beer that remained of his first helping, then sighed as if deeply troubled. 'What d'yer mek o' Will Stokes's lad, Murdoch?'

Murdoch pulled a stick of tobacco from his pocket and began cutting it into workable pieces with his penknife as he pondered the question. 'Can't say as I know him that well, but he seems a likeable enough lad. Ain't he a-courtin' your Harriet? I've seen him a time or two come to meet her from the Drill Hall after our rehearsals, ha?'

'Between me and thee, Murdoch, that's what's troubling me. I ain't so sure he's quite up to the mark, if you get me drift.'

Murdoch laughed. 'I seem to recall as his mother was well up to the mark at one time, ha? Still is, if you want my opinion.'

Eli grinned conspiratorially. 'Aye, you'm right there and no mistake. Proper little poppet, was Clara Bunn. Many's the time I've wished . . .'

'And the daughter takes after her,' Murdoch remarked with a twinkle in his eye.

'Ain't set eyes on e'er a daughter so far's I know,' Eli replied. 'But is that right? Another poppet? Like her mother was, eh, Murdoch?'

'The image.'

'I ain't surprised. D'you see anything of Clara these days?'

'Calls in me shop regular.' Murdoch began rubbing the pieces of tobacco between the palms of his hands to render it into shreds. 'If there's e'er a boiling fowl or a rabbit spare

I generally let her have it cheap. She's grateful for that. I've always had a soft spot for Clara.'

'She could've done a sight better for herself,' said Eli, secretly meaning that she could have had *him* if she'd played her cards right. He gazed blandly into the clear golden depths of his beer. 'She could've had the pick of the chaps in Brierley Hill – and beyond, but she settled for Will Stokes. Who'd have thought it at the time, eh? Will was never gunna be anything but a lackey to the Stourbridge Canal Company.'

'Oh, Will's a decent enough chap, but we can't all be businessmen, Eli, ha?' Murdoch scratched his chin, then took his pipe from his pocket and filled it with the shredded tobacco. 'You got your drapery and I got me butchery. But it ain't in everybody . . . So do I conceit as you ain't too keen on young Algernon's attentions to your Harriet, ha?'

'I got no intention of encouraging it, Murdoch, let's put it that way. She can do better for herself.'

'Is she took with the lad?' Murdoch struck a match and lit his pipe, his head quickly shrouded in waves of pungent smoke as he sucked and blew to get it to draw.

'I wouldn't like to say as she's took with him. It's hard to say for definite. But these attachments have a way of creeping up on folk. 'Specially these young uns what don't know their own minds. I'm afeared that afore I know it, he'll be telling me as he's got to marry her and asking for me blessing. I don't want to be asked for me blessing.'

'Aye, well when she's one-and-twenty – and that can't be too far yonder – he won't even need to ask, will he, Eli, ha? If he wants the wench he'll just do it. Anyroad, I reckon as she could do worse. A lot worse, ha? The lad's young, he's working as far as I know. He might mek summat of hisself yet.'

'Well,' pondered Eli, lifting his fresh glass of beer, ''tis to be hoped . . . Got any more o' that baccy, Murdoch? Me pipe's gone out.'

As he walked along the towpath alongside his horse, Seth Bingham whittled a toy top from a piece of wood for his children. All that remained was to find a strong switch from which to make a whip to set it spinning. He could imagine their delighted faces when he presented it to them and showed them later that day how it worked.

Marigold jumped down onto the towpath from the butty, where she had left Rose, her younger sister, in charge of the tiller. They were approaching the flight of locks at Dadford's Shed, on the way back from Kidderminster, and would soon be outside the lock-keeper's cottage where Algie Stokes lived. She began walking alongside Seth, ready to run on and open the locks ready for the ascent.

'What you makin', Dad?'

'A whip 'n' top.'

'A whip 'n' top? For the little uns?'

'It'll keep 'em occupied while we'm moored up.'

'Will it spin?' she asked doubtfully.

'Course it'll spin, when I've made a whip for it.'

'But it'll want painting, won't it?'

'It'd look better painted, I grant yer,' Seth agreed. 'But let's see if it spins all right first. If it does, we can soon paint it.'

'I'll paint it,' Marigold offered. 'With the kids. But it might be an idea to make more than one, you know, Dad. They'll want a whip 'n' top a-piece once they see it.'

Seth laughed. 'I daresay they will, but they might have to wait.'

Seth continued whittling a second or two more, when neither spoke.

'Have you got some pennies for the lock-keeper, Dad?'

Marigold asked, breaking the pause. 'I'll run on and make sure we can get through 'em all, and pay Mrs Stokes.'

Seth felt in the pocket of his trousers and fished out a handful of change. 'Here,' he said inspecting it. 'And fetch me an ounce of baccy from the Dock shop while you'm at it.'

Marigold rushed to the lock. No other narrowboat was heading towards them from the opposite direction to occupy the lock and impede their progress. Rather, the last narrowboat through the locks had come from the opposite direction so all the levels would be set for them to enter without waiting for them to empty. She opened the first lock, while Seth led the horse towards it, then made her way to the Dock shop, where she bought her father's ounce of baccy and put it in the pocket of her skirt.

She glanced back, saw their horse boat, the *Sultan,* entering the lock, and waved cheerily to Seth. She opened the next lock, then hurried to the next, amiably passing the time of day with a couple of the workmen from the dry dock that lay in an adjacent arm of the canal. A dog, from one of the rows of terraced cottages, joined her as she headed for the next lock, and she stooped down to fuss it.

'Hello, Rex,' she cooed, having become familiar with the animal over the years. She stroked it under the chin and it looked up at her with round, trusting eyes. 'I ain't got nothing for you this time. But next time, I'll bring you some bones to chew on . . . I promise I will.' The dog seemed to understand, and returned with its tail swinging, seemingly happy with the pledge, to the cottage he'd come from.

She reached the lock situated outside the lock-keeper's cottage and she was aware of her heart pounding. What if Algie was there? What if he hadn't gone to work and he was at home? She would see him again. It would be lovely to see him again so soon. Before she opened the lock, she crossed it to get to the cottage on the other side and climbed the steps to the garden and the back door. She tapped on the door and waited, scanning the well-tended garden and its crop of spring flowers that were blooming like an array of bright lamps. The door opened, and Clara Stokes greeted her, wiping her hands on her apron.

'Hello, young Marigold.'

'Hello, Mrs Stokes,' she replied deferentially. 'We'm just coming up through the locks. Can I pay you?'

'Course you can, my flower.' Clara held out her hand and Marigold dropped the pennies into it. 'Ta.'

'I was just looking at your flowers, Mrs Stokes,' Marigold said, turning round to admire them again. 'Them choolips am really pretty. I would've thought they're a bit early, though, wouldn't you?'

Clara was making out a chit for the payment, but looked up to appreciate the tulips with her. 'Yes, they're grand, aren't they? They are a bit early, like you say. Mind you, we've had some nice weather to bring 'em on.'

'Me mom likes choolips. They'm her favourite flower. And those are a lovely colour.'

'How is your mom?' Clara enquired.

'She's well, thank you, Mrs Stokes. It's her birthday tomorrow. I'd love to be able to give her some choolips. Would you sell me some, Mrs Stokes?'

Clara smiled. 'I'll do better than that – I'll give you some to take to her. Let me get a pair of scissors to cut them with.'

'Are you sure?' Marigold queried, calling after her as Clara left the scullery for the sitting room. 'I'd just as soon pay you for 'em.'

'They cost nothing to grow, Marigold,' Clara called back. 'I'll charge nothing for them. I just hope they give your mom a bit of pleasure.'

Marigold smiled gratefully. 'That's ever so kind. Thank you ever so much, Mrs Stokes.'

Clara stepped back inside the room with her scissors, and Marigold followed her up the garden path.

'How's Algie?' she asked, with becoming shyness. 'Is he at work today?'

'Oh, he's at work all right,' Clara replied, diligently picking out the best tulips and laying them on the ground as she snipped them. 'Earning his corn. At least it keeps him from under my feet.'

'I was talking to him Sunday,' she volunteered. 'We went a walk afore he went to church.'

'Yes, he said so.'

'Did he?' Marigold sounded pleased with this revelation. 'He's nice, your Algie.'

'I daresay he'd be pleased that you think so,' Clara replied non-committally.

'Does he go to church every Sunday?'

'Most. Only the evening service, though.'

Marigold felt herself blush, and was glad that Mrs Stokes was bending down with her back towards her, unable to witness it. She wanted to mention that girl called Harriet whom Algie had told her about, but had no wish to sound as if she was prying. 'I suppose Mr Stokes is out and about on the canal somewhere?' she suggested, to deflect any further focus from herself.

'He's checking the locks. You'll very likely see him as you go by . . . There . . . that's about a dozen blooms.' Clara gathered the cut tulips from the ground and stood up. 'I'll wrap them in a bit of newssheet, eh?'

'That's ever so kind, Mrs Stokes, really,' Marigold said, following Clara back towards the cottage.

'Come inside while I do it.'

Marigold followed her inside, into the little scullery. She noticed the blackleaded range, pristine and shiny, with the fire burning brightly and a copper kettle standing on the hob. In front of the hearth lay a podged rug, made from old material, the colours and textures of the cloth organised into an appealing pattern. A scrubbed wooden table had four chairs around it, and beneath the window was a stone sink. There was little enough room to move, but to Marigold, used only to the tight confines of the narrowboats' cabins, it was enormous.

She watched while Clara wrapped the tulips in a sheet of newspaper and asked again if she could pay for them, but Clara only refused with a reassuring smile. 'Take them, young Marigold,' she said kindly. 'Your mother will like them.'

'That she will, Mrs Stokes. Thank you ever so much.'

'You're welcome. Give your mother my best wishes, won't you?'

'Oh, I will . . .' She did not move, hesitating at the door, and Clara looked at her enquiringly.

'Is there something else, Marigold?

'Yes . . . Will you tell Algie I called, please, Mrs Stokes? He said to ask you to. Will you give him *my* best wishes?'

Clara smiled knowingly. She did not dislike this slip of a girl. 'Course I will.'

On the afternoon of the following Saturday after he'd finished work, Algie purchased his bicycle, a Swift, made in Coventry. His intention was to ride it all the way back from the shop in Dudley, stopping at the Meese home on the way to show Harriet; he reckoned she'd still be working in their shop. At Holly Hall, however, a mile away, the chain came off, which gave him a nasty jolt since he was pedalling hard, trying to see how fast he could make it go. As a result, he banged his crotch awkwardly against the crossbar, making him wince with the sheer agony of it. With little alternative but to try and ignore the pain, he dismounted, glad of the opportunity to bend down and nurse his crotch as he replaced the oily chain carefully around the cogs. The job done and the pain slowly receding, he continued on his way, more gingerly this time. He would have to adjust the chain properly when he got home.

'Oh, I say,' Harriet exclaimed with approval when she saw the bicycle. 'Can I have a go on it?'

'Yes, but mind how far you're going.' He was afeared that the chain might come off again, and had visions of walking miles trying to retrieve both the machine and Harriet if that happened. 'And don't get the wheels stuck in the tramlines, else you'll be off.'

Harriet cocked her leg over the saddle, in what was for her, a most unladylike but forgivable manner. She set off from the kerb shakily, emitting a girlish scream of apprehension. 'I won't go far,' she yelled over her shoulder.

Algie watched with a grin as she rode no more than a hundred yards in the direction of Dudley, then turned around with a series of inelegant wobbles. She didn't have the confidence to use the pedals and merely scooted with her long legs astride the crossbar, the hem of her skirt unavoidably hoisted to an immodest height so untypical of her.

'I'll get arrested with my skirt up like this,' she said, laughing, as she returned to his side. 'No wonder girls don't ride these contraptions.'

'All you need is to wear a pair of trousers instead of a skirt,' he suggested with a measure of practicality.

'Don't be a goose,' she scoffed. 'Who ever heard of such a thing!'

'Well, I think it's a good idea. These machines can be just

as useful for women as for men . . .' The comment was prompted by what Marigold had said about cycling ahead of the narrowboats to open the lock gates. 'But you women won't benefit unless you change your attitude.'

'What attitude?'

'Your attitude to what you're prepared to wear. Trousers, for instance. Women used to wear trousers when they worked in the mines.'

'Some women that worked in the mines wore nothing at all, I've been told,' Harriet responded with scorn. 'But you won't find me going about with no clothes on. Anyway, can you imagine what I'd look like?'

'Lord, I daren't even begin to think about it, Harriet . . .'

'Seen the Binghams lately, Dad?' Algie asked one day on his return from work. 'I ain't seen 'em for a fortnight.'

Will Stokes looked at his son with a wry smile. 'They ain't been a-nigh, Son, not since that day your mother laid bare me tulip patch. Still got your eye on young Marigold, have yer?'

Algie smiled. He was able to admit such things to his father. He was able to talk to him about anything. 'Could be,' he answered with a wink. 'Would you blame me?'

'Nay, she's a bonny wench, our Algie. I can understand you being interested. But if you seriously want her, don't lead young Harriet on, that's my advice. It ain't fair. She's a decent young madam is Harriet, and I'm sure she wouldn't do that to you. So be straight with her.'

'Oh, I intend to be, Dad. Once I'm sure of me standing with Marigold. I got no intention of two-timing her.'

Will shook his head. 'If you got no serious intentions for young Harriet, you should tell her straight, Marigold or no Marigold.'

'I know, Dad, but I don't want to burn all my bridges . . . Not yet . . .'

On the Wednesday night, that last day in April, Algie accompanied his sister Kate to the town hall, which had been hired by the Brierley Hill Amateur Dramatics Society for two performances that week of two plays; *My First Client*, a farce, and a comedy called *You Know What*. Both had the audiences guffawing with laughter.

After the show, Harriet returned from backstage and formally introduced Kate Stokes to Murdoch Osborne, the society's leading light and principle organiser.

'Me and Miss Stokes are already partly acquainted, ha?' Murdoch said pleasantly. 'Her mother's a regular customer of mine, and I see Miss Stokes most days on her way to work at Mills's cake shop, ha, Miss Stokes? I can see a definite resemblance to your mother, you know . . . and that's a compliment, ha?'

Kate blushed becomingly. 'Thank you, Mr Osborne.'

'Now then. Harriet here tells me as you might be interested in joining our little theatre group.'

'I never thought about it before, but I think I'd like to try it,' Kate replied coyly, imagining receiving the audience's applause and appreciation, as rendered so enthusiastically for tonight's star, Miss Katie Richards.

'Have you been involved in drama before?'

'Never, but I'm a quick learner. I learn poetry ever so quick. I would soon learn me words, I'm sure. I'd really like to try me hand at it.'

Murdoch Osborne was watching her, fascinated by her large, earnest brown eyes. 'You're a very pretty girl and no mistake, Miss Stokes . . . and we're fortunate to be blessed with so many lovely girls in our Little Theatre.' He glanced at Harriet for a look of approval at his flattery. 'We start casting and rehearsing next Wednesday for our next production, a play entitled *The Forest Princess*, set in North America. I'm keen that we cast the part of Pocahontas right.'

'Pocahontas?' Kate queried, wide-eyed.

'Pocahontas was a beautiful Red Indian princess who lived in the seventeenth century, Kate . . . Can I call you Kate?'

'Oh, yes. Course.'

'Good. Thank you . . . I was about to say . . . I would be very grateful if you could attend.'

'Thank you, Mr Osborne, I will. What time should I get here?'

'Oh, we don't meet here. We meet in the Drill Hall—'

'Why don't you call for me on the way, Kate?' Harriet suggested helpfully. 'You could walk up with me and our Priss.'

'Oh, right,' Kate beamed. 'Could I?'

'Course. It's always best, I think, if you can go somewhere strange with somebody you know. Especially the first time.'

'Then that's settled,' said Murdoch Osborne with a triumphant grin. 'I shall look forward to seeing you then.'

Chapter 3

Clara Stokes, although adamant about not leaving her fireside in the evenings, was often faced with no alternative during the day. Her family, not unreasonably, expected to be fed, and not every morsel of food was delivered to the lock-keeper's cottage. So she had to make trips to Brierley Hill High Street for meat and provisions, for fruit and the fresh vegetables her husband could not grow himself.

Sometimes, they would be given a rabbit, a wood pigeon, or even a pheasant, any of which would make a cheap yet perfectly acceptable dinner. A bunch of beetroots or a bag of freshly dug potatoes often arrived with the compliments of a neighbour, but you could never depend on it. In fact, if you waited for somebody to donate something like that, just when you needed it, you'd go hungry. It was a perverse principle which dictated that such offerings were only ever presented when the larder was full, never empty. Naturally, Will Stokes would return the favour whenever possible; his rhubarb was coveted for its flavour and gentle but very definite powers to relieve the Buckpool and Wordsley constipated, and his kidney beans were noted for their tenderness and delicate taste when in season. Most neighbours, as well as many of the boat families, would trade food in this way at some time.

It was the second Thursday in May and a fine sunny

morning when Clara Stokes set out on her walk to Brierley Hill, shopping basket in one hand and gallon can in the other to hold the lamp oil they needed. The clatter and smoke of industry was all around her. Carts, conveying all manner of finished goods and raw materials, drawn by work-weary horses, passed in either direction, the drivers nodding to her as they progressed. Small children with runny noses, too young yet for school, were as mucky as the dirt in which they scrabbled; poorly clad and often even more poorly shod.

Clara went first to the cobbler to pick up a pair of Will's shoes that had been in for resoling.

'I heeled 'em an' all,' the bespectacled shoe mender informed her. 'It's on'y an extra tanner, but it'll save yer bringin' 'em again to be done in another six weeks.'

Clara smiled at his enterprise and paid him one shilling and ninepence, the cost of the repair. Next she visited the ironmongery of Isaiah Willetts, who filled her gallon can with lamp oil after she'd bought candles, washing soda and a bar of coal tar soap. She passed the drapery, mourning and mantles shop of Eli Meese, avoiding glancing into the window lest old Eli himself spotted her and she had to stop and talk. So that she could buy elastic, since Will's long johns were hanging loose around his waist and needed new to make them grip him comfortably again, she visited the haberdashery store a little further along the street. At the greengrocer's she bought a cabbage, onions, carrots, parsnips, spuds and a cauliflower, by which time she was laden down, and she hadn't been nigh the butcher's yet.

Of course, there was a queue at the butcher's. But at least she could rest her basket on the sawdust-covered floor, along with her gallon can and the sundry brown carrier bags she'd acquired. Murdoch Jeroboam Osborne, in his white, blood-flecked cow gown and navy striped apron, greeted her warmly as soon as she entered, and she watched him chop off the heads of various fowl, a hare and several rabbits, until it was her turn to be served.

'A quart of chitterlings, please, Murdoch,' Clara requested familiarly.

'A quart of chitterlings coming up, my princess,' Murdoch repeated with an amiable grin. 'How're you today, Clara my treasure, ha?'

'Aching from carrying all this stuff,' she replied, nodding in the direction of the purchases at her feet. 'Who'd be a woman fetching and carrying this lot?'

Murdoch smiled sympathetically and turned around to scoop up a quantity of chitterlings, which were pigs' intestines that had been washed and cooked and were a tasty delicacy. 'Have you got e'er a basin to put 'em in?' he enquired.

'Not today, Murdoch. Can you lend me summat?'

'I've got a basin in the back, my flower. Just let me have it back next time you come, ha?'

'Course I will.'

'I'll go and rinse it out.' He returned after a minute with the basin and filled it with the chitterlings. 'Anything else, my flower?'

'Will fancies a bit of lamb for his Sunday dinner.'

'Leg or shoulder, ha?'

'Shoulder's tastiest, I always think, don't you?' Clara asked.

'Just as long as it ain't cold shoulder, ha?' He winked, and Clara chuckled as he set about carving a section of shoulder. 'By the way, Clara, I was glad to see as your daughter's decided to join the Amateur Dramatics Society,' he added, while he worked. 'She'll make a fine little actress. Nice-looking girl, ain't she, ha?'

'For Lord's sake, don't tell her so. She's already full of herself.'

'Gets it off her mother – the good looks I mean,' he

commented warmly, heedless of the other women queuing behind her. 'I don't mean the being full of herself bit, 'cause you ain't full of yourself, are you, Clara, ha?'

Clara tried to pass off his compliment with a dismissive giggle. She always felt a warm glow talking to Murdoch Osborne, for they'd known each other years, and he made her feel like a young girl again. 'Oh, you do say some things, Murdoch.'

'I mean it an' all.'

'I bet you say it to all your customers.'

Murdoch Osborne grinned waggishly. 'For all the good it ever does me . . . Here's your shoulder of lamb . . .' He held it up for her to inspect. 'Does that look all right?' Clara scrutinised it briefly then nodded her approval. 'Anythin' else, my flower?'

'I'd better take four nice pieces of liver for our tea. And I'll have two pounds of bacon, as well.'

She watched him slice the bacon and the liver expertly, and wrap it. When he'd bundled all her purchases together in newspaper, he took his blacklead pencil from behind his ear and tallied it up, writing the amounts on the corner of the wrapping. Clara watched, trying to discern the upside-down amounts, then paid him. He handed the package to her, but Clara had no room in her bags for anything else.

'I'll struggle with this lot.'

'Tell you what,' Murdoch said, not oblivious to her difficulty and keen to curry favour, 'why don't you let me deliver that lot to you later?'

'That's ever so kind of you,' Clara answered with a grateful smile, 'but I shall need the liver for our tea.'

'Then just take the liver and whatever else you need, and let me deliver the rest.'

'I don't want to put you out, Murdoch,' she said, as he pulled out the parcel of liver and handed it to her.

'It's no trouble. Now give us the rest o' your tranklements.'

She handed him the stuff she didn't need and kept the bag containing the vegetables and the liver she'd just bought.

'There you go. I hate to see a lady struggle. Soon as I've shut the shop, I'll have a ride over to your house and deliver this little lot.'

'I'm that grateful, Murdoch.'

'Think nothing of it. Enjoy the rest o' your day, and I'll see yer later.'

It was just turned half past six when Murdoch delivered Clara's shopping. The magical aroma of liver and onions still lingered in the air as Will Stokes answered the door to him.

'By God, that smells good, Will,' Murdoch commented. 'I've brought the shopping. Your missus was struggling to carry it all when she left me shop, so I offered to bring it.'

'She told me,' Will replied, and took the basket and a carrier bag from him. 'And it's very decent of yer, Murdoch. Fancy a cup o' tea while you'm here?'

'I could be tempted. I'd be lying if I said otherwise.'

'Come on in then.'

Murdoch entered and Will led him into the small parlour. Clara and Kate were at the stone sink in the scullery, but ceased their chores as soon as they realised Murdoch Osborne was a guest.

'Thank you for delivering me things, Murdoch,' Clara said when she saw him. 'It's service you don't expect these days.'

'No trouble at all.'

'Our Kate, put the kettle on,' Clara suggested. 'Let's make Murdoch a nice cup o' tea. Can I get you something to eat, Murdoch?'

'I don't want to put you to any trouble, Clara, ha?'

'One good turn deserves another,' Clara responded, while

Kate went out to fill the kettle and Murdoch's eyes followed her. 'I bet as you've had nothing all day.'

'It's true enough.'

'Well, I can imagine how it is for a man who ain't been widowed long. It must be hard for yer, Murdoch, since your poor wife passed on, but you need to look after yourself.'

'Oh, I don't go without, Clara.'

'Well, let me get you something to eat. What d'you fancy? It's a pity all the liver's gone – it was beautiful, by the way . . . I could always fry you bacon and eggs . . .'

'Bacon and eggs?' Murdoch said with a smile of enthusiasm, directing his comment to Will Stokes. 'What more could a man ask for but bacon and eggs and a bit o' fried bread, ha?' Will noticed how Murdoch cunningly added the fried bread to the meal. 'But only if it's no trouble, Clara.'

'I told you, it's no trouble.'

'You're a lucky chap, Will, having a wife who's handy with the frying pan.'

'I'm reminded of it every day, Murdoch,' Will answered dismissively.

Kate returned and hung the kettle on a gale hook over the fire. It spat and hissed as a few drips of water fell into the burning coals.

'So how's our Kate shaping up in this here amateur dramatics group?' Will enquired as Clara set about frying Murdoch's treat.

'Oh, she'll do very nicely, Will. I've got her to agree to play the part of Pocahontas in our next play.'

'Poker who?'

Murdoch guffawed. 'Pocahontas. A celebrated Red Indian princess from the Americas who became a Christian and married an English chap. She was very beautiful, if recorded history's to be believed. Kate's got the right sort of colouring and figure for the part, I reckon, ha? She read it well an' all, when we tried her out for it.'

'I'm glad to hear as she's some use for summat,' Will remarked dryly. 'Even if it is only acting up.'

Kate, who had been preening herself in the mirror, turned round and shot daggers at her father, who she felt had not only never understood her, but had signally failed to realise her latent talents as well.

'Oh, I reckon she'll be a valuable asset to us,' Murdoch affirmed. 'We've been lacking a wench with your Kate's qualities.'

'What qualities am they then?'

'Good looks, a certain grace . . .'

'Gets it off her mother and no two ways,' Will said.

'I wouldn't argue with that, Will . . .'

At that, Algie appeared and stood in the scullery doorway wiping his hands on a towel.

'How do, Mr Osborne,' he greeted cordially. 'You brought our stuff then?'

'Aye, I brought it, lad . . . We was just talking about your sister Kate and the Little Theatre.'

'Oh? Think she'll be any good?' he asked, as if it would be a surprise if she were.

'I reckon so. I was just saying as much to your father. And if you reckon you could act as well, young Algie, we'd be pleased to welcome you into the group, a good-looking young chap like you.'

'No thanks, Mr Osborne,' Algie replied unhesitatingly. 'I don't think it's my cup of tea, all that reciting lines. Anyway, I see enough of Harriet Meese without going to the Drill Hall with her as well. It's a good excuse for a night off when she goes to the Amateur Dramatics rehearsing.' He winked knowingly at Murdoch, who smiled back conspiratorially. 'But if

52

our Kate enjoys it, all well and good . . .' He turned to his mother in the scullery. 'What's that you're cooking, Mother? It smells good.'

'I'm doing bacon and eggs for Mr Osborne. He's had nothing to eat all day, poor chap. He's got nobody to look after him, like you and your father have.'

'Can you drop some in the pan for me as well? I'm famished.'

'But you ain't long had liver and onions.'

'I know, but I'm hungry again.'

Clara tutted. 'I can't seem to fill him up, you know, Murdoch,' she announced over her shoulder.

'Oh, I was just the same when I was his age,' Murdoch replied. 'It's to be expected, ha?'

The following Sunday, Algie decided to put his new bike, his pride and joy, through its paces along the towpath. The weather remained settled and it was a lovely warm, sunny day. He cycled first towards Wordsley, waving to the boatmen he knew and their wives, whose narrowboats he passed. Since it was the Sabbath many were moored up, generally close to a public house, their horses left to graze the tufts of grass that lined the canal. Algie had had no more trouble with his chain coming off since he had tightened it by moving the rear wheel back sufficiently in its forks. He cycled confidently now, in the certain knowledge that it would not come adrift again.

When he reached the Red House Glassworks with its huge brick cone towering over everything, he reckoned he'd gone far enough in that direction. He was keen to try the uphill ride back. The towpath followed the topography of the canal so it was flat for the most part, the ascent appearing in stages at the ten locks on that stretch of the canal, and the humpback bridges that spanned them. His intention was to cycle in the other direction as far as the Nine Locks at the area known as the Delph, about a mile as the crow flies, but nearly two miles along the meandering canal. He hoped he might espy the Binghams. But long before he reached the Nine Locks, he spotted a pair of narrowboats lying low and heavy in the water, plying the bend in the canal at the Victoria Firebrick Works. Thirty yards in front, a piebald horse was hauling them, its long face in a nose-tin. The stocky figure of Seth Bingham was leading it.

Marigold! Algie's heart skipped a beat. He smiled to himself and raced towards them. He bid Seth good day as he whizzed past, looking for Marigold, and saw her bending down at the tiller of the butty, the *Odyssey*. She was wearing a sunbonnet and failed to see him at first. It took a shout to draw her attention, whereupon she stood up and looked about enquiringly. When she eventually spotted him she smiled and waved.

'How do, Marigold,' Algie called, an amiable grin on his handsome face. He turned around and rode alongside her, matching the sedate pace of the narrowboat she was steering.

'Hello, Algie. You got your bike then.'

'What d'you think of it?'

'It looks nice. You ride it well.'

Mrs Bingham, at the tiller of the *Sultan*, the horse boat, turned around when she heard her daughter calling to Algie, and smiled to herself, not averse to the romance she perceived blossoming between them. This Algie Stokes was at least likeable, unlike that ne'er-do-well she'd taken to in Kidderminster.

'I'm getting used to it now, Marigold.'

'How long you had it?'

'A couple of weeks. Hey, I ain't seen you for ages. Ain't you been down this cut since last time I saw you?'

'No,' she called. 'We've been up again' Cheshire and back a few times, though, and to Birnigum.'

'So you're on your way to Kiddy again?'

Marigold nodded coyly, aware of all it implied.

'So you'll be doing a spot o' courting tomorrow night then?'

She shrugged and felt herself blush.

'Are you mooring up by the Bottle and Glass?' he asked.

'I reckon so. Me dad likes the beer there.'

'Yes, you said. So d'you fancy coming a walk with me again when you've had your dinner? It's a nice day for a walk.'

'If you like,' she answered, and Algie was encouraged by the spontaneity of her acceptance.

'I'll give you a ride on the crossbar, eh?'

She shrugged, still smiling with pleasure at seeing him. 'If you like . . . So how fast can you make the machine go?'

'Here on the flat I can make it go proper quick.'

'Show me, then.'

The lad that was in the man grinned boyishly at the welcome challenge; at the opportunity to impress. 'All right. Watch this.'

He raised himself from the saddle and exerted all the pressure he could muster onto the pedals for a rapid acceleration. Just as he was drawing level with the horse, the chain came off the sprocket and, because of its sudden and unexpected lack of tension, his right leg slipped off the pedal and he banged his crotch again on the crossbar. The instant, unbearable pain caused Algie to wince and he veered straight into the horse, its head still in its nose-tin. Shocked out of its wits, the animal panicked, but it had only one place to go – into the canal, followed at once by Algie and his new bike.

Animal and lad thrashed about looking very undignified. Algie surfaced with a look of disgruntled surprise on his face. He gasped for air as the chill of the water, coupled with the excruciating agony of testicular pain, robbed him of breath. His normally curly hair was a black, wet mop clinging to his head and he spluttered foul water in indignant astonishment. The poor horse, meanwhile, its eyes white and wild with fright, was drowning in its own nose-tin as it flailed about, desperately trying to regain its feet on the slimy bed of the canal. Seth realised the animal's plight and at once threw himself down on his belly at the edge of the towpath, reaching out, frantically trying to free the nose-tin from the horse so that it could breathe air without either choking itself with feed, or drowning.

'Hey up!' he cried, in a panic of concern. 'Steady on, old lad. Let me get thy nostern off, else you'm a goner.'

He managed to loosen the strap, which was attached to a metal ring riveted to the nose-tin on the side nearest to him. The horse coughed and spluttered and, in its continuing terror, lost its footing again in the slime.

The trailing narrowboat, by virtue of the impetus of its sheer uncontrolled weight, was in danger of crushing the horse between it and the canal wall. Seth yelled to Marigold to watch her steering. Suddenly, Marigold's eyes were filled with apprehension as she immediately understood the danger. She grasped the tiller, holding it with all her strength to alter the course of the heavily loaded craft, to bring it to the bank without maiming the horse. Seth, meanwhile, rushed to his feet and tried shoving the *Odyssey* away from the horse, mustering all his strength. He succeeded, but stretching too far in his urgency, he, too, dropped into the canal with an unceremonious splash.

Algie was too concerned with his own predicament to notice the commotion he'd caused. He was submerging himself repeatedly as he tried to locate his new investment, his precious bike, obscured in the murky water. 'I can't find me bike,' he declared in horror. 'It'll be ruined. What if the narrowboat's mangled it as it's gone over it?'

'Never mind the blasted bike, you daft bugger,' Seth Bingham rasped angrily, freshly saturated and surfacing behind him next to the increasingly perplexed horse. 'My hoss is more important than that blasted thing o' yourn. Mek yourself useful and fetch somebody who can help we get the hoss out the cut.'

'When I've found me bike,' Algie called defiantly. 'It cost me twelve quid.'

'And a new hoss'll cost yer a sight more. You barmy bugger, what did you think you was a-doing, eh? Wait till I tell your fairther. Now get out of the cut and help me. *You* caused all the bloody trouble, showing off like that. You bloody imbecile!'

Algie cringed under the tirade, but was diverted by a piercing scream that came from Marigold. One of her young brothers, a mere child, had suddenly appeared from the cabin to see what all the fuss was about, and was standing alongside the tiller. She had instantly perceived the danger as somebody, thinking they were helping when the danger of crushing the horse was over, was pulling the stern in towards the towpath. She yelled a warning and shoved him out of the way a mere fraction of a second before the rudder hit the bank, which in turn caused the tiller to swing violently across the stern, just missing the child's head. She sighed, a profound sigh, having just averted what would have been a tragedy. Marigold breathed a sigh of relief and picked up the child, taking him out of harm's way.

Algie found his submerged bike at that very moment. He lifted it over his head, mucky water and weeds cascading over him, and placed it on the towpath with a look of demoralised anguish. Then he clambered out, forlorn, bedraggled by the same cold water. By this time, the pair of narrowboats had come to a stop.

'Catch this rope, Algie.' It was Hannah Bingham's voice.

Algie turned and looked just as Hannah tossed it to him. When he stepped forward to catch it his boots squelched, oozing slime and mud.

'Chuck one end to Seth,' Hannah yelled. 'He'll fasten it to the hoss. You can help pull the poor thing out.'

Algie tried not to look at Marigold, but could not resist casting her a glance. He felt immensely stupid. She was obviously concerned at the sudden plight they all found themselves in, and she looked bewildered and flustered. She must think him such a fool. Surely, she must blame him for all this. He had ruined any chance he'd ever had of success with her.

Seth seemed to be making some progress calming down the frightened horse. He spoke to it as softly as the desperate circumstances would allow, and patted its trembling neck reassuringly. He fastened the rope to its collar, then tried to get the horse to limber up the vertical side of the canal.

'Pull the rope,' he called to Algie.

Algie pulled, but the horse resisted.

By this time a small audience had gathered, people using the towpath as a shortcut, and advice was not long in coming. 'Tie some planks together and put one end in the cut, the other on the towpath, and walk him out,' one man advised. 'But planks'll float,' reasoned another. Somebody else suggested that they fix a blanket under the horse's belly, then yank him out with a crane.

'Where are we gunna find a crane of a Sunday?' Algie queried impatiently, quietly shivering from the icy cold water that was running down his back, squishing inside his clinging clothes.

'They must have one at the firebrick works.'

'That bloody saft Algie ought to be made swim with the hoss to the nearest steps,' Seth declared from the middle of the canal.

For half an hour they endeavoured to coax the horse to jump up onto the towpath, but in vain, for the sides were too high and too steep. Until Algie, desperate to avoid swimming to the nearest escape steps with the horse, and to redeem himself in the eyes of Marigold, had an idea.

'Got any carrots, Mrs Bingham?'

'Yes, by God,' Hannah replied, at once catching on.

By this time, the pair of narrowboats had been hauled alongside the towpath and moored. She delved inside her cabin and emerged clutching several carrots. Algie squelched towards her and took them.

He made his way to the horse, sat on his haunches and offered the animal a carrot, which it sniffed suspiciously, then took in its mouth and chomped.

'Here's another,' Algie said, dangling it in front of the horse's long face, but about a foot out of its reach. 'This time, though, you gotta come and fetch it.' He stood up and moved away, but still held out the carrot for the horse to see.

'Goo on, lad,' Seth encouraged, acknowledging the vain possibility that this ploy might work. 'Goo on, get the carrot.'

The animal fidgeted about fretfully in the water, evidently lacking the confidence or the will to attempt a leap. Algie moved towards the horse again, allowing it another sniff of the carrot, then backed away once more. The horse shifted backwards, and for a moment looked poised to leap, then seemed to change its mind. Seth, Algie and all the others offered more vocal encouragement until, with a monumental effort, the plucky little horse leapt up. Its front hoofs scraped on the compressed ash of the towpath, while its hind legs flailed to and fro, trying to find some purchase on the smooth blue bricks that formed the edge. At the same time, the men pulled on the rope. For a moment it looked as though the horse would fail and hurt itself as it tumbled backwards into the cut again. But miraculously, it made it, and a loud cheer rang through the spring air.

'Thank God,' Hannah exclaimed with a sigh of relief.

Algie kept his promise to the horse, which was now only concerned with acquiring the carrot, and popped it into its mouth. 'Good lad,' he said, patting its neck. 'I'm just sorry as I caused you so much trouble in the first place. Now enjoy your carrots, 'cause they was sure to be for your master's dinner.'

'Well, at least you got him out,' Marigold said, sidling up beside him. 'That was a good idea to tempt him with a carrot.'

He turned to her. 'I didn't think for a minute that it'd work,' he admitted, relieved and surprised that she was still speaking to him. 'But I reckoned it was worth a try. I felt I had to do something, since it was me that caused all the upset in the first place. And I know that horses like carrots better than anything.'

'It's a good job as yo' did,' Seth Bingham interjected, his pique subsiding. 'Else Lord knows how we would've got the poor bugger out.'

'I'm really sorry, Mr Bingham,' Algie remarked with earnest repentance. 'The chain came off me bike just as I was going past the horse. It caused me to fall into him, and it startled him, I reckon.'

'Did you hurt yourself, lad?'

Algie grinned self-consciously. 'Gave me taters a right bang.'

'Aye, well it's over and done now. Now all we need do is change into some dry clothes. Hannah, find me another pair o' trousers and a shirt, and chuck me a towel, eh?'

'I feel I ought to make it up to you, Mr Bingham,' Algie said. 'To say how sorry I am.'

'Like I said, lad, it's over and done with.'

'Let me buy you a drink in the Bottle and Glass.'

Seth managed a smile at last. 'If yo' insist. But we'n gotta get there fust. I'll gi' the hoss five minutes to get over the shock afore I get him to haul we there. The poor bugger was frit to death.'

'I'd better get home and change into dry clothes as well, Mr Bingham.'

'That you had, lad. Is your two-wheeler any the wuss for having took a look in the cut?'

'It'll dry out,' Algie replied with resignation. 'It'll very likely dry out as I ride it home. I just hope the rust don't set in.'

'Aye, well just be careful where you'm a-going next time.'

'I will, Mr Bingham. I promise.'

Algie retrieved his bike from the towpath and inspected it. As he reinstalled the errant chain on its sprockets, Marigold stood beside him, watching and waiting.

'I don't suppose you want to come a walk with me now, do you, Marigold, after making a fool of meself like I have?'

'Why should it make any difference?' she said pleasantly. 'It was an accident. Anybody could see that. At first I thought it was funny, till I saw Victoria was in trouble. Then, when that ninny pulled us into the bank and the tiller swung round . . .' She put her hands to her face with the horror of recalling it. 'Well, our Billy's lucky he didn't get his head wopped off. Anyway, Algie, you did well to get Victoria out.'

'Victoria? Is that what you call the horse? Victoria?'

'Yes. After the queen. What's wrong with that?'

'But it ain't a mare, is it?' He grinned amiably, amused at the incongruity of the horse's name and its gender. 'Even I can see it's got a doodle.'

Marigold chuckled at his irreverence. 'The horse don't know it's a girl's name,' she reasoned.

He chuckled. 'I suppose not. Anyway, if it's good enough for a queen, it's good enough for a horse, I reckon. Male or no.'

Chapter 4

While Algie was at the Bottle and Glass trying to get back into Seth Bingham's good books, Marigold picked up her mother's basket and made her way to the lock-keeper's cottage. She tapped on the door and Kate answered it.

'Oh, hello, Marigold,' Kate greeted pleasantly. 'Our Algie ain't here, he's at the Bottle and Glass.'

Marigold blushed at the implication. 'I've come to see Mrs Stokes, not Algie,' she said. 'I've got something for her.'

'You'd better come in then.'

Marigold followed Kate into the scullery where Clara was at the sink. She greeted Marigold with a warm smile, which was returned.

'Hello, Mrs Stokes . . . I just wanted to bring you these . . .' She placed the basket on the table and invited Clara, by her demeanour alone, to peer into it.

'Eggs!' Clara declared. She looked up at Marigold and smiled. 'For me?'

'For being so kind, Mrs Stokes. For letting me have those choolips for me mom last time we was through here. She loved 'em, you know. As soon as I gave them to her she put them in a vase and they took pride o' place in the *Sultan*'s cabin. They lasted ever so long, as well. She was ever so pleased with them. So when I knew as they'd got some new-laid eggs at a farm up by the viaduct when we came past this morning, I thought getting you a dozen would be a good way of saying thank you.'

'You didn't have to do that, Marigold,' Clara said, touched by her thoughtfulness, 'but it's very kind of you. Thank you. It's a lovely thought. Algie will enjoy having eggs for his breakfast in the morning, especially since it's you that's brought 'em. So will Mr Stokes.'

'Did you hear about Algie falling in the cut this morning, and taking our horse with him?'

Clara laughed. 'He told me all about it. I can just picture it.'

'The silly devil,' Kate chimed in with scorn. 'I suppose he was acting the goat.'

'It was an accident, Kate,' Marigold said gently, immediately coming to Algie's defence. 'He couldn't help it. It could've been much worse than it was, but it was an accident. Nobody was hurt, thank goodness. Him and me dad just took a look in the cut with the horse, and got wet.'

'And now they're celebrating the fact in the public, I suppose,' Kate replied.

'I hope so,' Marigold said. 'It's just a pity our poor horse can't be there with 'em as well. I think he deserves a drink after what he's been through.'

Washed, dried and wearing his Sunday best suit, Algie Stokes left the Bottle and Glass after imbibing more beer than he was used to, in his endeavour to redeem himself in the eyes of Seth Bingham. He stepped unsteadily round the back of the public house, and winced at the bright afternoon sunshine that lent a dazzling sparkle to the canal's murky water. He headed at once for the pair of narrowboats moored abreast of each other in the basin. The *Odyssey* was furthest from him.

63

'Marigold!' he called.

Marigold emerged from the *Sultan*. She stooped down to say goodbye to her mother, who was below in the cabin. She saw that Algie was wearing his best Sunday suit, his silver Albert stretched across his waistcoat.

'How did you get on with me dad?' she asked, clambering out of the narrowboat onto the towpath.

'We're the best of mates,' Algie affirmed, with a misplaced sense of pride that amused her.

With an unspoken consensus they headed towards Wordsley, the direction he had taken at the beginning of his eventful ride that morning. Serenity enveloped them, a sort of reverential Sunday silence, punctuated only by the trickling songs of blackbirds. On other days such wistful and lovely birdsong went unheard, muffled by the intense throb of industry. Ducks and geese basked at the edge of the canal and a pen sat with propriety and elegance on a huge nest overlooked by the Dock shop.

'How many drinks did you have to buy him?' Marigold enquired.

'Two.'

'No wonder he's the best o' mates with you.'

'He bought me one back as well.'

'So you've had three pints?'

'No, four, to tell you the truth. Somebody else bought us one besides. I never drink that many as a rule. 'Specially of a Sunday dinnertime.'

Marigold gasped. 'Your hold must be awash. I wonder you can still stand.'

'Oh, I can still stand all right.' He teetered exaggeratedly, pretending to be more unsteady than he really was. 'I don't think I can walk very straight though.' The sweet sound of her laughter appealed greatly to him and he focused his admiring eyes on her.

'Then it's a good job you ain't riding your machine, else you'd be taking another look in the cut.'

'I was intending to give you a ride on it,' he said with a broad grin. 'Shall I go and fetch it?'

'Not on your nellie. Not if you've had four pints o' jollop and you keeps plaiting your legs. Look at you, you'm all over the place.' She chuckled again good naturedly at his seeming unsteadiness.

'When we come back, I mean.'

'We'll see.'

'How come it's been so long since you came this way?' he asked. 'I thought you'd be through our lock well before today.'

'I told you, we had work that took us up to Cheshire. It's a good earner to Cheshire and back to Birnigum, 'cause we generally loads up wi' salt for the return.'

'So you ain't seen that chap in Kidderminster either?'

'Course not.'

'I bet you got your eye on somebody in Cheshire, though, eh?'

'Me?' she queried, with genuine surprise. 'Course I haven't.'

He was teasing her, but something in her voice suggested she was taking him seriously, and convinced him she was telling the truth. 'I'd be surprised if nobody was interested in you, Marigold.'

'Why?' she fished, an expectant smile lighting up her lovely face.

'Well, I mean . . . Somebody as pretty as you?'

'Oh, I ain't that special, Algie,' she protested pleasantly, with no hint of coquetry. 'I'm just ord'n'ry. Anyroad, what about you? I bet you've been seeing that Harriet.'

He shrugged non-committally.

'I bet you have,' she persisted.

'There's nothing serious between me and Harriet. I told you.'

'I bet you'll be going to church with her tonight again, whether or no.'

It was true, worse luck; Harriet was expecting him, and there was no sense in denying it. 'Not if *you* agree to come out with me tonight, I won't.' He looked at her again to discern her reaction.

'All right,' she agreed, returning his look with a distinct twinkle in her eye. If she refused, then he would certainly spend the evening with this Harriet, and she must prevent that happening. 'I'll come out with you tonight, if you like. You'll have sobered up by then, tis to be hoped . . .'

They walked along the towpath in a companionable silence for a moment or two, each considering the implications of what they had said. Algie casually kicked a loose stone and it plopped into the canal. He would have to give Harriet an explanation for failing to show up for church. But he was not sorry. It would afford him the opportunity to make the break from her as honourably as he could, as his father had said he should. Such a break from Harriet would be to their mutual benefit, freeing her to accept the advances of other young men, more deserving of her.

'How far are we going?' Marigold asked.

'Not far, eh?' Algie replied. 'I'm tired. All that buggering about in the cut.'

'Oh, well, you can bet it's nothing to do with the beer you've had.' Marigold glanced at him sideways with a knowing look, with no hint of recrimination, then burst out laughing at his peeved expression.

'I can take my beer, you know,' he replied sheepishly. 'It's the mucking about in the cut that's done me in. I just hope I haven't caught a chill. Anyway, let's get off the towpath by Dadford's Shed . . . There . . .' He pointed to a huge new timber construction named after Thomas Dadford Junior who had supervised the building of the canal more than a century earlier. 'We can go over the bridge there to the fields at the back of the sand quarry and have a sit down.'

'If you like,' she agreed. 'I don't fancy walking far. I got some new second hand boots on as I got from Penkridge Market the other day, and they'm a bit tight. I need to break 'em in afore I walk a long way in them.'

It was a short walk from Dadford's Bridge and the wharf of the Glassworks, along a back way called Mill Street and then Water Lane, where they passed the sand quarry Algie had mentioned before the lane dwindled to a footpath. Marigold was surprised to find herself at a lovely quiet spot, nestling between steep hillocks and sandstone crevices, out of sight of the quarry, the glassworks and the rest of civilisation. A small and very clear stream rippled idyllically between clusters of young trees. Wafts of almond-scented gorse rose to meet them as they stepped over the soft grass, like velvet beneath their feet.

'Let's sit down here,' Algie suggested. He sat himself on the ground with his arms around his knees and looked up at Marigold who was still standing. He held his hand out to her. 'Come and sit beside me, Marigold. I thought you said your boots were hurting you.'

She did as he bid compliantly and with an inherent daintiness. Algie tugged at a stalk of grass, one end of which he put between his teeth. In the distance a cuckoo made its wilful call, while a pair of young rabbits bobbed about playfully close by. Marigold drew his attention to them.

'Ain't they beautiful?'

'They're all right in a stew,' he quipped, deliberately taunting her. 'I reckon there's too many uncooked rabbits knocking about.'

She responded by giving him a playful tap on the arm. 'Tell me about Harriet.'

'What d'you want to know?'

She shrugged. 'How long you've been seeing her, what she's like . . .'

'She ain't that interesting,' he replied dismissively.

'She can't be that bad if you see her regular.'

'I told you, it's nothing serious. We aren't courting proper.'

'So how long have you known her?'

He shrugged. 'About two years.'

'Two years and it ain't serious? It's time she got the hint . . . Unless you've just been stringing her along.'

He shrugged again, but made no reply.

'So you don't love her?'

'Love her?' he repeated, disparaging the notion with overstated disdain. 'If I loved her I wouldn't be here with you. That doesn't mean to say I don't *like* her, though.'

'But not enough to wed.'

'Any chap would be a fool to marry a girl he doesn't love, don't you agree?'

'Course.'

'It wouldn't do Harriet much good either, would it?'

She shook her head. 'I suppose not. Does she work?'

'Yes. For her father, in his drapery shop.'

'Drapery shop?' Marigold repeated in awe. 'Oh, I'd like to work in a drapery shop. I bet she's got some nice clothes.'

He took the stalk of grass out of his mouth and turned to her. 'I'd rather not talk about Harriet,' he said softly. 'I reckon you're a lot more interesting.'

The comment elicited a shy smile and she lowered her lids.

'You know what I'd like to do?' he said, as if confiding a great secret.

'What?'

'I'd like to kiss you.'

'You *must* be drunk.'

'I never felt more sober in my life.'

'Get away with you,' she chuckled. 'You'll be asleep in a minute. Me dad always nods off when he's had a drink.'

'I've never felt more wide awake. I want to kiss you, Marigold.'

She offered her cheek, teasing him.

'On the lips, you nit,' he said with a boyish grin.

She looked into his eyes earnestly for a few seconds, wondering whether to accede to his request. For Marigold this was a momentous step. As he leaned towards her in anticipation, she slowly tilted her face to receive his kiss. His lips felt soft and cool on hers, as gentle as the fluttering of a butterfly, a sensation she enjoyed.

'Wasn't too bad, was it?'

She focused on her new boots to avert her eyes. 'No, it was nice,' she answered softly. 'It was really nice . . . 'Cept I can smell the beer on your breath.'

'Never mind that. Kiss me again.'

She lifted her face to his once more and their lips brushed this time in a series of soft, gentle touches. Marigold's heart was pounding hard.

'You kiss nice,' he said softly.

'Nicer than Harriet?'

'A lot nicer than Harriet. Harriet ain't got kissing lips like you. Her lips are too thin. When you kiss her they feel as if they're worked by springs. I ain't that struck on kissing a set of springs.'

'So you reckon *I've* got kissing lips?'

'For certain.' He smiled with tenderness.

'I bet you've kissed loads of girls.'

'Not really . . .'

'A lot, I bet,' she suggested.

He allowed her to believe it. It could do no harm. 'How about you?' he asked. 'Have you kissed lots of chaps?'

'Me? No . . . Only Jack from Kidderminster.'

'Who kisses the best?' he enquired. 'Me or him?'

'Dunno,' she answered shyly.

'Does he kiss you like this . . .' Algie put his arm around her, and his lips were on hers with an eager but exaggerated passion.

She turned her face away. 'Algie, it's not so nice when you kiss me that hard. You hurt me mouth. It's much nicer when you do it gentle. Gentle as a butterfly . . . Butterfly kisses.'

'Sorry . . . Like this, you mean?'

He resumed kissing her tenderly again.

'That better?'

'Yes, that's much nicer. I don't reckon as you've kissed that many girls if you think they like it done hard.'

'I never tried to kiss anybody that hard afore, to tell you the truth. There's nobody I ever wanted to kiss that hard.'

She glanced into his eyes briefly with a shy smile.

'Will you be my girl?'

She picked a daisy from the grass at her side before she answered, and twizzled it pensively between her thumb and forefinger. 'Will you give up Harriet if I say yes?'

'Course I will. Will you give up that Jack in Kidderminster?'

She hesitated and Algie imagined she was torn which way to jump. Perhaps he was rushing things.

'Well?'

'I dunno, Algie . . .' she replied with a troubled look.

'What's to stop you?'

She sighed deeply. 'I do like you, Algie . . .'

'But?'

'Well . . . I can't say as I know you that well yet. How do I know you won't still see Harriet behind me back? I mean, if we keep going to Cheshire and Birnigum and back it might be weeks afore I see you again. I don't see the sense in promising to be yourn if you'm still gonna see that Harriet behind me back while I'm away.'

'I wouldn't do that,' he asserted, trying to sound as convincing as he could. 'Anyway, if you keep going to Cheshire you won't see Jack either, so you might just as well decide to pack him up as hang on to him. 'Specially if you got me. I could ride to Kidderminster on my bike to see you if you were moored up there the night. You wouldn't end up having nothing to do. As a matter of fact, I could ride to see you at lots of places if I knew where you intended to moor up nights.'

'I dunno, Algie . . .'

'Is it because you love Jack, then?'

'No, it's because I ain't sure of *you*.'

'Do you still want to see me tonight?'

'Course, if you still want to,' she said quietly.

The Meese household, with the exception of their maid and the cook, whose afternoon off it was, had assembled in the parlour. Harriet sat in an upholstered chair expectantly while Priss was perched on its arm, awaiting the imminent arrival of Algie Stokes.

'He's very late,' remarked Priss, twiddling her gloved thumbs impatiently. 'I don't think we should wait any longer. He'll see you in church, Harriet, I'm sure, if he's coming at all.'

Eli shuffled impatiently, and donned his hat. 'I'm hanged if I'm going to wait around any longer for that ne'er-do-well. As churchwarden I have a responsibility to be at church in good time.'

'Yes, please go on, Father,' Harriet urged. 'All of you. Except you, Priss, if you don't mind. I'd rather you wait to walk with me in case he doesn't show up. I do hope he hasn't had an accident on that bicycle of his.'

'He'll get no sympathy from me if he has,' Eli said self-righteously. 'Right, come on, you lot. Let's go. We'll see Priss and Harriet at the church with Lover Boy, if he ever deigns to show his face.'

In a swish of satin skirts, the younger Meese girls and their mother left the house and walked down the entry behind Eli in an orderly, if chattering, single file. Emily, the third daughter, eighteen, closed the door behind them with a wave, a smile and a flurry of audible footsteps as she ran to catch them up.

'What if he *has* had an accident, Priss?' Harriet speculated fretfully.

'Well, it would hardly surprise me. But how will you know? You can't walk all the way to their cottage tonight to find out. Anyway, we can afford to wait ten more minutes yet. He might show up.'

'Yes, he might,' Harriet sighed. 'But it's unlike him to be late. You can normally set your clock by him. He's normally so punctual that Mr Bradshaw could write his timetable by him.'

'Except there'd be a printing error for today's times,' Priss commented airily. 'But you know what a palaver Father makes of getting to church early. You'd think he was the vicar instead of the churchwarden, the fuss he makes.'

'Maybe Algie has had an accident and his fob watch got broken, and he doesn't know the time . . . Maybe we should invite him to tea of a Sunday in future. Then he'll be here ready, fob watch or no.'

'Steady on, Harriet,' Priss said. 'That's taking things a bit too far. But I suppose it depends how serious you are about him. Personally, I wouldn't shed any tears over him. It's not as if he's serious about *you*. Besides, has it ever crossed your mind that you could do better for yourself? I've noticed how the curate looks at you . . .'

Harriet shrugged. 'Oh, no, Priss, the curate admires you.'

Priss sighed and smiled sadly. 'I only wish he did.'

'I had a feeling you liked him like that, Priss.'

Priss felt herself blushing. 'Oh, I'd be very good for him,' she said candidly. 'I'd make an excellent clergyman's wife, you know. But I bet he thinks we're dreadfully plebeian, being a family of drapers.'

'At least we've got gas and water laid on, Priss. Anyway, I suspect it would be rather dull being married to the curate,' Harriet speculated. 'Living with him would be like taking board and lodgings in the church.'

'Oh, I don't agree. The curate is an ideal sort of person to marry, with his high principles and conscientiousness.'

'Yes, you could sit up in bed with him at night and discuss Constantine the Great's contribution to Christianity,' Harriet suggested. 'Or the relevance of the Book of Revelations to the Second Coming. That would be very stimulating, and be sure to beget you lots of offspring.'

'Don't be coarse, Harriet. I think the curate is too superior a person to fall in love with anybody anyway,' Priss surmised sadly. 'Like Algie Stokes in a way, except that Algie Stokes is not superior at all.'

'I know Algie's only a brass worker, Priss, but so what? I've known him ages and he's a dear, gentle soul. Just remember, our father came from nothing. If he hadn't had a bit of luck in the early days, *he* might have ended up a brass worker or an iron worker.'

'Yes, and look where we'd be . . .'

'It is honest employment after all, though, Priss.'

'Anyway, from what I hear, it was not luck that brought Father his prosperity, but sheer hard work, determination and a belief in himself.'

'And who's to say Algie won't develop along the same lines?'

'Of course, he might,' Priss conceded. 'But he shows no sign of it. He's far too immature.'

They waited the whole ten minutes, but Algie did not materialise. So the two sisters hurried to church in the warm evening air without him, curious as to what had become of him.

'Where you taking me tonight?' Marigold asked when Algie called for her again that evening.

'We could go for a drink.'

'I'd have thought you'd had enough to drink for one day.'

'I feel all right now. Sober as a judge in fact. I had a nap after my tea. Tell you what, why don't we go and have one drink, then go back to that spot down by Dadford's Bridge again? It was nice and peaceful down there.'

'If you like,' she said, content to go along with it. It would mean that they could lie in the grass and kiss to their hearts' content. The experience earlier had set her heart pounding and she'd enjoyed the exhilaration.

To avoid Seth Bingham, who had installed himself at the Bottle and Glass, they stopped first at the Samson and Lion, which backed onto the canal a little further along. Algie fetched the drinks and took them outside where Marigold waited.

'Does your mother go on to your dad about him drinking of a Sunday?' Algie enquired as they stood outside the public house overlooking the towpath, drinking glasses in hand, enjoying the warm summer evening.

'No, never. Why should she? She reckons he deserves his day of rest in the public bar, if that's what he enjoys. He works hard every other day, never stops. Up at the crack o' dawn, he is, to see to Victoria and get him ready for when the locks open so's we can be on our way. He don't stop neither till dusk when we moor up for the night and he's found a stable.'

'D'you like living in a narrowboat on the cut? Wouldn't you rather live in a house like ordinary folk?'

'I don't know nothin' any different, do I? I see folk like you living in houses, but I've never lived in a house . . . well, not as I can remember. My mother lived in one, though. She comes from somewhere round here.'

'Fancy,' he said. 'I didn't know . . . So, how d'you manage, living in so small a space?'

She smiled into his eyes. 'Oh, we manage. We've got everythin' we need. It's just all in a small space. I sleep in the butty on the cross-bed with two of my sisters, and one of my brothers sleeps on the side-bed. Me mom and dad sleep in the *Sultan* with our Billy, the youngest.'

'I often wonder how very young children get on, living on narrowboats. I mean, what do they do?'

'All sorts of things,' Marigold replied. 'Me dad makes 'em fishing rods, and he's taught us all to fish. They spend ages fishing. It keeps 'em busy. They know every type of bird, every fish we ever catch . . .'

'What about schooling?' he asked.

'Never had much schooling.' She sighed with regret. 'Oh, I'd have dearly loved to have had some proper schooling, all of us would, but we'm never in one place long enough. The inspectors came once or twice asking to see our attendance books, but even they know what it's like travelling 'tween towns all the while, pressed for time and money. It must be nice to have had some schooling, so's you could see words wrote down and be able to read 'em proper, instead o' mismuddling 'em, like I do.'

He smiled with admiration for this slip of a girl. 'Finish your beer and we'll go, eh?'

Soon, they left the Samson and Lion.

'Give me your hand,' he said.

She found his hand, and turned to look at him with tenderness in her eyes. They walked on, hardly speaking but companionable enough, till they reached Dadford's Shed and the bridge. In the distance, the bells of Wordsley Church were pealing melodically, as they would be at St Michael's in Brierley Hill.

'You'd be with Harriet now if you wasn't with me,' she remarked, prompted by the sound of the church bells, as they crossed the road into Water Lane.

'I reckon so,' he replied frankly. 'But not anymore I won't, if you say you'll be my girl.'

'Did you send word as you wouldn't be able to see her tonight?'

'How could I? There was no time.'

'P'raps you should've gone to see her instead then. She'd have been waiting.'

'Well, it's done now. Anyway, she's got sisters to go to church with. She won't miss me . . . You know, I don't think her dad likes me that much. They never say so, but I can tell by the way he is towards me – a bit offish.'

Marigold offered no reply other than a sympathetic smile.

They reached the dell where they had been earlier. It was all in shadow since the sun, now low in the west, had traversed the sky. As before, he sat down on the ground and beckoned her to join him, which she did. He put his arm around her and drew her to him, hugging her.

'Have you thought anymore about what I said?' he asked her.

'What was it you said?' she replied, not quite sure what he meant.

'About being my girl . . .'

'I'm thinking about it.'

'What is there to think about?' he said. 'I told you I'd give up Harriet. By not going to see her tonight, I already have done.'

'I know,' she said seriously. 'And I believe you . . .'

'So why dilly-dally? Tomorrow night I'll ride to Kidderminster on my bike and we can be together again . . .'

'I couldn't meet you till after I'd told him.'

He grinned, impressed by her obvious integrity, but had no wish to appear too triumphant. Not yet at any rate. 'So you'll tell him then, that you don't want him anymore?'

She nodded. She had made up her mind. 'I might get to talk to him while they'm offloading the boats. I want to be straight with him, Algie.'

Algie beamed. 'Course you must. It's the only way. So you'll be my girl?'

'I will,' she said, as solemnly as if she were taking her wedding vows.

'You're sure?'

She nodded again and smiled. 'Yes, I'm sure.'

He hugged her and planted a kiss on her lips, hardly able to believe his good fortune.

Chapter 5

A high-flying, three-quarter moon afforded ample light by which Algie and Marigold retraced their steps to Buckpool. The occasional drunken shouts from some inebriate or other, lurching in the streets nearby, interrupted the evening's stillness, but could hardly intrude on the euphoria and tenderness they both felt at their newly established accord. It was nearing ten o' clock when they returned hand-in-hand to the brace of narrowboats tied up in the canal basin. Marigold had promised her mother she would be back by that time, for there was still work to be done, preparing for tomorrow's early departure. When they reached the narrowboats, the stove pipe of the *Sultan* was exhausting a near vertical column of smoke that rose up in the moonlight like some spectral genie just released from a tall lamp.

'So what time shall I see you at Kidderminster tomorrow night?' Algie asked, taking her hands as they stood facing each other, in readiness for parting.

'Let's say half past seven.'

'But what if you don't moor up there?'

'Then we'll be back this way in the afternoon.'

'Come and knock on our door and let my mother know then, eh? When I get back from work she'll tell me where you'll be. Then I'll just ride till I find you. If you don't show up, I'll know you're between here and Kidderminster, and I'll find you.'

Her eyes crinkled into an appealing smile. 'Just mind you don't take another look in the cut . . .' She turned around to see if her mother was there waiting, having heard them return. 'I'd better go, Algie,' she said softly. 'I'll see you tomorrow . . . all being well.' She stood on tiptoe and planted a kiss on his lips, lingering a couple of seconds, then let go of his hands and went.

Algie stood watching her as she skipped lightly into the cabin of the *Sultan* and disappeared. He sighed, smiling contentedly to himself. He had won the affection of Marigold Bingham, and she was a treasure. He exulted in the thought without conceit, merely content that a girl as pretty as she could be the least bit interested in him. It had been a wonderfully eventful day, but he'd had no inkling at all that it would turn out this way when he'd woken up that morning.

Marigold . . .

Lovely little Marigold Bingham.

She was a cut above the other narrowboat girls he'd seen, the most divine incarnation of delectability, worth giving up Harriet Meese for. He'd admired her from a distance for so long. Now she'd promised to be his girl and he could scarcely believe it. And he had to wait unending hours before he could see her again tomorrow.

He turned to go, back to the lock-keeper's cottage under the road bridge. First, though, he would go to the garden shed by way of the back gate, to check that his bicycle was all right and locked away from thieves. There would be sufficient light from the moon to see if there were any globules of water still clinging or dripping from it after its ducking, which he ought to wipe dry and so save the machine rusting before he went to bed.

As he approached, he heard what sounded to him like the muffled sobs of a girl – it might even be a child – evidently in some distress. He halted in his tracks to listen more intently, his heart pounding at the sudden discovery and the anticipation of just what he might have stumbled across. The whimpers were coming from behind the shed. If it was somebody hurting a child, or even a woman, he'd kill the culprit. He looked about him for a stick or suitable implement with which to thrash him, but could see none in the darkness.

Stealthily he crept towards the shed, praying that no twig would crack underfoot to give away his presence and rob him of the element of surprise. Then, as he reached the corner he peered around it circumspectly. A man was pressing a young woman against the shed. By the pale reflected moonlight he could see that her skirts were up, her pale, slim thighs a visible contrast to the dark material of her skirt and her black stockings. The man's hands were grasping her backside, and he was thrusting into her energetically. Her arms were around his neck, but she could have been endeavouring to push him away; a subtle difference in attitude that Algie could not discern in the dimness. To his horror, he could just make out that his sister Kate was on the receiving end of all this physical endeavour.

Algie was not sure how he should react as he watched incredulously. Was Kate a willing party to this, or had she been forced? Her anguished cries suggested she was not enjoying the experience, that the rogue was hurting her. Then, he realised the rogue was none other than Reggie Hodgetts, that vile son of a rodney boatman whom he knew she had been seeing. Well, Algie did not like Reggie Hodgetts anyway. He and his family were the scum of the canal network. Best to assume Kate was a victim here.

He rushed at the man, knocking him over. 'You vile bastard!' he rasped. 'What d'you think you're doing to my sister? I'll kill you, you bloody turd.'

At such a savage and unexpected interruption, Reggie was too shocked to know what had hit him. One second he was ecstatically coupled to his worthy companion, whom he saw whenever his work brought him her way, the next he was on the ground beneath an unexpected, mad assailant.

'Algie!' Kate hissed indignantly, trying to pull her brother off poor Reggie, and desperate that they should not wake her mother and father who were sure to be wrapped up in bed by this time, though not necessarily asleep yet. 'Leave him be, leave him be. What's got into you, you stupid fool?'

'I'll kill the sod.' Algie took a swipe at Reggie and caught him high on the cheekbone with a resounding crack.

'Leave him be, Algie, for God's sake!'

'Why should I? He deserves all he's getting, treating you like that. I won't have you treated like an animal, Kate. You're my sister.'

By this time, Reggie had oriented himself to this unanticipated situation and wriggled his arms free while his adversary was discussing him with the girl. He traded an equivalent punch to Algie's mouth, which sent him reeling.

'Who does he think he is, your mad brother?' Reggie fizzed as he got up from the ground, his manhood suddenly deflated, dangling limp in the cool night air, his anger all at once frothing over like a bottle of ginger beer violently shaken. 'I'll teach him not to part a man from his pleasure.' He lurched after Algie and grabbed him by the lapels.

'Stop it, you two!' Kate urged in a hoarse whisper, but desperate to be heeded.

Reggie was just about to throw another punch at Algie, when Kate grabbed his arm. 'Stop it, the pair of you!'

'He attacked me, the bastard,' Reggie protested vehemently.

'I'll kill him,' Algie rasped, his indignation overwhelming his apprehension. 'Just—'

'Stop it!' Kate placed herself between them, stumbling over a line of potato shoots.

Both men seemed to calm down. Reggie surreptitiously checked his flies to ascertain if any material damage had been occasioned to his courting tackle during the scuffle.

'You'll waken the dead, you pair,' Kate added, perceiving that the worst of the incident was passed. 'Algie, do us all a favour and clear off, and in future don't be such a damn fool. Next time mind your own business.'

'But he—'

'Yes, I know . . .'

'But you—'

'But me what?'

'He was hurting you.'

'Clear off, Algie,' she repeated impatiently. 'And go and wipe your mouth. Your lip's bleeding, by the looks of it.'

'My lip?' He put his fingers gingerly to his mouth, then inspected the ends in the moonlight for signs of blood. 'You've split my lip, you swine,' he complained to Reggie, his indignation surfacing again.

'Serves you right. Come near me again and I'll knock seven bells out o' yer.'

It was all about to flare up again. Kate placed herself between her brother and her clandestine lover once more.

'Go, Algie . . . clear off. I'll see you inside.'

Algie turned to go, his shoulders hunched in humiliation at having perceived the situation between Kate and Reggie so wrongly. 'If I catch you here again, Reggie bloody Hodgetts, I'll do the same,' he said as a parting shot, trying to salvage some credibility.

'Balls!' rasped Reggie, determined to have the last, meaningful word.

Once inside, Algie stood on the hearth looking into the mirror by the light of an oil lamp at his bleeding lip. He didn't like the look of the cut and tried to stem the bleeding by dabbing it with a rag moistened with cold water. If it hadn't healed sufficiently by tomorrow night his ability to engage Marigold in some earnest spooning would be seriously impaired.

Kate eventually returned, shutting the door behind her grumpily.

'You article!' she scoffed in an angry, grating whisper, trying to keep her voice down so as not to arouse her mother and father. 'In future, if you ever see me with a man, whoever it is, just don't poke your nose.'

'I thought he was hurting you,' Algie muttered defensively. 'I thought you didn't want his . . . his . . . *attentions*. I thought he was raping you.'

'Raping me!' she gibed. 'You idiot.'

'I was trying to protect you.'

'I don't need your damned protection. A fat lot you know about women . . .'

Algie turned round to face her. 'I always had the feeling you might be a bit loose, our Kate, but I never reckoned you were that much of a slut. Couldn't you find somebody with a bit more about him than Reggie Hodgetts? He's the scum of the earth. He stinks. I swear I could smell him.'

'Oh, shut up,' Kate replied sulkily.

'Can't you see it? What if he's put you in the family way and you have to marry him? Would you like to spend the rest of your days living on his filthy narrowboat with no room to swing a cat?'

'Don't be stupid, Algie,' she protested, but calming

down. 'I'd never marry *him*. I ain't in love with him, am I?'

'Then what's the big attraction?'

She turned away, reluctant to answer that it was sexual pleasure, for fear of debasing herself further in her brother's estimation. Instead, she lifted the kettle off the hob, checked to see if there was water in it, and then lifted it onto a gale hook over the dying fire so it could boil.

'Tell me, our Kate, what's the big attraction?'

'Does it matter?'

'Yes. It does matter. He's a nothing. He's lower than slime in a duck pond.'

'It doesn't matter, Algie, 'cause I shan't be seeing him no more.'

He welcomed this unexpected nugget of information. 'That's a bit sudden, eh? Are you sure?'

'I ought to know.'

'So it's done some good, my parting you? Was it your decision or his?'

Kate made no reply.

'At first I thought I'd have to fetch a crowbar and prise you apart,' Algie continued derisively. 'Aren't there no decent chaps at the Amateur Dramatics Society you could take up with, if you're that desperate? Don't nobody decent ever come into the bakery shop?'

Kate didn't answer and they remained silent for some minutes. She went to the brewhouse to swill out the teapot.

'D'you want a cup of tea?' she asked, a little more civilly, when she came back inside.

'I might as well. Is my mouth still bleeding?' He dabbed his lip again and inspected the rag for blood.

'No, but it's swelling up . . . And it serves you right.'

'I can't believe you're such a trollop, Kate,' he commented, still preoccupied with what had occurred. 'My own little sister.' He shook his head to emphasise his disdain. 'I'd never have thought it of you.'

'Leave it be, Algie.'

'Why should I?'

'Because you're being stupid. What about if the boot was on the other foot?'

'Well it ain't, is it?'

'How should I know? Haven't you ever tried your luck with Harriet Meese?'

'Oh, I've tried,' he admitted. Then he saw an opportunity to belittle his sister further. 'But she wouldn't let me. And you know why? 'Cause she's a lady, not a trollop. She's got something about her. She deserves respect for it.'

'She's a stuck-up cat. Anyroad, I can't see young Marigold Bingham being as stuck-up, I'll say that for her. So when you get your way with her, just consider whether *she's* a trollop, eh?'

'Leave Marigold out of this.'

'How can I, when you've been with her most of the day? Have you had your way with her already?'

'What's it got to do with you?'

'Exactly my point, our Algie.'

'For your information, Marigold ain't a trollop,' he added in the girl's defence. 'And like I say, it's nothing to do with you what me and Marigold do.'

'Likewise, what me and Reggie were doing had got nothing to do with *you*,' Kate riposted. 'But it didn't stop you interfering.'

'I'm going to bed,' Algie announced grumpily. 'I don't see the sense in stopping up and arguing with you . . . trollop!'

Algie had eaten and gone to work by the time Kate went down for breakfast. She was employed as an assistant in the shop at Mills's Bakery in Brierley Hill High Street, and didn't have to be there until eight. She had not slept well, preoccupied all night at being discovered with Reggie Hodgetts, and her sudden plunge in Algie's already low esteem. Maybe she was a trollop. She'd never looked at it like that before; she'd never had to because she'd never been found out before. But if it was all done in private then what did it matter to anybody else? It was simply that she enjoyed the physical contact of men; the exhilaration, and all those sweet sensations. When Algie had pondered it all a little longer, when he was more familiar with the ways of women and the world, he might work it out for himself. It pained her to admit it to herself, but yes, she must be a trollop in his estimation and, if he thought it, so might the rest of the world. The encounter tonight must not become common knowledge for fear of her losing her reputation.

A significant thought struck her: polite society, on the brink of which she was now poised – by virtue of being invited to join the Brierley Hill Amateur Dramatics Society – would recognise her as such if they rumbled her, or if word got out. Let's hope that Algie would not be so indiscreet as to mention it to Harriet Meese.

As she walked to work that morning, she pondered this sudden fragility of her reputation and how she could protect it. Perhaps she should call and see Harriet at the drapery shop during her dinnertime, and preclude any possibility of the girl believing anything that Algie might reveal about her. But how could she do that without making Harriet suspicious?

Well, she thought she knew a way . . .

Dinnertime rolled round. Kate put on her bonnet and made her way in the warm sunshine to Meeses' shop. As she opened the door a bell tinkled, triggered by the door parting company

86

with its frame. Bolts of cloth by the score, in hundreds of colours and patterns, lined the walls of the shop edgeways, restricting space, while others were stacked on the counter. The place was a pomander exuding the dry, musty smell of cotton.

In seconds, Harriet, relieving her father who had gone to the Bell that dinnertime for his customary ale, was at the counter in the mistaken belief that she had a customer to attend to. 'Kate! How nice of you to call,' she said, wearing a smile of apprehension. Kate could only be bearing bad news of Algie.

'Hello, Harriet—'

'Is anything the matter?' she blurted anxiously. 'Is Algie all right? Oh, I do hope you haven't called to tell me he's met with an accident . . .'

Kate smiled sweetly to reassure her. 'Oh, no, nothing like that.'

'Then is he all right? I hardly slept last night, I've been so worried since he didn't show up for church.'

'You needn't have bothered, you poor dear,' Kate responded, a look of disdain for her brother upon her face. 'It's him I've come to talk to you about.'

'So what happened to him?'

'Nothing . . . If I were you, Harriet,' she said in a whisper of conspiracy as she leaned towards her, 'I wouldn't bother my head over our Algie ever again.'

'Why? What's he done?' Her face bore a look of intense apprehension.

'Well, for ages, it's been my opinion that he cares not tuppence for you, or for anybody else for that matter, other than himself. And yesterday proved it. He spent all day and all evening with another girl.'

Harriet's expression was one of surprise and incredulity.

She put her hands to the counter to steady herself. 'Are you sure, Kate?'

'Oh, quite sure, Harriet. I can even tell you the girl's name – Marigold Bingham.'

'Do I know her?'

'You? I'd think it unlikely. She's the daughter of a boatman on the cut. A common little piece if you want my opinion. But then, that's what some men want, I reckon – girls who they think are easy. I thought you ought to know, Harriet.'

'Well,' said Harriet, not sure how to respond, her eyes misty with tears, 'it's not exactly the sort of news I welcome, or had expected . . . But I would have thought that if Algie was tired of me he would have had the common courtesy to tell me himself.'

'Yes, you'd take such simple consideration for granted, wouldn't you?'

'I take it then, that he has sent you to do his dirty work, Kate.'

Here was a further opportunity to condemn Algie in Harriet's eyes, and Kate embraced it wholeheartedly. 'Well, yes he has, as a matter of fact.' She lowered her eyes, feigning shame. 'And I certainly don't admire him for it. I told him, "Do your own dirty work," I said. But he begged and pleaded. He said he couldn't face you, but that he recognised as you ought to know.'

'I see,' Harriet answered sadly.

'But when I thought about it, Harriet, I decided to come and see you anyway. I would've, whether he asked me to or not. You see, I'm really doing it for your benefit, not his. He doesn't deserve a decent, respectable girl like you, and to my mind you're well rid of him. Just forget him, Harriet.' She waved her hand dismissively. 'You can do so much better for yourself.'

Harriet sighed profoundly and brushed an errant tear from

her cheek. 'To be frank, Kate, you're not the first person to have said so,' she said dolefully. 'And you, his own sister, now saying it. Maybe I should take heed.'

'I know him better than anybody, Harriet. He's not worth wasting your time on, believe me. I don't think he could ever remain faithful to one woman. He thinks he's God's gift to women.'

Harriet slumped down on the stool that stood behind the counter and sighed. 'I'm deeply disappointed in him, you know, Kate. I would never have thought—'

'I would've thought one of the chaps in the society would have suited you much better than our Algie, you know,' Kate suggested, provocatively turning the focus of their conversation. 'Ain't there nobody there who interests you?'

Harriet shrugged. 'I hadn't thought about it. I'm not the type of girl to go flirting with all the men anyway. I'm really quite shy.'

'Best way and no mistake,' Kate agreed with a nod. 'Saves trouble in the long run.'

'And you, Kate?'

'Me? I ain't particularly interested in men, although I try and be pleasant to 'em all. As long as nobody reckons it's flirting, 'cause I ain't a flirt neither, you know. Us girls have our reputations to consider.'

So the subject of Algie Stokes was soon dropped, in favour of a discussion about the Brierley Hill Amateur Dramatics Society, its personnel, and the new play, rehearsals for which were due to start that week, now that the cast had been decided upon. They discussed each of the characters in turn.

'I'm so glad you were picked for the part of Pocahontas, Kate,' Harriet remarked generously, trying hard to push from her mind all thoughts of her erstwhile swain. 'I think you'll do it justice.'

'Oh, I intend to. Although I ain't had much experience at this acting lark, I reckon I shall make a decent fist of it. And how about you, Harriet?'

'Oh, I am content with the role of Mistress Alice. I don't have too many lines to learn.'

Late that afternoon, the Binghams passed through the locks at Buckpool. Marigold tried to persuade her father to moor up for the night in the winding basin close to the lock-keeper's cottage. Seth smiled indulgently, aware that his daughter had become attached to Will Stokes's lad, and that she would relish the opportunity to walk with him that fine spring evening before they had to move on. He recalled those days years ago when he was courting her mother, who was a landlubber then; how they had both looked forward to the days when he would moor up in Brierley Hill and they could spend tender moments together before he moved on again for more weeks of travelling. But for all his sentimentality and regard for Marigold's love life, he had to get as far along the canal as he could. And while there was still daylight left . . .

'We'll moor up at Parkhead Locks by the tunnel,' he said, knowing full well they could go no further that day. Parkhead was close to the entrance of the Dudley Tunnel and he had no intention of loading up with bars from the ironworks close by and travelling through that night. It would have to wait till tomorrow. 'Young Algie'll be able to bike it if he wants to see you, it ain't far – unless he falls in the cut again.'

'Thanks, Dad,' Marigold said with an appreciative smile, at once excited by the prospect of seeing Algie again. 'I'll go an' pay the toll and ask his mother to let him know. Have you got some loose change?'

He felt in his trouser pocket and coins jingled. 'Here . . .'

She crossed the lock to the cottage, and Clara answered the door.

'You making pastry, Mrs Stokes?' Marigold greeted amiably, seeing Clara's arms floured up to her elbows.

'I'm making a cheese, onion and tater pie for their tea,' Clara confirmed. 'Come in if you want to.'

Marigold smiled gratefully and entered. 'I brought the toll money.' She handed it to Clara.

'Ta, my love . . . Remind me to give you your chit when my hands are clean . . . Are you mooring up close by?'

'Parkhead Locks tonight, me dad says. He wants us to get to the ironworks so we can load up first thing in the morning.'

'You'll be going through the tunnel tomorrow then?'

Marigold nodded.

When they'd done asking each other how everybody was, Clara commented, 'I can never get over how a family the size of yourn can manage to be so comfortable living on a narrowboat. You must be under one another's feet all the time.'

Marigold laughed. 'Oh, it ain't so bad, Mrs Stokes. We got all we need and we do spread out between the two boats.'

'I know, but there's all the stuff you have to carry as well.' Clara said, rolling out a ball of pastry. 'All your clothes, tools, a mangle, a dolly tub and what have you.'

'Oh, that reminds me, Mrs Stokes . . . me mom wants to do a bit o' washing while we're moored up. Can we use your tap in the brewhouse for some clean water? She asked me to ask you. There ain't a pump at Parkhead Locks. We can fill some buckets and the tin bath if you don't mind.'

'Course I don't mind. Course you can, my flower. Shall you be helping her with the washing?'

Marigold nodded emphatically, as if there could be no other way. 'We each help her all we can. We've all got our jobs to do. But she says I can still see your Algie after, if we get it done in time and hung out to dry. Will you tell him, please, Mrs Stokes, as we'll be moored up at Parkhead Locks when he comes back from work?'

'Course I'll tell him,' Clara said. 'Have you got time for a cup o' tea?'

'That's ever so kind, but I'd better not,' Marigold replied, regretting the lost opportunity to get to know Algie's mother better. 'The sooner we get on, the sooner we'll be finished. You wouldn't believe how black your clothes get carrying coal, like we've been doing last trip. I daresay we'll have to get in the tin bath as well, while we've got it out, heating buckets o' water up.'

Clara smiled. 'As long as you've got a tarpaulin to put round you, eh? You don't want no peeping Toms.'

'Oh, we got a tarpaulin, all right.'

Clara dried her hands and wrote out the promised chit, which she handed to Marigold. 'I've made some jam tarts already this afternoon. Would you like to take some for the family?'

'Oh, if you can spare them,' Marigold said, and Clara found a paper bag to put them in.

'There's seven there. One a-piece.'

Marigold took them gratefully and rewarded Clara with a smile. 'That's ever so kind, Mrs Stokes. Thank you ever so much. They'll love these.'

'Well, go and fill your buckets, my flower, and I'll see you next time you're this way.'

'I hope it'll be soon, Mrs Stokes.'

On his ride home from work, Algie decided that he must call on Harriet Meese to explain his absence last night and to tell her he wished to end their courtship, unaware that Kate had already done so. He turned over in his mind the things he would say, mentally rehearsing them, imagining her replies and reactions. He was not looking forward to it, but it had to be done. It was for Harriet's own good, too, for it would release her, make her available to somebody more deserving of her refined qualities.

It was not that Algie didn't like Harriet. He liked her well enough, he respected her. She was exactly the sort of girl he should court seriously, exactly the sort of girl he should marry. He could hardly conceive of her ever going against his wishes, of her ever doing anything without his consent. She would be eternally faithful and loyal, raise his children faultlessly, and seldom, if ever, be shrewish. If only he could have fallen in love with her . . . But he had not fallen in love with her, nor ever would. It might have helped if she'd been blessed with a pretty face. But she had not, and that would never change either, and so her face, the foremost obstacle to her potential to fascinate, remained irresolvable. He regarded her as cold and aloof, as shying away from physical contact, but in this Algie was mistaking her instilled chastity for frigidity. Anyway, he did not enjoy kissing her at all; she had a faint, furry moustache that really put him off. On those occasions when he had kissed her he'd imagined he could feel it tickling him; hardly a pleasant sensation, and he could not foresee having to endure that for the rest of his virile manhood. He could not imagine fulfilling his marital bedtime duty without wishing he were fulfilling it with somebody else. In any case, as she grew older she was bound to become stout – you only had to look at her mother to see how the daughter would turn out . . .

It was best that he ended it, he reassured himself. He had the perfect reason now. He had found a girl he wanted, a girl he liked, with whom he would be less half-hearted.

Algie rode on, assiduously avoiding getting his wheels

trapped in the tramlines as he was jolted over the cobbled surface. Between Queen's Cross and Brierley Hill town it was mostly downhill, save for a slight uphill gradient at Holly Hall, which was hardly likely to trouble him. He coasted to a halt at Meeses' drapery shop and leaned his bicycle against the stone window sill.

The bell chinked with reliable monotony as he thrust the door open and there, facing him over the bolts of cloth that adorned the counter, was the stern, fat, uncompromising countenance of Eli Meese. Eli rose from his stool at sight of Algie, bridling like a frenzied bull that had been goaded by the proverbial red rag.

'What do *you* want?'

'I'd like to see Harriet, please, Mr Meese.'

'Oh, yes?' He nonchalantly scratched his fat backside, partly for effect, partly because it itched. 'The trouble is, our Harriet don't want to see you.'

'Oh? Why not?'

''Cause you'm a bad un, that's why.' Eli looked Algie squarely in the eye. 'I know all about you and your shenanigans. I know you was off with some slattern from the cut last night when our Harriet was here waiting for yer like the true soul she is, mythered to death over yer 'cause yo' hadn't showed up and she knows no better. I waited with her an age meself, like a mawkin, till I could see as you was never gunna show your ugly fizzog. I'm churchwarden, you know . . .' He prodded his chest importantly with his forefinger. 'And I tek me responsibilities serious. Not to be hindered by the likes of you.' With consummate contempt, he wagged the same forefinger at Algie. 'So from now on, I *forbid* you to see our Harriet. Besides, you'm neither use nor ornament. Her can do better for herself, can our Harriet, than a ne'er-do-well like you as'll never mek anythin' of himself. So bugger off, lad, and if I ever see or hear of you sniffing round our Harriet again, I'll draw blood, so help me.' The bull swelled up threateningly and seemed to snort. 'Now sod off!'

Algie considered that to retreat while he was still standing was his best option.

'Will you just tell her I called, Mr Meese?' he said feebly, opening the door to make his ignominious exit, which made the bell chink annoyingly again.

'I'll tell her all right, have no fear. I'll tell her what I've just told you an' all.'

Outside in the warm early evening air, Algie blew out his lips, perplexed, which hurt the fragile split that he'd acquired last night. As he cocked his leg over his bicycle to ride away, feeling ever so humble, he gently touched the wound and looked at his fingers circumspectly to see whether there was blood on them. There was, and he rode away, nursing it.

How in God's name had the Meeses found out that he had been with Marigold last night? News travels fast in communities like Brierley Hill, but surely never that fast. It would never have occurred to Algie that his own sister was the culprit.

Anyway, he had better things to contemplate. He had Marigold to see. He wondered if the Binghams had passed through Buckpool yet, or whether they were still stuck in Kidderminster. Either way, he would ride along the canal's towpaths till he found her. And he would wallow in her warm, newly won affection . . .

Chapter 6

'I'm hungry,' Algie complained to his mother when he returned home. 'Is tea ready?'

'Your tea won't be ready for another half hour,' Clara replied, peering into the oven. Its cast-iron door closed with a reassuring clang, but the aroma of roasting cheese and onion had seeped out long before and filled the cottage with a tantalising aroma, making Algie feel even hungrier. Clara regarded him quizzically. 'What've you done to your lip?'

'My lip? Oh . . . I did it at work.'

'It looks as though you've been fighting.'

'Me, fighting? No, I walked into a brass rod somebody was carrying.'

'You want to be more careful. You could've poked your eye out.'

'How long's my tea gunna be, Mother?' he asked again, anxious to divert her from the topic lest he dig himself into a hole and let slip some clue that might reveal the sordid truth of how he'd really acquired his injury.

Clara began slicing a cabbage at the table. 'It won't get served till your father comes back from mending a lock gate by the dry dock.'

'What's up with it, then?'

'Winding gear's broken, he said. Why don't you go and see if you can help him?'

'But I'm starving hungry.'

'Then have one of those jam tarts.' She nodded at the tray on the table. 'I've already given a few to Marigold.'

'Marigold?' He picked one out and took a bite. 'She's been here?'

'She called to say they'd be moored up just beyond the Parkhead Locks.'

Algie beamed. 'Good. That's all I wanted to know.'

Clara gave him a knowing look. 'Just mind what you'm up to with that young girl,' she said.

'Course I will,' he said. 'What d'you think I'm gunna do?'

'I'm just afeared she might get too attached to you, and I wouldn't want you to hurt her.'

'Hurt her?' he queried.

'Yes, hurt her,' Clara replied. 'I wasn't too keen on you seeing her at first, our Algie, but she's won me over good and proper. She's a lovely girl. Now . . . if you're going to start seeing her regular, just be kind to her.'

What a strange thing for his mother to suggest, as if he was capable of being unkind. He shrugged at her apparent lack of understanding. 'I don't intend to hurt her, Mother. I think the world of her. I really like her. Can I have another jam tart?'

'Help yourself.' He turned around and took another. 'What I mean is, Algie, Marigold has it hard enough on the cut. So does her mother, who was never brought up to live life on a narrowboat. It ain't like living in a nice comfortable house with a warm hearth, soft feather beds and running water laid on, 'specially when that's what you've been used to.'

'Did you know Marigold's mother?' Algie asked, his curiosity roused. 'Afore she lived on the cut, I mean?'

'Yes, I knew her. Not well, mind. But I knew *of* her.' Clara transferred the cabbage to a pan containing cold water and immersed the shreds.

'Marigold told me her mother came from round here. So I suppose you could've known her before, eh, Mother?'

'Not that well, like I say.'

Algie took another bite out of his jam tart. 'So what brought her living on the cut in a narrowboat?'

'Because she wed a boatman, I suppose,' Clara answered dismissively. 'I ain't so sure I would've done, but *she* did.'

'There's good families on the cut, Mother,' he commented, more in defence of Marigold than anybody else. 'Old Seth Bingham's all right. He's a decent bloke.'

'I'm not saying he isn't. And I'm sure Hannah must've thought so to marry him . . .'

He shrugged as if it was of no consequence. 'As long as she's content, I say. She seems content. So does Marigold.'

''Tis to be hoped she is. 'Tis to be hoped they all are. So does this mean you've given up Harriet?' Clara lifted the pan of cabbage onto the hob. The coals in the fire shifted and a flurry of sparks flitted up the chimney.

'Yes . . .' He took a last bite of jam tart.

'Shame . . .' Clara sighed. 'She's a nice respectable girl.'

'I know she is.'

'Have you told her yet?'

He shrugged nonchalantly. 'I've tried. I called to see her on my way home tonight, but old Eli wouldn't let me. He told me to clear off. Says he's forbid her to see me ever again. He already knew somehow as I'd been with Marigold yesterday. How d'you reckon he found that out, eh? He knew almost as quick as I knew it meself.'

'Oh, I bet your name's mud,' Clara said, with some conviction. 'Word travels fast in a place like this. Everybody knows everybody else's business.'

'But it made me look as though I hadn't considered Harriet at all, and I had. I had, Mother, honest. I wanted to be straight with her . . . Oh, well . . .' He shrugged, and turned to go. 'I think I'll go and see if my dad wants any help. If not, I'll clean my bike. It could do with an oiling after its dunking in the cut yesterday.'

'Go on, then, and I'll give you a shout.'

'Is our Kate back yet?'

'She's upstairs, a-changing.'

'Changing?' he queried disdainfully. 'Let's hope she changes for the better.'

The implication was lost on his mother, as he knew it would be.

Algie lumbered outside. Out of curiosity he decided to inspect the far side of the shed, where he'd witnessed Kate and Reggie Hodgetts up to their antics, to see if there was any evidence of what had happened. He kicked over the traces and noticed a small footprint in the line of sandy earth where his father's potatoes were planted, obviously that of a woman – Kate's, of course. He kicked over that too, else his father was bound to see it and wonder what a woman had been doing there, and under what circumstances, trampling his precious produce. Despite Kate's unsavoury wantonness, he still had to protect her; she was his sister, after all.

After that, he passed through the gate, clambered over the lock gates and onto the towpath, heading towards the dry dock, where they repaired ailing narrowboats. Will Stokes was bolting a new cast-iron pinion wheel and brake to the lock's winding gear. Narrowboats from both directions waited in the basins above and below while he completed the job, so they could continue their journeys. Meanwhile, the boatmen gathered around him watching, enjoying good-natured banter and swapping gossip with the workers from the dry dock, who lived in the row of cottages on the other side of a little cast-iron bridge.

'Hello, Son,' Will greeted.

'Did you see the Binghams pass through earlier?'

'Aye, just before I started work on the lock.'

'I've come to see if you need any help.'

'It's the time to come now I've nearly finished,' Will quipped with a grin. 'Just gotta tighten these bolts, check the alignment and grease it. You can pass me that tub o' blackjack, though, our Algie.' Will pointed with a huge spanner to the pail of thick, black bitumen grease.

'Will it want warming up?' Algie queried as he went to fetch it from the towpath where it was standing along with Will's thick canvas toolbag.

'No, it'll be a bit on the stiff side, but in this warm weather it should be workable.'

Algie picked it up and took it over to his father. 'I read today in the newssheet at work that Lord Sheffield's eleven took a beating by the Australians.'

'Did they?' A look of disappointment clouded Will's face as he looked up from his work. He was a keen follower of cricket and liked to keep abreast of all the first class matches. 'I never heard. What was the score?'

'The Aussies won by an innings and thirty-four runs.'

'Damn! Was W. G. Grace playing?'

'Yes, but he only scored twenty in the first innings and nine in the second. I reckon he ain't half as good as what he's made out to be.'

'Wait till the test match in July. He'll show 'em who's the best batsman in the world.'

'Pooh, I doubt it, Dad,' Algie argued. 'Not on his showing this week.'

A discussion ensued, also involving all the men gathered

around, about the merits or otherwise of the world famous W. G. Grace. It seemed to go on for ages, by which time Will finished his task and collected his tools together. Father and son walked back to the cottage, but Algie removed himself to the shed, to tend to his precious bike.

Algie was so proud of his Swift bicycle with its pneumatic tyres. It was in desperate need of a thorough clean after its unscheduled dip in the cut, so he set about polishing it up. When it was gleaming again, he picked up the oil can and oiled the wheel hubs and the brake linkages, then trickled a few spots over the chain. Rust was the arch enemy of the conscientious cyclist, especially when the machine had cost twelve pounds of hard-earned and hard-saved money.

As he applied the oil, he became interested for the first time in the engineering that had gone into the bicycle's manu-facture. It struck him that with the proper jigs and fixtures at his disposal he could make a machine like this. It was hardly like building a complicated steam engine. His research into bicycles, before making his purchase, had revealed that the frames of some were made from bamboo, for lightness. But bamboo would not do for him. He would prefer to sacrifice that inherent lightness for the durability of steel. And so would most other folk who had to save hard and long to be able to afford a bicycle. They wouldn't want to see their bamboo frame warp and split. The only obstacle he foresaw to building a machine like his would be making the wheels – all those spokes. A wheel seemed like a perfect work of art; so precise, so finely balanced. If only he had enough money to start a business making bikes . . . maybe he could even buy the wheels already finished from another firm. He would start designing bikes anyway. They were all the rage. Everybody was mad about bikes.

Such enterprising thoughts eclipsed the immediate guilt he

felt about Harriet Meese. However, it niggled him to realise that Eli, the grumpy old devil, had prevented him from seeing her when Algie believed he had a perfect right. He'd been anxious to explain to Harriet how he felt; that he honestly believed she would be better off released from any obligations of loyalty to himself. Their courtship, however apathetic on his part, had left him with a great deal of respect and admiration for her. Perhaps he should write to her, explaining his side of the story.

The ride along the towpath towards the Parkhead Locks took Algie through the most squalid, intensively industrialised landscape on the face of the earth. From the lock-keeper's cottage at Buckpool the canal followed the contour around the hill, meandering first between a tile works, a small iron-works, workshops, and several collieries. Some of the collieries were still active, others defunct, but all had their forbidding black spoil encroaching everywhere. There were gas works, brick and firebrick works with their attendant clay pits, gener-ally filling up with dangerously murky water. Huge red-brick cones loomed, presiding over the bottle works and potteries to which they were attached. And all this before the area's industry got to be really densely packed.

Algie rode up the incline at the Nine Locks, keen to see the fresh, new girl in his life, not minding the visual blight which so much heavy manufacturing had engendered. Rather he wondered at it, when he bothered to contemplate it at all, as a symbol of a richer life; it brought relative prosperity, giving folk some opportunity to pick and choose what work they did; it sucked up like a sponge the young men from the countryside who came in search of their fortunes, as well as country girls who sought excitement, husbands, more lucra-tive work in factories, or the guarantee of ample food and a clean bed that working in service offered.

At Round Oak it was overwhelming. The vast ironworks owned by the Earl of Dudley, and known to all as 'The Earl's', surrounded him on every side. Its massive furnaces released roaring pillars of flame that would redden the midnight sky like a storm at dawn. The canal here vied for space not only with the furnaces, the rolling mills and vast travelling cranes, but with the network of internal railways and their clanking, hissing locomotives. Chimney stacks pricked the sooty sky; a haphazard array of obelisks erected in celebration of man's daring enterprise. Beam engines dipped and withdrew their gigantic arms, pumping water out of deep mines, where night and day were ever one, and work never ceased. There were lesser ironworks, another glut of collieries with huge circling wheels atop their tall headgear. Glowing slag laced the tops of black spoil banks like the flame-licked soot at the back of a fire grate. The stoke-holes of brick kilns glimmered through their own smoke, and fountains of fiery sparks spat from under black-roofed workshops with sides open to the elements. Forges, where monstrous thudding hammers shook the earth, crudely smote and shaped yellow-hot metal into preordained designs.

Algie reached Parkhead, spanned as it was by an impressive viaduct that bore the Great Western Railway between Oxford and Wolverhampton, and all points between. At last he spotted Seth Bingham's highly decorated narrowboats moored abreast, at the basin near the entrance to the canal tunnel. Hannah was pushing some garment or other through the cast-iron mangle, while Marigold was amid the flutter of drying skirts and shirts, pegged out on a line which stretched from the chimney pipe to the front of their butty, and propped in the middle.

'Marigold!' Algie called, as he pulled up alongside and dismounted.

She turned to greet him with a perky smile. 'Hello, Algie. Your mother gave you the message then?'

He nodded and grinned. 'Course she did.'

'I won't be a minute. I've just gotta hang these last few things.'

'What time did you go past our house?' he enquired.

'About four, I think. Your mom gave me some of her jam tarts.'

'Nice, aren't they? I had a couple meself.'

She nodded. 'Beautiful. Shan't be a minute,' she said, and disappeared into the cabin.

While he waited, Algie chatted affably with Hannah, who was wiping down the mangle. Seth appeared from inside the *Sultan* and passed the time of day while he emptied the dolly tub in the long grass that lined the towpath. He was still talking as he carried it off and stored it in what they called the laid-hole. Soon, Marigold re-emerged, and stepped off the *Odyssey* onto the towpath. She took his arm affectionately and they began walking away.

'You didn't have to stay in Kidderminster last night then?' Algie commented.

'No,' she replied. 'When we got to the carpet factory, Jack was there. I told him straight away as I didn't see any point in us seeing one another anymore. I told him it was because I never knowed when I was gunna be there.'

Algie smiled with relief at this news. 'And what did he say?'

'That I'd been taking him too serious, and that it was nice just to see me when we did go to Kidder, even if it wasn't all the time. Anyroad, we was offloaded in no time.' She chuckled at that. 'Just goes to show, I'm sure he used to fix it that we couldn't get offloaded, just so as he could see me of a night time, just like you said. Lord knows how much that cost me dad, losing time like that, but I ain't said nothing.'

They walked past the locks, towards the bridge that would lead them away from the canal. Three canals met at this point and, in whichever direction the couple went, there were collieries and wharfs. There seemed no escape from the sights, sounds and smells of industry.

'If we go up this way, we get to Scott's Green,' he told her, wheeling his bicycle beside him. 'Beyond that there's some fields. We could sit on the grass there.'

She smiled at him admiringly.

'Where're you bound for tomorrow then?' Algie asked.

'Wolverhampton. But we gotta go through the tunnel first, loaded with iron bars . . . And Victoria don't like the tunnel's blackness. He can hardly see where he's going, poor horse.'

'So who'll lead him?'

'Our Charlie. He always does . . . Anyway, what've you done to your lip? It looks ever so sore.' Marigold peered at it with evident concern.

'I walked into a brass rod at work,' he said glibly, repeating the excuse he'd given his mother. 'It's much better now. It won't stop me kissing you.'

'Ooh, I ain't so sure as I want to kiss that,' she said squeamishly, scrutinising it with a little more zeal as they strolled. 'Are you sure you walked into a brass rod? It looks more like you've been fighting.'

'That's what my mother said.'

He had no particular wish to expose Kate's disgracefully immoral behaviour, yet neither did he see any point in concealing it from Marigold. He felt he could confide in her, so he confessed that he'd had a scuffle with Reggie Hodgetts and what it was over.

'That slime?' Marigold commented. 'What does she see in *him*? My dad hates the whole family of 'em. Troublemakers, they are. Thankfully, we don't see 'em that often.'

'I just hope he hasn't put her in the family way, that's all.'

'Oh, that would be *terrible*,' Marigold agreed.

'Anyway, they must have moored up somewhere close to our house last night. Let's hope they're miles away by now.'

They crossed the Stourbridge Road at Scott's Green near the Hope Ironworks, then ambled over an area of rough ground before crossing the busy mineral railway that operated between the Himley Colliery and the wharf at Springs Mire in Dudley. From that point they found themselves in undulating open fields at an area known as Old Park. Algie rested his bike on the grass, then they sat down in a hollow behind a grassy hillock. Marigold inched herself close beside him.

'Did you tell Harriet about me?'

'She knows I'm stepping out with you,' he replied ambiguously.

Marigold smiled with satisfaction while Algie remained quiet for a few seconds, looking out onto the distant headgear of the pits that lay towards Gornal.

'I think our Kate's a trollop,' he remarked. 'Don't you think so, Marigold?'

'Depends.' She teased some stray strands of dark hair from over her eye. 'With him, yes, 'cause he's horrible.'

'Would you do such a thing?'

'Lord, no,' she protested. 'Not with him at any rate.'

'And not without being married either, I expect, eh?' he suggested experimentally, trying to glean whether she felt the same as Harriet about such things.

'Some o' the couples that live on the narrowboats ain't proper wed,' Marigold said guilelessly. 'But they share a bed all the same, and I know zackly what goes on between 'em when they'm abed, 'cause I often used to hear me mom and dad at it when we was all abed in the *Sultan*. They'm proper wed at least, though, me mom and dad,' she added, to set the matter straight. 'But the way I see it, you don't have to be proper wed to do such things. It ain't as if marriage is some sort of key what opens a lock to that sort of thing.'

'You don't go to church, I suppose, Marigold?' he asked, somewhat astonished by the candidness of her response and yet encouraged by it. 'I mean, it's obvious you don't follow the Church's teaching.'

'Me? Go to church?' She laughed at the notion. 'When do I get the chance? The only time I ever went to church was when I was christened, me mom said. What would I know about what the Church learns you? Anyroad, what do I care?' She paused, pondering Algie's question before she spoke again. 'Am you religious, then, Algie?'

'Me?' he guffawed with exaggerated scorn. '*I* ain't religious.'

'But you've been going to church regular with that Harriet.'

'And never listened to much of it.'

'Too busy whispering sweet nothings into her ear, eh?' she fished.

'No. I preferred the singing, to tell you the truth ... Are you sure you don't fancy kissing me, Marigold, with my bad lip?'

Their spooning was seriously impaired by Algie's poorly lip, but that did not prevent him from endeavouring to see how far Marigold would let him go. Yet he began to feel guilty that perhaps it was too soon in their courtship to expect her to be submissive. She rebuffed his advances repeatedly, but without rebuke, which only served to enhance his esteem of her nature.

'No, Algie,' she replied firmly, after he'd attempted several times to fondle her breasts. 'I ain't a girl like that, to give in to a chap when I ain't known him that long.'

'But you've known me years.'

'Not like that, I ain't.'

'So how much longer d'you need to know me?'

'Dunno.'

'A week? . . . Two? . . . A month?'

'I don't *know*, Algie . . .'

'Don't you like me enough?'

'Yes, I do . . . That's the trouble.'

He was heartened by her candid admission. 'But I want you, Marigold.'

'What if I let you go all the way and you put me in the family way—?'

'I wouldn't.'

'You can't say that.'

'I just did. And I'll say it again. I wouldn't put you in the family way.'

'I was about to say, what if you put me in the family way and then scarpered?' She looked into his eyes, her sincerity and emotion shining through like beacons. 'I ain't sure of you yet, Algie. You might still go back to Harriet, for all I know.'

'Never.'

'My dad says you should never say "never".'

'But I mean it.'

'Well . . . maybe when I'm sure of you . . .'

'You can be sure of me now, Marigold.'

'Not yet I can't.'

Algie and Marigold did not see each other after that night for several weeks. The Bingham's haulage work took them serially up and down the Shropshire Union Canal between Cheshire and Wolverhampton and Algie did not know where he would be able to find her. He could have ridden fruitlessly for miles. He would have written her a letter, but even if Marigold could have read it, he would have no idea to where he should address it. So they had parted tenderly with the promise that she would leave a message with his mother again when they next returned to Buckpool.

Algie's thoughts were usually with Marigold while she was away. He was well and truly taken, and she a mere boatman's daughter. Hardly a minute would pass when he did not think longingly about her, aching for the time when she would be in his arms again.

Meanwhile, he kept himself occupied at night. Sometimes he would meet the chum whom he worked with, Harry Whitehouse, and they would tour the local public houses and assembly rooms. With a bravado that was entirely assumed they would laddishly ogle and talk to any likely females they encountered, but none measured up to Marigold. Other times, he would stay at home designing bicycles, dreaming vainly of the day when he could start his own business manufacturing them. Of course, it was a pipe dream. He did not have the finances, and he knew nothing about the ins and outs of embarking on such a venture. It was the sort of undertaking that should sensibly be shared with a solvent partner who was prepared to stump up some cash and take the attendant financial risk, but finding somebody like that was another matter. So there was little hope of ever accomplishing it.

One evening, for want of something better to do, he even forced himself to write to Harriet:

Dear Harriet,

I thought it was about time I wrote to you to say what I called round your house to say when your father wouldn't let me see you. I hope that by now the dust has settled and that you don't think too badly of me, and that you are keeping well, your sisters included.

The truth is, Harriet, my heart had not been in our

courtship for some time, and I believe you sensed it. Priss seemed to, at any rate. It would have been unfair of me to keep you tagging along believing that at some time there would be something at the end of it. You are too decent a person and too loyal to be treated like that and I wanted to talk to you about it even before I met Marigold, my new sweetheart. Somehow I always seemed to lack the courage to get round to saying it.

I suppose that, because I wasn't committed enough to you, it was easy to be captivated by another girl. The trouble is, I wanted to tell you all this myself. I didn't want you to hear it first from somebody else. However you found out, you knew almost as soon as I knew about Marigold myself. I don't suppose I'll ever know who told you, but gossip can be a wicked thing. The benefit for you, Harriet, is that you are now well rid of me and free to do as you please. There are plenty of other fish in the sea. So if another young man pops up who you like, well, you'll be able to go out with him with a clear conscience if he asks you.

I am only sorry that your father has forbidden us to meet ever again. Despite everything, I would still like to consider you my friend, and I suppose I always will. If ever I see you about, I hope that you will not ignore me because of my actions, which I realise must appear very unseemly to you.

I remain, therefore, your friend,
Algernon Stokes.

During those long weeks, Marigold pondered deeply this unanticipated love affair which had so radically changed her outlook and expectations of life. She seemed to have grown up, almost overnight. She was no longer the frivolous adolescent girl who ran ahead to the locks as she'd done, even as a child, to help her father, but a woman, with a woman's feelings. Her love for Algie was earnest, and growing more intense the longer she was away from him. She did not want to lose him, but was fearful that he might lose patience waiting so long, and so seek Harriet's company again. Harriet was a perpetual concern, somebody Marigold worried about constantly. What if Harriet, eager to welcome Algie back, felt obliged to give in to any sexual demands he might make, just to make sure she held on to him? Such thoughts plagued her incessantly, especially when she went to bed at night. They kept her awake, rousing her jealousy and her anxiety to intolerable heights. It was an unremitting fear, a fear that made her all the more anxious to be with Algie and beat Harriet to it. Consummation of their love was the one factor that she believed had the potential to bind them together irrevocably, totally, both mentally and physically. It was the one single factor which would make sure Harriet Meese was forever shut out of Algie's thoughts and Algie's life. And although Algie had implied that that one single factor would at some time be expected in his relationship with Marigold, he had never actually pressed her too hard into feeling that it must happen immediately and at all costs. Whenever she had gently rebuffed his amorous advances, he had never shown any resentment, merely good-humoured resignation.

Any reluctance had been on her part. Yet it was not a reluctance in the sense that she was unwilling. Oh, she would have been willing enough already. Her uncertainty about Algie had precluded her so far, and she'd told him so honestly. If, when next they met, he was still as keen on her as he had been last time, she would feel much more at ease, much more inclined. They had talked about it, and he had asked her views on whether she felt it was right before marriage. Since then, she had considered everything there was to consider on the subject, and with some preoccupation, including the risks, the shame on her family if she became pregnant, the subsequent worry it would most certainly cause her mother, who had worries of her own without adding to them. She'd anticipated the guilt she might feel doing something which would only collect her mother's and father's total disapproval. She'd also pondered the life she could expect if Algie was dishonourable and left her with a child, to a life on the narrowboats with all that it entailed. It was not an arrangement she would wish for. Rather she looked forward already to a life on dry land in a nice warm house with a cosy fireplace . . . with Algie.

Yet she had to trust him. For her own peace of mind there was no alternative. She could hardly go through life mistrusting this man she loved so much. It was not that he did not inspire her trust, more that she lacked confidence in her ability to keep him interested, and she was increasingly apprehensive about Harriet in consequence. If she submitted to Algie, she would be doing it out of sheer love and respect for him; to better their relationship; to add a deeper, more understanding dimension to it, to render it more secure.

Naturally enough, she had no idea of what physical sensations to expect from full-blown lovemaking, but its promise was tantalising. She'd heard other women talk about it from time to time – usually married women – and their comments, whether sincere or boasting, whether guileless or bravado, led her to believe that it must bring some sort of pleasure as yet unimaginable, but intense enough for them to ignore the risks, whatever some might claim.

She was not too young for that sort of thing, either, especially when she considered that her mother must have been already carrying her at the same age. She was big enough and old enough to bear children, old enough to be married, so certainly old enough to conceive a child. She even knew of girls who'd had babies at sixteen.

She thought about talking it all over with Algie first, but dismissed the idea. She knew his opinion already. It would be like inviting a hungry man to share a meal with her. In any case, there was nothing he could say that might significantly alter her position. The more she considered it, the clearer it became: it was time to break any hold that Harriet might still have, and achieve it by allowing Algie to make love to her, body and soul. She had already discerned his susceptibility. Besides, the prospect of it thrilled her; she was sure she would enjoy it at least as much as him . . .

Chapter 7

Kate Stokes had quickly fallen into the habit of calling for Harriet and Priss Meese on Wednesday nights so they could arrive together at the Drill Hall for rehearsals. This particular Wednesday towards the end of June was no exception, and Kate tapped on the side door at the top of the entry that led to the Meeses' house. She was not invited in, however, nor was she likely to be as the sister of that bluebeard Algie, yet neither did Harriet and Priss keep her waiting out of deference to her; after all, she was not Algie, but his sister who had no control, no dominion over him. As they all walked down the entry together, the clickety-tap of their dainty boots echoed off the blue-brick floor.

They dispensed with the small talk within the first fifty yards and got down to the more serious business of discussing *The Forest Princess*.

'How are you getting on with your lines, Kate?' Priss asked.

'Pretty well, I reckon,' she replied brightly. 'It's a big part, but I'm determined to learn the words by heart till I'm sick to death of 'em. I don't want nobody moaning to Mr Osborne that he should've picked somebody with more experience to play Pocahontas.'

'All that archaic language,' Harriet remarked. 'All those *thees* and *thous*.'

114

'I know . . . Still, that's how they used to talk in the olden days.'

'Even the Redskins, according to whoever wrote the play . . . What do you think of Mr Osborne as Powhatan?'

'As Pocahontas's father? I reckon he'll be all right, 'specially when he's wearing that feather headdress, and he's got some o' that grease paint on to make his fizzog brown.'

Priss smiled. 'I think so too . . . He's quite a character, you know, is Mr Osborne. So dedicated to the society.'

'You know that Katie Richards who played the lead part in that comedy you did before?' Kate asked.

'In *My First Client*, you mean?'

'Yes. She hasn't spoken to me at all, but I've tried to smile at her and that.'

'I suppose she feels a bit put out that you've taken the lead role from her,' Harriet suggested. 'Not that any of us take for granted that we're going to get plum parts.'

'Well, it ain't my fault, is it? I mean, I didn't ask for it. Mr Osborne asked me.'

'What's your opinion of Mr Froggatt?' Harriet enquired falteringly.

'Mr Froggatt?' Kate looked at Harriet and perceived that she was blushing. 'Oh, he's a sweetheart.'

'You like him, do you?'

'I'm glad it's him playing the part of John Rolfe—'

'The man you marry,' Harriet added coyly, as if there were some hidden ironical twist to it.

Kate laughed. 'I know . . . Now he'd be a fine catch for you, Harriet. Still unwed, handsome—'

'And excellent prospects . . .' Priss remarked typically. 'The only son of Dr Froggatt. You could certainly do worse for yourself than Dr Froggatt's son, our Harriet.'

'But it's foolish of you to think of Mr Froggatt and me in

that way, Priss,' Harriet protested mildly. 'It's like comparing us with the princess and the frog, only the other way round. I'm sure he'd be far more interested in Kate.'

'Do you think so?' queried Kate, affecting surprise.

'I'm sure of it . . . if he thought you were available.'

'Oh, I'm available.'

'Oh, are you, Kate?' Harriet sounded surprised. 'Algie told me not so long ago that you were seeing some chap . . . Somebody called Hodgetts, I believe he said.'

'Our Algie told you that?' Kate became suddenly alarmed. If news of her wantonness at the back of the shed had reached Harriet after all . . . 'When did he tell you that?'

'Oh, before he . . . before he became interested in that . . . that other girl.'

'Well, our Algie was wrong, Harriet,' Kate said emphatically. 'And I'll tell him as much when I get back home. I ain't tied up with nobody. 'Specially nobody called Hodgetts. I don't know where he got that daft idea from. Wait till I see him.'

'He was quite concerned for you,' Harriet persisted, loyally defending Algie. 'He said he didn't like him very much. The thing is, Kate, you could have your pick of men, if you don't mind me saying so, a girl with your looks. It's why I mentioned Mr Froggatt. He seems to look at you with such great interest.'

'Me? I don't think so, Harriet. I think you must be mistook.'

'Well, I don't believe so. I've witnessed it with my own eyes. How he looks at you when he's reading the part . . . And, oh, my goodness, how he held your hand so tellingly in the scene where he proposes to you in front of Powhatan. Even though you were only reading, and not yet acting.'

'Oh, I think he was just trying to get into the mood of the part, Harriet,' Kate responded dismissively. 'Anyway, he'll have a long wait if he thinks I'm going to be interested in *him* . . .

116

I could always tell him that *you* fancy him, though, Harriet. I'd be happy to give *your* chances a boost.'

'Oh, no, please don't, Kate. Oh, I beg of you, don't say anything.'

'Are you sure? I could have sworn I detected some interest in him.'

'Oh, I think he's very nice, to be sure, but he's hardly for me . . .'

'What do you mean, *hardly* for you?' pried Priss.

'Well . . . it wouldn't be fair on him . . .'

'Oh? Why on earth not?'

'Because I'm still smarting over Algie, to tell you the truth.'

'Lord knows why,' Priss remarked disdainfully, and rolled her eyes.

Harriet shrugged. 'It's easy for you to scoff, Priss, but losing him has hurt me far more than ever I thought it could.'

'Good gracious, Harriet!' Kate exclaimed. 'You really do surprise me.'

'I surprise myself, Kate. He wrote to me, you know, apologising for not being straight with me sooner.'

'He wrote?' Kate queried. 'What did he say?'

'As I say, it was just an apology. I ought to reply soon.'

'I wouldn't,' Priss said. 'After the deceitful way he treated you.'

'But there's no reason why we shouldn't still be friends, Priss. I like Algie. He's basically very decent . . .' She turned to Kate. 'So what's he been doing lately? Seeing his new lady friend, I imagine.'

'I don't think he's seen her for weeks. She hasn't been our way at all lately, as I know to.'

'Maybe it's all over with her then?'

Kate shrugged. 'I couldn't say. He don't tell me his secrets. But I wouldn't trouble myself over him, if I was you. He ain't

117

worth it. I told you . . . And the best way to get over one love affair is to get started with another. It's better than any poultice, you know.'

Harriet smiled demurely.

They arrived at the Drill Hall and entered. The Little Theatre group was a mix of all the social classes, people with a shared interest in being involved, in however small a way, for the satisfaction it gave them. Seats had been set in a circle in the middle of the room, and several were occupied already by an assortment of women, some not so fashionably dressed, others in tight-bodiced costumes and the latest in toques and bonnets. Harriet, Priss and Kate sat down and said good evening to those already seated. Murdoch Osborne was standing by the stove, talking to the assembled males of the group and Katie Richards. Presently, Clarence Froggatt, well-dressed in a smart jacket and a necktie, arrived and made his way at once to the three girls.

'Good evening, Pocahontas,' he greeted, beaming with abundant good humour. 'Good evening, Miss Alice. Good evening, Miss Anne.'

'Good evening, Mr Rolfe,' Kate answered for all three, likewise using his character name, while Harriet blushed decorously and averted her eyes.

'Learned our lines yet, have we?' He looked from one to the other expectantly.

'I've been working hard learning mine,' said Kate.

'Splendid. Maybe we should attempt a first run through without the script, you and I at any rate, Miss Stokes.'

'If you like, Mr Froggatt.' She smiled at him, more coquettishly than previously, after hearing Harriet's observations of his apparent regard for her. 'But I would've thought that was up to Mr Osborne.'

'Oh, he'll be delighted that we're both being so conscientious, I'm sure.'

More of the players arrived and eventually Murdoch Osborne called them all to order. Accordingly, the men drifted towards the vacant seats within the circle.

'Miss Stokes says she'd like to go through the play without the aid of her script, Mr Osborne,' Froggatt announced, glancing at Kate for her approval. 'Is that all right by you? I'll endeavour to do likewise.'

'Learnt your parts already, ha?' said Murdoch. 'Well, let's hear it then. Let's see if you can get through it without referring to the scripts. I'll be pleased as Punch if you can.'

So they began running through the play. Some received coaching from Mr Osborne as to how they should express their lines, including Kate and Clarence Froggatt. Kate felt herself blush as Clarence harkened to Murdoch Osborne and gave greater expression to Rolfe's admission of love for Pocahontas.

'You've just got rid of your comrades and you're thinking aloud about her, as you've been left to keep watch over that part of the forest,' Murdoch directed, interrupting Rolfe's flow. 'But you ain't seen Pocahontas yet, remember. All you know about her is what you've been told, and that she saved the life of Captain Smith. Try it again.'

Clarence Froggatt cleared his throat. '*How I wish I could catch sight of her. Such a gentle maid would be much pleasanter acquaintance in these wilds than yon rough comrades. I am already half in love with this forest maid for saving my friend Smith . . .*' He glanced at Kate hoping for some unfeigned reaction, watched closely by Harriet. But Kate's eyes were in her lap.

'That's more like it,' Murdoch said with approval. 'Now . . . you see a panther stalking his prey and you follow it. Suddenly, you spot a Red Indian girl reclining under a tree and you realise the panther is about to attack her. You begin to tremble at the responsibility that befalls you . . . Carry on . . .'

119

'*Beneath the shade of yon tree a Red Indian girl reclines. I'll nearer steal . . . Is she the panther's prey? Yes, there he is, crouching low, unseen.*' He pretends he is levelling a gun. '*Heaven nerve my arm! . . . Well shot! The brute is down, the maid unhurt . . . She comes this way.*'

'Aye, that's passable for now,' Murdoch claimed with a nod to Froggatt. He turned to Kate. 'Right-ho, then, Pocahontas. What have you got to say to this pale-faced stranger who just saved your life?'

Pocahontas looked at Rolfe with contrived coyness. '*So thou art the stranger whom the forest maid must thank. Within yon shady nook where she a moment sat to rest, a panther lies dead. One instant more, without thy aid, and it is she who would have been the dead one. How shall the forest maid thank the stranger?*'

'*Nay, no thanks, sweet maid. It is enough to have saved thee. Mention it no more . . . May I ask thy name?*'

'*Matoka is my name. The tribes of this land, which your people call Virginia, know me as Pocahontas . . .*'

'Well spoken, both,' Murdoch Osborne remarked with an amiable smile.

They continued their reading. At each attempt the company's confidence grew, the meaning they put into the words became more earnest, and the whole play more believable. At the end of it, Murdoch Osborne took Kate to one side.

'I'll give you a lift home in the gig, Kate. I should hate anything to happen to our leading lady for want of seeing her home safe. It's a rough part of Brierley Hill you have to walk through, and there's no lamps to speak of.'

'That's very kind of you, Mr Osborne,' Kate replied. 'But you needn't trouble yourself. I'll come to no harm. I normally walk part of the way with Harriet and Priss Meese.'

'Listen, it's no trouble. I'd rather I took you than not.'

She smiled sweetly. 'Thank you.'

'Just give us the nod when you're ready.'

She was about to return to the company of Harriet and Priss, who had moved towards the door to make their exit, when Clarence Froggatt approached her.

'Kate, would you allow me to walk you home?'

'Stone me if there isn't a sudden outbreak of gallantry hereabouts,' she exclaimed dryly. 'I've just accepted Mr Osborne's offer to drop me off in his gig. Save my legs, it will.'

'Oh,' Clarence said, disappointment manifest in his eyes. 'That's very thoughtful of him. I can offer you nothing as grand as a gig. Merely Shanks's pony. Another time, maybe?'

'Who knows?' Kate smiled sweetly. 'In the meantime, Clarence, my friend Harriet Meese might appreciate your company if you're going her way. She could do with an escort.'

'But won't her sister be with her?'

'Two for the price of one, eh? Maybe your luck's in, Clarence . . .'

That same evening in June, Algie Stokes had returned home from work to the news that Marigold had called, and that the Binghams would be moored up in the basin at the Bottle and Glass. Before even he had his tea, he hurried to their narrow-boats, full of excitement, to cast his eyes over her lovely face again and to arrange to see her later.

He was enchanted, and it showed. Marigold, too, was suddenly on top of the world after all the nagging doubts she'd harboured; doubts which she now recognised were stupid and unreasonable. Algie still loved her, and she felt uplifted, relieved, ecstatic. It was obvious he did, else he would not be so happy and so keen to see her. She made an effort to look her best for him when he returned after he'd eaten and, when she smiled, affection oozed from her clear blue eyes.

'You look nice,' Algie remarked as she stepped off the gunwale of the narrowboat to be with him.

'Do I?' she said, needing his reassurance.

'You look nice enough to eat.'

'I want to look nice for you, Algie.'

'Well, you do,' he confirmed.

'It's lucky the weather's been so fair, don't you think? . . . And I'm glad to see your poorly lip's mended.'

He grinned waggishly, aware of what she meant. 'Yes, it's very serviceable now, I reckon.'

They headed, with an unspoken accord, in the direction of the secluded dell close to Dadford's Bridge. There, they might have expected to find at least one more courting couple, but again they were alone and sat down on the grass, hidden from the rest of the world in their own private little hollow, surrounded and hidden by gorse bushes and the steep, grassy knoll behind them. Algie took off his jacket, rolled it up and laid it on the ground behind them.

'Rest your head on my coat, eh?'

She did as she was bid and smiled up at him adoringly. He lay beside her, his head propped up on his arm, looking at her lovely face.

'I've missed you such a lot, Algie,' she whispered softly. 'I was thinking about you nearly all the time I was away.'

Touched by her openness, he bent his head and kissed her gently on the lips. 'I missed you as well, my little flower.'

'We kept getting loads up to Cheshire and back. It seemed as if I was never going to see you again.'

'Well, you're here now.'

'Have you really missed me?' she asked earnestly, delaying receipt of another kiss.

'Yes . . . I really have.'

'And you ain't snuck off to see Harriet?'

'No, never,' he protested sincerely. 'I promised I wouldn't, and I haven't. She doesn't mean anything to me anymore. She doesn't interest me. I thought you understood that.'

She lifted her face to his and her kiss was an apology for making the suggestion. 'I just have to be sure, Algie. You must've guessed by now that I can be a bit jealous . . . Besides,' she added wistfully, 'I was away so long . . .'

'You don't have to be jealous, Marigold,' he said with evident concern for her feelings. 'There's nothing to be jealous about. I told you I'd wait for you. And I have. I'll always wait for you. I promise.'

She smiled, her anxiety dispelled. 'Kiss me again, Algie. Long and gentle this time. A butterfly kiss. I always think of your gentle kisses as "butterfly kisses".'

He obliged her, lingering, tenderly savouring her sweet lips.

'I've been dying to come down here with you again, Algie.'

'Honest?'

'Honest.' She snuggled up to him contentedly, her head resting on his shoulder, relishing his arms around her.

A certain rigidity inside his trousers, unruly as ever, was insisting on more adequate accommodation, and he shifted his position to relieve the discomfort. He thrust his knee tentatively between hers, and she allowed it. Her long skirt was a frustrating barrier between them, but still he could feel the tantalising warmth of her thighs caressing his. He kissed her again, more ardently this time. His tongue probed her mouth while he held her small backside and pressed himself against her.

'I want you, Marigold,' he sighed heavily. 'I want to go all the way with you.'

'So it seems, by the feel of that thing against me belly,' she replied, feigning disregard, even though she enjoyed the sensation and her heart was pounding like a drum because of it.

'I suppose *you* don't want to?'

'Why do we have to talk about it, Algie? It spoils it all, talking about it.'

'Would it spoil it if I were to tell you I love you?' he asked.

'It's easy to say as much just to get your way,' she said challengingly. 'You have to mean it.'

'I do mean it. I missed you like hell while you was away. I was thinking about you all the time.' She melted in his arms at this admission, and he hugged her. 'If only I'd known where to find you . . .' He lifted her chin and planted another kiss on her lips. 'I'd have been there, believe me. Like a shot from a gun.'

'I think I'll always love you, you know, Algie,' she said dreamily. 'I thought about it a lot while we was up and down the cut.'

He took that as an invitation to undo the buttons of her blouse.

'What are you doing?' she said, feigning surprise, but with no indignation.

'Undoing your buttons.'

'What for?'

''Cause I want to feel your titties.'

'Well, you won't feel them proper through my chemise . . . Let me loosen it first.' She undid the buttons at the side of her skirt, slackening it, then pulled her chemise up above her waist. 'There . . .'

His breathing came heavier. He placed his hand on her bare stomach and the smoothness and tautness of her skin astonished him. Gently, he explored higher and reached one cool, silky breast. It was the first time he had ever felt a girl's breast like this, and he gave it an experimental squeeze. To his amazement it returned immediately to its original delightful contours as soon as he relaxed his gentle grip. To make sure it was not a unique phenomenon, he repeated the experiment with the other.

'They're so smooth,' he whispered, his voice a tight thread of emotion. 'They're ever so nice to feel, even though they ain't that big.'

'I think they're plenty big enough, Algie,' she replied, smiling to herself at his candidness. Then, feeling the need to be rewarded with a show of affection for allowing him unfettered access to her breasts, said, 'Kiss me, Algie. Another butterfly kiss.'

He was entirely content to kiss her again, and did so more passionately. While he was working her lips he wondered what it might be like kissing these delightful breasts, and pulled up her chemise a little further before nuzzling each in turn. To his astonishment, her small pink nipples hardened in response to his moist caresses.

'Oh, that's ever so nice, Algie,' Marigold sighed.

He was encouraged and, deeming it his bounden duty to venture south in the interests of seeking even greater mutual pleasure, took a handful of skirt and pulled the hem up above her knees. When his fingers ventured through the elasticated leg hole of her long drawers and found the soft, warm flesh of her thighs there, he thought his chest would burst with the intensifying pounding of his heart.

He returned to her mouth, plying her lips with gentle little bites and kisses, while he located the slit in her drawers and thereby gained access to the warm mound of hair secreted within.

'Oh, Algie . . .' Her whimper was a mix of anxious resignation and pleasant expectation, but not discouragement. Certainly not discouragement.

He caressed the soft, moist place between her legs with the greatest care and devotion. This was a moment he had only ever tried to imagine before; to be allowed such extreme liberties by a girl he really loved and admired. But the reality far exceeded the capability of his imagination. He was actually touching, feeling a girl . . . *there* . . . in this, the most mystical, the most privileged, the most private of places. It was a landmark in his life. It would be a landmark in the life of any young man – the first such extraordinary intimacy . . . Surely, it could only lead to that ultimate familiarity which he had always feared was going to elude him. Without doubt, this was a red letter day. He found it difficult to control his trembling at the electrifying prospect.

To add to his private elation, he encountered no resistance from Marigold, only complicity. After all her teasing last time they met, she seemed as anxious as him after all to fulfil what must have since become a mutual wish.

She in turn, was convinced of Algie's love. With this wondrous shared experience of total commitment to draw on, further doubts would not plague her next time they were apart.

Algie reluctantly removed his hand from the split in her drawers. But it was necessary in order to progress to the next stage and unfasten his fly. His trapped and aching manhood sprung free, like a jack-in-the-box released, while she virtuously avoided sight of it. Breathing heavily again, and feeling as nervous as he'd ever felt in his life, he rolled on top of her and guided himself back to the place he had just vacated. She parted her legs a little wider in anticipation, closing her eyes as she felt him press against her for entry.

'Oh, Algie . . .' The girlish tremor in her voice betrayed her nervousness, but she resigned herself to the inevitable outcome, welcoming it.

After an abortive series of gentle pushes, he confessed with frustrated inadequacy, 'I can't get him in, Marigold.'

'You ain't lined up right, I s'pose,' she whispered tenderly.

'Help me then. Guide him in.'

'It's like steering a narrowboat into a lock, ain't it?' She gave a little giggle to hide her embarrassment. 'It only just fits and you've only got a little opening to aim at.' She held him, and he felt her cool fingers gently embrace him as she carefully guided him into her, raising her knees and her back-side to make his entry easier. 'There,' she breathed, suppressing a little cry of pain; pain she had expected, pain which she was prepared to endure in her willing submission to this man she loved with all her heart.

'Well, Kate, this'll save your shoe leather and no mistake, ha?' Murdoch Osborne said, as they rode in his gig down Moor Lane's incline towards Buckpool.

'I said something of the sort to Mr Froggatt when he asked if he could walk me home,' Kate replied.

'He asked to walk you home, did he? He must have his eye on you, Kate. Still, who can blame him, ha?'

'I said he should go with Harriet Meese and her sister instead.'

Murdoch guffawed. 'Any wench would be glad to be took home by Clarence Froggatt, I would've thought. He's a smart enough young chap. I got a feeling that Miss Katie Richards was keen on him an' all at one time.'

'Katie Richards might still be, Mr Osborne, and she can have him for all I care. I better like chaps a bit older. He's only about the same age as our Algie, and he's as green as a cabbage.'

Murdoch laughed again. 'You're a canny wench, and no two ways, young Kate.' He flicked the reins and the horse broke into a steady trot.

'I reckon Harriet Meese would suit him better,' Kate continued. 'She's more of a lady than me. More up his street.'

'Oh, she's a decent young woman is Harriet, and no mistake. I reckon your Algie will live to regret passing her over, ha?'

'How long you been a widower, Mr Osborne?' Kate enquired, changing tack.

'Nigh on three years now.'

'D'you think you'll ever get wed again?'

'Me? I doubt it. Who in their right mind would have me?'

'I reckon you'd be a good catch,' she said brightly, deliberately to flatter him.

He grinned. 'You reckon so, ha?'

'Well, you can't be short of a shilling or two.'

'Nor am I,' he said with a deep belly laugh at Kate's forthrightness, which he found a refreshing change from the constricting piety of some women from his own generation. 'But I wouldn't get hitched to a woman just 'cause she took a fancy to me, ha? I'd have to tek a fancy to her as well.'

'Ain't there nobody you fancy?'

'Oh, one or two . . . but none o' the grim-faced harridans from hereabouts. Women mostly a sight younger than me. Too young to have any truck with me, at any rate.'

'You never know your luck, Mr Osborne,' Kate advised. 'Like I said, you'd be a good catch for somebody.'

'Mebbe so, mebbe not. Anyroad, I'm content to let things be. I got a maid to do me housework and a cook to feed me. Why should I want to tie meself to somebody else – unless I really took a fancy to her – ha?'

'How old are you?' she asked. 'You can't be that old.'

'I'm forty-five.' He glanced at her in the dimness.

'About the same age as me dad.'

'Aye, about the same age as your dad. I used to envy your dad, you know, when he was courting your mother.'

Kate smiled to herself at the candid admission. 'How many children you got, Mr Osborne?'

'Two daughters. Both wed. Not that I see much of 'em since their mother died. If I did, they'd only be after money, I daresay. As it happens, they both married well, so that problem don't arise, ha?'

'It must be grand to have a dad with plenty money,' Kate mused. 'My dad ain't got two ha'pennies to scratch his backside with.'

Murdoch roared. 'I shouldn't think he needs any for a wily daughter like you. If anybody's capable o' getting on in life without help from her father, I reckon it's you, Kate Stokes, ha?'

They soon arrived at the bridge over the canal. Murdoch stayed the horse while Kate alighted and, with a cheery wave, she disappeared with a patter of dainty footsteps into the darkness.

Marigold lay in the cross-bed of the butty that night with her younger sister Rose, her mind full of Algie Stokes and what they had shared so tenderly. She was finding it difficult to sleep, reliving over and over in her mind the dreamy hours they'd spent together that evening. She was entirely content that she had given herself to Algie. In return, he had loved her considerately, gently, and she had felt closer to him afterwards than she had ever felt towards anybody in her whole life before. Well, now the deed was done. She was no longer a virgin, no longer a young girl, but a woman. And she was not sorry. Virginity mattered not one jot to Marigold.

Besides, she had to exude much more appeal than that Harriet Meese, whom she still considered her deadly rival. And what better way? Sex had to be the surest magnet. Marigold was certain that she had gone far beyond what

Harriet would have allowed, and she was right. She had given Algie what he wanted. With the promise of more, he was less likely to drift back to Harriet's stricter, meaner embraces.

She was, however, a little disappointed with the physical aspect of love-making. If that's all there was to it, then she failed to see what all the fuss was about. It had been over before she had really got into the swing of things, but it had been pleasant enough once the initial sting had subsided to show some promise; pleasant enough at any rate for her to fancy a repeat. And that would be tomorrow night, provided they could get offloaded at Kidderminster in time to moor up at the Bottle and Glass again.

Chapter 8

Dear Algie,

Thank you very much for your letter. I was so glad to receive it, and to read your version of events at first hand. Yes, it is a pity that I heard about your dallying with this girl called Marigold from a source I am honour bound not to reveal. I can understand how the alacrity of gossip beat you into second place when it came to appearing in person to tell me, and the frustration it might have caused. I am sure I do not have to tell you how hurt and shocked I was. I do know, of course, that you called to see me, and I am sorry that my father did not allow me to speak with you.

As I say, it was all a dreadful shock to me. I had hardly expected it, since you had given me no inkling at all that you were so discontented. I suppose there is a lesson there, that we can sometimes be complacent in our affairs and just drift along, believing all is well when patently, in your case at any rate, it was not. I personally would have been content to continue as we were, but your own sensitivity obviously deemed it necessary that I be released into the fearful marriage market, when I'm not entirely sure that I ever want marriage anyway, nor the children and the attendant responsibilities that must inevitably ensue. In that respect, maybe you jumped too rapidly to conclusions

131

about what I wished for my future. So, if marriage and children are things that you eventually want, then it might well be for the best that our affair is ended.

Of course, I shall deem it a privilege to remain your friend, Algie. I have never harboured anything but affection and respect for you. So if we see each other out and about someday, then I shall be happy to acknowledge you and even stop to talk, if circumstances permit.

I am pleased to report that your sister Kate is doing splendidly well in the Amateur Dramatics Society's next offering, and I believe you will be surprised and delighted once you eventually come to see her perform when The Forest Princess *is staged at the end of October and beginning of November.*

I remain, your friend always,
Harriet Meese

The Drill Hall was buzzing with greetings and conversation as members of the Brierley Hill Amateur Dramatics Society assembled for their weekly rehearsal. Kate, Priss and Harriet had been discussing men in general and Algie Stokes in particular, as they ambled to join the rest of the cast. Marriage had cropped up in their conversation and differing points of view inevitably followed about the duties of a wife, which caused some laughter and some controversy between them. The discussion continued, amid the increasingly voluble chatter of the others.

'But why should a wife have a duty to adapt to her husband rather than a husband adapt to his wife?' Priss asked truculently.

'Maybe it's 'cause us women are more adaptable,' Kate suggested.

'And less important,' Harriet added. 'Somebody has to give

way in an argument, Priss, and that somebody is nearly always the wife.'

'I fail to see why.'

'So do I,' said Kate, changing her allegiance.

'I merely perceive it as the rule,' Harriet explained. 'As far as I can see, exceptions to the rule don't make for happiness on either side. I merely try to see things as they are, and order my life accordingly.'

'Which is why you allowed Algie Stokes to walk all over you,' Priss scoffed.

'He didn't walk all over me,' Harriet replied indignantly, glancing at the subject's sister Kate. 'I merely adapted myself to him.'

'I'd like to meet the man who could make me adapt myself to him,' proclaimed Priss.

'So should I,' Harriet countered. 'He might make you a happier woman . . . But whether you would make him a happier man is another matter.'

Priss chuckled at that, prepared to willingly suffer a joke at her own expense, and Kate laughed too. Kate had some sympathy with both points of view.

Clarence Froggatt sidled up to them, placing himself between Priss and Kate. He offered a jovial good evening to each and asked if it was possible to share the joke.

'I don't think you would appreciate it, Mr Froggatt,' Priss declared, still laughing.

'But rest assured, you are not the butt of it,' Harriet was careful to explain, to spare him any embarrassment.

'I'm glad to hear it . . . So, are we all prepared for a fault-less rehearsal?'

'A faultless stage performance would be a first, let alone a preliminary rehearsal,' said Priss. 'I believe you expect too much too soon, Mr Froggatt.'

'Better to live in hope, I always say.' He leaned towards Kate, and spoke quietly into her ear. 'May I have a word?'

'Yes.' She looked at him expectantly. 'What about?'

Clarence addressed the Meese sisters. 'Would you excuse us a moment, ladies?' he said apologetically, and detached Kate from the trio. 'I just wonder if you will allow me to drive you home afterwards, Miss Stokes.'

'Drive, did you say?'

'Yes.' He smiled nervously. 'I borrowed my father's dogcart so as to get here more quickly . . . I would've been late otherwise, you see.' He smiled pleasantly. 'I thought I would make the most of it and ask you before Mr Osborne had the chance. Unless, of course—'

'Thank you. That would be very nice.' Kate was smiling sweetly. 'But didn't you escort the Meese girls home last week?'

'Oh, indeed I did. But that surely doesn't mean, does it, that I've set a precedent which I have to abide by for eternity?'

She smiled radiantly. 'No, I reckon not. Although *they* might be disappointed. Or one of them at any rate.'

'They are both charming girls, and good company . . .'

'And you might get yourself a reputation as a Romeo.' She leaned towards him and whispered in his ear. 'I understand that even Miss Katie Richards used to be sweet on you.'

'Who told you that?'

'Never mind. Anyway, I'm not trying to push you away, Mr Froggatt,' Kate asserted with a warm smile. 'Nor push the Meese girls' interests either. I'm very happy to accept your offer of a lift.'

'I'm happy to hear you say so, Miss Stokes. My only hope is that Mr Osborne will not think me a Romeo in usurping his position as the conveyor home of the company's precious forest princess.'

'Why should he? He has no prior claim.'

'I wouldn't have thought so either, but I'm glad to hear it confirmed, all the same.'

Kate smiled demurely as Murdoch Osborne then called the gathering to order.

'I hope we've all memorised our lines by now,' he declared, ''Cause I'd like us to stand and begin to act our parts. If anybody isn't sure of their lines, then Miss Bennett will prompt.' He smiled patronisingly at Miss Bennett, a squarely built, middle-aged woman with an enormous mouth, who nodded her acknowledgement. 'Let's begin at page eighty where I, Powhatan, have given a belt to Dale, who has handed me the peace treaty in return.' The actors all began turning over pages hurriedly. 'We'll take it from the "Flourish of trumpets" . . . *Doo-doo-to-doo*,' he sang, trying to imitate a fanfare, to everybody's amusement. 'Mr Casey . . . you are Hunt, are you not?' Casey replied that he was. 'Then speak . . . He evidently needs a prompt, Miss Bennett. Would you?'

Miss Bennett looked at Mr Casey and prompted, '*Now hear me . . .*'

'*Now hear me,*' Casey responded with a grateful nod to his prompter. '*If this peace ye cherish, there is a way to make it endure. This youthful pair, thrown together by Providence, have looked into each other's heart and seen the same fond characters in each . . .*' Clarence glanced at Kate, their eyes met, and exchanged a very private smile. '*Let Powhatan wed his forest princess unto young Master Rolfe, and in that marriage strife will breathe its final breath.*'

'*This gives me happiness I dared not hope for,*' quoted Clarence. '*What does Virginia's king reply?*'

Murdoch spoke, as Powhatan: '*The pale-face is brave and young. He saved my daughter's life when the panther was about to strike. But he will take my daughter away, to his wigwam across the sea . . . Pocahontas clings fondly to Powhatan,*'

Murdoch Osborne added, looking at Kate expectantly. 'It's a stage direction, Kate . . . Cling fondly to me . . .'

Kate stepped forward and put her arms around Murdoch and he reciprocated by holding her around the waist, rather tightly, she thought. He continued his lines, still attached to Pocahontas. As Powhatan he gave his consent that Pocahontas could wed the pale-face, so Clarence, as the character Rolfe, duly advanced to Kate, who freed herself from Murdoch's enthusiastic embrace.

Kate looked into Clarence's eyes kittenishly and he was uncertain whether she was acting or not. If it was pure acting, it was very convincing. '*Stranger, Pocahontas will be thy wife.*' She laid her hand on Clarence's.

'I don't quite know what to make of Kate Stokes,' Harriet remarked in a half whisper, as she and Priss left the Drill Hall. 'She gave me the impression that she wasn't at all keen on Clarence Froggatt. I even believed that she might step aside for me if I'd wanted her to, but after their little *performance* tonight she was quick enough to clamber onto his dogcart as soon as they stepped outside.'

'Like a bitch on heat,' replied Priss disdainfully. 'She tries to put on a demure face, but deep down I wonder whether it's all an act. Considering she's never performed before in a drama, she does it well enough. Which makes me believe she must be a natural . . . Maybe a natural liar, for that's what acting is, after all . . . lying.'

'Maybe she's one of those conceited girls who always imagines that every man they meet is in love with them,' Harriet said, 'and they can scorn all but the finest, knowing full well there will be one finer still just around the corner.'

'And well she might,' Priss answered, 'with her looks.'

'That would explain her devil-may-care attitude to him at first. But beauty is only skin deep, Priss.'

'And so say all of us . . . all of us plain girls, that is.' She uttered a little laugh of irony. 'But from a man's perspective, I rather suspect not. Girls with pretty faces and flawless skin are the be-all and end-all from a man's point of view. That's why I have no beau, Harriet, and it's why Algernon Stokes has forsaken you. It's why Clarence Froggatt has taken Kate home tonight and not walked with us as he did last week.'

'Maybe he didn't find us entertaining enough,' Harriet suggested, in defence of her looks.

'No, Harriet. It's because you weren't at the front of the queue when they were handing out pretty faces . . . And nor was I. Let's be realistic.'

Harriet sighed. 'I suppose you're right,' she conceded pensively. 'And yet it seems a bit demeaning to write ourselves down as gargoyles when our figures are truly statuesque.'

'I hope you don't mind a bit of a gallop,' Clarence Froggatt asked Kate Stokes over the clatter of wheels.

She held on to her bonnet defiantly lest the breeze take it, her ribbons flaring out behind her. With her other hand she was clinging to the handrail of the dogcart for fear of being thrown off as she was jolted about. 'No, I don't mind going fast,' she replied with a grin of exhilaration. 'It's a change. I'd like it better, though, if we could see where we was going.' She was referring to the darkness of the unlit street down which they were hurtling.

'I'm sure the horse can see.'

''Tis to be hoped.'

'Whoa!' he yelled to the horse, realising he was perhaps frightening his prize passenger. The animal settled down to a steady trot.

'I really don't mind going fast,' she repeated, not wishing to be considered delicate, like some girls she could think of.

'In fact, I quite like it. My mother would die, though. She was scared by a runaway horse in the dark one night. Ever since then she's refused to go out at night.'

'I must remember not to offer your mother a lift . . . How far are we from your house?'

'Not far now. I'll tell you when to stop.'

'So did Mr Osborne offer to drive you home?'

'Yes.' She looked at him and grinned. 'I told him as you'd offered though, and that I'd accepted.'

'I bet he was put out.'

'Why should he be? He didn't show no signs at any rate.'

'Well . . . judging by the way he was clinging to you during rehearsal.'

'You mean before he agreed Rolfe and Pocahontas should be wed?'

'Yes. Didn't you notice?'

'It did cross my mind,' she answered modestly.

He turned to her and smiled. 'There you are then, you see.' Her eyes were reflecting the light of the dogcart's lamps and he thought she looked like an angel. 'I always knew he had a keen eye for a pretty face. Who asked you to join the Little Theatre in the first place, Kate? Him?'

'I heard about it first from the Meese girls.'

'The Meese girls?'

'My brother used to court Harriet. Harriet asked him to ask me.'

'Harriet and your brother were courting?' He sounded inordinately interested.

She nodded.

'I wonder if I know your brother . . .'

'You might. You're of an age, I reckon. His name's Algernon . . .'

'Oh, Algie Stokes. Of course. Yes, I know Algie. Your brother, is he? Well, I never. I should have made the connection. I haven't seen him for years. Not since I left that school we were at when we were kids. How is he?'

'Horrible . . . I hate him . . .'

'With a sisterly zeal,' Clarence remarked, amused.

'You can stop there, Clarence.' She pointed to the bridge just ahead and he pulled the horse to a halt before it.

'Why don't you call me Clarry?'

She smiled. 'If you like . . . I live just beyond the bridge alongside the cut . . . Clarry.'

'Handy for that public house.'

'The Bottle and Glass. Algie finds it handy. And the Samson and Lion.'

'So, Kate . . . I'd like to see you sometime, if you've a mind to . . . if you're allowed.'

'Course I'm allowed.'

'Good. Sometime other than rehearsal night, though.'

'If you like.' She smiled, pleased with her conquest.

'Are you free tomorrow night?'

'Yes,' she answered softly, lowering her lids. 'Will you call for me, or what?'

'Could we meet somewhere?'

'Meet?'

'Well . . . because I can't guarantee that I'll be able to borrow the dogcart again tomorrow,' he said apologetically. 'My father might have been called out, you see. He's the local doctor. Otherwise I'd gladly call for you.'

'Oh . . . all right, then. Where?'

'How about the top of Moor Lane? Can you manage eight o' clock?'

'I reckon so.'

'Excellent. I'll see you there then.'

* * *

While Marigold was absent, Algie Stokes was once more at a loose end every night. He spent more time designing bicycles on the scullery table, fathoming ways he could build them. The prospect of fulfilling his dream of manufacturing them seemed to recede the deeper he delved. He was beginning to accept that expensive – too expensive – machinery would be required to draw and bend the steel tubes from which they would be manufactured, the stamping presses needed to press out components for flanges and the chain, the new-fangled welding equipment. Then there were rods to be cut for the brake mechanism, threads cut and tapped so they could be linked together, sprockets forged and machined. Some things could be bought in already finished, things like wheels and bearings, rubber handle-bar grips and tyres. But still he had not discovered where he could source the wheels. Once he knew where, he could actually build a bicycle, making every other part by hand. If it was successful he could build another and maybe sell it. It would be a long-winded process making bicycles that way, but at least he would build up a knowledge that would be invaluable. It was the only way he could accomplish his dream – and even then only in a very small way.

But big oak trees from little acorns grow . . .

Summer rolled on in weeks of shimmering heat; a long, hot summer. England beat Australia in the first test at Lords, and Marigold had her nineteenth birthday miles away from Algie. They grew used to being apart, sometimes for weeks at a time. When they were reunited, however, they generated a smouldering heat of their own that vied with the summer's. Marigold was certain that Algie was intent on marrying her eventually to obviate the pain of being apart. Certainly, she was intent on marrying him, and she looked forward to the day when they would be together always, looking after the little house which they would rent, close to the canal of course, so that she could see her family regularly and entertain them when they travelled her way. She dropped many hints about marriage.

As they lay in their hollow one evening near Dadford's Bridge, hot after making love, she decided to broach the topic again. She was committed to him entirely and was anxious to know just where she stood in his future.

'D'you ever think about us being together always, Algie?' she asked softly.

'How d'you mean, together always?' He plucked a piece of straw from the ground and put it between his teeth, gazing up at the sky as he lay on his back, his shirt hanging out, his trousers still loose about his waist.

'I mean, wouldn't it be nice if we didn't have to be apart from one another for weeks on end, like now, with me traipsing up and down the cut?'

'It would, I grant you,' he replied.

She smiled, encouraged, and snuggled up to him. 'It could happen, Algie.'

'How?' Of course he knew how, but he wanted to hear it from her.

'If we get wed. If we was to get wed I'd be with you all the time – 'cept when you was at work, o' course.'

'I've been thinking about that myself, and I think I'd like to marry you,' he said, gazing at the sky. Then he turned to her and smiled his affection. 'But I'm not sure you're old enough yet, my flower.'

'Course I am. I'm nineteen.'

'Oh, I know you're nineteen,' he said gently, 'but in my book, nineteen's a bit too young to get wed.'

'But not too young to do what married folk do?'

'That's different, Marigold. You can't compare the two things.'

'Why is it different?'

'It's nature at work. Human nature. Just remember, not long ago it was legal for girls to be wed when they was twelve. In that case, they weren't considered too young by some to conceive.'

'All right, so I ain't too young to get pregnant.'

He looked at her suspiciously. 'You're not pregnant, are you?'

'No. I had a show only a fortnight ago, and I ain't seen you since.'

He smiled with relief, still gazing at the sky. A skylark was soaring overhead; he hoped he was not in its line of fire if it dropped its dinner. 'That's a blessing. So what's brought this on, this yearning to be wed so soon?'

'It's just that we'd be together, Algie. We'd sleep together every night. Just think . . . Oh, you've no idea how much I miss you when I'm away, how much it hurts. I pine to be with you. I do, honest. I love you. I want to share your life.'

'There's nothing wrong with having dreams, my flower,' he said softly. 'But where would we live? I'm not living with my folks when I get wed. They'd drive us both potty.'

'We could rent our own house. Our own little love nest.'

'It costs money to rent houses, Marigold. Money up front. Then we'd have to furnish it. I haven't got that sort of money. It'll take a year or two to save for that.'

'You could sell your bike.'

'Sell me bike?' He stirred at that, and sat up, half indignant at such an alarming suggestion. 'I ain't selling me bike.'

'But that'd give us the money we needed, Algie.'

'So it might, but I'm not selling it. Not for nobody. I worked hard for that bike. I'll never sell it.'

'I'd work then,' she said earnestly, offering a viable alternative. 'I'd get a job. They'm always after willing workers at glassworks or brickworks, and there's enough of them here-abouts. I could work in a shop, maybe, like your Kate. Maybe she could put a word in for me where she works . . .'

He took her hand and squeezed it. 'I love you, Marigold, with all my heart, but it's too soon yet. It's much too soon.'

'But I want to be with you, Algie. Not a couple of nights every two or three weeks, but every night . . . every day of every week.'

'I'm trying to be sensible . . .' He turned to look at her, at the intense expression in her lovely eyes. He could have hugged her. It touched him to the core that she loved him so much, that she wanted to be with him all the time. He felt blessed to be so adored by this delightful waif, but marriage was a step too far yet. You got married when you were about twenty-five, and not before if you had any sense; not twenty-two like he was, nineteen like she was.

'What about if you got me pregnant?' she asked.

'Then that'd be different,' he responded reassuringly. 'But I always try to be careful, so don't ever try and trap me by saying you are when you aren't.'

'Oh, Algie,' she whispered, her disappointment manifest in her eyes at a notion that was so alien to her nature. 'I'd never do that. I couldn't. I could never lie to you about *anything*. And you know why?'

'Why?'

''Cause if you ever found me out in a lie you'd never believe me again, would you? That's why. So I won't lie to you. Ever.'

He planted a kiss tenderly on her lips and lay down again. 'I'm lucky to have you, Marigold,' he acknowledged warmly. 'I know I am. And I don't rule out ever getting wed to you. I hope we shall wed someday. You'd be a good wife. But it's too soon yet, my flower. It really is. So just have a bit of patience.'

'I'll try,' she conceded, disappointed.

'Anyway, I got dreams of my own as I want to see come true first . . .'

'What dreams? Tell me.'

'You might laugh.'

'I won't laugh. Course I won't laugh.'

He propped his head up on his arm as he lay facing her. 'I want to start my own business making bikes. I want to be my own gaffer. I want to be rich.'

She beamed. 'That's a great big dream,' she said enthusiastically. 'I'll help you if I can.'

'There's just one problem.'

'What's that?'

'I haven't got the money. You need money to start up a firm, same as you do to start your own home.'

'Borrow it.'

'Who from?'

'A bank?' she suggested with a shrug. 'They'm the ones who lend folk money, ain't they? On the other hand, you could find somebody wealthy who'd be prepared to come in with you as a partner.'

'I don't want a partner, Marigold. I want to do it on my own.'

'But if you want it that bad, maybe you got no choice but to find a partner. It don't mean you wouldn't be your own gaffer, even if you had a partner, the way I see it.'

He grinned, impressed with her surprisingly mature grasp of things. 'You're not daft, are you? Maybe you're right. To tell you the truth, I'd wondered about a partner. I'll have to think about it.' He kissed her again as a token of his thanks, a kiss they lingered over, a kiss that reignited their mutual desire.

Dusk was falling fast. The sky was darkening, decorated

144

with crimson-edged feathers of cloud. The land, the trees, the gorse, the buttercups and dandelions had become smudged with the limpid redness of the sun which was hidden by the high hill behind them. Colours were rendered indistinguishable one from another.

He was tempted to say so much that was in his heart but it was difficult to find the right words. He was inclined to tell her just how much he loved her; that he would not only be prepared to marry her when the time was right, but proud to. He could not trust himself to deliver such potent words sincerely enough, believing it would sound laboured and contrived if he did. He was inclined to tell her that she was just right for him. Her demeanour, her natural warmth, her intelligence, all these qualities he adored. Yes, she would make a wonderful little wife. Anyway, if he said too much it might all come out funny and make her think he was too keen. So he left it unsaid . . .

Chapter 9

Benjamin Augustus Sampson, twenty-five years old, was the only son and sole beneficiary to the estate of his father, the late Benjamin Prentiss Sampson; self-made man, industrialist and brass founder. Benjamin Augustus inherited from his father the Sampson Fender and Bedstead Works at Queen's Cross in Dudley, which he continued to run. But he lacked the acumen, commitment and foresight of the old man. He was not particularly interested in the manufacture of bedsteads and fenders, so the business merely drifted. The factory continued to produce what it had always produced with no earnest effort at improvement or innovation. It was a tap that provided an endless supply of wealth, which young Benjamin rather took for granted. As an only child he'd wanted for nothing and, while he was a conventional enough chap in the normal way of things, he would stop at nothing to have what he wanted. Part of the problem was that he knew little about, and appreciated less, what his father had achieved, or how he had achieved it.

Benjamin Sampson Snr, on the other hand, had been one of three children, born to Enoch Sampson and Eliza Crump, his common-law wife, both nailmakers from Lye, which was little more than a shanty town that lay between Stourbridge and Halesowen. Enoch and Eliza had died young of consumption within a year of each other, before they could procreate more. Their children were subsequently taken into the care of the workhouse. Benjamin had lived his young life within sound of the clinking anvil and roaring bellows, taking for granted the conditions he was born into, knowing nothing else. He had learnt to make nails, and toiled with his mother and father from dawn every day till late into the night . . . for his keep. Fresh bread was a rare delicacy to be savoured and he knew nothing better. But as he was carted to the workhouse some miles away he saw the way other people lived; fine houses, neatly tended gardens, and children with clean, fresh faces and beautiful clothes. In the workhouse Benjamin was separated from his sisters amid tears which went unheeded by the sour-faced officials, who manifested harsh voices and rattled bunches of keys. He was stripped and bathed unceremoniously, dressed in strange clothes, then cast into a pack of other boys, all dressed alike, all with sullen faces and furtive glances. It was the catalyst Benjamin Prentiss Sampson needed to better himself. At ten years old he was given work in a brass foundry and learnt all about the trade. He worked hard and long, harder and longer than he had ever worked making nails, learning all the time. He learnt to do the jobs of others who fell absent, and learnt that above all he could rely on himself, if on nobody else. His two sisters died in the tender care of the workhouse, but Benjamin managed to escape it and he thrived. He saved what money he earned and, in 1856, had enough to start his own business making fenders and hearth ware, employing more and more men as the years went by. He developed a morbid fear of being short of money, for he quickly learnt what privileges money brought, compared with the quality of life without it. In 1862 he met and married a respectable girl, and found time to father a son, Benjamin Augustus, born in 1865.

Old Benjamin was canny enough to realise that an education would ensure that his son would never be subjected to the misery and ignominy he had suffered, so gladly paid for his schooling; another privilege that money could buy. Young Benjamin was merely an average pupil, though, excelling in nothing, mediocre in most things. When the lad left school, he was drafted into the prosperous Sampson firm to learn the business, being no good at anything else. Young Benjamin, however, was not interested in the business. He lacked imagination and could muster enthusiasm about little, except cricket. He wanted to spend his life playing cricket. The fact that cricket was a game played only in summer was a fact that he ignored. Nor did his accent ever become particularly refined. He could, however, be utterly charming, but only when he chose to be, something that schooling had taught him about fine manners and the art of getting what you want.

It was in mid-September, towards the end of the cricket season, when young Benjamin Augustus Sampson was at the factory he'd inherited, poring unenthusiastically over some ledgers in his office upstairs. He heard footsteps on the floorboards of the landing, followed by an apologetic tapping on his door.

'Enter.'

The door opened tentatively and Benjamin looked up to see the face of Algernon Stokes apprehensively peering round it.

'Algie!' The acknowledgement was more a statement of fact than a greeting, and thus not particularly welcoming. Not a time to ooze charm. 'What's up?' he growled.

'Sorry to trouble you, Mr Sampson . . .'

'Well, come in and shut the door.' He regarded Algie with the grand impatience of God-given superiority. 'What's up?'

'Oh, er . . . nothing's up, Mr Sampson . . . I . . . I wanted to ask your advice on a particular matter, that's all . . . But if you're too busy I could come back another time.'

Mr Sampson, however young, was senior to Algie. He made a show of taking his watch out of his fob and noting the time. 'Make it quick then. It seems to me, that since this is your working time, I shall be paying for me own advice.'

'Then I'll come back when work's finished.'

Benjamin smiled patronisingly. 'No, I want to leave this place on time. Sit down and tell me what's up. A burden shared is a burden halved, they say. I suppose it's to do with work?'

'Not altogether, no . . .'

Mr Sampson almost bridled, as if about to conclude the interview at once, but Algie was not about to be overawed having got this far.

'Mr Sampson, I'd like your advice – you being a successful businessman and all – on how best to go about starting a business.'

A mite flattered at being thus described, Benjamin visibly straightened his back with some pride. He also regarded his lowly employee a little more curiously. 'You want to start a *business*?'

'Well, not right away, Mr Sampson. But sometime soon.'

'Doing what?'

Algie couldn't help but smile, pleased that he had gained the interest of his gaffer. 'Manufacturing, sir. That's why I thought as you'd be a good person to ask.'

'Manufacturing what? Not bedsteads and fenders, I hope.'

'Bicycles, sir.'

'Bicycles? Ah . . .' Benjamin swept his fingers through his long and dark wavy tresses, and leaned back importantly in his padded leather chair.

Algie nodded. 'Bikes are all the rage. And they wouldn't

be too hard to cobble together, once you'd got the right equipment.'

'Bikes,' Benjamin mused. 'I don't know much about bikes. I drive a gig and a carriage meself, as you know. Are you sure folk will buy bikes with all the damned hills we've got round here? It'd be hard work pushing the pedals, I reckon.'

'Oh, yes. But everywhere ain't so hilly as it is round here.'

'Maybe not . . . Maybe you'm right. Norfolk's flat, they say . . .' He cogitated for a second, trying to formulate a response that might make him sound plausible. 'My advice, Algie, is that you should only mess with something you know about. Better the devil you know . . . You know the old saying.' Benjamin was quite full of old sayings.

'Oh, I know a bit about bikes, Mr Sampson. I bought one. You might have seen me riding it. And I've been studying it. Matter of fact, I was studying bikes long afore I even bought one. You could make a good strong bike with steel tubes, you know, so long as you got the right jigs and tools to bend them and draw them in the proper places. The only thing I couldn't make is the spoked wheels and the ball bearings – oh, and the pneumatic tyres and rubber handle grips.'

'So how would you reckon to join all these here steel tubes together, Algie? Rivets, or nuts and bolts?'

'By resistance welding, I believe, sir.'

'Resistance welding?' Benjamin Sampson looked bemused. He'd never heard of resistance welding. He was way out of his depth when it came to innovative engineering processes. 'What the devil is it? What do you know about resistance welding, Algie?'

'It's a new way of fusing metal, and I don't know much about it yet, except it could save riveting pieces together. Anyway, I'm prepared to find out.'

'Just one of many hazards you'll come up against, I reckon,

150

Algie,' Benjamin declared dismissively. 'You see, to start a business you have to know the ins and outs of the business you want to go into, like I say. It helps to know the manufacturing processes involved, like this here resistance welding you'm on about, for instance. But before you can even think about any of that, you have to have some money in place, I would've thought. And that could run into hundreds and most likely thousands, *especially* in manufacturing. Have you considered the investment you'd have to make in machinery, for a start?'

'Well . . . I have *sort* of considered it. I should have to go to a bank, I reckon.'

'Cap in hand at that. If you've got enough behind you – property, I mean – they *might* loan you something on the strength of it,' Mr Sampson said, safely assuming that the presence of any property behind Algie was highly improbable. 'Then you'd need suitable premises and trained workers. Above all, you need customers. You need a network of wholesale and retail outlets to sell things like bikes – same as for bedsteads and fenders. Have you thought about all this, Algie?'

'Well . . . no, not all of it, Mr Sampson,' Algie admitted reluctantly. 'Not yet. I've only considered the manufacturing part. How to make them.'

Benjamin Sampson afforded Algie a smile as he rose from the chair his more enterprising father used to sit in. 'I reckon you've got a lot more thinking to do afore you could ever start such a project.' He walked round his desk towards the door, anxious to be rid of Algie Stokes and his crackpot idea which, in any case, was way above the lad's station. 'It would be too big an undertaking,' he went on. 'Mind you, the idea has got some merit,' he added patronisingly. 'It's just a pity that a stream can't rise above its source . . .'

* * *

151

Kate Stokes took to seeing the doctor's son, Clarence Froggatt, two or three times a week. He couldn't use his father's conveyance every night they met. He was always careful, however, to see her home safely, dogcart or no, dutifully walking her to the lock-keeper's cottage and trudging back alone in the darkness to his family's home at Holly Hall, which lay between Brierley Hill and Dudley. Kate enchanted Clarence. She was ravishingly easy on the eye, and affable. Despite her lowly origins she made the best of herself, and was never out of her depth, even with those Meese girls who had befriended her. Of course, he had no plans to take her home to meet his family yet; he wasn't quite sure how they might react to his befriending the daughter of a humble lock-keeper, however ladylike, intelligent, and pretty, for outward demeanour was not everything. There had to be some substance, and preferably a little ancestry besides, to render her entirely suitable. But, for the time being, her big brown eyes and lovely face captivated him.

Something that surprised him, for a girl from such an inferior background, was her obvious innocence. The working class were not noted for it. Several times he had engineered situations when they were alone so that he could take advantage of her, but she allowed no hanky-panky, spiritedly refusing anything more than kisses. This was to her credit. The fact that she was not *easy* was yet another fine characteristic that enhanced her worthiness. However, she did kiss rather nicely, an attribute that evidently came naturally to her, despite her obvious lack of actual experience in the kissing department.

Clarence's lively imagination began to run riot when dress rehearsals for *The Forest Princess* began. Kate's outfit consisted of a short tunic – considerably shorter than her usual skirts – sewn together from pieces of chamois leather. Neither could she realistically wear stockings, and she ran across the imaginary stage of the Drill Hall in bare feet, flashing two well-turned ankles and pale, shapely calves. Kate was astutely aware that the eyes of all the men would be upon her and she revelled in the knowledge. When she squatted, as any forest princess was wont to do, she revealed, without turning a hair, tantalising glimpses of smooth, pale thighs. These same tantalising limbs were destined to be browned with stage paint for the actual performances. If only Kate would allow him personal access to those alluring nether regions. If only she would allow him to apply that stage paint . . . The thought troubled him, particularly at bedtime.

His imagination was working overtime at one such rehearsal, the week before Harriet Meese's twenty-first birthday party, to which they had both been invited, and his lust was overflowing. He watched her, mesmerised, in one particular scene. She was sitting on the floor, her hands clasped round her knees revealing besotting tracts of alabaster thighs as she stared into an imaginary camp fire. Her mouth was solemn but pouting as she listened to the pontificating of Powhatan, but so kissable, her eyes exotic pools of darkness, deep and inscrutable. She had never, Clarence thought, looked so ravishing.

That evening he walked her home, and stood pressed against her, out of public sight at the side of the lock-keeper's cottage. The image of her exposed, alabaster thighs was still fresh in his mind. It was vital to confess how much he wanted her before he imploded with sexual frustration. There was, after all, just a chance that she might take pity on him and allow him just to touch her somewhere very private for a second or two. That, at least, would be a start.

'You must surely know by now, Kate, how much I *want* you,' he breathed.

She laughed. 'Don't be daft, Clarry.'

She looked so amazingly pretty by moonlight. Her eyes were pools of dark, sweet sherry, her smooth, rounded cheeks so sensually soft against his. If only he could overcome her innate propriety.

'Why won't you let go?' he asked intently.

' 'Cause it ain't right,' she answered, looking him straight in the eye. Then, more kittenishly, she said, 'Such goings on are for the marriage bed, Clarry. Not before.'

He sighed, a profound sigh. 'You must understand that I respect your opinion on the matter, Kate, my love, but I want *you* to understand how *I* feel . . . that it's driving me mad.' He squeezed her tight around her waist.

'Clarry!' she protested, but with a giggle. 'What are you doing? You'll squeege the life out o' me.'

'We could have such lovely times together,' he murmured, his breath warm in her ear, sending delicious shivers up and down her spine, shivers that she had to disguise at all costs. 'And nobody else would know. It'd be our secret.'

'But you're asking me to go against all my principles,' she answered, feigning mild indignation that he should esteem her so little.

'It's my opinion that the pleasure you would derive would far outweigh any feelings of guilt you might at first encounter.'

'You daft thing! And what if you was to put me in the family way?' She gave him a hug to demonstrate that she was not trying to drive him away, that maybe she actually wanted to be persuaded, calculated to ensure his continued interest.

'I'm sure my father has some potion somewhere that could quickly remedy that.'

It was not the sort of remedy she'd anticipated and it narked her. 'That wouldn't be very nice, Clarry.'

'But it might be expedient under such circumstances.'

'You're not likely to put me in such circumstances,' she said provocatively. 'I told you, such things are reserved for the marriage bed. Then everybody expects you to get pregnant, and thinks there's something amiss if you don't within the first six months.'

'Well, it would be wonderful now,' he sighed. 'If only you were willing.'

'I reckon it's unfair to expect me to do that sort of thing, Clarry,' she said with a distinct air of propriety. 'I mean, there's no certainty as you and me would ever wed. I mean, I'm ever likely to meet some other chap, really well-to-do and that. Can you imagine what it'd be like for me if I had to confess as I wasn't a virgin? Have you thought about that?'

'I confess, I hadn't.'

'See? You ain't really thinking about my feelings, Clarry. Only your own.'

'Of course,' he said smoothly. 'I understand what you say. But what if it looked as if we *might* marry eventually? . . . You and me . . .'

'*Might* wouldn't be enough,' she asserted, lowering her lids with an innocence that was entirely convincing. 'A *certainty* might make a difference. But in any case, it's way too soon to be thinking of such things . . .'

He gave her a hug and a kiss on the lips, and she responded deliciously. 'Oh, Katie, you're such a sweet, innocent and very sensible girl. There's no wonder I want you so much. There's no wonder I want to be the first and only.'

They kissed again, ardently, lingeringly. His hands wandered over her clad body, only to be rebuffed.

Underneath all this pretence she was smouldering. He only had to touch her . . . If only he knew. If only he had the remotest idea how much she craved physical love, to feel him moving inside her, he would be shocked to the core. But she could not allow him to know – at least, not without a convincing show of virtuous resistance first.

'I'm working myself up into a lather again,' he whispered with a rueful grin. 'I'd better go before I'm unable to control myself.'

She gently pushed him away with decorous propriety then, just to confuse him more, gave him another sympathetic hug, another passionate kiss.

'Don't forget the party Saturday,' he said. 'Do you still want to go?'

'Yes, course I do,' she answered with playful appeal. 'I've had a lovely frock made just for it. I don't want to be outdone by them Meese girls, 'cause they always have such lovely frocks.'

'I'll have the dogcart. Mother and Father are away for the weekend at my aunt's in Nottingham. So I'll collect you about eight. I presume you remembered to ask your mother and father for permission to be back home late?'

'Yes, I told you. I think you should thank them, and settle their minds that I'll be in good hands.'

'Oh, you'll be in very good hands, Katie, my love.' He caught her smile, angelic in the moonlight. 'Goodnight, Kate. Sweet dreams . . .'

From the gate she watched him cross the lock in the moonlight. He turned and waved as he walked up the towpath opposite, and she could just about discern him picked out by the moon's silvery lambency as he ascended the road bridge till he was out of sight. Oh, if only he knew . . . If only he had the slightest inkling of what she had to endure to maintain this odious but necessary pretence of virtue. But how long could she keep it up, when at every opportunity he was assaulting her agonisingly potent feminine desires? She had to appear chaste. It was vital. He must not know of her past experiences. If she allowed herself to be seduced easily and it became known, she would be shunned by the people she now mixed with. Especially with no prospect of marriage in view, no engagement. And what if she did fall pregnant?

She turned from the gate to go inside.

'Kate!'

She stopped and turned round, startled at hearing a man's whispered call coming from the towpath. But it was a familiar call.

She went back to the gate and peered over it. 'Who is it?' She knew very well who it was, and her heart lurched.

'Me. Reggie.'

'Reggie?' At once she pretended to be indifferent. 'What d'you want?'

'I came to see you. I ain't seen you for ages. And we've got some unfinished business, you and me.'

'Where are you moored?' she said, sounding more amenable.

'Down there in the basin by the dock. Come a walk with me, Kate.'

'But it's time I went in.' This offering excuses on moral grounds was getting to be a tedious habit.

'Just a short walk, eh? Up the cut a bit.'

She tiptoed over the lock gates towards him, the winding mechanism catching at her skirt. They headed under the road bridge and walked on the towpath around the basin at the Bottle and Glass.

'I've missed you, Kate,' he said as they sauntered along in the moonlight. 'But it looks as if you'm a-courtin' nowadays, eh?'

'You saw me with Clarry, then?'

'Clarry? That's a dandy name.'

She didn't answer.

'Decent respectable chap, is he?'

'Very,' she affirmed. 'The son of a doctor.'

'Handy, eh?' He regarded her knowingly. 'Does he keep you happy?'

She knew exactly what he meant. 'We don't . . . do that. I have to be a decent, respectable girl for a doctor's son.' She grinned at the irony of it, while Reggie guffawed.

'More fool him, eh?'

'Yes, I reckon. More fool him.'

'Is it serious?'

'Course not.'

He took her hand, sure of his standing now. There was a patch of spare ground, between two old properties. He led her through a gap in the hedge, and sat down.

'Come and sit by me.'

'I ain't gunna do *that*,' she said, but without any conviction whatsoever. 'I don't want to . . .'

'You?' He laughed, almost mockingly. 'If I know you, you'm dying for it. 'Specially after you've been spooning with him, with bugger all at the end of it. Sit down.'

She sat beside him. He raised his hand and tickled the back of her neck, then drew her to him. She submitted to his caress and he kissed her full on the mouth, his tongue probing for hers. Why should she resist? He'd shaved and his skin felt smooth, he'd made some effort with himself and seemed more presentable than usual. She was aching for some honest, physical contact; not the polite, apologetic fumblings of the doctor's son. She was tingling, itching in all the right places, and those places needed attention. She'd had enough of pretence, of dancing around her emotions with respectful words and restrained innuendo, denying her natural desires, however wanton. She needed some good, hard, unpretentious loving. She needed to be herself; her burning, carnal needs satisfied. She would get that satisfaction with Reggie, no holds barred, no frills and no strings attached. And no condemnation either.

He shoved her back so that she was lying in the rough grass. He took a handful of skirt and pulled the hem up to her waist, then knelt between her legs and untied the ribbon of her white drawers. She raised her backside and he yanked them down, casting them aside, a double pennant of surrender lying limp and pale on a tuft of grass beside them. His hand gently stroked her inner thigh, his goal that delectably wet place he hankered for.

'By the living Christ, you'm dying for it,' he whispered when he felt her.

'You don't say. Get on with it.'

He undid his fly and the thing sprang out like some pale serpent, stiff with rigor mortis, except that it was far from dead. 'Here, cop this,' he muttered. He rolled onto her and buried himself inside her without further ceremony.

'Oh . . . Jesus!' she gasped, her gratitude audible in her shuddering sigh.

Although she was wily enough to use a douche, it occurred to Kate that if she had the gross misfortune to be pregnant anyway as a result of that encounter with Reggie, she would be regarded as one of the simple-minded and corrupt women that litter society. She could never entertain the thought of marrying Reggie and spending the rest of her days being towed up and down the Midlands' canal system with his disgusting family, in that floating squalor they called a home. Her mother and father, too, would be likely to disown her rather than tolerate derisive whispering behind cupped hands, the finger pointing, and the scorn that would be poured on them for harbouring a wanton daughter, for wanton is how she would be perceived. She would have no alternative but to seek refuge in the workhouse among the poor sick, the crippled, the insane. Her only redemption might be taking to the streets and selling herself, but even that would be only short-lived, for she would inevitably end up back in the workhouse, diseased and ruined. Gone would be her dream of willing acceptance by her respectable peers, such as those she had befriended in the Amateur Dramatics Society. Gone would be all possibility of a good marriage to a worthy and respectable gentleman . . .

Maybe she should provide herself with some insurance against such an eventuality.

On the Saturday, during her dinner break from serving cakes, bread and pastries, Kate scoured Brierley Hill High Street for a pair of the finest silk stockings and the flimsiest undergarments. They cost her more than she could reasonably afford, especially since she had already forked out for an expensive dress, but she consoled herself with the knowledge that they would all turn out to be sound investments. After all, Clarry's folks would be away from home, he'd said . . .

At seven, when it was dark, she went upstairs and began to get ready. She sponged her body at the washstand in her bedroom and put on her new flimsier underclothes. There was not a lot she could wear beneath the new dress she'd bought, designed as it was to flaunt her bare shoulders and display a goodly amount of cleavage. She pulled on her stockings and enjoyed the feel of cool silk against her skin. Then she did her hair, piling it up, allowing dark brown wisps to fall waywardly in front of her ears, others to fall in a girlish fringe across her brow. She put on the dress. Some impressive contortions were needed to fasten it, but she was lissom enough to manage it without calling for her mother's help. By the light of the oil lamp she looked at herself in the long Cheval mirror and was satisfied that whoever saw her that night would turn round for a second glance . . . and maybe even a third.

Clarence called at eight, as he had promised he would. He thanked Mr and Mrs Stokes for bestowing their permission on Kate to return late, assuring them that he would look after their precious daughter and return her safely.

'Enjoy yourselves,' Will Stokes said heartily, somewhat jealous because his wife would never be forced out at night, even if he exploded a keg of gunpowder under her. He was relieved that his daughter was different, and proud that she had won herself a respectable man, after all the rumour and uncertainties about her going off with boatmen. 'Mek the most of it, my flower.'

'I'll try, Father,' she replied, with an enigmatic smile.

Chapter 10

September had been mild, but that particular evening, as the sun went down, Algie and Marigold began to realise that it was too cold and damp to lie in the grass near Dadford's Bridge. The summer, though mostly hot, had yielded some similarly damp evenings after rain and when the grass was too wet they walked, stopping frequently for tender kisses, but nothing more. It was at such times that the lack of a soft, warm featherbed and somewhere to house it seemed to highlight the need for one, a need which could feasibly only be remedied through the mystical union of marriage and setting up home somewhere, with such fundamental comfort readily to hand. Algie was, at these times, vulnerable to being swayed.

'Why can't we ever go to your house?' Marigold asked as they set off on a draughty walk along the cut.

''Cause my mother never goes out nights.'

'Why not?'

'Because once, when she was carrying our Kate, she was walking back to our house from her mother's one night, and a horse took fright in Moor Lane. It was hauling a cart, and heading straight towards her. She managed to throw herself to the ground and roll out of its way just in time. It frightened her to death. Ever since then she won't go out at night for fear of it happening again.'

'I'd have been afeared as well, Algie,' Marigold proclaimed sincerely. 'But horses don't take fright that often, do they? I've never seen one take fright meself. It shouldn't stop her going out, though. What about in the day? Doesn't she go out in the day?'

'She doesn't mind going out in the day so much. If a horse took fright in daylight she reckons she'd see it and hear it and have plenty of time to get out the way.'

'But she could go with your dad to a public house,' Marigold reasoned. 'There's two close by. She very likely wouldn't even see a horse, the time it'd take to walk to either of them.'

'She wouldn't be seen dead in a public house, she thinks they're common and not a good place for a woman to be seen. She thinks everywhere's common.'

'Shame.'

'I know,' he admitted ruefully. 'We could go to our house now if you're cold, but we'd only end up pulling faces at each other and making each other laugh. Maybe when the weather gets a lot colder we might have to go and sit there just to keep warm.'

'We could go to a public house,' she suggested. 'At least we could have a drink while we pulled faces at each other.'

He laughed at that, and they walked on, arms entwined, each tormented by the other's body warm against them. Beyond the basin and the lock east of the Bottle and Glass the canal split, the left hand arm reaching to an ironworks, the right hand meandering around Brierley Hill towards Dudley. A footbridge switched the towpath of the Stourbridge Canal away from the left hand arm, across to the other bank, and they took it. A gust of wind stirred through the hawthorn trees and trailing brambles that lined it, carrying dank air, laden with the smell of damp leaves that had fallen early. The musty aroma of tired and rotting vegetation mingled with the smell of tawny canal water. Through a gap in the brambles a dog emerged, and stopped to sniff them.

Algie stooped down and stroked the dog, speaking softly to it. The animal wagged its tail enthusiastically and lingered. It licked his hand as though it had discovered an eternal friend, then padded on its way without further ado when he stood up again.

'He soon realised I'd got no food for him,' Algie remarked.

'Poor thing. I wish you had. He was a nice, friendly soul. I wish we'd got a dog, but that'd be another mouth to feed, and I don't suppose me dad could afford it.'

'We had a dog once. When I was a little lad.'

'What was its name?'

'Harry.'

'Harry?' Marigold chuckled. 'It reminds me of Harriet. Have you seen anything of Harriet lately?'

Marigold dropped this same question into their conversation every time they met, as if she still hadn't got it through her head that he was no more interested in Harriet than in jumping voluntarily into the murky waters of the cut.

'Why should I have seen her?' he responded, his impatience at once evident in his tone, for he was tiring of the question and the doubting trust it implied. 'I never see her. I hear about her from time to time from our Kate, when she decides I'm worthy enough to be granted some snippet or other. It's her twenty-first birthday party tonight.'

'Whose? Kate's?'

'No, Harriet's.' He rolled his eyes. 'We'd be at Kate's if it was hers. Anyway, our Kate ain't even twenty yet.'

'Fancy you not being invited,' Marigold remarked. 'To Harriet's party, I mean.'

'It's hardly likely they'd invite me.'

'*She* might've.'

'Her father wouldn't allow me within a mile of her.'

'Well, if she's twenty-one she'll be able to do as she pleases, never mind her father. I bet she wanted to invite you. I bet she did.'

'She invited our Kate and Clarence Froggatt. Kate was all dressed up to the nines. I reckon it's a do just for the local mashers.'

'Never mind . . . You're my masher, Algie . . .' She gave him a hug and he bent his head and kissed her briefly for her unerring sweetness, which made up for her irritating habit of mentioning Harriet in connection with himself. 'Has Harriet got a new beau in her life yet?'

'I haven't a clue,' he said. 'I don't ask. Why? Would you feel better if she had?' He looked at her sideways to gauge her reaction.

'Oh, Algie . . .' She turned to him with a sigh, thrusting her arms around his waist.

She reminded him of a vulnerable kitten which was impossible to resist and which had to be protected. He put his arms around her and huddled her to him.

'What?' he whispered gently. 'Tell me.'

'It's just that . . . that while she's still got nobody else, she's ever likely to come after you again and pinch you from me. I would feel safer if she'd got another chap.'

'You nit,' he answered tenderly, looking into her tearful blue eyes that dazzled him even in the gloaming. 'You don't think I'd give you up for her, do you?'

'I don't know, do I? I'd feel more sure if you told me you loved me a bit more often. You hardly ever say it these days,' she pouted.

'Course I love you, else we wouldn't be seeing each other still, would we?'

'I dunno. Sometimes I think you only want me for . . . for *it* . . .'

'No, I don't,' he protested.

'So why don't you tell me you love me?'

'All right . . . I love you, Marigold,' he said. Then, more tenderly, 'I *love* you. I really do . . . Honest . . . Never doubt me.'

She squeezed him ardently around his waist, thankful that she had been able to elicit this profoundly important declaration from him. 'And I love you as well, Algie Stokes,' she whispered. 'With every bit of my heart.'

'Oh, Marigold, I do wish there was somewhere warm we could go. Let's walk on a bit.' Then he had a bright idea. 'We'll sneak behind a brick kiln at the firebrick works further on . . . It'll be warm leaning against the kiln wall.'

Harriet's party was being held in the assembly rooms at the Bell Hotel. All day the Meese family had been anxious about its impending success or failure. They tried vainly to maintain the normal rhythm of daily routine, but it was regularly interrupted by visitors bringing gifts and best wishes. And these visitors had to be rewarded with cups of tea or snifters of whisky or gin, as the preference took them. Jane, the maid, cleared the breakfast table, only for the dining room to take on the appearance of a dressmaker's workshop when Mrs Palethorpe, the seamstress who had been entrusted with the making of the girls' dresses, arrived along with the various creations to be worn that evening. Mrs Palethorpe officiated over the mayhem with unruffled dignity, while the besieged Jane scurried in and out, trotting upstairs and down, then to the shop below fetching pins, bits of lace, needles, cotton and, not least, more cups of tea.

Old man Meese put in a brief appearance to check what

all the fuss was about, but the sight of all that satin and chiffon, which he had dutifully supplied free of charge, as well as being told by Priss that he was in the way, made him realise it was hardly a place for a man. As he wandered disconsolately down their dimly-lit stairwell back to his solitary stool behind the counter of his drapery shop, he speculated how different his life – and his bank balance – might be if he had fathered sons instead of seven daughters, all taken with expensive fripperies.

Harriet's ensemble for her special day was a dark green satin dress. It was sleeveless and tight-bodiced with a low, scalloped neck which, by her standards, revealed a spectacular amount of enchantingly heaving cleavage – sufficient enough to incline Priss to describe it as 'utterly reckless'. Harriet's dress was readied first and in good time, but Priss's, the last of the family's to be dealt with, was subject to some last minute, panic-stricken improvisations.

On the evening, Kate Stokes and Clarence Froggatt entered the Bell Hotel by the main door and climbed the stairs that led to the assembly rooms. Lit by gas lamps, the room was already dense with wafting cigar and cigarette smoke, and the dark, sickly smell of beer and spirits, all of which had permeated the curtains and even the wallpaper over long years, to become eternally entrapped. A four-piece band had been hustled into the corner where the piano stood. The players were providing music that was turning out, unintentionally perhaps, to be mere background noise to the chinking glasses, and the buzz and yelping laughter of various conversations.

Kate and Clarence made their way over to Harriet. She was standing with a group, some of whom were her younger sisters. The couple wished her a happy birthday and handed her the small gift which Kate had purchased during her dinnertime a couple of days earlier.

'I love your dress, Harriet,' Kate said admiringly. 'Green don't half suit your colouring.'

'Thank you,' Harriet replied sweetly, realising that Kate was actually being sincere and intended no slight by her reference to the colour. 'But yours, too . . . You look lovely. Doesn't she, Mr Froggatt?'

'I've never seen her look otherwise,' Clarence responded with truth and tact. However, he could not help but cast a covert glance at Harriet's pushed-up breasts, squeezed together quite deliciously, her cleavage rising and falling tantalisingly with every innocent breath she took. He glimpsed Kate's for comparison. It was a job to know which girl was sporting the most revealing tract of contoured bosom, which was the most appealing . . . But Kate was so much the prettier girl; vastly prettier. 'Oh, and do call me Clarence,' he said amiably. 'Enough of this *Mr Froggatt* malarkey.' He smiled, a warm, friendly smile, and Harriet felt her knees buckle beneath her pretty petticoats.

'Thank you,' she replied coyly, and Kate smiled to herself as she discerned a blush from her friend.

Kate looked about her to see who else had arrived so far. Many faces from the Amateur Dramatics Society were already present, some half hidden as they dipped their noses into drinking glasses, particularly the men. Murdoch Osborne, looking and acting much younger than his forty-five years, was holding court, entertaining a couple of the younger females, including the company's ex-leading lady, Katie Richards. Kate Stokes caught his eye, and he flashed a private smile across the room at her.

One or two couples, showing regard for a suggestion by the musicians, encroached onto the space allocated in the room for dancing. Priss, however, joined the gossiping group.

'I've just been talking to the curate.'

Harriet looked at her expectantly. 'Has he asked you out yet?'

'Unfortunately not,' Priss replied. 'He's been waffling on about his ancestors.'

'Ancestors? Well, he does come from an aristocratic family, Priss. Descendants of William the Conqueror, I bet you tuppence. And he's the sort of person that drags his ancestors about with him all the time.'

'I know the sort,' Clarence commented.

'He was harping on to me about his precious forebears last Sunday,' Harriet said, 'when I thought a little mockery might not come amiss. So I told him we'd mislaid our great-great-grandmother. I said we'd searched up hill and down dale, in the dirty washing bag, the privy, everywhere, but we couldn't lay our hands on her. He didn't think it funny in the least. You should have seen his face.'

The others laughed, but Priss looked aghast. 'Oh, Harriet, you never!'

'I did.'

'I bet he thought you were off your rocker,' Priss remarked. 'Still, I'm surprised he couldn't see the joke.'

'Ancestor-blindness,' Harriet suggested. 'Too sacred to be trifled with. I'm glad I belong to a new family.'

'Fancy you fancying the curate, Priss,' Kate exclaimed.

'Oh, I doubt if he has the sense to realise it,' Priss admitted. 'But it would do him the world of good if he did. I'm exactly the sort of girl he needs, if only he knew it.'

'Such humility!' Harriet said. 'What is there about you that would induce any man to look at you twice?'

'The same that would induce him to look at you twice – or not, as the case may be.'

'I've always believed,' Harriet bantered, 'that of two sisters, the second is always the better-looking, from the days of Leah and Rachel downwards. If there are any brains going about, then I concede that the older one generally gets them. But since there are no brains in our family, that doesn't apply to us.'

'I don't see why the curate shouldn't fancy you, Priss,' Clarence interjected kindly. 'And he should have no scruples about indulging it if he does.'

'I daresay he can't afford to marry, being only a curate,' Priss responded. 'Unless he married a girl much richer than me. After all, as a man of the cloth, it's likely he'll only be a second or third son. Not in the line of inheritance.'

'Oh, I don't think it's that,' Harriet suggested.

'Then is Priss not poor enough?' Clarence queried.

'Oh, I don't think money enters into it either way, Clarence,' she replied. 'Having a string of aristocratic ancestors himself, I suppose he thinks she's common.'

'And no wonder, if he thinks we keep our great-great-grandmother in the privy. Really, Harriet, you are the limit.'

'It's time we went over to say hello to Mr Osborne, Harriet, if you'll excuse us . . .' Kate interjected with a charming smile of feigned regret, looking at Clarence for his approval. She got it and they moved away from the group. 'They can be a bit daft sometimes, those two. Priss especially. Man-mad she is. Only because she can't get one.'

Clarence smiled his acknowledgement of the truth of her words. 'Harriet's not half so bad though, is she? She does try to shut her up. Look, I'll get us a drink while you talk to Mr Osborne. What would you like?'

'Gin,' she said brightly. 'With lemonade.'

'You're looking lovely enough to eat, young Kate,' Murdoch Osborne declared with a superb grin as his eyes delved into her cleavage. 'The belle of the ball tonight, and no mistake.' That comment ensured that Katie Richards was less than impressed, however, since it reflected badly on her own notions of qualifying for that particular honour. She duly excused herself, along with her female companions, to find more appreciative company.

Kate thanked Murdoch for his compliment with a bright smile. 'It does me good to hear you say it. But I was thinking, Mr Osborne . . . you're looking sprightly yourself.'

He chuckled at what he regarded as her directness, which he liked. 'I try to. How's your mother keeping?'

'She's all right, thanks,' she replied, then added, 'And my father.'

'Glad to hear it. You and our Mr Froggatt seem to be courting strong now.'

'I wouldn't put it quite like that, Mr Osborne.'

'Oh? You surprise me, Kate. A fine lad like that from a well-respected family, and with a bright future ahead of him as an architect. I'd have thought he'd be a good catch for any young madam, ha?'

'Oh, he'd be a good catch for somebody, I daresay,' Kate said. 'But I might still chuck him back into the pond.'

'Oh? How's that then?'

Kate shrugged. 'He's a bit young for me . . . in the head, I mean. He's a bit of a pushover. We'll see how he shapes up.'

Murdoch guffawed into his drink and took a swig. 'Pushover?' he queried. 'I ain't heard that word afore but I can guess what it means. You'd be a proper handful, I warrant, young Kate, ha? By the living Christ, I wish I was twenty years younger. You'd not find me such a pushover.'

'Quite a blade with the young women in your day, I bet, Mr Osborne, eh? I can just imagine.'

'Oh, me and Eli Meese used to have some fun together, I can tell ye.'

'Eli Meese? Lord! Don't let Priss or Harriet hear you say that. He's a churchwarden, they tell me, whatever that means.'

'And a Justice. A Justice and a churchwarden. There's no flies on Eli Meese, ha?'

Clarence returned, carrying their drinks. 'How do, Mr Osborne. Sorry. I could've got you a drink as well . . .'

'No matter, lad. I can easy afford me own.'

'I wasn't thinking of the cost, Mr Osborne. I simply never thought. What are you drinking? I'll go and get you another.'

'No, leave it, lad. It's of no consequence. I ain't in no rush to get legless anyroad. I can think of nothing more degrading, ha? Moderation's the thing where drink's concerned.'

Eli Meese waddled up to Murdoch and spoke. Kate decided it was her cue to move on and she took Clarence's hand.

'We'll leave you to it, Mr Osborne,' she said apologetically. 'See you at rehearsal Wednesday.'

'That you will.'

'I don't like that Eli Meese,' Kate whispered to Clarence when they were out of earshot. 'He gives me the creeps.'

'He seems all right to me, Kate.'

'I ain't very fussed with this music they'm playing either, Clarry,' she said forlornly, and sipped her drink. 'It's a boring old party, this. All these folk from the Amateur Dramatics Society, all with a bob on themselves. And these boring old fogeys what'm Harriet's relatives . . .'

'So what would you like to do?' Clarence asked. 'We can't just announce that we're leaving yet. We haven't long arrived.'

'Why announce it?' she suggested, glad that she'd planted the idea to leave in Clarence's head.

'You mean, just go without saying a word?'

'Who's going to miss us? They're all too wrapped up in themselves to notice anybody else.'

'But it's cold out. Where would we go?'

Kate shrugged, disappointed at his lack of imagination. 'I

dunno. Somewhere warm, I would've thought, where we can be on our own.'

His eyes lit up. 'My folks are away in Nottingham, aren't they?' he said at last. 'If you fancy going back to my house . . .'

She smiled smugly to herself. 'Without a chaperone?'

'Since when have you needed a chaperone? You're well able to fend off my advances all by yourself, if past experience is anything to go by.'

'Well . . . all right . . . Your house. If you promise to be on your best behaviour.'

'I can't promise any such thing, Kate, my angel,' he said triumphantly. 'We would be by ourselves, except for Myra – the maid. And she's hard of hearing, so unlikely to hear us.'

She smiled coyly, enchanting him with her big brown eyes that glanced up at him so temptingly from under her lovely brows. 'When we've finished our drinks then . . . We'll just slip out . . .'

Doctor Froggatt's was a large house set in its own grounds, well back from the Stourbridge Road where it met the Pensnett Road at Holly Hall. It overlooked fields at the rear. Because of its elevated position, you could see in daylight the locomotives and trucks of the mineral railway, articulated reptiles volleying steam and smoke as they snaked in the middle distance between the Himley Colliery at Old Park and the wharf on outlying Wellington Road in Dudley.

When Kate had alighted from the dogcart, Clarence tethered the horse to a post and looped a nosebag over its head. As he unlocked the substantial oak front door to let her in, he put his fingers to his lips to ensure her silence. He ushered her into the drawing room and took a spill from the mantelpiece which he ignited in the fire, then lit the gas lamps in turn, which exploded one after the other with a little pop. He turned them down low.

'Can I get you a drink?'

'Another gin would be nice, if you've got any.'

'Of course . . .'

Kate sat primly erect at one end of a vast sofa, waiting, taking in the ambience of the room. It didn't look anything at all like she'd expected. The furniture was hardly contemporary, although a grand piano stood at one end, and a handsome mirror hung over the fireplace. Rather, it looked as though it had been furnished in the first flush of old Dr Froggatt's prosperity, and hardly in the best of taste, and it reminded her of the town hall. It harboured a peculiar smell as well, a crosscurrent of strange medicaments that wafted in from the adjacent surgery. A canary emitted a tweet of protest at the intrusion, from a cage of brass wire shaped like the Crystal Palace, lithographs of which Kate had seen in the newssheets and magazines.

Clarence returned presently with two drinks.

'Here . . . Bottoms up.'

'Bottoms up,' she repeated. The words, as she took a sip, elicited an image in her mind of his naked bottom aimed squarely at the ceiling with herself pinned secure beneath him.

He sat at the other end of the sofa swigging the whisky he'd poured for himself, and smiled at her.

'Aren't you going to sit a bit closer?' she enquired with a hurt expression.

'I'd be delighted. I was merely trying to maintain the good behaviour you require of me.'

'There's nothing wrong with sitting closer,' she cooed. 'As a matter of fact, there's nothing wrong with a kiss or two neither, so long as you don't imagine it's going to lead to anything else.'

He grinned. 'You're such a tease,' he declared resignedly. 'And if I kiss you, I'll only get myself worked up into a lather.'

'I quite like to see you get worked up into a lather, Clarry . . .'

'Do you? Then since I aim to please . . .' He put down his drink, took hers and put it next to his on the occasional table in front of them. Then he took her in his arms and kissed her, a long, lingering kiss. 'I love the way you kiss,' he murmured.

'Do you?' she whispered kittenishly.

'I'd die for your kisses.'

He kissed her again and his hand wandered, drawn inexorably to her cleavage which had been tormenting him all evening. She allowed the tips of his fingers to enjoy the feel of the soft smooth skin of her breasts for a second or two before she playfully removed his hand in token resistance, knowing full well that he would attempt another raid soon.

And he did.

But she got such immense pleasure from his kisses that she herself was too overwhelmed with desire, without pretence, to repel him next time anyway, and he delved deeper into her bodice, managing to cup one breast entirely in his hand, squeezing it amorously. It all fell in beautifully with her plan, and her lack of resistance encouraged Clarence.

'I should hate to tear your dress,' he breathed. 'May I unfasten it?'

'You're taking a lot for granted, Clarry,' she felt bound to say, to let him think she was still safeguarding her virtue.

'Not at all, my angel. I have no doubt you'll refuse me.'

She smiled at him enigmatically and rested her head momentarily on his shoulder, as if in helpless submission, and resigned to it. 'Well . . . maybe I won't . . . Just this once . . .'

They broke off their embrace and he attended to the back of her bodice. He found a hook, fumbled inexpertly with it, and eventually released it from a loop of thread. Then another . . . and then a line of tiny buttons . . . He slid the shoulder straps down her arms and the front of the bodice peeled away from her, exposing her breasts, like firm, round peaches.

Clarence gulped, unable to think of anything suitable to say, lest it was the wrong thing, that might make her realise she had made a scandalous error of judgement in allowing him such outrageous liberties. So he gently took her chin, turned her face to him and kissed her succulently again instead. At first, he did not touch her breasts, illogically believing she needed some time to get used to the idea that they were naked and at his disposal. Also, he was gallantly affording her the opportunity to draw back.

But she did not draw back. She showed no inclination to draw back as they kissed again, more ardently. Rather, she seemed to melt under the pleasure of all these kisses and limply swayed backwards so that she was lying stretched along the sofa, naked from the waist up. Clarence eased himself onto her, heartened by this sudden surprising power of seduction that he evidently had after all, and confidently took a handful of breast, kneading it with loving care, savouring the firm but soft, feminine smoothness of her flawless flesh.

'Oh, Kate . . .'

'Oh, Clarry . . .'

Mouths met again, as if they were trying to chew each other's lips. Greatly encouraged, he lifted the hem of her skirt and petticoats and risked ruining all his hard work hitherto by running his hand up her leg. Silk stocking, so smooth and sensual . . . a garter above her knee. Then the warm, creamy smooth skin of her thigh . . . Oh, *God* . . . He thought his heart would burst forth from his chest, it was pounding so hard. Yet still he encountered no resistance. He was breathing hard, finding it difficult to keep his lips in contact with hers as he reached down and let his fingers glide up the inside of her thigh till it came to the obstacle of her silk drawers, also erotically smooth.

'I'm afraid of ruining your dress,' he murmured, with the sort of mistimed gallantry that could ruin the moment and mar forever what he had thus far achieved. 'I was thinking . . . it might be better if we removed it . . .'

'If you'll turn the gaslight out, Clarry . . .' she responded with a whisper and a shy smile.

'Yes, yes, of course,' he rapidly agreed, content to accede to her commendable modesty.

He reached up and pulled on the chain that shut off the gas as she began undressing herself. He began fumbling with his own clothes, but his nerves were so unsteady that he could not unfasten his shirt buttons so he tore off his shirt and pulled off his trousers, almost losing his balance in the process. He glanced at Kate and was bewitched by the sight of her naked body as she stepped out of her silk drawers, bathed in the warm glow of the flickering fire. The dancing coruscations played over the soft curves of her breasts and the taut skin of her belly, caressing her delta of lush dark hair below it, which seemed to glisten by the light of the frolicking orange flames. He could scarcely believe this was happening, and took a slug of whisky to steady his nerves.

They reached the sofa together and fell onto it in a frenzy of longing, lips drinking lips in delicious kisses. She could taste the whisky he'd just had, still lingering in his mouth, loving this sort of sensual intimacy. His hands, meanwhile, explored her urgently, savouring as much of her as was possible before she inevitably changed her mind.

But Kate was not about to change her mind. She manoeuvred herself so that she lay directly beneath him, perfectly positioned for his inevitable entry, for she could feel him hard, pressing hungrily against her.

'Promise to be gentle, Clarry,' she sighed.

'Oh, my angel,' he simpered. 'As if I could be otherwise with you.'

'But they say it hurts a girl first time.'

'So they say.' He lined himself up and pressed forward, anticipating some difficulty, but was amazed and gratified by how effortlessly, how smoothly he was sucked into her, despite her little gasps that suggested otherwise.

They rocked together gently, their arousal becoming more profound.

'Get closer into me,' she said, almost impatiently, he thought. 'Firmer . . . Rub yourself against me more . . .'

He tried and, for a couple of minutes or so, his efforts seemed to elicit a more animated response from Kate. The effect on him was significant; he could no longer contain himself and he squirted his seed into her, groaning silently as the ecstasy of intense but premature orgasm overwhelmed him. Kate was thrusting herself against him still, with a phenomenal enthusiasm that astonished him, emitting a series of very worrying gasps and cries before she fell into total stillness, as if suddenly relaxed by some ethereal sedative his father might have invisibly administered.

They lay together unmoving for some minutes, Clarence still in a state of incredulity that this had really happened. If it had been a dream, it was the most amazing, the most lucid dream he'd ever had in his life, and hoped he would dream it every night.

'You're going to pop out,' Kate said with cruel reality, making him fully understand that this was no dream at all.

'Yes,' he answered, and it happened exactly as she predicted. He rolled away from her.

'You won't tell anybody about this, will you, Clarry?'

'Of course not,' he said earnestly.

'You mustn't. It would ruin my reputation. I'm already ruined now as it is . . .'

'What sort of man do you think I am? Of course I wouldn't breathe a word. It's our secret . . .'

She smiled at him. 'You let go inside me, didn't you?'

'I couldn't help it, Kate. I'm sorry.'

'Let's hope nothing comes of it.'

'Yes . . . Let's hope.'

He lay snuggled up to her and they both fell asleep, each content that their mission had been accomplished.

They were still asleep when Myra the maid came down from her garret to make up the fire. The light from the hallway fell on the young couple as she opened the door. Mr Clarence was curled up on the sofa naked alongside an utterly striking young woman, also naked except for her pale silk stockings. She gasped with shock and made a silent but very rapid exit.

Chapter 11

Algie and his workmate, Harry Whitehouse, were working together one morning at the beginning of October, assembling yet another of a seemingly infinite series of brass bedheads. That area of the factory reeked of metal polish, paint, and the lubricating tallow they used for cutting threads; a fusion of heady chemical smells that neither of the men disliked. In the centre of the workshop stood a stove, its chimney piercing the tin roof through a hole only approximate in diameter to that of the hot pipe, so that during a good rainstorm, water trickled down it and onto the smouldering surface of the stove where it bubbled and hissed. Thus it was that morning.

'Piss-begotten weather,' Harry declaimed with high rhetoric, eyeing the gap in the roof with some contempt.

'Piss-begotten roof,' Algie replied.

'It's a long time till next summer, Algie, my mate. I don't know if I can stand the thought of another cold winter.'

'Nor me,' Algie agreed, his mind at once turning to thoughts of Marigold and the prospect of months of cold and draughty courting.

'How's that wench o' yourn? Still getting your leg over even while the weather's rotten?'

'Where there's a will, Harry.' He winked waggishly.

'What yer doing tonight?'

'Nothing much.'

'Not seeing her?'

'I doubt it. They only left Brierley Hill Monday. I doubt if I'll see her again for another fortnight.'

'Fancy a pint then? We could have a wander to the Bricklayers. There's generally a doxie or two knocking about as we could have some fun with. Keep you in practice while Marigold's away.'

'If you like,' Algie said, but without enthusiasm, as he took a rag to a length of brass rod to polish it.

'So how often do you get to see this Marigold?'

'It depends.' He eyed up the length of the brass rod for signs of any blemish. 'It depends on what work they've got, to bring 'em our way.'

'So how d'you know when to expect her?'

'I don't. I never know till Marigold knocks on our door to say as they'll be moored up somewhere close by. Her old man's keen on the beer at the Bottle and Glass, if he can find a mooring there. If they're within striking distance next night I'll generally bike along the cut to find her.'

'You don't half sound keen, biking along the cut. Think you'll marry the wench?'

Mr Benjamin Sampson appeared at that precise moment, obviating the need for Algie to admit that it was his private intention eventually. He walked straight up to Algie, looking cursorily at what they were doing.

'A word, if you please, Algie. Would you follow me to my office?'

'Yes, course, Mr Sampson.' Algie glanced at Harry with a puzzled frown as he put his work piece down on the bench they shared, then followed the gaffer, believing he must be on the carpet over some misdemeanour or other.

Benjamin Sampson walked with deliberate briskness; it was

181

yet another way of demonstrating his superiority, his aloofness, a means of making his bone-idle men realise that he was in charge and that they had to go at his pace, not he at theirs. Neither did he speak again until they were inside his office and he'd closed the door behind them.

'Sit down, Algie,' he invited, sounding surprisingly amenable.

Algie sat down, and his apprehension began to diminish.

'I expect you're wondering why I've asked you up here,' he said, his face even erupting into an expansive smile.

'I was wondering, like.'

Benjamin took a silver cigarette case from his pocket, opened it and offered Algie one.

'I don't smoke, Mr Sampson.'

Benjamin put a cigarette in his mouth and lit it, and his head was enveloped in a miasma of blue smoke. 'Your little scheme to manufacture bikes, Algie . . .'

'Oh!' Algie registered some surprise, especially as he believed the idea was dead as far as Mr Sampson was concerned.

'I've been thinking . . . and I've done a bit of investigation into the things you told me . . .' Algie smiled, delighted that his scheme had elicited a flicker of interest after all. 'I've took a look at some bikes – one or two different makes – and I reckon you might have a point about manufacturing 'em. I reckon we could make 'em easy. There seems to be a good market for bikes, as far as I can make out, and they look easy enough to chuck together. Not only that, they'd fit easy into our own way of doing things. You have to keep an open mind about such things these days. In other words, hoist your sail when the wind's fair.'

'What about the question of resistance welding, Mr Sampson?'

182

Benjamin drew on his cigarette and pensively blew out smoke in a gust. 'I need to look deeper into resistance welding, Algie. But such as I've heard, I reckon it would be the right way to go about it.'

Algie beamed, and nodded. 'Good, sir. I'm glad you think so.'

'I'd like to talk this over with you a bit more, Algie. I reckon we could be of some help to one another. We could come to some arrangement whereby we could all benefit from getting our heads together.'

Algie continued beaming. 'Well . . . I'd like to think so, Mr Sampson.'

'Well, no bird ever flew on one wing, you know. What I'd like to do is to talk the whole thing over a bit more informally – bandy about a few more ideas. If you and your missus would like to come to my house on Friday evening – say seven o' clock – we could talk it over a bit more . . . over a nice bit of dinner, eh? We could get to know one another a bit better. It's all well and good us making bedsteads for ever and a day, but maybe we should be looking to broaden our horizons. Sampson's needs to look at other things. It's daft to have all your eggs in one basket, I'm thinking.'

'Over dinner?' Algie gulped. This was an unanticipated honour. Either he or his idea must be considered worthy to warrant such a signal honour being bestowed upon him; Mr Sampson must be serious about manufacturing bicycles too, to be willing to go to such lengths. 'That's very kind, Mr Sampson. I'd love to. There's just one thing, though . . . I don't have a wife. I'm not married yet.'

'Then bring your sweetheart. I presume you've got a sweetheart, a young chap of your age and looks?'

Algie grinned self-consciously. 'Oh, yes, I've got a sweetheart all right.'

'Well, there you are, then.' He inhaled on his cigarette again. 'Then my missus and me will look forward to meeting her.' He stood up, making it plain, despite the smile, that the interview was over. 'Friday, then. Seven o' clock.' Mr Sampson held out his hand, and they shook on it. 'In the meantime, Algie, keep this little chat we've had to yourself, eh? There's no sense in inviting speculation from anybody yet. After all, the best laid schemes of mice and men . . .'

'Oh, I agree, Mr Sampson. Don't worry, I won't breathe a word.'

The invitation left Algie with a problem. From the pattern of the Binghams' work hitherto, he knew it was extremely unlikely that they would be passing through the Buckpool Locks for at least two weeks and possibly more. Marigold would therefore be unable to accompany him to dine at the Sampsons' grand home on Friday. So what should he do? Should he try and locate her and get her back to Brierley Hill by train? By this time she could be miles away, well out of reach, even if he cycled for hours. Besides, where should he cycle to? In which direction, on which canal? He decided instead that if Kate could be trusted to be on her best behaviour, and not of a mind to embarrass him, she might make a very presentable stand-in.

'Kate,' he thus addressed her that evening, when she and their mother had finished the washing up. 'Can I ask you a favour?'

'A favour?' she queried suspiciously. 'It depends. What sort of favour?'

'I need you to help me out Friday night.'

'Friday night? How?'

He explained.

'I can't go with you,' she said flatly. 'I'll be seeing Clarence

Friday night. We'm meeting some of his old school friends with their wives and sweethearts. It's been arranged ages.'

'Damn!' he said. 'And I really want this to go well. It's the opportunity of a lifetime, Kate. I can feel it in my water.'

'You'll have to ask somebody else. Ain't Marigold likely to be about at all? Mind you, Marigold ain't got the polish to pull it off like me, has she? And you can bet she ain't got a decent frock to go in neither.'

'Don't be so snotty about Marigold,' he protested defensively. 'What a vile thing to say – "she ain't got the polish". She's more of a lady than anybody I know . . . you included.'

'Well, she ain't borrowing my best frock, whether or no. I'll need it myself.'

'She won't be here anyway,' he said ruefully.

'Then you'm up the cut with ne'er a paddle . . . Course, you could always ask Harriet Meese.'

'Harriet . . .' he mused for a second. 'No,' he said decisively. 'Harriet wouldn't come with me. Her father wouldn't allow her, anyway.'

'She is twenty-one, Algie,' Kate reminded him. 'She can do as she pleases.'

'But she wouldn't go against her father, twenty-one or no.'

'He don't need to know,' she suggested mischievously. 'Ask her.'

'How can I ask her? I shan't see her.'

'I shall,' Kate declared. 'I'll see her tonight at rehearsal. She's still keen on you, you know, our Algie, though the Lord only knows why. I'll ask her for you if you promise me one thing.'

'What?'

'That you won't tittle-tattle to her about me and Reggie Hodgetts. I don't want anything to get back to Clarence.'

'Fair enough, our Kate. I wouldn't say anything anyway.'

'Good. Then I'll see how the land lies.'

'If she's agreeable, tell her I'll meet her at quarter to seven Friday, on the corner by the Elms.'

Clarence Froggatt was wallowing in a fog of perplexity, suffering sleepless nights, wracked by doubt and anguish. The problem was, of course, Kate Stokes. Her avowed words did not seem to coincide precisely enough with his more recent perceptions of her. He did not know exactly how to express in simple terms what was to him becoming more apparent, so he was unable to discuss it with any of his friends – not that it was an easy thing to talk about – but he was tormented all the same.

At first he was troubled by the fact that Kate had allowed him to seduce her at all. Because he was twenty-three now and contemplating his future, accustoming himself to the likelihood of marriage at some foreseeable time with a well-presented and respectable girl, he was more concerned with the virtue of eligible candidates. The fact that Kate had been so feckless as to allow herself to be seduced by *him*, of all people, only lessened his esteem. No girl worth having would have allowed him such intimate access without a marriage already arranged at the very least. This is how Clarence viewed it.

But there was something else, something more fundamental. Something was radically amiss. His concern was triggered after they had made love the first time, naked in front of the fire in the drawing room after attending Harriet Meese's birthday party. Kate had professed she was a virgin. Indeed, many were the times she had protested it adamantly. Nor would you expect anything less from a sweet, respectable girl of nineteen, however pretty and appealing to men. But recalling that first heady evening, he began to realise not only how readily her high moral principles had been overturned, but also how easily he had penetrated her, when she was supposed to be a virgin. Indeed, it had been so slick and instant that it belied her claims to innocence. Kate was not the first girl he had known intimately, and the previous one truly had been a virgin, giving him not only all hell's game trying to puncture her seemingly inviolable hymen, but also the experience to know how awkward and unromantic such a thrilling event could turn out to be. But with Kate he had slid right in, like an otter slipping into deep water, and with about as much resistance.

Something else . . . 'Get closer into me,' she'd said. 'Rub yourself against me more.' He recalled it so accurately, and with such a thrill at first; her breathy, urgent voice, how she had raised her long, shapely legs, still clad in silk stockings, to a sort of inverted crouch, to render herself more accessible. Where had she learned that? Then she'd sighed and groaned with ecstasy as he ground into her. That could surely only have been the supplication and reaction of a woman experienced in such things, a woman who required that sort of sexual play because she *knew* it would bring her more surely to a climax, when half the decent girls in Christendom had only half a notion of what a climax might be.

At first, he'd been pleased with his apparent prowess and her response, delighted that his technique had made her wriggle beneath him with such toe-curling pleasure, but the more he thought about it, and the more they practised these techniques which she craved, the graver became his doubts.

Until they had *known* each other in that way, Clarence had been becoming quite serious about Kate. He had had it in mind to announce to his parents sometime soon that the delightful young woman they'd recently met would, in a year or two, make him a virtuous and devout wife, despite her lowly upbringing. She was personable enough despite the handicap of her social class, and would certainly have fitted in with his family. After all, his father was only a doctor; educated, yes, but hardly aristocracy. The introduction into the family of a pretty girl, albeit only a lock-keeper's daughter, would hardly cause them any acute social embarrassment. Of course, he would have expected a frown of disapproval from his mother, who tended to be the snob of the family, but once she got to know Kate . . . Unless, of course, he found it necessary to marry her because she was pregnant . . . Oh, perish the thought!

But – always assuming that she was not pregnant – he had changed his mind about Kate. She was certainly not the innocent young girl she'd purported to be, and it had been his unswerving intention to marry a girl who had been deflowered by nobody but himself. Somebody had previously deflowered Kate, though. He was not particularly interested who, or even how many had been before him, merely that she had been wanton enough to allow it in the first place, and then become so practised at it. To lead him into thinking that no such thing had ever happened was an even bigger mistake, because it implied that she considered him a fool. Well, he was not quite such a fool as she imagined.

The Forest Princess, as performed by the Amateur Dramatics Society, was about as close to perfection as they would ever get within the confines of the thespian and material limitations of the company. After another successful and confident run-through with only one minor slip, the members broke up into relaxed but enthusiastic groups, discussing the play and speculating on the opening night a week on Friday. Priss Meese was tying up the ribbons of a fashionable new toque, having resorted to them, as she laughed with her younger sister and Mr Higgs, another member of the cast, when Kate

Stokes, by now changed back into her ordinary clothes, approached them.

'Well done, Kate,' Harriet said generously. 'Another flawless performance.'

'Thank you, Harriet. But I don't know about flawless,' she answered modestly. 'You were good, though.'

'Me? Oh, my part's hardly demanding. We were just laughing at how Miss Bennett fed poor Mr Froggatt the wrong line when he forgot his words.'

'I know, ain't she a gooby?' Kate remarked. 'Half asleep, I reckon she was. If he forgets them again I'd be better prompting him.'

Clarence himself joined them. 'Kate and I can walk part of the way with you girls, if you like,' he announced to Harriet and Priss.

'Actually, Mr Higgs is walking us home,' Harriet said, almost apologetically.

'Oh? . . . In that case—'

'I wonder if I could have a quick word, Harriet,' Kate butted in, keen to say what she had to say before the Meese girls left.

Harriet stepped aside and turned to Kate. 'What is it?'

'It's our Algie.'

Her eyes widened with interest. 'Oh?'

'He'd very much like you to go out with him on Friday night, Harriet.'

'Algie?' Harriet's eyes lit up. 'Really?'

'Some important do. Actually, he asked me to go with him, but me and Clarence are going to another do, so I can't oblige him.'

'What is it?' Harriet asked. 'What sort of do?'

'Oh, it's a reunion of some of his old school mates and their wives and sweethearts.'

'Oh?' she said again. 'Isn't he taking that girl Marigold

Bingham to his reunion? Has he fallen out with her or something?'

'No, no,' Kate exclaimed, realising that Harriet had got the wrong end of the stick. 'It's me and Clarence what'm going to the old school friends' reunion.' She laughed at the easy mistake. 'Our Algie's been invited to dinner at his gaffer's house. He needs to take a lady friend. It looks like they'm about to start up in business together making bikes.'

'Algie's starting up a business?' Harriet beamed with pleasure at the prospect. 'I always said—'

'Anyroad, he wants to take you along 'cause you'd be the right sort of person to have at his side for dinner at his gaffer's.'

'He asked for me? Fancy.'

'But he knows as your father mightn't be too pleased. Like I said to our Algie: what his eyes don't see, his heart won't grieve about. I mean to say, you'm twenty-one now, Harriet. You can do as you've a mind.'

'Well . . .' Harriet mused, 'I'd dearly like to see Algie again . . . If it can be done discreetly.'

'Course it can be done. Can't you just dress up and slip out the house without him knowing?'

'Oh, on Friday, yes, I could. My father goes out Friday afternoons playing cribbage and he never comes back till late. He wouldn't even know I'd been out.'

Kate smiled triumphantly. 'There you are then. Our Algie says to meet him at quarter to seven outside the Elms.'

'The Elms? That big house on the corner?'

'That's the one. Far enough away from your place not to be seen, eh?'

'Tell him I'll be there,' Harriet said smiling eagerly, trying unsuccessfully to suppress her excitement. 'I'm keen to help, if he thinks I'm able.'

'Oh, and, Harriet . . . Dress to kill. Take a tip from me and wear that green dress you wore for your party.' Kate winked saucily, aware she was about to shock her friend. 'You got a fine bosom, you know, Harriet. Might as well make 'em do for you. 'Specially if you feel inclined to get our Algie interested again. He's only human, after all.'

Harriet was already waiting. She saw a tallish man walking towards her up the hill, and recognised his jaunty gait in the dusk. As he got closer, she could see he was wearing his best Sunday suit beneath an open topcoat that flapped in the breeze. His silver Albert, looped across his chest, glinted by the light of the gas street lamps. She smiled in anticipation of being close to him after so long, trying to check her trembling. She had hardly slept since Wednesday thinking about this meeting and whether it would lead to a resumption of their courtship, which had ended so abruptly and unexpectedly nearly six months earlier. Kate had been right; her father would not condone its revival, and it would certainly present some serious family difficulties, but she would deal with those if and when the need arose.

Algie had not seen Harriet since their split. As he ambled towards her, he perceived that she had lost a little weight, become a little leaner, but not unbecomingly so. Her face looked thinner, as were her lips, which did not enhance her features, and her nose had a more pronounced bump, but her figure looked more refined. Maybe it was the dimness that exaggerated the effect, for her eyes were warm on him as she smiled her greeting.

They began walking together, about a yard apart, with polite enquiries as to each other's health and the health of their nearest and dearest. When the pleasantries were exhausted, it was Harriet who volunteered to raise the topic of the evening in hand.

'It was such a surprise when Kate told me you'd asked her to ask me if I'd go with you tonight. I had the shock of my life. How far is it?'

'Holly Hall. We'd better get a move on. My gaffer wants us there for seven.'

'Oh, well, Holly Hall's not far. We can walk it in less than a quarter of an hour. And in any case it won't hurt even if we're five minutes late.'

A tram huffed and rattled past them in the other direction, in a clangour of metal and steam, its iron wheels rumbling over the iron rails that bore it.

'You don't mind walking, do you, Harriet?'

'Oh, no,' she reassured him. 'We might wait ages for a tram to come our way at this time . . . Kate said something about you and this Mr Sampson going into partnership. You must be very excited.'

'I don't want to count my chickens yet, Harriet. Ever since I bought my bike I've had the notion that I'd like to set up a firm to make them. But, money being tight like it is, I knew it wouldn't be possible to do it on my own. Anyroad, I told Mr Sampson about my idea and he must've pondered it, 'cause he said he wanted us to talk more about it. I think he might be about to make me an offer, seeing as how he asked me to bring along my wife.'

'But you haven't got a wife,' she grinned.

'I told him that, and he said I could bring my sweetheart.'

'But I'm not your sweetheart, Algie . . . am I?'

'No, but you used to be . . . sort of.' He smiled at her amiably, a little embarrassed that she might be asking if she could be once again. 'And you said in your letter as we should still be friends. Anyway, I'm grateful to you for helping me out.'

'So where's Marigold? Why aren't you taking her?'

192

He shrugged. 'Because she could be anywhere between Kidderminster and Nantwich, or Wolverhampton and London. Or anywhere else on the blasted canal network for that matter. Too far away to be able to go with me tonight, anyway.'

'So you haven't fallen out with her?'

'Oh, no.'

Harriet concealed her sigh of disappointment. 'How often do you see her then?'

'Oh . . . a couple of nights every two or three weeks.'

'Not too often then?'

'Not often enough. If she'd been moored up by our house tonight she would have come with me, but I knew she wouldn't be. That's why I asked you. In any case, you'll be more at home hobnobbing with the Sampsons than Marigold might've. She isn't used to hobnobbing. I reckon she'd have been out of her depth a bit, and I wouldn't want to put her through that.'

'That's very thoughtful,' Harriet said. Privately, she felt put down by his inference that she was his second choice, but delighted that he thought her more suitable for the occasion than Marigold. She could have made some disparaging comment about the girl being deprived of culture and home comforts as a canal worker's daughter, but suspected Algie would not appreciate it, especially since he was merely the son of a lock-keeper. In any case, she would not win back his affection by being catty. It was not Marigold's fault that she was where she was, or who she was. It must be difficult for a girl born to commonplace circumstances with a commonplace intellect to make her world a larger one.

'I understand she's very pretty,' she said instead.

'Oh, she is,' Algie replied emphatically. 'She's really beautiful . . . and bright with it, considering she's had little or no schooling.'

'I feel quite sorry for her,' Harriet remarked.

'Sorry for her?' He looked at her questioningly. 'Why?'

'Having had no schooling.'

Algie laughed aloud. 'You don't have to feel sorry for Marigold just because she can't read a newssheet or the latest novel. What's she missing, after all? What you have to remember, Harriet, is that she ain't tainted or influenced by all that stuff. She's natural and unspoilt, and she's a delight because of it. She's just pure Marigold. You'd like her, I know you would.'

'I'm sure I would,' she replied, knowing perfectly well that she would despise the waif, for that was how she imagined her. 'But, on the other hand, you can't write to her or she write to you, which would be a boon since you don't see each other very often.'

'That's true,' Algie admitted.

They were walking through Round Oak by this time. On their left was the railway station, on their right the massive ironworks belonging to the renowned Earl of Dudley. Columns of smoke belched forth, accompanied by the clatter, the smells, the dross and the mullock of heavy industry and the Great Western Railway, all assaulting their senses.

They discussed at length the forthcoming play and whether Algie and his parents would be going along to the town hall to see it. Kate, Harriet unstintingly reported, was dazzling in the role of Pocahontas, and would be the talk of Brierley Hill for months to come. This in turn switched the conversation to her liaison with Clarence Froggatt.

They were walking less than a foot apart now along the drive of Holly Hall House, the home of the Sampsons, and their boots crunched the gravel beneath their feet. A pair of carriage lamps, set either side of the impressive front door, flared a welcome and lit their way towards the front steps.

Bright lights glared from within, also spilling out onto the driveway, throwing into relief the parallel wheel tracks of a carriage.

'Do you know if Kate and Clarence are seriously contemplating marriage?' Harriet enquired conversationally.

'Not if he's got any sense.'

'Oh? What makes you say that?'

'Marry our Kate?' Algie scoffed. 'He'd want his head looking at.'

'She's not so bad as you make her out to be, Algie. She's my friend now. I like her enormously.'

'The world is full of surprises, Harriet. You're chalk and cheese, you two.'

'Oh, yes, I realise we're quite different. But that, I think, could be the reason we are such good friends.'

'Yes, they say opposites attract,' he remarked obscurely, as he rang the door bell.

Chapter 12

A maid answered the door of Holly Hall House and stood back to let Algie and Harriet in. Algie seemed to quake with apprehension as he stood on the threshold. This could be the moment when his dreams became a reality. He ushered Harriet in before him. There was the sound of a piano playing gentle music. Algie was not aware what the music was, but it seemed to have a tranquillising effect on him. He looked around. The impressive square hall, gas lit, held a sweeping staircase, a dresser and an ancient grandfather clock, its long pendulum sedately, heavily measuring time.

The servant, a girl about the same age as Harriet, bowed her head deferentially.

'Shall I take your mantle and bonnet, miss?'

'Thank you,' Harriet said, unfastening both while the maid waited.

The girl tossed Harriet's cloak over her arm. 'Your coat, sir?'

'Thank you,' Algie echoed self-consciously, unused to such lavish attention.

As soon as Harriet's mantle was off, Algie noticed her dress, how it accentuated her more refined figure, and his eyes almost popped out of his head. Her bosom looked so inviting in the flesh, a sight he'd never before had the privilege to behold.

'Mr and Mrs Sampson are in the drawing room,' the maid said. 'If you'd like to come this way . . .'

'I like your dress, Harriet,' Algie felt compelled to say in an aside as they followed the maid. 'A bit of a bobby-dazzler tonight, aren't you?'

She turned to him and smiled graciously, pleased to receive his compliment, and noticed the impish look in his eye. 'I'm aware that I might have been hiding my light under a bushel, as you might say.' Secretly she thanked Kate for advising her to wear it.

The maid opened a door to the right and, as the sumptuous drawing room was revealed, the piano playing stopped. The room was filled with elegant furniture, and the walls were bedecked with a rich red flock wallpaper in swirling arabesques. Gilt-framed mirrors, and oil paintings of stags standing noble and proud against the Scottish Highlands, hung from a picture rail that traversed each wall. Another grandfather clock stood in one corner. Several highly decorated vases were dotted around, each overflowing with fresh blooms, and a whatnot in another corner bore an aspidistra. On the mantelpiece over the marble fireplace with its rich swags, sat an ornate marble shelf clock, flanked on either side by shining brass candelabra. Red velvet drapes hung at the windows, and an elaborate arrangement of four gas ceiling lights, fizzing softly, provided ample illumination.

But Algie was oblivious to this domestic extravagance, for the woman he had just cast his eyes upon, about to leave the piano, was a domestic extravagance more in his appreciation. She was compellingly beautiful, and her presence before him at once shattered his contentedness and turned his world upside down. Till that moment he had believed his life to be ordered, uncomplicated; he had looked forward to a future of contentment with Marigold. This woman, however, was so heartbreakingly desirable. She was also the wife of his gaffer;

legally, consummately, sovereignly unattainable. Fate was so cruel, so ruthless, so unthinking by tormenting him with such unparalleled loveliness.

Benjamin Sampson smiled, and stood to greet them . . .

And so did she.

'Algie . . .' Algie heard his name, spoken amiably by Benjamin as if they had been close friends for years. He was barely conscious of their handshake, heedless of anything bar the vision before him. 'And this must be your sweetheart.'

'Oh, no, I'm just Harriet Meese,' he heard Harriet say.

'Delighted to meet you, Miss Meese. But let's agree to use first names, shall we? I'm Benjamin, and this is Aurelia, my wife . . . Aurelia . . . Harriet Meese . . . and Algie Stokes.'

Algie was blinded by Mrs Sampson's azure gaze, held like a rabbit mesmerised by a bright light. She stood before him expectantly, a welcoming smile on her face, her eyes full upon him. Their clarity made him catch his breath, their softness staggered him, and Algie trembled in their sapphire radiance. In that one enchanting look he glimpsed heaven and hell. In that single, unforgettable moment he witnessed the height of human aspiration and the depth of despair. Beholding such beauty enraptured him, but her unattainability was a down-right torment. She was way beyond him in every respect.

Yet no other woman in the world could compare.

'Thank you indeed for coming,' Aurelia chimed, and her tone was warm and sincere. 'I've been looking forward to meeting you . . .'

As they shook, the feel of her hand, so cool and soft, thrilled Algie to the core. His eyes devoured the sweet curve of her mouth as she spoke to him; a mouth so delicately moulded, so obviously formed for the pure pleasure of kissing.

'I've been hearing something of your ideas for making bikes,' the vision said, easily. 'It all sounds very exciting.'

It seemed to him that she was of another world, another time, some other plane of existence of which he was not a part, that he was seeing her remotely through some ethereal telescope which rendered her unreachable. She was so astonishingly young as well – younger than himself – and so stunning that his tongue seemed stuck to the roof of his mouth, and he could offer no more than an awkward smile in response.

'I take it you walked here,' she suggested to Harriet, for she seemed to be getting no response from Algie.

'Oh, yes. It's not far. I only live on Brierley Hill High Street, and Algie lives at Buckpool.'

'Oh, Buckpool?'

'Yes, Buckpool,' he answered inadequately.

'You know, Algie,' Benjamin said matily, 'you might think about building a bicycle made for two, eh?' and laughed at his own little joke. 'Don't you think that would be a good idea? Get the woman to help with the pedalling? A problem shared is a problem halved, you know . . . Think about it, eh? . . . What would you like to drink?'

'Do you have lemonade?' Harriet said.

'Of course. And you, Algie?'

Algie was just then beginning to notice what Aurelia was wearing. She had on a plain, blue chiffon dress that matched her eyes superbly, and seemed to complement the lush dark brown of her hair, so elegantly swept up from the nape of her neck and piled up on her head in a swirling mass of feminine curls. An image of Marigold in her muslin frock, which had impressed him all summer with its simple femininity, leapt to mind, but by comparison with Aurelia's it seemed rustic. Her chiffon bodice was buttoned demurely up to her throat, where a blue and white cameo brooch was fastened, but her breasts tantalisingly nudged the material of her bodice with every breath she took.

'What would you like to drink, Algie?' Benjamin repeated.

He managed to divert his gaze away from Aurelia. 'I'll have whatever you're drinking, Mr Sampson.'

'It's dry sherry, and I'm Benjamin tonight, Algie, remember. Not Mr Sampson. Didn't you hear what I said about first names?' He smiled magnanimously. 'The same goes for all of us. Sit down, Harriet. You, as well, Algie.'

Algie nodded.

'Would you like to sit on this sofa with me?' Aurelia suggested, and he willingly assented.

Benjamin seated Harriet next to himself on the opposite sofa, rang for the maid and offered his cigarettes, which everybody declined. He lit one for himself.

The maid entered and he requested drinks for his guests. 'Leave the bottles there when you've poured 'em, Mary. We'll help ourselves.'

Mary handed out the drinks, bobbed a curtsey and left them.

'How long have you been married?' Harriet enquired, her question directed at Aurelia.

'Nearly three years.' Aurelia glanced at her husband as if seeking his permission to say more, but he was not looking at her, his eyes were lowered, furtively glancing at Harriet's diverting cleavage. 'I have a little boy, coming two years old.'

Algie felt a deep twinge of agony as Aurelia plunged the knife of despair deeper into his heart and twisted it. Already she had a child . . .

'Oh, how lovely,' Harriet cooed. 'What's his name?'

Aurelia smiled proudly. 'Benjamin. After his father, and his grandfather before him.'

'Is he like his father?'

'More like his mother at present, I'd say,' Benjamin declared. 'And about as soft.' He drew on his cigarette, turned to Algie and blew smoke down his nostrils in two parallel gusts. 'Aurelia is turning my son into the biggest softy imaginable. Lord knows what she'll do when we send him packing off to boarding school.'

'It will break my heart,' Aurelia said softly.

Algie felt like clasping her to him to shield such a sensitive soul from the emotional terrors of the wicked world. 'I wouldn't put you through that,' he heard himself say quietly, and his heart lurched when he noticed her warm smile, intended only for him, in response.

'Then you're as soft as she is,' Benjamin guffawed. 'You can't be soft with sons, you know, Algie. Course, you're not a father yourself yet, so you're hardly likely to know. But let me tell you – a child can have too much of his mother's softness. Sons have to be brought up in a way that prepares 'em suitably for the rough and tumble of the world we live in, whatever their station.'

'I'm sure you're quite right,' Harriet said amenably. 'All the same, I can see Aurelia's point of view. I would hate to be parted from a little child of mine even for a few days. Providing I'm ever fortunate enough to be blessed with children.'

'Oh, children are all right so long as you keep them in their place,' Benjamin proclaimed archly. 'Spare the rod and spoil the child.'

They talked on, switching from one subject to another, until they were led into the dining room and took their places on mahogany chairs upholstered in red velvet, at the beautifully laid table. The fire grate was low and brilliantly blackleaded. Above it, a tall mirror had been installed, which emphasised the room's height. The top of a mahogany sideboard was taken up with a dessert service, ornaments and unused table decorations. And there were more flowers.

Mary served the soup. It was hare, Aurelia announced, and Algie waited to see how his host and hostess set about consuming it before he committed himself to doing the wrong thing.

Benjamin said, 'This idea of making bicycles, Algie . . .'

Algie was studying the soft skin and slender fingers of Aurelia's hands, wishing the bright gold band she wore on her wedding finger was his, before he looked up expectantly in response to Benjamin's words.

'I reckon it could be viable, and that we should have a go, but on a limited scale at first, to test the water, so to speak.'

Algie beamed, glancing at Aurelia, who met his admiring look with a smile of encouragement.

'I propose to put you in overall charge of the manufacturing side, Algie. It'll be a big responsibility. First, I intend to start a new draughtsman who's got the engineering knowledge and skill to convert your designs – *your* designs, Algie, mark you – into workable engineering drawings. We'll need jigs and fixtures made, based on these drawings. While all that's going on, I want you to sort out that welding process you mentioned.' He took a slurp of soup.

'Resistance welding,' Algie prompted.

'Aye, that.' Benjamin dabbed his mouth with his table napkin. 'Get to the bottom of it, Algie. Do some digging and delving. Find out which companies can offer us the tackle we need to do it, and what it's gunna cost. We shall need some sort of enamelling facility an' all, since we can't despatch the machines without first painting 'em. As you said, we'll have to source wheels as well, till we learn how to make 'em ourselves. And them new-fangled tyres that you pump up with wind.'

'Pneumatic tyres.'

'Aye, pneumatic tyres . . . That's something else I'll want you to look at.'

'Shall you want me to do this while I'm still working on bedheads?'

'Good Lord, no.' Benjamin laughed, and Algie felt stupid for having asked it. 'You'll be too busy for that. I'll transfer you to the offices. You'll have your own office, Algie . . . Close to mine.'

'My own office!' He grinned with delight at Harriet.

Harriet regarded him proudly. Aurelia pushed her half-consumed soup away from her and listened quietly, glancing from one to the other from time to time and smiling indulgently.

'O' course, one of the things we shall have to do quick is assess the potential market. We'll need to appoint a network of wholesalers. That'll involve a fair amount of travelling up and down the length and breadth of the country. That will be up to me, Algie, to travel, to seek out good, reliable wholesalers and get 'em signed up accordingly. Even abroad, maybe, since it would be my intention to export what we make. Everybody else does.'

'You have it all mapped out,' Algie commented familiarly, and was delighted to see that Aurelia considered the comment with approval enough to warrant another generous smile. 'When d'you want me to start on all this work?'

'Let's say from the beginning of November – the first Monday, eh? In the meantime, I'll have you an office whitewashed, and a decent desk and chair found.'

Algie smiled with satisfaction at the prospect. This is how he would make his name. 'You said we should come to an . . . an arrangement to our . . . our mutual benefit,' he said hesitantly, not wishing to push his luck too far, but anxious for some appropriate financial consideration for all the effort he was being expected to put in. And this was as good a time as any to broach the subject.

'You mean money.'

'Yes . . . But not just money.'

'What d'you have in mind, Algie? A seat on the board?'

Benjamin was mocking him, and Algie reddened, for he could never aspire to that. 'No, Mr Sampson,' he said, ridiculing the notion with an embarrassed laugh. 'Course not.'

'Nor would you get one. My mother and me are the only

company directors, although it's just me that gets involved with the day-to-day running of the business.'

'Oh, yes, I—'

'Having said that, Algie, if things go well there's no reason why you shouldn't be allowed eventually to buy shares in the firm,' he went on more amenably. 'And your wages would reflect your new status. But let's not count our chickens afore they're hatched, eh? There's many a slip twixt cup and lip. Nor was Rome built in a day.'

'But if a job's worth doing it's worth doing well,' Algie felt justified in saying. It was obviously socially acceptable to bandy about hackneyed proverbs so indiscriminately, as Benjamin often did.

'Well,' chimed in Aurelia, with a mischievous grin that made her blue eyes sparkle, 'if you don't, it'll be no good crying over spilt milk afterwards.'

Harriet subdued the inclination to burst out laughing. She realised that Benjamin had not tried to be clever or even amusing rattling off so many sayings consecutively; they simply fell from his lips unheeded. He was too uncultured to comprehend that what he was saying was unoriginal, just so long as it conveyed his meaning. She felt an inclination to riposte with 'a still tongue makes a wise head', but decided to heed her own advice and say nothing.

'So what about money, Mr Sampson?'

'I don't discuss money over the dinner table, Algie,' Benjamin said flatly. 'We'll talk about it later.'

Benjamin kept his own counsel thereafter, at least during the first remove, content to let his guests and his wife have their conversational heads while he sank the wine.

'So forgive me for asking, Harriet,' Aurelia said, after some minutes of small talk, 'Are you and Algie engaged? Or what?'

'Oh, definitely or what,' Harriet chirped, to Aurelia's amusement. 'We used to step out together, until . . . But we remain friends.' She looked at Algie, smiled with mild embarrassment, and then reverted her gaze to her dinner plate and the well-done roast beef that Mary had served so unobtrusively.

Aurelia put down her crystal goblet after taking a sip of wine. 'But Algie seems to be an ideal candidate for marriage,' she suggested with an interested glance in his direction. 'He seems so homely and comfortable.'

'So is bread pudding, and flannel petticoats,' Harriet responded.

Aurelia giggled deliciously. 'But so handsome, too. What a pity you are neither of you in love.'

Benjamin rolled his eyes but kept silent.

'Oh, I'm not even sure that Algie is capable of falling in love, Aurelia. He is so matter-of-fact, if you know what I mean. So *un*romantic.'

'Is that true, Algie? I'd be very surprised . . .'

'No. I think Harriet has a tainted view of me.'

'Is your view tainted, Harriet?'

'I think not. I am a realist, if nothing else, and I think I know him as well as anybody.'

'I don't think you do,' he answered defensively.

Aurelia turned to Algie once again. 'So do you think you'll ever marry?'

'Do you mean, will I marry Harriet, or marry anybody?' he asked, unsure of her meaning.

'Oh, he'll marry right enough,' Harriet butted in. 'A sweet homely girl who darns his socks while he talks to her about building bicycles and the price of pneumatic tyres.' She smiled to show that she bore no ill-will. 'He'll believe he is making love to her with all this small talk and, what's more, she'll very likely believe it too. Until a prettier face comes along to divert him from his domestic bliss.'

Algie recognised the truth of Harriet's perception and

glanced at Aurelia to gauge her reaction as he took a sip of the fine Bordeaux his hosts had provided, but which he could hardly appreciate.

'Is that true, Algie?'

'At heart I'm a very loyal person,' he answered. 'I'm not swayed just by a pretty face, although a pretty face helps. There are other qualities I like in girls.'

'Money, for instance?' Harriet suggested provocatively.

'Yes, if a very pretty girl came along with plenty of money, I could be tempted,' he said unapologetically. 'I am single, after all, Harriet. I'm still free to pick and choose.'

'Don't fall into the trap, Algie, of thinking money can make you happy,' Aurelia said, with all the callowness of one who has never known what it is to be without, yet with all the sincerity of one who knows the truth of her own words from experience.

That comment made Algie think. Maybe Aurelia was not happy, surrounded as she was by the trappings of wealth. Something else he realised at that moment: he had not seen or heard Benjamin speak to her directly. All the time he and Harriet had been in their company, the man had spoken to him and to Harriet, but he had not once addressed Aurelia. Maybe something was amiss in this marriage of theirs.

'Tell me, Algie,' Aurelia said with an earnest expression. 'Have you ever fallen in love?'

'I really believe I have,' he answered with reckless ambiguity, and looked into Aurelia's eyes with such burning intensity that she had to avert hers. He noticed her blush. He believed she had caught his meaning. But she had asked for it, and he had no qualms about letting her know it.

Despite the wine, or because of it, Algie felt himself redden at his foolhardy admission and had to avoid her eyes momentarily. He glanced at Benjamin, whose head was down over his plate as he tucked into his dinner and swigged more wine, still content to let the others make their own conversation.

'What about you, Harriet?' Aurelia persisted. 'Have you ever fallen in love?'

'Oh, I think I fell in love with Algie,' she answered candidly. 'But I just can't be sure. I wish I could be.'

'There's no mistaking the feeling,' Aurelia proclaimed. 'If you say you can't be sure, then you haven't. Falling in love is like nothing else this side of heaven, especially when it's reciprocated.'

Well, maybe he was wrong. Maybe she was happy in her marriage after all. She would hardly speak so openly of love in front of her husband if she did not love him and he was aware of it.

'Oh, I've known girls get lit up like a hollowed-out turnip with a candle inside,' Harriet said flippantly. 'Just because some man or other said something flattering. It just seems a bit silly to me to get yourself worked up into a stew over a man. Oh, I've done it myself, I know I have, but I'm still not convinced it was love that caused it. More likely my injured pride at being cast aside. I've known myself go to pieces like a linen button through a mangle just because *somebody*—' she glanced at Algie, '—did the inevitable and preferred a girl with a prettier face than my own.'

'Was it you, Algie, who caused Harriet such distress?' Aurelia sounded disappointed.

'She makes it sound like it. But we were never betrothed, Harriet and me, nor ever likely to be.'

'So you don't have a current sweetheart then?'

'Yes, I have a sweetheart,' he replied.

'So how come she's not here with you this evening, instead of Harriet?'

'Because she . . . Well, because she's away at present . . . She goes away quite a lot. And because Harriet and I are still friends, she agreed to come here with me tonight in her place.'

'You don't mind being a stand-in then, Harriet?'

'As Algie says, we remain friends, although we don't see each other often these days.'

'And shall you tell your absent sweetheart that you have been here tonight with Harriet?'

'I don't know,' he replied honestly. 'I haven't thought about it yet.'

'I think honesty is pref—'

'I say,' Benjamin chimed in indignantly. 'Do we have to put poor Algie on the rack just because he preferred somebody else to Harriet here? Every Jack has his Jill.'

'We're not putting Algie on any rack,' Aurelia bit back. 'As a bachelor, he is perfectly entitled to step out with whomever he wants. I was only trying to establish in my own mind the relationship between him and Harriet.'

'And now that you have – so blatantly – even though it's none of your damned business – why don't you change the subject? Your talk of love is so . . . so tedious, Aurelia . . . Now . . . Algie and I have something more important to talk about.'

'Then Harriet and I will retire to the drawing room, Benjamin,' Aurelia said obediently, and rose gracefully from her chair. Algie was irritated and embarrassed for her over the way Benjamin had spoken, belittling her. Yet she retained her dignity and he watched with longing the feminine sway of her hips as she left the room behind Harriet.

Over several glasses of port, Algie and Benjamin talked about the manufacturing of bicycles and everything they imagined it might entail. Benjamin, however, would not be drawn yet on details of remuneration for Algie, other than to say that he could expect an increase in his wages in recognition of the new responsibilities Sampson's would impose upon him, with a review in three months.

* * *

As they walked back towards Brierley Hill, Harriet said, 'I hope you didn't mind my saying what I did about you preferring somebody with a pretty face to me.'

'No, I didn't mind. It livened up the conversation.'

'I'm not sure that I like Benjamin Sampson. Especially the way he spoke to Aurelia. I thought she was very pleasant though.'

'Yes, so did I.'

'*You* quite fancied her, Algie. I could tell.'

'Was it that obvious?'

'To me it was. But then, I know you. I know what you're like. Still, you can't have her, and that's a fact . . . She's way out of your reach.'

'It sounds as if you're pleased about that,' he said grumpily.

'And you not at all.'

'I get the feeling that she isn't happy, wed to Mr Sampson,' Algie said, fishing for Harriet's opinion.

'You mean, you hope she isn't happy, wed to him.'

'I wish she wasn't wed to him at all.'

'Even if she wasn't, Algie, she'd be no nearer you. On the other hand, maybe it's Mr Sampson that isn't happy wed to her . . . Maybe he's not in love with her. He didn't seem it.'

'But she's so damned beautiful! How can he not be in love with her? I'd give my right arm . . .'

'But that's typical of you, Algie. Only ever attracted by what you can see. Beauty is only skin deep, you know. *He* married her for her beauty, I suppose, but that's just typical of men. Who knows? She might be a very obnoxious person when you get to know her.'

'I can't believe that. Never in a million years.'

'Then you are a romantic after all, despite everything I said about you earlier.'

Another couple passed them walking in the opposite direction, and they all bid each other goodnight.

'Do you mind if I take your arm, Algie? I'm a bit unsteady on these cobbles in these boots.'

'Help yourself,' he said, and offered it.

'Thank you. I've seen her before, you know, that Aurelia. I really feel that I ought to know her. It was ages ago, but I can't place her. I didn't dare ask her, of course . . . Was she familiar to you?'

'Never seen her before in my life. But what's so surprising about that? We only ever see the people who cross our paths at the same time every day, as our own routines dictate. Of all the thousands of folk who live in Brierley Hill, I reckon I've only ever seen a fraction of them in all my life . . . and most of them I've forgotten. Look at *you*—'

'Oh, yes, I realise I'm eminently forgettable.'

'I didn't mean that, you ninny. I was going to say that I haven't caught sight of you in, what? Five months? If we'd never met before that, I'd never have known you existed.'

'You still don't know I exist, Algie.'

'That's a daft thing to say, Harriet.'

'Is it? Who knows? It might be another five months before I hear from you again.'

Meanwhile, they were getting perilously close to her home.

'I'd best leave you here,' she said, 'for fear I'm seen with you.'

'All right.' They stopped walking and she let go of his arm reluctantly. 'Look, Harriet, thanks ever so much for coming with me tonight. It means a lot to me. As you can tell, there's a lot at stake for me in this bike building thing.'

'I've enjoyed myself, Algie.' She stood before him and looked up at him smiling expectantly, the meagre light from the gas street lamps reflected in her eyes. 'It's been really lovely seeing you again. I've had a jolly good feed, and even a glass of wine, which I shouldn't have, because it went straight to my head. I should sleep well, anyway.'

He smiled at her with genuine admiration. Why couldn't Harriet have been blessed with a beautiful face like Aurelia Sampson, or even Marigold? There again, if she had been – and with her body – she wouldn't be standing in front of him right now gazing into his eyes waiting for a goodnight kiss. No, she would be like Aurelia; already the wife of some wealthy ironmaster's son or suchlike who didn't deserve her, snapped up for her ability to adorn, to be admired, to titillate, to be a submissive and playful bed-partner and bear an unending succession of children.

'Will you mind if I give you a goodnight thank you kiss?' he enquired, the alcohol clouding his judgement, and with as much passion as if asking a policeman the time.

'Do you need to ask?'

'In view of the way things are, yes. I don't take such things for granted.'

'How noble of you.' She swivelled her head to check that nobody was watching them. 'Then you'd best make it quick while there's nobody about.'

He kissed her briefly. 'Goodnight, Harriet. And thanks again for going with me.'

'Goodnight, Algie. See you sometime. By the way, are you coming to see the play?'

'I might.'

'Shall you bring Marigold?'

'Course, if she's around.' He smiled. 'Goodnight, Harriet.'

Chapter 13

The following week, on the Saturday dinnertime – it was the 1st of November – Algie returned home from his last day of bedstead making. It was a grey, chilly day and damp. Typical autumn weather. Brown leaves eddied and swirled in the breeze as he rode his bicycle to the lock at the rear of the house. He was hungry. He'd not eaten since he'd got up and, because he had been late getting up, he'd had no time to prepare any snap. So, he'd had to do without. He carried his bike across the lock gate and left it in the shed before he entered the house by the back door.

Clara, her arms dusted in flour, was rolling out pastry on the scullery table. Sliced apples, which occupied a basin, were destined to become the contents of several pies. Algie sidled up to his mother and gave her a kiss on the cheek.

'Apple pie, eh? Where'd you get the apples from?'

'I'd got some stored in the cellar. There's still some left. We ought to make some cider one of these days, save them going to waste.'

'I don't mind helping my dad do it,' Algie said, hanging his cap on the nail that had been hammered into the door for that very purpose.

'Your dad's poorly, our Algie.'

'Poorly?' Algie frowned with concern. 'I didn't know he was poorly. What's up with him?'

'Bad pains in his belly. He's been ailing the last couple of days. Now he's feeling sick.'

'Something he ate, I suppose.'

'He's only eaten the same as the rest of us, what bit he's had, and none of *us* are poorly. He hasn't been to work neither, and that's unlike him. He's still abed.'

'I'll go up and see him, Mother. Should I take him a cup of tea?'

'He'd like that. The kettle's boiled. Just swill out the teapot and brew a fresh pot. I wouldn't mind a cup myself, our Algie.'

Algie took off his coat, and hung it on the nail under his cap, then set about making a pot of tea while his mother distributed evenly the slices of apple into the pastry-lined plate before her.

'I don't suppose you've seen Marigold today?' he queried, spooning tea leaves into the crock teapot.

'Marigold? I haven't seen any of the Binghams. Missing her, are you?'

'It's been more than a fortnight since I saw her last. They must be due down this way soon, I'd have thought. I was hoping it'd be this weekend. It's just that I bought a ticket for her to go to see the play tonight, thinking she might be here.' He poured boiling water into the teapot. 'Still, if she don't come, I'll take you instead, eh, Mother?' He looked at Clara, hoping for her tentative agreement.

'Me? Oh, it's a nice thought, our Algie, but you know very well I shan't want to walk up to the town again tonight, especially when I'll already have been there this afternoon.'

'Even though your only daughter is playing the lead role?'

'Oh, our Kate'll manage well enough without me there. She won't be expecting me to go.'

'I'll go to the town for you, if you want some errands running.'

'Would you, our Algie?' She smiled her gratitude.

'Course . . . If you'll go to the play.'

'Bless you. But I don't particularly want to leave your dad, anyway, him being so off the hooks.'

'Just tell me what to get, and I'll get it,' he said, exasperated that he couldn't get her to leave the house, irked that she couldn't seem to get over her ancient fright with the runaway horse and cart all those years ago. Yet her excuse to stay home and look after his father was perfectly valid.

Clara reeled off a list of groceries and household goods she wanted while she placed the top layer of pastry over the fruit. As he listened, making a mental note, Algie gave the tea a stir and covered the pot with their knitted tea cosy that had been singed many times due to its proximity to the fire.

'Have you seen our Kate this morning?' he asked eventually. 'I wondered how the first night of the play went.'

Clara held the pie up to eye level and trimmed off the overhanging pastry with a knife. 'A bit of a touchy subject, I think.'

'Oh? Why?'

'I think she and Clarence have had a row. She said he's been funny with her lately and it's affected the play's love scenes. He kept looking at her funny, she said. I think it put her off her lines.'

'Lord, that means we'll all have to suffer,' Algie said ruefully. 'She's miserable enough, without things like that to make her even worse.'

'Well, maybe they'll make it up with one another.'

'Let's hope not. Clarence is better off without her, if only he knew it . . . I'll pour the tea and take one up for my dad.'

Algie went upstairs and into his parents' bedroom. It was cold in there. Already it seemed that autumn's dampness had penetrated through the walls. Will Stokes was lying huddled beneath the blankets, his hair awry. He stirred as Algie greeted him.

'Feeling a bit better, Dad?' he said chirpily.

'I feel lousy, Son,' Will groaned, his voice weak. 'Me guts feel as if they'm on fire.'

Algie saw how pale and drawn his father looked. He looked a hundred years old. 'I brought you a cup o' tea.' He placed it carefully on the bedside table beside Will.

'Ta, my son,' Will said piteously. 'I'll try and drink it in a minute.'

'Shall I light you a fire, Dad? It's cold in here.' He hunched his shoulders to emphasise the point.

'No, don't bother. We need to be thrifty with the coal now winter's a-nigh. Besides, I'm sweating like a pit-bank hoss as it is.' Will raised himself on one elbow and picked up the cup. He took a token sip then lay down again.

'Is there anything you want me to do, Dad? Any jobs you want doing on the cut?'

Will Stokes shook his head. 'Nothing as can't wait till I'm feeling better. I should feel better tomorrow, when all this has passed over.'

Algie moved over to the window that overlooked the canal and peered out. 'I see as the Tomlinsons have moored up in that new boat o' theirs, the *Jubilee*. They've got it tarted up real pretty, ain't they?' Scanning the landscape, he peered to his right and saw, to his utter delight, the Bingham's piebald horse come into view under the road bridge, straining against its collar and led by Seth as it hauled their lead boat, the *Sultan*. 'Dad!' Algie exclaimed with a grin, 'I'll see you later. Marigold's just turned up.' He rushed down the stairs to go outside and greet her.

* * *

Marigold stood on the narrowboat's gunwale, her back towards the towpath. In her well-worn coat and bonnet she looked, from behind, like any other working girl, except that she had this particular way of standing so elegantly; no slouching for Marigold. Then she heard footsteps, turned and saw him, and her blue eyes shone as she skipped off the barge to rush to him.

However, Aurelia Sampson had not yet faded from Algie's thoughts. She was still present, haunting him, not only with her polished and flawless beauty, but her apparent vulnerability as well from her unappreciative and overbearing husband.

It was inevitable that he compared the two girls. Marigold's face was no less beautifully constructed than Aurelia's, but it lacked the pampered glow that affluence brought. They shared similar colour hair and eyes. Her figure was no less perfectly proportioned, but lacked the enhancement that fine clothes afforded. Algie wondered how they would compare if they both stood naked before him, washed and bedraggled having just stepped out of a hot bath, with no visible hint of their different backgrounds to colour his view. Which one would he choose, if a choice he were forced to have? He imagined they would look decidedly similar, little or nothing to choose between them in looks and age. Of course, he would choose Marigold. But something about Aurelia was gnawing at his soul . . .

'Why'm you looking at me all queer?' Marigold asked, as she sidled up to him and took his hand.

'Am I?' He hadn't realised. He planted a kiss on her lips and smiled affectionately. 'I didn't mean to.'

'You was looking at me as if you've seen a ghost.'

He laughed. 'It's because I haven't seen you for so long. I forget what you look like while you're away, and so I have to feast my eyes on you to try and imprint you, like a photograph, on my rotten memory.' It was no lie; he did tend to forget what she looked like, try as he might to picture her lovely face. 'So where have you got to the last fortnight?'

'We been to Birnigum. Then we been to 'Emel 'Empstead, then across to Hoxford and Banbury.'

'What've you been carrying?'

'Oh, all sorts. Iron bars, iron stone, flour, gravel . . .'

'So you're off to Kidderminster next?'

'Worcester this time. We'm carrying china clay for the porcelain factory. But we shan't leave here till Monday. I aksed me dad special to try and get here early today, so as I'd see you for two days running. Three if you get up early Monday to see me off . . . You still look as if you've seen a ghost, Algie.'

'My dad's poorly,' he announced.

'What's up with him?'

'Something he ate, I think. He's got terrible guts ache. He must be bad, because he hasn't gone to work. He's still abed.'

'Poor soul,' Marigold said with sincerity. 'Give him my best wishes, will you? I hope he feels better soon.'

'Oh, I daresay he'll be better tomorrow. Anyway, I've got a surprise for you, Marigold.'

She beamed with anticipation, and her eyes sparkled like polished sapphires. 'A surprise? What?'

'More than one surprise, to tell you the truth. There's been a lot happening.'

'Go on then, tell me,' she implored girlishly.

'No,' he teased. 'I'll keep you in suspense a bit longer. Will you come a walk with me this afternoon into Brierley Hill town when I've had my dinner? I've got to go and get some shopping for my mother, 'cause she doesn't want to leave my dad while he's poorly. It'd be nice if you could come with me. Then I could tell you all my surprises.'

'Course I will, Algie.' She squeezed his hand reassuringly. 'I'll tell me mom. She might want some things fetching as well.'

The weather that Saturday was overcast as they walked to the town by road hand-in-hand, each carrying a basket. October's relative mildness had been ousted by a definite autumnal nip that foretold that bitter cold must inevitably follow.

'So, what's this news you've got to tell me?' Marigold prompted. 'I could hardly eat me dinner for wondering what it was.'

'Well . . . you know I asked Mr Sampson for advice on starting a business making bikes?'

'Yes.'

'Well, he's asked me to go in with him. I get a new job on Monday, with my own office, sorting it all out and getting it under way.'

'Oh, Algie . . .' She looked up at him in admiration. 'That's just . . . just brilliant.'

'I get a rise in wages too, and if we do well I'll be able to buy shares in the firm.'

'But it ain't like having your own firm, by the sounds of it?' she queried.

'Oh, no, course not. I could never afford to have my own firm anyway – I'd already worked that out. But this is the next best thing. I'll be a sort of partner to Mr Sampson. His right-hand man. We'll be building bikes to my designs and I'll be in charge of making them most of the time, 'cause he'll be away signing up wholesalers who'll sell the bikes. Just think, Marigold . . . If I do well . . .'

'So when was all this arranged?'

'A fortnight ago. He asked us round to his house for dinner.'

'Us?'

'Yes . . .' He must be careful here not to let slip about Harriet. 'But you couldn't go with me, 'cause you wasn't here.'

'I don't know if I would've felt comfortable anyroad, Algie, with swanky folk like that. I bet they live in a great big house with all the trimmings, and servants to wait on them hand and foot, eh?'

'Oh, yes, course,' he replied, as if it could be no other way.

'I couldn't be doing with that. I wouldn't know how to act. I mean, I'm from the cut. I ain't no better than one o' them servants they've got, and that's the truth.'

'Course you are, Marigold,' he said kindly, upset that she should demean her own worth. 'Brush your hair tidy and put you in your best frock and nobody would know the difference between you and a lady.'

'Till I opened me mouth, I suppose. Anyway, did you have a nice time?'

'Mr and Mrs Sampson were very hospitable. Especially her . . . She was *very* nice . . . and beautiful with it. I reckon she's one of the most beautiful women I've ever seen in my life, you know.'

'Fancy,' she said, peeved that he should think so, let alone having noticed another woman.

'Like I said, put you in your best frock, and you're just as lovely.' He smiled reassuringly, aware and sorry that he'd offended her sensitivity. 'You are just as beautiful in your own, more simple way.'

'Simple now, am I?'

He cursed himself for not having chosen his words more carefully, words that would not have invited her innate jealousy. 'I didn't mean simple in the sense that you're daft, Marigold. I know you're not daft. I mean you're just . . . less cultured—'

'It ain't my fault if I am,' she pouted. 'What schooling have I had? I do me best.'

'I know you do, and I'm full of admiration for you, else I wouldn't be here with you. What I mean is, you're more natural, you got no airs . . .'

'So I'd have been like a fish out of water, what with all their wealth, their put-on airs, and maids running about all over the place.'

'There was one maid that I saw. Only one.'

'But I bet they got more.'

'If they can afford it, all well and good, but I didn't see any more.'

'What was the maid like? Does Mr Sampson pick 'em for their looks? Did you fancy her as well?'

'No, I didn't fancy the maid, as it happens.'

'That's a wonder.'

They walked on in silence for some minutes, Algie determined not to speak until she made some apology. He made allowances for their enforced absences being responsible for exaggerating her notions that he might be unfaithful to her between times. But he had not been entirely unfaithful. Any disloyalty had been only in his mind. It meant nothing. Absolutely nothing.

It was Marigold, predictably, who broke the silence.

'You said you had more than one surprise for me,' she said meekly, the closest thing to an apology he was likely to get.

On reflection, maybe he did not deserve an apology. Maybe she was spot-on with her assessment of him. Maybe she was blessed with the same sort of intuition that informed Harriet of what he was like where handsome women were concerned. In any case, maybe he ought to take Marigold's sensitivity into account more often, that she loved him and loathed being away from him for weeks on end, that she didn't want to be taunted with how lovely other women might be, with whom he'd been in contact.

He smiled forgivingly, his eyes brimming with affection, and he put his arm around her as they walked. 'That play our Kate's in . . .' he said. 'Tonight's the last performance. I got tickets for me and you to go and see it.'

So he did think about her sometimes. 'Oh, Algie . . .' She beamed up at him. 'That'll be lovely. Will it be a grand do?'

'Yes, a grand do. Best frock for you tonight, my girl. All the bigwigs of the town will be there.'

'What's the play about?'

'About a Red Indian princess, and how she falls in love with an Englishman.'

'Ah, that sounds right up my street . . . A Red Indian princess, did you say? Do they have a royal family then, them Red Indians?'

'Seems like it. Anyway, our Kate's taking the part of the princess.'

'Well, she is nice-looking, your Kate. She'll make a lovely princess, I bet. Is she still courting?'

'By the skin of her teeth, by the sounds of it.'

And so they chatted on in their desultory way, all the way to Brierley Hill. There, Marigold was enchanted by the variety of little shops, but Algie studiously avoided the Meeses' drapery, mourning and mantles emporium, not only wary of seeing Eli, but apprehensive of bumping into Harriet as well.

Algie had received instructions to call into Murdoch Osborne's butcher's shop for the Sunday joint, and Murdoch was quick to greet Algie amiably.

'Have you been to see the play yet?' he enquired, as he placed a small joint of beef on the scales and juggled his weights.

'We're going tonight, Mr Osborne,' Algie replied.

'This your sweetheart, young Algie?' Mr Osborne asked, wiping his blood-stained hands on his already soiled apron.

Algie smiled self-consciously. 'Yes, she's the one.'

Murdoch eyed her up and down, while Marigold likewise weighed him up. 'A bobby-dazzler, ain't she?' He flashed a wink of bravado at Algie. 'I can see why you've took to her.'

Algie smiled again, uncertain how to reply.

'Anything else, young man?'

'That's the lot for me, Mr Osborne.' Algie paid and took the meat, all wrapped in newsprint.

'Oh, and give your mother me fondest.'

Algie grinned uncertainly. 'My sweetheart wants serving as well . . .'

Murdoch looked at Marigold with anticipation.

'No, it's all right,' she said, and glanced at Algie with embarrassment. 'I don't need nothing today.'

Algie apologised for his mistake, bid Mr Osborne goodbye and left the shop with Marigold in tow.

'I thought you wanted to buy some meat,' Algie said when they were outside and out of sight.

'I didn't like him,' Marigold replied with a shudder. 'That's why I wouldn't buy off him. Did you see how he looked at me? Eyed me up as if I was a prize side of bacon, he did, then talked to you about me as if I wasn't there.'

'It's just his way,' Algie said. 'He doesn't mean anything by it.'

'Whether or no, I don't like him. He gi'd me the creeps. Fancy having his hands roaming all over you. Ugh!' She screwed her face up in distaste at the thought. 'I'll go to another butcher for our meat . . . Why did he ask if you'd seen the play?' she added. 'What's it got to do with him?'

'Because he's in it. He runs the show.'

'Damn and blast! Have I got to see him again?'

Marigold looked a picture when Algie called for her that evening to go to the play. Her face shone from the effects of soap and water and she had acquired a new dress for Sunday best. Her mother had suggested it some weeks before, when she perceived that Marigold and Algie were courting more seriously. Since they were often in the vicinity of the Stokes's home on Sundays she was ever likely to be asked in for tea, and she couldn't go to Sunday tea looking like a dishmop. The dress was plain, ultramarine in colour, and made from cotton, and was suitable for all sorts of occasions. It was eminently suitable for attending a play at the town hall. Over it, she wore a new darker blue mantle and matching bonnet, and Algie was delighted with what he saw.

Clarence Froggatt had collected Kate from the bakery shop and delivered her home in good time to get washed and changed for her evening performance. He had collected her again later and whisked her off to the town hall to get into her stage make-up and flimsy costume in good time for the play.

'How's your dad?' Marigold asked as they embarked on a steady walk to the town for the second time that day.

'He's no better. Worse, if anything. I'm a bit worried about him. So is my mom. She's even been rubbing Elliman's Embrocation over his belly, and giving him Lamphrey's pills, but neither seems to have done him any good.'

'You think a lot of your dad, don't you?'

'Course I do. He's my dad.'

'I think a lot of my dad as well.'

The rain had kept off, even though the sky had looked ominously grey all day. The town hall that night did not reflect the day's drabness, however. The gas lights, brilliantly flaring, cast a warm glow over the carriages that rolled up outside depositing the wealthy and the local dignitaries – who all milled about, chatting with friends and acquaintances who happened to be arriving at the same time. The approach of a steam tram ensured that the horses and carriages could not tarry, occupying the tramlines. When it pulled up outside the town hall it disgorged passengers by the score, to the rattle and hiss of the little engine that hauled it. Unused to such activity and the excited atmosphere, Marigold stood and watched spellbound, her eyes wide, a smile of expectancy brightening her delightful face.

'Oh, Algie, ain't it grand watching all these fine folk?' she said dreamily. 'I could watch 'em for ages.'

He smilingly allowed her this preoccupation for a few minutes, then said, 'I reckon we'd best get inside and find our seats.'

'Tickets please,' said a military-looking man with a waxed moustache who was standing by the door to the auditorium.

Algie fished in his pockets and drew out his two tickets. The man inspected them officiously.

'Right at the front,' the waxed moustache said, as if begrudging them such a privilege.

Algie turned to Marigold. 'Hey, fancy that. We got seats right at the front. Fancy our Kate being able to get tickets for seats right at the front.'

As he pushed open the doors, the glare of the house lights met them, and Marigold became even more thrilled. Several men, heavy swells, all tall, all moustached, turned to stare at her lovely smiling face as Algie led her towards their seats at the front. As the town hall filled up, a buzz of anticipation ran through it. Brierley Hill was normally only privileged to host concerts from its Amateur Dramatics Society a couple of times a year, and so they were always well-attended. Occasionally a choir would put on a performance, either in the town hall or in St Michael's Church, sometimes an organ recital, but church music, which is how even Bach's 'Toccata and Fugue' was perceived, was not everybody's cup of tea.

The lights went down and a hush fell over the audience. The curtains swept open to reveal a painted backdrop of a river bank depicting a wooden fort flying the Union flag. In front of various crude, distant dwellings players stood, dressed as seventeenth century colonists. The action began when they assembled round a group of seven military men who entered, Clarence Froggatt among them.

Marigold listened to the dialogue for a few seconds then whispered to Algie, 'They don't half talk funny, don't they? Can you understand what they're on about?'

'It's supposed to be how they spoke in the sixteen hundreds, I think.'

'Oh . . .' She was content with the explanation for a minute or two, then whispered, 'When does your Kate come on?'

'Soon, I would think.'

The next scene was the inside of a wigwam. Powhatan entered, whom Marigold immediately recognised as the butcher she'd met earlier and didn't like.

'That's him from the butcher's,' she whispered, heard by those behind who tittered with amusement at the remark. Algie laughed too.

'*The sun has set,*' cried Powhatan poetically, but to Marigold he was still the odious butcher. '*And Pocahontas returns.*'

At which point, Pocahontas made her entrance. There was a collective gasp, especially from the ladies, when they saw how revealing her short costume was, rendered from pieces of yellow chamois leather stitched coarsely together. Her lissom legs, slender arms, face and elegant neck had been browned with stage paint to give a tanned effect, and her dark hair, hanging loose over her shoulders, afforded her a look of exotic authenticity. She looked strikingly different, but also disturbingly, almost indecently lovely, and a deathly hush enveloped the auditorium in anticipation of her first line.

She spoke.

'. . . *The pale-faced men whose homes are where the sun doth rise, are come unto our shores once more in their white-winged canoes.'* Her voice and delivery were crystal clear, and in earnest.

'*They come to seize our lands – to slay—*' spoke the butcher again, rather too woodenly.

'*Though some were false,*' replied Pocahontas, '*my father will not judge all harshly, I hope. Even amongst our own and other tribes there are oft wicked and deceitful men. So it may be with these. Yet in years past when they came to our shores before, you yourself told me, many stood eminent for their bravery.*'

'*Thy voice breathes kindness ever. Pocahontas is her father's dearest child.*'

'See, he's talking about her as if she ain't there,' Marigold whispered to Algie. 'Just like he did with me in his shop.'

Algie was beginning to wonder if Harriet would ever appear. The story had progressed considerably, Pocahontas having met and fallen in love with the character Rolfe, played by Clarence Froggatt, just as they had seemingly done in real life. And by now the forest princess had been converted to Christianity, renamed Rebecca, transported with her English husband to England, and had been blessed with a child. Her costume too had changed. She was now dressed in the style of an English lady with all her lace and finery.

It was indeed very close to the end when Harriet made her

appearance as Mistress Alice. At once she spotted Algie on the front row and her eyes at that moment gleamed brightly at him, reflecting the specially hired arc lamps in a faint smile of acknowledgement. Then she noticed an extraordinarily pretty girl sitting attentively beside him, her arm linked through his . . . and she understood.

Marigold was watching. At that precise moment, she looked at this girl who was playing the part of Mistress Alice, and could have sworn she detected a look – intended directly for Algie. Algie, meanwhile, glanced at Marigold, trying to discern whether she had noticed the barely concealed greeting.

'D'you know that girl?'

He nodded economically, turning his head for a brief glance and flashing her a reassuring smile.

Maybe it was not the time to ask who she was, although Marigold didn't think she had much to worry about, a girl with a face like that. Algie would only ever be interested in pretty girls, and this girl was anything but. She did have a good figure, though.

And then came the end. Literally and with extreme poignancy.

Pocahontas, dying, said to Rolfe, *'I lose thee now. My eyes behold Virginia's grassy turf . . . I hear my father . . . Husband, fare thee well. But we shall meet again – in heaven . . .'*

And there she died, in a strange land, leaving her little son and the husband she loved behind. Rolfe remained on one knee, clasping her hand and gazing upon her in utter despair.

Algie heard a little sniff from Marigold and turned to her to see a tear trickling down her cheek. He squeezed her hand as the curtain swished to. Thunderous applause filled the auditorium. The curtain opened again and the entire cast were lined up, taking their bows.

'Did you enjoy that?' he asked, with a grin as proud as if

he himself had been taking part, when the curtain closed for the last time.

'Oh, it was lovely,' she answered, wiping her tears with a handkerchief. 'Wasn't she good, your Kate? I can hardly believe it.'

'She's surprised me,' he agreed. 'She was ever so convincing.'

'And she looked lovely in that costume, flaunting her lovely legs. It's a pity us girls can't flaunt our legs a bit more.'

He laughed at that. 'I don't think the old ladies would be very impressed.'

'Well, that's 'cause the old ladies ain't got nice legs anymore, have they, like us young girls? That's why. That's why they don't want anybody to see nice legs on younger girls. Their men would turn and have a good look, then they'd have to have a moan at them for looking.'

People were gathering in the aisles, queuing to get out into the cool night air. With an unspoken accord, Algie and Marigold tagged on to the end of the queue in the nearest aisle.

'It's a pity your mother couldn't have come,' she said. 'She'd have loved to see that play. Especially her own daughter so good in it.'

'It's true,' he sighed.

Algie felt a gentle tug on his arm. He turned around to see Harriet, still in her stage costume.

'Hello, Algie,' she said, breathless. 'I'm so glad you could come. Did you enjoy the play?'

'It was great. I thought our Kate was very good.'

'What did I tell you?'

She'd already told him? When? Marigold was watching with piercing eyes, a look of indignation settling on her face.

'We're having a party afterwards at the Bell Hotel,' Harriet blustered on, apparently heedless of his pretty companion, which irritated the pretty companion even more. 'We've reserved the assembly rooms. Why don't you come along? It should be very convivial. Kate and Clarence will be there. I'm certain she'll want to wallow in everybody's praise, including yours, Algie. I know I would, if I were her.'

Algie looked at Marigold, but received only a stoney look which suggested he should decline the invitation.

'I don't know, Harriet. I ought to get back. My father isn't very well and I want to see how he is.'

'Then stay for just a short while. But do come.'

'Harriet, this is Marigold. Marigold, this is Harriet, who I've told you about.'

Marigold forced a very reluctant smile. 'Hello, Harriet.'

'How do you do, Marigold. I was beginning to wonder if Algie would ever introduce us. He's already told me plenty about you, of course.'

Had he? When?

Marigold looked at him with that same urgent query in her eyes. But he seemed not to notice, and she heard him say, 'Yes, all right, we'll come. But we shan't be able to stop for long.'

Chapter 14

It was drizzling with rain, and as Algie and Marigold stood at the top of the town hall steps they heard the clock above them strike ten. They were looking over a spread of bobbing and tilting umbrellas, whose taut, wet fabrics glistened in the gas lights.

Algie led Marigold down the steps and they turned, heading towards the Bell Hotel at the other end of the town. Harriet's words were still ringing sharply in Marigold's ears, and she was eager to get away, keen to escape the suddenly oppressive atmosphere of the town hall, and into the cold outside air. Neither did she want to go to the party, for there she would encounter Harriet once more.

'What did that Harriet mean when she said you'd already told her plenty about me? And when did she tell you how good your Kate was?'

'Oh, a couple of weeks ago.'

'You never said.' She adjusted her mantle to keep out the rain, feeling slighted and deceived. 'You should've said, Algie. Why didn't you say?'

'Why? So you could get queer about it?'

'Well, I'm queer now, 'cause you hadn't told me. How did you come to see her?'

'I bumped into her.'

'Where? How? Tell me. You don't tell me anything.'

He quickened his step to get away from a knot of people who were strolling leisurely along the pavement, volubly discussing the play. He had no wish that they become witnesses to an argument with Marigold. Marigold tripped along behind him agitatedly, under the impression he was trying to get away from her, but desperate to get her fears into the open and cleared up.

'Tell me,' she said again, when he had slowed down and she was walking at his side again.

'There's nothing to tell,' he said. 'I happened to see her one day and we talked for a while.'

'So why didn't you tell me? If you'd got nothing to hide, you could've told me.'

'If I'd told you, you would've got queer in any case, like I said. Why should I invite your moans?'

'You could've said, "Oh, by the way, Marigold, I bumped into Harriet the other day and I told her all about you", but you didn't . . . Because you've got something to hide, I reckon.'

'I've got nothing to hide,' he insisted. 'Anyway, Harriet's still a friend. If I want to talk to her, why shouldn't I?'

'I didn't like the way she looked down that long nose of hers with her squinty eyes, as if I'd just crawled out o' the woodwork. Who does she think she is?'

'I didn't notice.'

'Oh, now you're taking her part,' she complained 'You ain't being straight with me, Algie. You won't look me in the eye. If you don't tell me the truth, I'm going back home.'

'No you're not. You're not walking through dark streets by yourself.'

'Tell me the truth then, else I will.'

'Lord! Women!' he exclaimed, exasperated. 'And if I tell you everything, will you let it drop?'

'I might. It depends.'

'Marigold, you're driving me mad with your daft jealousy over Harriet. I swear, you've got no reason to be jealous.'

'So you keep saying. So tell me everything.'

'Well . . . when I got invited to Mr and Mrs Sampson's house, I took *her*, because you weren't here. I would've took you – course I would – if you'd been here.'

'You took *Harriet*?' Marigold was horrified. She remained silent for a second or two while the seriousness of what this implied sank in. 'So they thought *she* was your girl, and I suppose you let 'em.' Her indignation was rising inexorably.

'It wasn't like that, Marigold. I explained that she wasn't my girl, just a friend. In fact, I told them all about you.'

'So how did you arrange it if you don't ever see her, like you always say you don't?' she persisted, determined not to be put off. 'Did you write her a letter, or what?' She asked the question with the frustration of her own inability to read and write evident in her tone.

'No, I didn't write. In the first place I asked our Kate to go with me. She was my first choice after you. But she couldn't go either, 'cause she was going to a swells do with Clarence. It was Kate who suggested I take Harriet instead, and she asked her for me.'

'I always had an idea as your Kate didn't like me.'

'Oh, don't be daft.' He rolled his eyes at her apparent wish to misconstrue everything. 'It just seemed a good idea at the time . . . I was expected to turn up with a girl . . . with you. I would much rather it had been you. But you weren't here, were you?'

'Algie, I can't believe you done that, after all you said about how you ain't interested in her. It was lies, lies, lies, all the time. Right from the beginning, lies.' Tears, a liquid blend of hurt and anger, were glistening in her eyes.

'Don't get upset, Marigold—'

'What d'you expect?' she sniffed, bitterly aggrieved and wounded. 'You've lied. You've lied to me all along . . . took me for a mawkin . . . and I've been daft enough to fall for it. I've been dead straight with you, an' all. I ain't never looked at another chap since we started going out, but I ain't been short of offers, I can tell yer.'

'I'm sorry, Marigold. But it meant nothing—'

'I bet you kissed her goodnight, as well.'

'Course I didn't.'

'I don't believe you. Look at you . . . I can tell when you're lying, Algie. You're a rotten liar . . . I'm going home.'

She turned with the intention of running across the road to escape him. A hundred yards away, a tramcar was huffing its way towards Stourbridge, carrying people who had just turned out of the town hall. Algie caught Marigold's arm and prevented her from leaving.

'You're upset, Marigold. I can see that. Honest to God, my seeing Harriet meant nothing, you have to believe me. She was just handy at the time. I used her, I suppose. It's you I want, it's you I love. Not Harriet.'

'You been distant with me ever since I seen you at dinner-time, as if you got somebody else on your mind, Algie Stokes. I ain't daft, you know. I can read you like a book.'

'You are being daft, Marigold,' he argued guiltily.

'If you don't want me no more, why don't you just come out with it and say so? Anyway, I don't want to go to this party with *her* there – Miss Squinty-eyes – having a laugh at me behind me back.'

'She won't be laughing at you. She isn't like that. Anyway, we don't even have to speak to her again.'

'I'm finished with you, Algie Stokes,' Marigold said with sudden decisiveness. 'So you can please yourself what you do.

I ain't playing second fiddle to nobody, least of all her. You ain't treating me like some rubbing rag. There's plenty other fish in the sea, you know.'

The tramcar and its steam engine passed them, clanking and hissing, its iron wheels growling over the iron rails at the bend in the road where the rails of the single track split into two to form a double track. Here, trams coming from the opposite direction could pass.

Then something terrifyingly unexpected happened. The engine that was drawing the tramcar swerved, taking the right hand curve instead of the straight, but the tramcar itself was guided onto the straight. Engine and tramcar were taking two different lines.

'Get back!' Algie shouted as he realised what was happening, and shoved Marigold away.

The tramcar began to tilt, very slowly at first, as the tension on the linkage between it and the engine became critical.

They were directly beneath it.

Marigold had hesitated, but Algie had the presence of mind to grab her hand, and he pulled her back along the pavement, out of harm's way. They both turned in horror to see what was happening.

He believed there was a chance that the tram's centre of gravity would pull it back upright, and it teetered for a few seconds as if deciding which way to go. But then, as the weight of its cargo of passengers shifted in anticipation of the inevitable, it tilted further and toppled over. As it crashed to the ground, just missing the buildings that lined the pavement, there was the terrifying sound of smashing glass, squeals from the passengers inside and gasps of horror from passers-by.

'My God! Watch out for flying glass, Marigold.' Algie held his arm out as a barrier to protect her as he watched the tram topple, like a huge felled animal. 'Jesus Christ! There'll be folk maimed here. We'll have to help get 'em out . . . Look, Marigold, go back along the road and tell everybody you meet that help's needed.'

'Should I ask if anybody's a doctor?'

'Yes. Good idea.'

Marigold hurried off in the direction from which they'd come.

High Street was suddenly in uproar. People were trying desperately to scramble from the wreckage, screaming and shouting. Women were crying, clambering out whichever way they could, while the steam engine, which had also been dragged onto its side by the weight of the tramcar toppling over, was still huffing and puffing with the driver still inside, trying to shut off the steam. Algie rushed to a young woman who was frantically trying to limber up through a window on the upper deck. He climbed onto the upturned side of the tram and held his hand out to her. She took it, holding on while she scrambled through. Then he slid down the roof of the tram and caught her in his arms as she followed him. She thanked him with overwhelming gratitude, and he could see her gloveless hands were torn and bleeding, lacerated by the window's broken glass.

'You need to get those cuts seen to,' he said kindly. 'Let's hope there'll be a doctor here soon. I bet you'll need stitches.'

She nodded, unable or unwilling to speak again.

'Why don't you sit down on that step?' he suggested. 'Are you by yourself?'

The young woman shook her head. 'My husband is in there as well. I hope he's not badly hurt.'

'I'll have a look for you.'

He clambered up onto the side of the tram once more but with all the folk desperate to escape it was impossible to know who the woman's husband was. Another woman was struggling to push a child out who was crying, terrified. It was a little girl.

He took the child's hands and pulled her out, cut and bleeding, then bade her to sit tight on the metal skin of the tram's side while she waited for him to pull out her mother. Everybody was waiting their turn to clamber out, but nobody seemed to be seriously injured, suffering only from shock, lacerations and a few bruises. They urgently needed a doctor to sew up the worst of the cuts and administer some surgical spirit to clean them up.

A myriad of folk, many of whom had been to see the play and were walking home, gathered and wondered in disbelief at the toppled tram. A policeman arrived, then another, and they took charge of things.

Algie had no idea how long he'd been there when he saw the dogcart bearing Clarence Froggatt and Kate heading towards the Bell Hotel and their celebration party. They stopped as Algie waved them down.

'What the devil happened?' Kate asked.

Algie explained what he'd witnessed. 'Some of these folk need medical attention, Clarence. Mostly cuts, I reckon, but one or two are shocked stupid. I think you ought to fetch your father.'

'I think so, too,' he agreed, and hastily arranged to see Kate later in the assembly rooms of the Bell. He turned the dogcart round and sped off.

'Have you seen Marigold?' Algie asked Kate as she stood beside him surveying the wreckage.

'No. Why?'

'I sent her to get help. Damn. Where the hell has she got to?'

'If you sent her to get help, maybe that's what she's doing, Algie. Don't fret. She'll be back in a trice.'

'But we had a row.'

'Oh, me and Clarence are always having rows. Everybody has rows. She'll have calmed down a bit when she gets back.'

Algie rolled his eyes with frustration. 'I hope so . . . You were good tonight, our Kate,' he felt bound to say. 'We both enjoyed it.'

'Struth! Praise, from my own dear brother.'

'Why don't you get off to the Bell, away from all this, and I'll see you later when I've found Marigold. I shan't stay long, though – I want to see how Father is.'

Algie looked around at the turmoil that was beginning to subside now, wondering if there was anything else he could do. He went to one of the policemen and offered his services as a witness to the accident, if they should need him later. The policeman jotted down his name and address in his notebook and thanked him, and Algie went off in search of Marigold.

He scoured the street, but there was no sign of her. Harriet and two of her sisters were heading towards the Bell, and she told him they hadn't seen her either. A little later, as he walked further along High Street and even beyond the town hall, still he had not seen her. He saw a dogcart coming towards him carrying two men, and guessed correctly that it was Clarence conveying his father to the scene of the accident. He hailed them, asking Clarence if he'd seen Marigold. Clarence drew the dogcart to a halt briefly.

'No, I haven't seen her. I'm sure you'll spot her though soon. Is it possible she might have gone home?'

'Yes,' he replied miserably.

'Maybe you'll catch her up if you hurry.'

'What time is it?'

Clarence felt inside his cape and withdrew his fob watch. 'Ten to eleven.'

'Already? I'd best get a move on.'

Algie felt like asking for a lift, but realised that conveying the doctor to the overturned tram was infinitely more important than his trivial tiff with Marigold, so he raised his hand in a parting gesture and hurried homewards on foot.

Marigold was indeed returning home to the pair of narrowboats moored near the Bottle and Glass. She hurried through the dark streets, unsure of her way, frightened and watchful of drunks that lurched towards her so menacingly, running if she thought she was being pursued. Tears stung her eyes. Algie had lied to her. He'd been lying to her all along. He'd been seeing Harriet behind her back while she was traipsing up and down the canal network in the *Sultan* and the *Odyssey*, tied to her family and their work. It pained her to acknowledge the fact. He might as well have plunged a dagger in her heart, it hurt so much. She had harboured such cherished dreams of the future, happily settled with Algie. To be suddenly faced with his deceit was heartbreaking. She could not forgive him. How could she? Never would she be able to trust him again. There was no other course open to her now but to forget him. For her own self-esteem and future peace of mind she had to give him up, no matter how much it hurt. No more would she allow herself to be used and abused. Never again would she yield to his sexual desires. However much those pleasurable times had meant to her, they were in the past now and would not be repeated.

Just what had been going on with that Harriet? And for how long? To think he had taken *her* to meet his gaffer . . . What did he see in her? Her face was like the stern of a narrowboat, her nose its rudder. It was the ultimate insult to be cast aside for a girl so plain. Well, at least she had found out about the two of them before it was too late.

She arrived at the basin by the dry dock and slipped surreptitiously along the towpath where their two narrowboats were barely distinguishable silhouettes against the blackness of the night. A light shone feebly from the window of the *Sultan*'s cabin. She stepped onto the gunwale and opened the door.

'I want to sleep in here tonight, Mother,' she said, wiping tears from her eyes with the rag she kept in the pocket of her skirt.

'Whatever's the matter, our Marigold?' Hannah enquired, raising her eyes from the sewing she was doing by the yellow light of an oil lamp. 'You're crying.'

The youngest child was asleep on his bed. Marigold pulled a stool from under the folding table that would later convert into the cross-bed. She sat beside her mother and father.

'I've given Algie up,' she whimpered. 'If he comes after me he'll go to the *Odyssey*, not this boat. He's been seeing another girl while I've been away. Every time I've been away, I expect. I ain't having nothing else to do with him.'

'If it's the truth, then I don't blame you, our Marigold. Are you sure it's the truth?'

'Oh, yes . . . He as good as admitted it.'

'Then you'm best off without him and no two ways . . .' Hannah severed the thread between her teeth and put down her sewing. 'But I *am* surprised, our Marigold. I wouldn't have thought it of young Algie, he's always so pleasant, he seems so open. And his father's such a nice chap as well. Which reminds me, I haven't seen Mr Stokes today.'

'He's bad a-bed.'

'That explains it. It might explain why young Algie's a bit strange as well, our Marigold. Maybe he's worried about his dad.'

'He is, but that ain't it, Mom. His father ain't that bad.'

Algie was intent on going straight to the Binghams' narrowboats when he returned, but his mother was outside waiting for him, a shawl thrown about her shoulders. By the dim reflection of the lights from the Samson and Lion she looked fraught.

'What brings you outside in the dark?' he asked. 'Have you seen Marigold?'

'Marigold?' His mother queried, totally unaware of her son's anxiety over his sweetheart. 'No, I haven't seen Marigold. I thought she was with you.'

'She was, I was just about to see if she'd come back.'

'Can it wait till morning, our Algie? It's your father. He's took a turn for the worse.'

'He's worse?' Algie's attention was immediately diverted. 'What d'you mean, he's worse?'

'He's in terrible pain, our Algie, and feverish. I don't believe it's what he's eaten after all. I think it's more serious.'

'Like what?'

'I wish I knew. I was hoping as Clarence would bring our Kate back soon, so's I could ask him to fetch his father to come and have a look at him. I'm sure he could give him something to ease the pain, if it was only laudanum.'

'Doctor Froggatt's attending to folk in the town, Mother. A tramcar toppled over. I saw it happen with my own eyes. I never saw anything like it. Dozens are hurt. Clarence went and fetched him to tend to them. He might be hours yet. Some folk had got dreadful cuts, kids an' all.'

Clara sighed agitatedly. 'Just when we need him . . . It's one thing after another. D'you think you could go back and find him and ask him to come and see your dad. I bet Clarence would bring him.'

'Course I will. I'll be quicker on my bike though.'

He rode as fast as he could back to where the tram had overturned. Engineers had arrived and were trying to right it, so that the debris could be cleared and the wreck hauled back to the depot. Algie looked around. Many of those hurt had left by then, as had the bulk of the crowd. Dr Froggatt was still there, however, sitting on a low wall as he attended to the wounds of the crash's victims, working by the light of a naphtha lamp the police had supplied. He approached, and Dr Froggatt looked up at him enquiringly.

'Begging your pardon, Dr Froggatt, my father's very ill, and my mother wondered if you could come and see him. D'you think you'll be here much longer?'

The doctor studied him for a second. 'I'll be here yet a while, lad,' he said apologetically. 'There are still a few people to tend to. It's been a hectic night . . .' He looked down again at the gaping cut he was stitching in a man's lower arm, then back at Algie. 'Aren't you the chap who stopped my son and me earlier, when he came to fetch me?'

'Yes, that's right, Doctor. Clarence is courting my sister, Kate.'

'Oh, you're that Kate's brother, eh? My son said you live in the lock-keeper's cottage at Buckpool. Is that right?'

'Yes, that's right, Doctor.'

'Course, I'm acquainted with your father. So what's the matter with him?'

'We don't rightly know. He's got terrible pains in the gut, he's been sick, and now he's feverish. We thought at first that it was something he ate, but now my mother isn't so sure, he's in that much agony.'

'How long has he been suffering?'

'Since the day before yesterday.'

'Hmm,' murmured the doctor. He stood up and dismissed the man he had been attending to, telling him to call and see him at his surgery in a week's time to have the stitches removed. He turned to Algie again. 'While I see to the next person here, would you like to alert my son? He's in the Bell, I believe. If he can get the dogcart brought to me I'll certainly go and see your father.'

'I wonder, Dr Froggatt . . . If you would be so good as to drive the gig yourself. My sister could go with you, maybe. My mother could do with her help, I reckon.'

'Very well. While you round them up, I'll deal with these last couple of people.'

Algie hurried on to the Bell, leaving his bicycle leaning against the hotel's wall. He rushed upstairs to the assembly rooms where the party was in full swing. The first person he saw was Murdoch Osborne, who greeted him cordially.

'I'm looking for my sister and Clarence Froggatt,' Algie said. 'My father's poorly and he's taken a turn for the worse. Mother needs our Kate back home.'

'Your father's bad?' Murdoch queried. 'What's up with him?'

'We don't know. Dr Froggatt's going to have a look at him if Clarence takes the dogcart to him.'

'There's your sister, look.' He pointed towards her.

Algie thanked him and barged his way through the crowd of folk. Kate was accepting the plaudits of her fellow performers and her smile was radiant, until he interrupted her. He explained what had happened and she tugged at Clarence's jacket to alert him while he was speaking to somebody else. She repeated what Algie had told her, and he looked with alarm at Algie.

'My father wants the dogcart?' he queried.

'Yes, he's still outside at the crash. He says he'll take our Kate back home, because Mother will need her. I'll walk back there with you, if you like, Clarence, and you can go back home to your house with your father when he's done at ours.'

'Sounds fair,' Clarence agreed, and they all left, bidding a brief farewell to Murdoch Osborne.

'Let me know how he is,' Murdoch entreated as Kate swept past him.

* * *

When the doctor and Kate were on their way, Algie walked with Clarence to the lock-keeper's cottage, wheeling his bike in the gutter.

'What an eventful night, eh?' Clarence remarked. 'The success of the play, that tramcar crash with all those poor folk hurt, and now your father being so poorly. My father will have had quite a night of it, don't you think?'

'And it's not over yet,' Algie replied grimly. He thought of Marigold and his stomach churned. 'To top it all, me and Marigold have had a row,' he admitted. 'I haven't seen her since before I saw you. I wanted to see if she'd got back to their boat all right, but I never had the chance. First thing in the morning I must go to her and make my peace. It's bad enough the worry over my father, without worrying over her as well.' He wondered which was bothering him more, his father's illness or Marigold's abrupt departure.

'Strange creatures, women,' Clarence said. 'At certain times of the month some of them are prone to behave very irrationally. My father reckons it's something to do with their monthly cycles. I must say, I sometimes find it difficult to make out Kate. She can be very queer at times.'

'Marigold has got this streak of jealousy in her,' Algie confided, as if they were blood brothers. 'And she can be bloody obstinate. She's convinced I'm still seeing Harriet Meese, and once she's got something into her head there's no shifting it. To tell you the truth, I'm not the least bit interested in Harriet Meese, but you try telling Marigold that.'

'Harriet's a fine girl, though, Algie, old man. She can be very charming . . . and what a figure . . . And you did take her to dinner at the home of some friends, did you not? Or so Kate tells me.'

'Only because Marigold wasn't around. I would've taken Marigold. I would rather have taken Marigold. She's my girl.'

They stepped out purposefully, anxious to get to the lock-keeper's cottage as soon as they could.

'How are you and Kate getting on?' Algie enquired. 'You reckon she's hard work as well sometimes, do you?'

'Kate worries me, Algie.'

'Oh?'

'Can I be frank with you, Algie? I mean quite brutally frank? Man to man?'

'Course. What's bothering you?'

'Well . . . you know how it is with us men and our girls . . . We have the need to . . . well . . . not to put too fine a point on it . . . to release some of our pent-up energies.'

'Oh, I know exactly what you mean, Clarence,' Algie replied with a matey grin. 'And I reckon I'm lucky with Marigold . . . you know what I mean? But that's just between you and me, Clarence.'

Clarence looked at Algie and smiled knowingly. 'I am the soul of discretion, Algie. Depend on it. You're a lucky chap, you know – she's a very pretty girl, is Marigold.'

'Oh, she's lovely,' Algie agreed.

'So is Kate, of course. I thought she would never come across with the goods at one time. Fought me off virtuously for ages. But then, suddenly, she changed. Needless to say, I didn't need any second bidding.' He wondered whether he was being too frank and looked apologetically at Algie. 'I really hope you don't regard—'

'I ain't in the least surprised,' Algie replied.

'Oh? What do you know that I ought to know?'

'I oughtn't to say, Clarence. Already I think I've said too much. Kate *is* my sister. It wouldn't be fair to say anything else.'

'No, come on, old man, out with it. You've made a comment. You must either substantiate it or withdraw it.

Whichever way it is, I beg of you to tell me the truth, since I've formed my own conclusions. A great deal may depend on what you say.'

'Well, the thing is, Clarence, I don't think you're the first.'

'Really? She led me to believe I was.'

'Our Kate?' Algie said scornfully.

'My God . . .' Clarence rolled his eyes as his own doubts suddenly seemed justified. 'It's interesting you say that, Algie. The first time it happened . . . you know . . . after she'd claimed so insistently that she was a virgin, I . . . well, it all seemed too easy . . . Look, I hope you don't mind me talking about your sister like this, Algie?'

'Me? Course not.'

'But you know how it is first time for a girl – bloody hard going – quite literally . . . It struck me at the time that she was no more a virgin than I was.' Clarence sighed and they walked on in silence for a little while. Then he said, 'I wish it were not so, Algie, old man, because I'd quite taken to Kate. But if a girl with her looks, who could really have any man she wanted, is inclined to looseness, then what peace of mind would I have if we ever got wed? I'd be afraid to turn my back lest she was flat on hers with somebody else. Good Lord, no.' He shuddered at the thought. 'Ah, well. It was great fun while it lasted, but I think that will be the end of it. It just remains now to tell her.'

Just as Algie and Clarence arrived at the lock-keeper's cottage, Dr Froggatt was upstairs pronouncing his diagnosis on Will Stokes.

'Peritonitis,' he said grimly to Clara. 'All I can do is treat him with comforting applications. Mr Stokes is obviously in a great deal of discomfort, and running a temperature. I'll need bread for poultices, Mrs Stokes, and hot water.' He rummaged through his black bag. 'I have some laudanum here that will deaden the pain for your husband. If he could be persuaded to take a few drops in a small amount of brandy . . . And do you have another lamp?'

It was shortly before midnight when Dr Froggatt treated Will Stokes with comforting poultices by the light of two oil lamps. Clara watched anxiously. Dr Froggatt hardly spoke while he worked, except for the occasional grunt, from which Clara was unable to discern satisfaction or concern. All she knew was that her husband was suffering.

'I have done my level best, Mrs Stokes,' Dr Froggatt said forebodingly, looking at Clara with sympathy. 'Tell me, are you a praying woman?'

'Not especially, Doctor.'

He smiled benignly through his tiredness. 'It wouldn't hurt to start, you know. Your husband is going to need every bit of God's help he can get, as well as your careful nursing.'

'You don't sound very encouraging, Doctor,' Clara said.

'Unfortunately, we do not know very much about peritonitis. We don't know what sets it off, but by the time we've diagnosed it, it's generally too late. The effects of its poisons, you see, are rapid and generally lethal, which makes it a very dangerous illness.'

'Do you think he'll recover?'

'That I cannot promise. Your husband should sleep now after the laudanum. Keep him comfortable and warm, and apply more poultices if you think they are beneficial. I'll call again tomorrow. If you need me in the meantime, don't hesitate to send for me.'

Chapter 15

Algie, Kate and Clarence sat in the scullery awaiting news of Will. The floorboards above them creaked as Dr Froggatt shifted his weight from one foot and one plank to another as he worked on the patient. Kate's enthusiastic recounting of her successful evening irritated Algie, who was listening with his other ear for the doctor's muffled comments and his mother's softer, anxious replies. He could only conjecture on what might be happening. One thing was certain; Will's illness was infinitely more serious than any of them had hitherto imagined.

The sporadic comments, deadened by the barriers of bed, mat, a layer of linoleum and floorboards, then became a conversation, but unintelligible to Algie. The sound of water being poured into a basin from a jug telegraphed to him that the doctor's work might be over.

'Hark!' he said, interrupting Kate's unremitting flow. He looked at his sister with apprehension, and she clung to Clarence's arm. 'The doctor's finished, by the sounds of it. They're coming down.'

Dr Froggatt descended the stairs carrying his bag and entered the room.

'How is he, Doctor Froggatt?' Algie asked, his face an icon of anxiety.

'Your father is very poorly, Mr Stokes, and I shall repeat what I have told your mother.' He explained his diagnosis, and Algie was aghast. 'If you need to send for me in the night, don't hesitate.'

'Thank you, Doctor Froggatt,' Algie said, rising from his chair. 'For everything.'

The doctor nodded his acknowledgement with a tired smile. 'In the meantime, I'll bid you goodnight. Are you coming home with me, Clarence?'

'No, Father. You go on in the dogcart. I'll walk back later.'

'As you wish.'

'Goodnight, Father.'

When the doctor had departed, Clarence said, 'Kate, if you'd like to take a walk with me in the fresh air . . .'

'What? At this time o' night?'

'Please. There's something I need to discuss with you.'

'Can't it wait till tomorrow?'

'I'd prefer not to wait.'

Kate got up reluctantly, tutting. 'Fancy having to venture out into the cold on a night like this.'

'I'll go up,' Algie offered. 'You can do your talking here, save going out into the cold.'

'Save yourself the trouble, Algie.' Clarence flashed him a knowing look from beneath his telling frown. 'We'll go for a walk.'

Clarence's voice sounded full of pent-up emotion. He'd spoken and heard little while they had been waiting downstairs awaiting news, immersed in his own thoughts. Kate's effervescing over her stage success had gone largely over his head, and seemed, in any case, to exclude him, as if he'd had no part in the play. Nor did Kate show any signs of anxiety over her father. The severity of his suffering had hardly sunk in. She donned her mantle and bonnet, and followed Clarence outside.

'What's so important as can't be said in the house nor wait till tomorrow?' she asked expectantly, fully believing he had decided to propose marriage, prompted by her new-found local celebrity status. It would, after all, be a fitting tribute to what had been a day of overwhelming personal triumph for her.

'I want to talk about us, Kate. The future.'

'Are you about to ask me to marry you?' she said, her eyes widening with pleasure and forgiveness, for being dragged out into the chill night air.

'On the contrary, Kate. I'm telling you that I'm giving you up. I don't envisage any future for us as a couple.'

Kate was stunned, uncertain how to react. 'Well!' she exclaimed, deflated and struggling to find an appropriate response. 'That ain't exactly what I expected to hear.'

'I'm sorry, Kate. It's not been an easy decision to make.'

'Have you got somebody else?' she asked, as if such a thing would be a cardinal sin.

'No. Of course there's nobody else. When do I have the time to see anybody else?'

'You've picked a great time to tell me, when me father's so bad,' she said, her indignation rising at his thorough lack of consideration. 'As if he ain't enough to worry about. Now this.'

He wanted to say that she had not even mentioned her father while he was being attended to, that she had been oblivious to the poor chap and his plight, only interested in herself and how much people might admire her after the performance in the town hall. But he thought better of it.

'So what's turned you against me?' she asked. 'For ages now I've sensed as something was wrong.'

'Oh, it's not you, Kate, it's me,' he said softly, willing to shoulder all blame. 'It's something that's been occupying me a while. You see, I really don't want to be tied down just now. I have examinations pending. Important examinations. I need time for more study, without distractions.'

'Shall you still belong to the Amateur Dramatics Society?' This was a relevant question, for seeing him there in future might be too embarrassing, and she had no intention of giving up the literal limelight now.

'Possibly not. I may well have to give it a miss next year.'

Well, at least that was a blessing.

Their footsteps crunching on the towpath's ash surface were deafening in the silence that surrounded them. Kate fell quiet for long seconds, ruminating over what this all meant. 'Of course, you've ruined me,' she pronounced at last. 'Who else is gonna be interested in me now?'

He felt like saying that she could pretend to be untouched, like she had pretended with him. She might even fool a more naïve or more besotted suitor.

'I ought to sue you for breach of promise,' she went on, 'ruining me like you have.'

'You'd have your work cut out,' he replied evenly. 'Even if you could afford it. We were never engaged. I have never asked you to marry me.'

'So I'm left on the shelf now to rot, am I?'

'Come on, Kate. You're hardly on the shelf at nineteen.'

'Nearly twenty. Soiled goods, I am, though. What decent, respectable chap is gonna want me when he knows I ain't a maid?'

'I believe any girl as beautiful as you are, Kate, can have her pick of men,' he said sincerely, 'whether or not you are a maid, as you so quaintly put it. Just beckon – and men will come running.'

'Except you. You're running in the opposite direction. And what if I'm pregnant, Clarry? What then?'

'If you are pregnant, Kate, we shall deal with it. There are ways and means . . . However, you can rest assured that whatever transpires, I shall not marry you.'

'Not? Even if I do turn out to be pregnant? . . . You swine!'

'How would I possibly know that any child would be mine?'

'How d'you think? I ain't been with nobody else.'

'I only have *your* word for that, Katie . . .'

While Kate was out walking with Clarence, and his mother was upstairs sitting with his father, Algie decided to take a walk along the canal in the other direction to make some sense of what had happened. The rain had ceased and holes were visible in the clouds, through which the moon sailed briskly, lighting up his way. The narrowboats belonging to the Binghams lay in darkness, which told him that Marigold had indeed returned safely; if she had not, her mother would still be waiting up for her with a lamp burning. That in itself was a relief; something less to concern him. Tomorrow, after breakfast, he would make his peace with Marigold.

He walked on, towards Dadford's Shed and its adjacent bridge, passing the numerous locks, the winding holes and weirs that made the descent into Wordsley possible. He began to realise how remarkably perceptive Marigold had been. She had discerned that he had been diverted by another woman, a diversion he could hardly deny to himself, however futile. Marigold, though, had picked the wrong woman. She had jumped to the conclusion that it was Harriet, when nothing could have been further from the truth.

Yet why had he allowed himself to become so preoccupied with Aurelia Sampson? She could never be his. She might as well live on the moon, for she would be just as close there as she was in Brierley Hill. Even if she were still unmarried she wouldn't look twice at him. She was way out of his reach. At that very moment she would almost certainly be lying in bed with Benjamin, probably doing what all young and virile married couples do. At least this rift with Marigold had brought him to his senses, made him realise how stupid he had been to allow himself to be so diverted.

Tomorrow, he would make a clean breast of it. He would tell Marigold all. He would confess how he had been boyishly infatuated with Aurelia Sampson, not Harriet, and tell her how daft he had been to let it affect his attitude and his true feelings. He would tell Marigold how much he loved her, how he hoped they would soon be able to marry, fulfilling her dreams and his. After all, if the new bicycle making venture was successful, he would be earning significantly more money than at present; enough to rent a decent house and live in comparative comfort. He would pledge eternal fidelity, and cross his heart and hope to die, to underline his good and true intentions. In time they would become highly respected members of the community.

He felt rain on his face again. Maybe he'd better go back home, save getting wet, and see how his father was. So, before he got as far as Dadford's Bridge, he turned around.

Dadford's Bridge . . . What lovely, romantic hours he and Marigold had spent in the fields nearby during the long, hot summer and early autumn, concealed from the world in grassy hollows and by gorse bushes. If only he were lying there with her now, and it were a warm, balmy evening. He would be sure to tell her how very much he loved her.

Only now was it clear to him how surreptitiously, but how surely, Marigold had stolen his heart. It had never been his intention to fall in love, but he just couldn't help it. At the outset he had only ever envisaged a casual courtship, just somebody to have fun with whenever she and her family moored up close by. Never more than that. What tricks life played on us, trapping us when we least expect it. Yet who could fail to fall in love with Marigold? Delightful, lovable, beautiful, forthright poppet that she was. How could he have been so puerile, so selfish? Well, only now, after she had had the courage to walk away from him, was he beginning to realise how privileged he had been to have her love. Their silly argument had been a timely reminder, forcing him to realise her true worth. Well, it had certainly served to make him appreciate her the more, and made him sincerely regret his cavalier attitude earlier.

As he walked quietly past their boats, he was almost tempted to tap on the window of the *Odyssey*'s cabin, in an attempt to wake her so that he could take her in his arms and just say, 'I love you'. But he didn't. He would only succeed in waking the other children who slept with her, causing ructions, and they would have no privacy in which to reconcile their differences. It must keep till morning. Then she would have slept on their argument and would be more inclined to forgive him. So he ambled past, crossed the lock gates and opened the garden gate to their own lock-keeper's cottage.

His mother was downstairs, sitting at the table, her head in her hands, holding a handkerchief to her nose. Kate was with her, also in tears, trying to comfort her.

'How's Father?' he asked apprehensively.

'Your father's dead, Algie,' Clara croaked, and then wailed with a stream of tears running down her anguished face. 'He passed away a quarter of an hour ago.'

'Dead?'

She nodded.

His father could not be dead.

His father was not an old man. He had years of life left in

him. He'd always been healthy, hardly suffered a day's illness in his life.

'How can you be sure he's dead, Mother?' he queried in anxious disbelief, but speaking softly lest it were true. 'He might just be sleeping sound, hardly breathing. The laudanum could've done that. I'm going up to see him. I'll see if I can wake him.' Algie could hear the tremble of panic in his own voice.

'Yes, go up and see him, if you want to,' Clara blubbered. 'But you won't wake him. I wish to God you could, but you won't, our Algie. He's dead. Dr Froggatt said as how we should pray for him. He didn't hold out much hope.'

Algie felt a tear trickle down his cheek. Already he was emotionally battered over his upset with Marigold. Now his father was dead. Could not the Lord have spaced his trials and tribulations more widely, so that he could come to terms with one before having to face the other?

'I'm going up,' he said. 'I want to see my father. I can't believe he's dead . . .'

He rushed up the stairs and into the bedroom. One oil lamp was still burning, casting a flickering orange glow onto the pale green floral wallpaper of the bedroom. Will Stokes was lying lifeless, the sheets and blankets folded neatly down over his chest, leaving just his head visible above them. His face was pale and waxy, but he looked at peace, with no sign of the agony he'd suffered lately. His hair had been brushed so that not one was out of place. It was typical of his mother to do that last service for her husband.

Algie knelt at the side of the bed where his father lay, and he wept.

He did not want his father dead. He wanted him to turn his head, to open his eyes and ask him to give him a hand with one of the locks that needed attention. He wanted to

254

talk to him, to discuss cricket and pick the best possible English team. If only he could ask his advice about the best thing to do about Marigold. His father would have known what to do, what to say. But now he could not ask him. He was gone from Algie. Gone forever.

Where was the justice? Where was the reason? If there was a God, why did He have to take his father? Why *his* father, a good and kind man who had never wished anybody any harm? Why did God see fit to take a man who had only ever helped folk, a man who had been a kind and gracious neighbour to all and respected by all, including the boat people? Why now? The questions were never ending and unanswerable.

But the grief was only just beginning.

None of the Stokes family slept well that night. Clara had lost her husband, Kate had lost her father as well as Clarence, whom she had grown to admire. Algie, however, thus far only believed he had lost his father, which was upsetting enough.

He got up that morning, lit a fire and put the kettle to boil, turning over in his mind exactly what he would say to Marigold. Of course, the fact that his father had died in the night would elicit all her sympathy, and ensure her reasonableness and forgiveness. He made a pot of tea and delivered a mug each to his mother and Kate, then went downstairs and outside to see Marigold. This was, he hoped, about to become the most important moment of his life. He was about to ask Marigold to become his wife.

But when he stepped outside he saw that the Binghams had gone. Their two narrowboats were no longer moored.

Only then did he realise he had lost Marigold too.

They must have left very early, and it was sure to have been at Marigold's behest. Otherwise, they would still be there, waiting till first light on Monday to leave for Worcester, as she had told him they would. Maybe he should ride along the canal till he caught up with them. He sat on the sturdy wooden arms of the lock gates and sighed, pondering this latest blow.

Obviously, Marigold did not want to see him, she did not want reconciliation. If she did, she would still be there, available and anxious for his apologies or, as she might choose to perceive them, his excuses. No, she had made it all too plain.

It was over.

Finished.

He tried hard to make sense of all this, but no sense would come. Would he ever come to terms with what he had lost? Would the world ever be the same again? If only he could turn back the clock to the time of Marigold's previous visit, before his fateful dinner at the home of the Sampsons with Harriet Meese. From that moment he would do things differently. He would politely decline Benjamin Sampson's offer and hold out until the time was ripe to start his own business, thus obviating the need to visit them. Then he would never have met Aurelia Sampson, whose loveliness and perceived vulnerability had so blinded him and clouded his judgement. He would have clung to Marigold. If he'd had any sense at all he would have gone to see the vicar of St Michael's and asked for the banns of marriage to be read out; he, Algernon Stokes, bachelor of the parish, and Marigold Bingham, spinster of the parish of . . . of what parish? How did you define your parish if you spent your life travelling the country's canal system?

But Marigold was gone anyway. His father was dead. Could his life get any worse? Hot tears stung his eyes, and he forced them back. How could he go back in the house blubbering like a baby? Think of the effect it would have on his mother, who would burst into tears merely at the sight of Will's hat, or even the tea mug he always used, let alone at sight of his broken-hearted son. He sat on the thick arm of the lock gate and listened to the sound of cascading water, trying to come to terms with all that had happened.

Clara and Kate had risen from the bed they had shared, so as to leave Will lying at peace till they could arrange for an undertaker to have a coffin made. They were sitting in their nightgowns with puffy eyes, brooding over mugs of steaming tea. Clara looked pale and drawn, and both shivered in the cold, although the fire had caught and was volleying swirls of grey smoke up the chimney when Algie returned.

'Marigold's gone,' he announced sombrely.

The significance of his words was not apparent to them, preoccupied as they were with Will's sudden death.

'It can only mean one thing – that she don't want me anymore . . . What with that, and my father dying all of a sudden . . .'

Tears came again, unstoppable and relentless. His shoulders shook with the double dose of grief, and he choked on a great, violent sob that seemed to tear its way out of his heaving chest. His father, whom he loved dearly, had died in pain, and nobody had realised how poorly he was. His one true love, Marigold, was gone, no doubt also wracked with the pain of a broken heart that he had so unthinkingly, so stupidly, so immaturely inflicted. He did not know, he could not tell, which hurt the most; the pain of losing his father, or the pain of losing Marigold. Combined, they were unbearable.

'She'll be back this way in a day or two,' Clara said kindly. 'I'll watch out for her.'

'Not if they get work to take 'em somewhere else,' he said bleakly. 'Anyway, she doesn't want to see me anymore. It's plain enough.'

'I feel sorry for you, our Algie, but your suffering's no

257

worse than mine,' Kate declared. 'Me and Clarence finished last night as well. He chucked me.'

He looked up at her through his tears. 'I'm sorry to hear that, Kate.' At once he felt guilty, for what he'd told Clarence must have caused it.

'So was I.' She drew a handkerchief from down her sleeve and dabbed at the tears filling her eyes. 'But there's plenty more fish in the sea,' she added stoically. 'I shan't grieve long over Clarence Froggatt.'

'I wonder what time Dr Froggatt will come,' Clara said, changing the subject. 'Of course, he won't know as your father's dead. We could save him the bother.'

'Well, I ain't going a-nigh his house, Mother. But our Algie could go.'

'I think Algie's got enough on his plate, our Kate. Anyway, the doctor will have to see him so's he can sign the death certificate.'

Dr Froggatt called shortly after twelve o' clock. He went upstairs and into the bedroom, took one look at his late patient and opened his bag. From it, he drew out a pad of pre-printed forms; death certificates. He sat down on the ottoman and began to write in copperplate swirls. Cause of death, peritonitis. The fact that Will Stokes had passed away did not seem to surprise him in the least, but he spoke kindly, and with the practised voice of compassion, to the man's grieving wife, his son and his daughter. He had seen this all before a thousand times. The sudden death of a hitherto well person, whether by accident or illness. The acute distress and upheaval it caused the families, who had neither expected, deserved, nor planned for such a traumatic event, which invariably turned their lives upside down.

Back downstairs, he handed the death certificate to Clara.

'I presume this house is owned by the Stourbridge Canal Company,' he said conversationally, 'and so tied to Mr Stokes's employment.'

'That's true,' Clara stated, and looked at Algie aghast as the implications suddenly dawned on her.

'I wonder how long they will allow you to stay here,' the doctor continued. 'They'll certainly want to install a new lock-keeper here very quickly, I would have thought.'

Chapter 16

'You know as much about the job as anybody, going about with your father like you did when you was a lad, our Algie,' Clara said tearfully when the doctor had gone. 'I think you should apply for the lock-keeper's job.'

'It doesn't necessarily mean that I'd get it, Mother.'

'But if you did, it'd mean we could stay on living here. I think you should try for it, our Algie.'

Our Algie gave a great shuddering sigh. 'But I don't want to be a lock-keeper, Mother. I've got my own plans. Anyway, I'm supposed to start my new job tomorrow. I can hardly let Mr Sampson down, he's depending on me.'

'I don't think you'll be going anywhere tomorrow, other than the canal company's offices to tell them about your dad, and the undertaker to arrange to bury him.'

'Won't I have to go to the town hall as well to report my dad's death?'

'Somebody will, I expect. I daresay our Kate will do that. She can go to the *Brierley Hill Advertiser* as well and have your father put in the Deaths as soon as we know when the funeral will be.'

'We're going to have our work cut out,' Algie said. 'I suppose I'd better have a ride over to Mr Sampson's house to let him know I shan't be at work. I wonder what'll be the best time to go.'

'Before they have their dinners,' Clara suggested without hesitation. She glanced up at the clock on the mantelpiece as she got up from her chair to give the fire a poke. The glowing coals shifted randomly and a flurry of sparks flitted up the chimney. 'Gentlefolk tend to rest of a Sunday afternoon. They did when I was in service. They won't want to be disturbed if they've got somebody round for Sunday tea. You could always leave a note, I suppose, if they're busy.'

'I'd better get a move on. Shall you two be all right while I'm gone?'

'I expect so,' Clara answered for herself and Kate, who had hardly spoken, secretly more indignant over being abandoned by her lover. 'Me and Kate'll get our Sunday dinner on to cook. I bought a nice joint of lamb . . . Your father was 'specially fond of lamb . . .' Tears moistened her eyes as she thought of Will, and Algie threw his arms about his mother to comfort her. 'I'll be all right, our Algie,' she said, mopping up the tears with a handkerchief. 'You'd better go. I've got to get used to your father not being here anymore to enjoy his Sunday dinners.'

'Nor any dinners, come to that,' Kate interjected carelessly.

'When they've taken him away, it'll be easier,' Algie comforted, casting an admonishing frown at his sister. 'It's hard when he's still here, upstairs. You think he's going to come down any minute and ask why we're all so maudlin.' He picked up his bicycle clips from the drawer where he kept them. 'I'll be as quick as I can,' he said, and bent down to fasten them round the bottoms of his trouser legs.

He rode as fast as he could to the house of Mr and Mrs Sampson, practising what he would tell them, anticipating their sympathy and hoping he would not break down in front of them. Soon, he was tugging at the bell-pull, his bike leaning against the house, beneath a window.

The maid answered the door.

'I called to see Mr Sampson,' he said. 'My name's Algie Stokes and I work for him at the bedstead works. You might remember me. I was here a week or two ago.'

'Mr Sampson ain't here,' the maid replied, eyeing him up and down. She thought she recognised him. 'He's out, visiting his mother.'

'Is Mrs Sampson in?' The prospect of seeing her, especially without Benjamin present, was an unanticipated diversion that lifted him momentarily from his sorrow, though he felt somewhat guilty that it should.

'I'll ask her if she can see you. What did you say your name was again?'

He repeated it and she left him at the door while she sought Mrs Sampson. Two minutes later she returned.

'Mrs Sampson will see you, Mr Stokes,' she said, sounding as if she thought Mrs Sampson was off her rocker. 'Would you follow me, please?'

He followed the girl through to a small sitting room at the rear of the house. Aurelia was playing with her little son, and wooden toys littered the carpet around her. She stood and smiled warmly when she saw Algie enter, and approached to shake his hand.

'This is a pleasant surprise, Algie,' she said amiably as they shook. 'Won't you sit down?'

'Thank you.' As pliable as moulding clay at the touch of her hand, he did as she suggested. She looked fresh and lovely, wearing a white linen morning dress that only served to enhance her youthful figure. He was painfully reminded of why he had been so diverted in the first place; she was so utterly beautiful, so desirable. 'Would you like a cup of tea or something?'

'Thank you,' he said again, suddenly aware that he was still wearing his cycle clips. 'I'd love a cup of tea, if it's no trouble.'

She turned to the maid, who was awaiting instructions. 'Mary, if you would be so good as to clear up Benjie's toys and ask Nanny to take him back upstairs, please? Then can you bring us a pot of tea?'

'Very good, ma'am,' the maid said, glancing at Algie once more. She quickly disposed of the toys, to little Benjie's apparent dismay, for he complained bitterly to his mother.

Algie took advantage of the distraction to remove his cycle clips which he slipped into his jacket pocket.

'No, Benjie,' Aurelia scolded gently. 'Mommy has a visitor and Mr Stokes doesn't want to be bothered by you, dear.'

'I don't mind, honest.' Algie felt sorry for the child, for being shepherded away and deprived of his toys, just because he had appeared unscheduled in the house. The boy reminded Algie of Aurelia, with his large blue eyes and long lashes.

'He's due for his lunch anyway,' Aurelia said. 'We try and keep him to a strict routine.'

Algie smiled to himself, acknowledging her refinement, which allowed her to call the child's dinner his 'lunch'.

'Benjamin has taken the gig and is visiting his mother,' she went on. 'She vacated this house in favour of us and moved to a cottage in Himley after his father passed on, you know.'

'No, I didn't know.'

'He won't be back yet awhile.' She sat down again, more relaxed now that she'd organised the maid and the nanny. 'It's so nice to see you again, Algie. I often think of the evening we all spent together when you discussed your new project with my husband.'

So do I, he wanted to say, but smiled dumbly instead.

'I really enjoyed it,' she went on. 'So how is Harriet?'

'Oh, Harriet. She's well as far as I know. Don't you remember that Harriet and me are not . . . not a couple . . . I mean, in the sense that we're not courting.'

Aurelia smiled brilliantly. 'Yes, of course I remember. And yet I thought she was very pleasant company.'

There was a tap at the door. Aurelia called, 'Come in,' and another young woman opened it. It was the child's nanny.

'Maude . . . Thank you for coming so quickly. Would you take Benjie for me? If you would give him his lunch now, please, since I have a visitor. And then you can go.'

Maude smiled, and said of course she would. She was also about twenty-one or twenty-two, slim and attractive, but wearing a sombre flannel dress in a dark green plaid. Attractive as she was, she was completely outshone by Aurelia, who stole a hug and a kiss from her son before the girl shepherded him away.

'It's Maude's afternoon off.' Aurelia explained. 'Where were we? Oh, yes, we were talking about Harriet . . .'

'I know,' he said, not realising how glum he looked. 'D'you mind if we don't?'

Aurelia laughed. 'Of course not . . .'

'Well, she's not my favourite person right now.'

'Oh?' Aurelia regarded him with wide-eyed curiosity.

He shook his head solemnly.

'Do you want to tell me why?'

'Oh . . . she made it plain to Marigold, my sweetheart, that she was here with me that night,' he replied. 'The trouble was, I hadn't told her. I hadn't mentioned Harriet had been here with me.' He shrugged woefully. 'It didn't go down very well.'

'Oh dear.' Aurelia sounded very sincerely concerned. 'That's unfortunate.'

'I realise now that it was wrong of me, that I should have told Marigold. Now she won't speak to me anymore. I don't think she'll ever have anything to do with me again. But I do wonder whether Harriet blurted it out deliberately.'

'Oh, I'm sure she wouldn't . . . It was most likely just a slip of the tongue. I thought you seemed a little preoccupied, Algie, if you don't mind my saying so.'

'Yes, I am, Mrs Sampson . . . But not just because of Marigold . . .' Algie heaved a sob of a sigh, a sigh that he could not smother despite being in Aurelia's company. 'My father died in the night—'

'Oh, *Algie*!' Aurelia sounded horrified. 'Oh, you poor, poor man. I am so sorry. *So* sorry . . . If there's anything I can do . . .'

Another tap at the door; the maid entered, carrying a tea tray. She placed it on an occasional table in front of the sofa on which they both sat. 'Would you like me to pour now, ma'am?'

'I think we'll let it steep for a minute or two, Mary.' She smiled amenably at the maid. 'You can go. I'll pour when it's ready.'

The maid curtsied and left the room. Algie was glad of the interruption, for he felt certain he would have burst into tears had she not broken into the conversation.

'Your poor father,' Aurelia continued. 'What caused his death? Was he in that dreadful accident last night that we heard about? A tramcar toppled over, didn't it?'

'Oh, the accident . . .' He'd forgotten all about the accident. 'No, he wasn't killed in the accident. He was nowhere near it. He died in his bed. Peritonitis, but we didn't know. We didn't know the symptoms, you see. We thought he'd got a bad stomach upset. By the time we got the doctor to him it was too late.'

'Oh, how dreadful. I've heard of these things before, you know, Algie. You can't be too careful with stomach and chest pains, it seems.'

'I witnessed the accident with the tramcar myself,' he said, wishing to veer off the subject of his father lest those threatened tears fall to embarrass him. 'I watched it topple over.'

'Oh, do tell me what happened,' she said, going along with his change of tack.

He recounted what he had seen.

'And you helped people out of the wreckage?'

'Oh, yes,' he said, as if it was the most natural thing in the world.

'My, what a hero!'

'Hardly that,' he said modestly. 'It was the very least I could do. People were frightened to death and a good many were hurt. There were some terrible cuts and bruises. Old Doctor Froggatt was sent for and he had a right old time of it, patching them all up. By this time Marigold had disappeared, because of our row over Harriet. I can understand why now . . . She'd gone back home, as it turned out.'

'But your father, Algie, meanwhile . . .'

'Oh, well . . . When I got back home my mother was waiting outside for me so I could fetch the doctor. Well, fortunately for once, I knew exactly where to find him.'

As he paused, she saw the grief return to his eyes, saw him fighting back tears, the troubled, distant expression that belies joy and contentment. She felt for him, understanding his grief and that he needed to give vent to it. Only by yielding would he gain any relief. She leaned towards him, deliberately reached out and took his hands in hers, stroking the backs of them gently with her thumbs. 'So you've two bereavements to contend with,' she said softly. 'Goodness me. One is enough to knock anybody for six . . . but two . . . I can imagine, Algie, that you don't know which is the harder to bear – losing your father or losing your sweetheart . . .' She looked into his eyes, hers overflowing with sincerity and sympathy, and squeezed his hands gently. 'You are obviously very fond of both.'

He nodded, aware of her soft, clear blue eyes studying his face as he watched her hands tenderly holding his, as if they were not his own, but somebody else's, somebody more deserving than him. Whilst he could easily wallow in her sympathy, he had not wanted it to be like this; him the over-sensitive fool, when he needed to appear masculine and in control of his feelings, especially with this woman he admired so much, whose admiration he would give anything to attain, a woman who was above his station anyway. What on earth would she think of him? She would think him a proper milksop, a nincompoop.

'Yet all may not be lost with Marigold,' she said softly and with genuine concern. 'She'll come back and make it up to you, I'm sure. Especially when she knows about your father. No woman could be that callous.'

He heaved another great sobbing sigh and tears filled his eyes again. But in the face of Aurelia's warm compassion he could stem the tears no longer. They flooded down his sorrowful face and he let out a half-stifled wail. Aurelia put her arm around him comfortingly, and his head was almost instantly on her shoulder, submissive, having no option but to weep like a child.

'Yes, yes, you must cry,' she whispered encouragingly into his ear, hugging him with a whole world of compassion. 'The more – the longer you let out your grief – the easier you will overcome it. Come . . . Come, Algie . . . Let those tears fall . . . Don't be afraid to show your grief. Let it go . . . Let it *all* go . . .' She felt his warm tears penetrate through the shoulder of her white blouse, and was moved to tears herself. 'I have lost a parent as well,' she whispered into his ear. 'I know exactly how it feels, believe me. It can only be twice as hard to have lost two loved ones simultaneously.'

'I'm sorry, Aurelia,' he blubbered. 'I had no intention of

letting myself down in front of you like this.' He sniffed, trying to stem his weeping. 'I don't suppose you'll ever forgive me.'

'For pouring out your troubles to me? On the contrary,' she said kindly, 'I am so pleased to be of some help, flattered that you feel enough at ease with me to let it go.'

'But I feel such a baby.'

'Never a baby, Algie. Never. A man who can cry is *not* a baby, but a giant of a man. A man of compassion, which you obviously are, cannot hide his real emotions and I have nothing but admiration for that. So many men think it is beneath their dignity to cry, even over something as sad as the loss of a loved one. So many men are obsessed with displaying their masculinity and that silly stiff upper lip which they think it pays them to nurture. If only they could see themselves . . . my own husband included. You have shown me that you are a caring, sensitive man, Algie. If only all men were like you . . .'

'But I only came to tell Mr Sampson that I wouldn't be able to go to work and start my new job tomorrow.' He lifted his head from Aurelia's comforting shoulder and gave another great series of shuddering sobs. 'I've got so much running about to do,' he said, wiping his reddened eyes on his Sunday best handkerchief, 'arranging things for the funeral, seeing how long they'll let us stay in the house.'

'You have to move out of your house?'

He nodded. 'It's tied to my father's work,' he explained.

'Don't worry, Algie. I'll see to it that my husband knows. Don't return to work until after your father's funeral. It is essential that you are there to comfort your poor mother in any case.'

'Thank you, Mrs Sampson.' He forced a smile through his tears. 'I feel so much better now . . . I reckon you're right about weeping – it does help pull the misery out of you.'

'It certainly does,' she said. 'In times of grief, the more you can cry, the better . . . I *know* . . .'

He dried his eyes and blew his nose. There was no longer any physical contact between them, but Aurelia sat erect intently watching him, her hands in her lap, her knees swivelled towards him.

'And please, Algie, don't call me Mrs Sampson. Friends call each other by their Christian names.'

He forced a smile that creased his reddened eyes. 'I'm sorry I troubled you with all this.'

'I'm not,' she whispered, and put her hand on his again reassuringly.

'But I scarcely know you, Aurelia.'

'I feel that I know you a good deal better already,' she said quietly.

'I think I know you better as well. Thanks for being so patient.'

'You have nothing to thank me for, believe me.'

He sighed mournfully. 'I'd better be going, I suppose,' he said, loath to depart from Aurelia's welcome tenderness. 'I should hate Mr Sampson to see me here like this.'

'Oh, I should love it,' she replied. 'It would show him it's not so hard to let go of some feelings, as you have done . . .' *He might even be surprised to witness my response to it,* she wanted to say, but did not have the nerve. 'Look, we haven't even had the tea. Do have your cup of tea before you go. It will be a pick-me-up for you before you go back home. And my husband will not return yet, I can assure you.'

She stirred the tea in the pot and poured out two cups without waiting for his response.

'Milk and sugar?'

He nodded. 'Thanks . . .' He stirred the tea and took a drink. 'I feel such a fool, you know, Aurelia.'

'Don't . . . Please . . . You have nothing to feel foolish about where I'm concerned.'

He felt tempted to tell Aurelia that he had been diverted by her, and had paid Marigold less heed as a result, but thought better of it. It might be information she did not want to hear and would not welcome; she was a respectable married woman after all. He finished the tea quickly.

'I'd best go. My mother will be anxious if I'm not back soon. Especially in her state.'

'Of course.'

He put down his cup and saucer and stood up. 'Thank you for being so understanding.'

She detected that he was embarrassed still. 'You're perfectly welcome,' she reassured him, laying a hand gently on his arm. 'Think nothing of it. I hope to see you again some time. In happier circumstances.'

He put on a smile. 'Yes, I hope so.'

She accompanied him to the front door, bid him goodbye and, with a sigh, waved as she watched him put on his cycle clips and ride away on his bicycle.

The Stokes' household was up and about its business early on the Monday morning. It was a grey November day, hardly yet light. Algie, unable to resist the temptation to look at his father, went into the bedroom where he was still lying in state. He brushed the backs of his fingers over Will's face. It was cold and clammy, but the previous stiffness of his skin seemed to have softened. Algie noticed his whiskers had grown since yesterday, yet he was supposed to be dead. Oh, there was no question that he was dead. Yet Algie felt no horror, no revulsion, a fact that surprised him. On those rare occasions when he had actually contemplated death, he'd imagined that he would find it impossible to look at a corpse for fear it contaminated him. But his father was lying there as if asleep, looking more at peace than if he were sleeping, and he half expected to hear a snore. He wondered whether his spirit had risen and was watching him unseen from some corner of the room, but still he was not troubled.

He went over to the window and glanced out. The canal looked like molten lead in the early morning greyness. Several canal boats were moored in the series of locks and basins that descended like liquid steps towards Wordsley, but not Seth Bingham's narrowboats. If only the Binghams had not left with Marigold so suddenly yesterday. If only they had waited till today, as they had originally planned, all would be well with her now. She would be supportive through his grief, she would help him overcome it in her gentle, loving way. And he needed her support, desperately. He needed to feel the soft, easy warmth of her love to steer him through this, the most traumatic time of his life.

He returned to his own room and dressed, then went down for breakfast.

'Did you sleep?' he asked his mother as she placed his breakfast before him.

'Not much. I seem to have been awake most of the night, but I reckon I must've drifted off. How about you?'

'I dropped off eventually.'

Clara sighed mournfully. 'The boatmen will have to sort out their own salvation if there's any problems with the locks on our stretch today. What time will you go to the canal company's offices to tell them about your poor father?'

'I'll be there as soon as they open.'

'Get them to let us stay here as long as we can, Algie.'

'I know, Mother.' He popped a piece of bacon into his mouth. 'But, in the meantime, we shall have to look for somewhere to rent. If you hear of anything . . .'

271

'When am I likely to hear of anything?'

'When you go shopping up the town. Have a look in Mr Green's window. He advertises houses to rent in his shop window.'

Clara sighed again. 'I never thought as I'd ever have to flit, our Algie. I always thought I'd spend the rest of my days here in this house.'

'There's one thing the last few days have taught me, you know, Mother . . .'

'What's that, my son?'

'That you can take nothing for granted . . . Ever . . .'

After his breakfast, Algie sped off on his bicycle to the offices of the Stourbridge Canal Company, overlooked at the end of the Stourbridge arm of the canal by a large bonded warehouse and on the opposite side of the street by a tavern. He rested his bicycle against the front wall of the office building and went inside. A young woman sitting at a high desk, seemingly swamped under chits of paper that he recognised as toll slips, asked if she could help him.

'Could I see Mr Munslow?' he asked. 'It's about my father, Will Stokes, the lock-keeper at Buckpool.'

The woman slid off her high stool and asked him to wait a moment. Presently Mr Munslow appeared. He was wearing a white India rubber collar and necktie that was tucked behind his waistcoat, a formal tailed jacket, and striped trousers.

'You wanted to see me?' he asked, scrutinising Algie.

'Yes, Mr Munslow,' Algie responded politely. 'I'm Will Stokes's son from Buckpool Locks.'

'D'you know, I thought I recognised you, but I couldn't place you. So what brings you here? Got a complaint about the old man, have you?' He uttered a short laugh, since he evidently considered his comment amusing.

'Not really, Mr Munslow. My father passed away suddenly Saturday night. I came to let you know.'

Mr Munslow stood open-mouthed at the news. 'Will Stokes?' he said, aghast. 'But he was fit as a fiddle. So what ailed him?'

Algie told him.

'You'd better step into my office, Mr Stokes.'

Algie followed the official into a small room that seemed to be all wooden partition and panelling, covered in ageing cream-coloured paint and glazed with heavily frosted glass. Framed sepia photographs of various canal scenes adorned the walls. Mr Munslow motioned Algie to sit on the chair in front of the desk, while he sat in a squeaking, commodious, swivelling, leather-clad, wooden chair behind it.

'This has come as a complete shock, Mr Stokes.'

'Imagine how we feel, Mr Munslow.'

'I can't even begin to. Please accept my sincere personal condolences and the condolences of the Company also . . . which I trust you will pass on to your good mother the moment you see her.'

'Course I will. Thank you.'

'Have you any idea yet when the funeral will take place?'

'The undertaker in Brierley Hill is my next call, Mr Munslow.'

'But please let us know when it's arranged. Just drop us a note. Naturally, at least one representative – certainly myself at any rate – will wish to attend to pay our last respects to a servant of the Company who has always been regarded very highly.'

'Of course, Mr Munslow . . . But there is another delicate question which I have to ask . . .'

'Please, ask it.'

'It concerns the house we live in, which belongs to the Company. How much longer will we be allowed to stay in it?'

Mr Munslow scratched his clean-shaven chin. 'Hmm . . . Of course . . . You appreciate, of course, that we shall have to appoint another lock-keeper as soon as is practically possible?'

'Yes, we understand that,' Algie replied.

'We have no wish to inflict hardship upon you and the rest of your family by eviction, naturally, but, since the house is tied to the job, we really have little alternative.'

'Yes, I know we'll have to find somewhere else to live, Mr Munslow, but what I really need to know is how long you can give us.'

'It depends. We shall have to appoint a person to replace your father, Mr Stokes, as I say. If you could see your way clear to vacating the house by the end of this month, say, I imagine we could accommodate that.'

'The end of the month . . .' Algie ruminated.

'That gives you four weeks. I would've thought it was generously ample time . . .'

Chapter 17

On Monday the 10th of November Algie watched his father's coffin being steered carefully down the winding narrow stairs. Later, he followed the hearse, with his mother and sister facing him, in the only carriage that followed it through the industrial wilderness of Brierley Hill, to the old red-brick Church of St Michael. It was hardly a grand funeral. Clara and her daughter had hired the long black dresses that custom dictated, from Eli Meese's drapery and mourning wear emporium. Clara was also heavily veiled in crepe, to hide her sadness from the collective gaze of curious onlookers, while Kate's unveiled face was white and expressionless, a far cry from the image she'd portrayed only a few days earlier as the fascinating and exotic Pocahontas. The family did not speak, the only sounds the clip-clop of the horses' hoofs and the rumble of the iron tyres on the uneven road. Algie watched his mother and his sister, curious as to how they both felt deep in their hearts. He was sure his mother was grieving more than she showed, but Kate? He was not so sure about Kate. Her face was inscrutable, her composure rigid. Was this pale, tearless face a mask? What were her thoughts?

Murdoch Osborne was at the church. Harriet Meese, too, had slipped the watchful eye of her father, but with his grudging consent as long as she was accompanied by her sister

Priss, who had taken the morning off from her teaching, and because the Stokeses had spent money with him on mourning dresses. Mr Munslow from the canal company was there, but the absence of Clarence Froggatt was noticeable, and a further twist of the knife for Kate.

There were some strangers too, mostly officials of the Stourbridge Canal Company, though not many other mourners in a town and district where the deceased was not particularly well-known to anybody but folk connected with the canal. But one elegant and very handsome young woman was at the back of the church and afterwards, watching the group surrounding the grave from a discreet distance. Algie did not see her, for he was very near breakdown and could hardly raise his puffy eyes to see anyone; but Harriet saw her and recognised her at once. She said nothing to Priss, but she thought to speak to Algie privately afterwards if the opportunity presented itself. However, she looked around at the end of the committal, and the young woman was gone.

Algie had arranged that after the funeral there was to be a small wake at the Bell Hotel, with sandwiches and beer laid on, which he paid for out of his own savings. This went on until after two, by which time all the not-so-closely related had left, except for one or two more hardened drinkers. Relatives and close friends congregated together and speculated about the future. Still present was Murdoch Osborne, holding court with the Meese girls.

The conversation between them beat backwards and forwards over the problems that the widow would have to face, how much money Will Stokes might have left, if anything at all, and how long Clara and her family would be allowed to remain in the lock-keeper's cottage while they sought and found a suitable alternative.

'I'm sure they will have got some sort of respite from the canal company,' Murdoch conjectured.

'Oh, I'm sure Algernon will have organised that,' Harriet said, keen to promote his sense of responsibility.

'It might well have been better if Kate had seen to it, if it meant discussing it with men, ha?' Murdoch replied. 'She'd have been able to win them a three-month stay, I'll wager, a girl of her charm.'

'We shall never know,' Priss commented sourly, envious of the approbation Kate stimulated.

Algie approached, and Harriet left the group to intercept him. It would be the first opportunity to speak to him since the fateful Saturday night after the performance of the play in the town hall.

'Oh, Algie, what can I say?' she said earnestly, laying a gloved, sympathetic hand on his arm. 'I am so sorry about your father. His death must have come as a complete shock. You must be devastated, all of you.'

He tried to smile. 'We are, but we'll get used to it. It'll be a bit easier now he's gone. I mean, while he was still lying in the house, I half expected him to get up and ask for his breakfast.'

Harriet touched his arm again and telegraphed her high regard with a warm smile. 'I'm so glad to see you haven't lost your sense of humour, despite all.'

'Haven't I?' he said glumly. 'I'm not so sure . . .'

'Well, this might put a smile on your face . . . Did you know that Aurelia Sampson put in an appearance?'

'Aurelia?' He was patently surprised. 'No, I didn't see her.'

'I thought not. You were too engrossed in the service and your thoughts to notice anybody. But yes, she was there. She left very soon after the committal.'

'Well, I'm blowed. Fancy . . .' His thoughts wandered to

last Sunday morning when he had visited the Sampsons; her caring kindness.

'So how is Marigold, Algie?'

'I don't know,' he shrugged resignedly. 'I haven't seen her since the night of the play.'

'Oh? Off on her travels, is she?'

'She got it into her head that I'd been seeing you regular while she was away. Nothing would persuade her otherwise.' He rolled his eyes, reconciled now to his fate.

'But why should she think that? Was it something I said?'

'Partly,' he replied. 'But it was my own fault, not yours. I made the stupid mistake of not telling her I took you to the Sampsons'.'

'Oh, Algie . . . You should have told her. And now you miss her.'

'Course I miss her. I love her. I need her . . . 'specially now, with my poor father suddenly gone.'

'Algie, I am so sorry,' Harriet said softly, lowering her eyes, feeling chastised and deflated. 'Whatever I said that made her suspicious, please don't imagine for a minute that it was deliberate. I would never do a thing like that knowingly. I'm sure she'll be back.' Harriet was anxious to redeem herself. 'Especially when she knows about your father. No woman could be that callous.'

'That's exactly what Aurelia said.'

'You've seen Aurelia?'

'Last Sunday. I went to tell Mr Sampson I wouldn't be at work to start my new job on Monday.'

'I see . . . So when shall you start this new job?'

'Tomorrow.'

'And when do you have to vacate your house?'

'By the end of the month.'

'It's just that Mr Osborne was wondering.'

He glanced towards Murdoch Osborne and caught his eye. Maybe he ought to go over and thank him for taking the trouble to attend the funeral.

So both Algie and Harriet joined the small group that contained Murdoch Osborne.

'How's your mother taking it?' Murdoch asked Algie.

'As well as can be expected, Mr Osborne. She puts a brave face on it, but she's grieving all the same.'

'Only natural,' Murdoch said. 'So how long afore you've gotta leave the house?'

Algie told him.

'Aye, well there seems plenty houses to rent. And you've got your work, young Algie, so you won't starve, ha?'

'No, we won't starve.'

'And how's young Kate taking it?'

'Hard to say, Mr Osborne. She and Clarence Froggatt have parted company. I think that's upset her as well.'

'Fancy . . . I didn't know . . . Ah, look. There's your mother now, Algie. I'll just go over and pay me respects.'

Algie returned to work next day. To his disappointment, the office he'd been promised was not ready and he wondered why Mr Sampson had said it would be if he had no clear intention of getting it done.

'Share with Mr Moody,' Benjamin Sampson pronounced. 'Meanwhile, you can paint it yourself and switch desks in your spare moments. We've got a new draughtsman starting Monday. Have you got your designs ready so we can discuss them and get them drawn up properly?'

'Yes, Mr Sampson.'

'While you've been away I've been looking into the question of tyres and wheels, you know.' Algie thought he detected a look of disdain. 'Did you know that Dunlop, the firm that make the pneumatic tyres, also make the spoked wheels?'

'I didn't know that, Mr Sampson.'

'Well, there you are.' He threw his chest out with superb pride in having discovered it. 'It didn't take much finding out. I've also sourced equipment for the welding process we'll be using.'

'Resistance welding equipment?' Algie queried.

'Exactly. Resistance welding equipment. The first machine will be delivered late next week. I'd like to have a prototype bicycle ready by Christmas. Do you think that's possible, Algie? You must have some idea.'

'I . . . I . . . reckon so—'

'No *reckon* about it, we must,' Benjamin declared icily. 'Time is money. The sooner I can bring Sampson bicycles to the market, the sooner the firm will be making money from them. Elementary logic, Algie. So let's all knuckle down to it. I trust you've got no more need of time off?'

'No, sir . . . Oh! Except maybe when we have to move our house. I'll maybe need a day off then.'

'You're moving house?'

Evidently Aurelia had not discussed it with him. Algie explained.

'Of course,' Benjamin responded with measured scorn, 'I would have thought you could manage a move like that in half a day. You surely can't have that many chattels. A lock-keeper's house is hardly a stately home. So I'd expect you at work in the afternoon.'

Another week passed, and Will Stokes had been dead a little more than a fortnight. Clara, Kate and Algie had cleared up after their meal and were sitting in the scullery. Algie was browsing the *Brierley Hill Advertiser* for a house to rent, when there was a knock on the back door. Kate got up to answer it, hoping it might be Clarence Froggatt come to make amends, which would give her the opportunity to tell him in no uncertain terms to bugger off. Two weeks into this upheaval and she was feeling angry at the way he'd treated her, especially at such a sensitive time as her father's illness and his subsequent death.

'Mr Osborne!' she declared pleasantly when she saw him standing there in the wind and the rain. 'This is a surprise. Come in out the wet.'

'Thanks, Kate, lass.' He took off his hat as he entered the little house and shook the rain off it onto the floor quarries. 'I just thought I'd come and see how you're all faring after your father's demise, ha?' he said. 'How are you doing, Clara?'

'Bearing up, thank you, Murdoch. It's nice of you to call, 'specially on a night like this.'

'I said I would when I saw you at the funeral, didn't I?'

'Our Kate, take Mr Osborne's cape . . . I bet you'd like a cup of tea. A drop of summat in it would be nice, eh? 'Specially if you've walked all this way in the rain.'

'No, I come in me gig, to tell you the truth,' he said, doffing his wet cape and handing it to Kate, who somewhat resented being treated like a maid. 'But a drop of summat warming in it would be welcome, Clara.'

'Sit you down, Murdoch.' Clara got up from her chair and rummaged in the cupboard at the side of the stairs, retrieving a half-full bottle of whisky which she put on the table. 'My husband liked a drop of whisky in his tea afore he went to bed at night, you know, Murdoch. It helped him get off to sleep, he always reckoned.'

'Very nice,' Murdoch concurred. 'A drop of whisky never hurt nobody, ha?'

'Have you decided what our next production for the

Amateur Dramatics Society is going to be, Mr Osborne?' Kate enquired, sensing an oncoming lull in the conversation.

'As a matter of fact, I have, Kate. We'll be doing a thing called *The Three Temptations*. It's a burlesque about King Arthur and the Knights of the Round Table. It should be very funny, and there's music and dance in it, so we'll need a damned good pianist – or even a band, ha? If we can find one as is capable of doing it.'

'Is there a part in it for me?'

'Oh, I should say so. La Belle Isolde. A beautiful young woman. Daughter of Sir Agravaine.'

Kate bridled with satisfaction and smiled. 'I can't wait to read it, Mr Osborne.'

'Call me Murdoch when we'm intimate like this, ha?' he said. 'I don't see the sense being formal when we're all sitting in the same house together like a family. What say you, Clara?'

'It's very nice of you to be so amenable with my son and daughter, Murdoch. I'm sure they appreciate it.'

'I got Clarence Froggatt marked down for the part of Sir Lionel, Knight of the Silver Shield, an admirer, Kate.'

'He ain't an admirer no more, Murdoch,' Kate informed him dryly. 'Not of me anyway. I'm finished with Clarence Froggatt. He can fizz up and burst as far as I'm concerned. And he won't be a member of the society no more, either. He reckoned he'd got too much studying to do for his architecting.'

'Well, it was nice of him to let me know, ha?' he said sarcastically. 'Ah, well, there's others as can fit the bill. It's a pity you won't join us, young Algie, a good-looking lad like you. You'd have all the young women after you.'

'I have enough trouble with young women as it is,' Algie declared, thinking of the tribulations with Marigold and Harriet. 'What with one thing and another.'

Murdoch roared, and even Clara smiled. 'He reminds me of meself when I was his age, ha, Clara?'

'Well, there was always plenty young women around you in them days,' Clara admitted.

'All except the one that got away, ha? The one as fancied somebody else more, ha?'

Algie noticed how his mother lowered her eyes at that remark, and it set him wondering.

'So how are you faring, Clara?' Murdoch went on. 'Are you all right for money? Do you want for anything?'

'We're managing. Course, Algie lost wages when his father died, but Kate was still at work, so we're managing.'

'Don't go short or get yourself into debt. If there's anything you need, tell me. If ever you need any help, let me know, and I'll fix it.'

'That's very nice of you, Murdoch,' Clara replied graciously. 'But, like I said, we're managing.'

Murdoch's visit was on the Monday evening. On the following Wednesday morning, Mr Munslow from the canal company paid Clara a visit. Algie and Kate were both at work, and she received him in the scullery, drying her hands on a towel that was riddled with holes.

'Would you like a cup of tea, Mr Munslow?'

'No, thank you, Mrs Stokes. My visit will be brief, as I'm anxious to get back to my office.'

'So, what can I do for you?'

'I've brought money for you, Mrs Stokes. The exact amount of your husband's weekly wage.' He handed her a sealed envelope. 'The company has decided, in its wisdom and generosity to pay a full week's wages, even after his death, as a token of our respect and thanks for the years of service he had put in with the company. There will also follow a small annuity to which your husband contributed each week. I don't have details yet as to the amount you will get back, but rest assured it will be paid as soon as we can arrange it, so please keep in touch.'

'Thank you, Mr Munslow,' Clara said graciously. 'It'll come in useful and no mistake. It'll go towards the cost of having to flit.'

'Yes . . . er . . . About the house, Mrs Stokes . . .'

'What about it?' Clara asked apprehensively, sensing that she had just accepted a sweetener to get them out of the house quickly.

'Well . . . I realise that I gave your son the impression that you would be able to stay here till the end of the month . . .'

Clara eyed him suspiciously. 'That you did. But . . . ?'

'But circumstances have changed, Mrs Stokes – as circumstances often do – and we find ourselves – unexpectedly, I should add – in need of it by Saturday. It means, I'm afraid, that you must vacate this house by Friday of this week at the very latest. If you don't agree voluntarily, we can of course apply to the courts for an eviction order.'

'But, Mr Munslow,' Clara gasped, 'we've got nowhere to go. We haven't been able to find a suitable house to rent yet.'

'I can't help you there, Mrs Stokes. This house is the property of the canal company, and you must appreciate that as landlords we have the right to do as we please with it. I am authorised to explain that a new lock-keeper has been chosen, and he wishes to move in with his family on Saturday, or else we lose him. He has the offer of two jobs, you see, and we'd very much like to engage him. But it is dependent upon vacant possession of this property.'

'I see,' Clara said, trying to remain unruffled. 'It sounds as if we haven't got a leg to stand on, doesn't it? It sounds as if we haven't got a choice.'

'I do appreciate your cooperation, Mrs Stokes. So you'll be gone by Friday. I thank you most heartily. Now, if you'll excuse me, I must go.'

'Heartless devils!' Algie exclaimed when he learnt of the canal company's decision. 'After all the years of faithful toil my dad put in, now they go back on their promise and want us out by Friday. Well, we don't need their charity, Mother. We'll get by. I shall make sure we find somewhere to live, and soon.'

'But what shall we do if we don't find anywhere by Friday?'

The urgent quest for a new home, this basic priority, was suddenly preoccupying them and eclipsing, for the time being, their grief over Will's death.

Algie shrugged. 'We'll put up at the Bell for a few days.'

'But we'll have to put our furniture and things in store. Where are we going to store it?'

'Lord knows. But I'll find somewhere.'

Harry Whitehouse, Algie's chum from work, had an uncle who owned a warehouse. By Thursday evening, they had received permission to store their goods and chattels in a corner of it for however long it took, at the exploitative rate of two shillings and sixpence a week. Into the bargain, however, he loaned them a horse and cart with a driver, who turned out to be useful lifting heavy furniture out of the house and onto the cart with Algie.

Stripping the house was a poignant occupation. Every item which they shifted, or cast aside to throw away, elicited some deep-seated memory of his father. It struck Algie how young his father must have been when he began life as a lock-keeper in this house, not vastly older than himself now. Will had seemed to be of an eternal, never-changing age. Although the years rolled by relentlessly, his father had never seemed any older – nor even any younger – and he searched his memory for mental images of him as a gentle, younger man.

His thoughts turned inevitably and sadly to Marigold. Since that fateful Saturday night he had heard nothing of her, no news, no sight of her. His mother hadn't seen or heard anything of the Binghams either. If they had passed through their locks they had done it stealthily. Yet it seemed extremely unlikely, for somebody would have seen them and reported the fact. Algie had asked several folk for news, including the gaffer of the Bottle and Glass, where Seth was ever likely to call for beer, if only to have a jug filled that he could sup on his way to some other mooring. But nobody had seen the Binghams. It was obvious they had not been along that stretch of the canal since. However, that fact alone was hardly conclusive evidence that they were avoiding the place, Algie realised; their work could take them anywhere in the vast network of canals that criss-crossed the country. So he remained hopeful.

But now he was about to leave this house, and it was here that Marigold would expect to find him. He must leave her some message as to where he had gone, in the hope that she would find it, otherwise he might never see her again. The appalling thought brought a chill to his bones. Never see Marigold again? But he loved her, he ached for her. Could life ever be so cruel as to deny him sight of her lovely face again? Of course, it couldn't. If need be, he'd scour every towpath, every winding hole, every lock on every canal in the country to find her. He would be sure to find her someday.

Until he realised he could be chasing around forever.

What if, on the very day he chose to scour the length of the Shropshire Union, for instance, the Binghams were at Oxford or Banbury, or even Northampton? It could go on like that forever. He could waste no end of time and energy, and cause himself no end of heartache in the process. The best way was to leave messages with as many people as he could. And he could start by leaving one pinned to the door of the cottage. Maybe the new lock-keeper would be so good as to either leave it there for her, or pass it on if ever she came enquiring.

Algie realised that his best bet would be to meet the new lock-keeper, explain his situation and ask him to pass on a message. He could hand him a letter to give her, and although she couldn't read or write, at least she would have the gumption to find somebody to read the letter to her. Perhaps her mother could read a little.

But what if she came tonight, or tomorrow?

No, he'd better write the letter now, and pin it to the back door, addressed to Marigold Bingham of the *Sultan* and the *Odyssey*, care of the new lock-keeper.

He was careful not to pack away their writing pad and envelopes and, just before they left the house, he wrote these few lines in indelible pencil, against the door that would be locked to them forever thereafter.

Friday 21st November 1890

Dearest Marigold,

If you had not already heard, my father died suddenly on the last night that I saw you. Because of it we've had to move from this house. As I write this letter I don't know where we shall end up living, because we haven't found a house yet, but I shall have asked the new lock-keeper to let you know, once I know who he is.

It has been very hard losing my father, but it has been just as hard without you. I hope you realise how much I love you and miss you, and I hope you still feel the same. I am truly sorry for what I did, not letting you know I had

*seen Harriet, but I promise you on my honour that it was
the only time and I would much rather have taken you to
Mr Sampson's house that night instead of her. I hope you
have already found it in your heart to forgive me my fool-
ishness.*

*Please get a message to me somehow, perhaps through
Mr Simpson, the publican at the Bottle and Glass, as soon
as you get this note. I am waiting for you, my angel.*
Yours eternally,
Algie.

He placed the note in an envelope and pinned it to the back
door, in the hope that she would receive it sooner or later.

Chapter 18

The 3rd of December was the first Wednesday the Brierley Hill Amateur Dramatics Society met after their roaring success with *The Forest Princess*, and the company was assembled in the Drill Hall for its introduction to their next programme. Murdoch Osborne handed out copies of the short comedy called *The Three Temptations*, described as 'A Masque for the Moderns; novel, allegorical, musical, and spectacular,' and written by E. L. Blanchard. There were never enough copies to go round, which meant several people sharing. Kate Stokes was blessed with sharing with Priss Meese.

'This is a short burlesque,' Murdoch announced, 'which will be the first part of our programme for next spring. It's very funny, but requires some clever acting by those I've chosen to participate.' He looked around, scanning the faces that formed a wide circle around him. 'Mr Mobberley, I would like you to read the part of King Arthur – "once a King of England, now a subject of Burlesque",' he read theatrically. 'Mr Carter, please be Sir Lionel, Knight of the Silver Shield, ha? And you, Mr Coates, Sir Tristram, his rival, Knight of the Brazen Mug.'

Everybody laughed, which Murdoch, with a grin, interpreted as a good sign.

'Now, Mr Homfray, I think the part of Sir Agravaine of the

Rueful Countenance would suit you, seeing as you're such a poker-faced man of the law, ha?' This observation elicited a few titters among the ladies. 'Mr Grafton, you can be Bruno, a servant, and Miss Kate Stokes . . .' He looked up at her expectantly and received a grateful smile. 'I'd like you to be La Belle Isolde, the beautiful daughter of Sir Agravaine of the Rueful Countenance. I shall play the part of Merlin . . . the Enchanter . . .' He took a mock bow. 'And the part of Morgana La Faye, the Welsh fairy, I would like our dear Miss Richards to play.'

He glanced at Katie Richards, and was pleased to see an agreeable smile on her pretty face, pushed out as it had been lately by her prettier namesake Kate Stokes.

'Mr Hartshorne, would you please be The Phantom Bill, a dangerous fiend . . . ha?'

'It depends how dangerous I'm required to be,' Mr Hartshorne jested.

'Oh, not half as dangerous as you can be, I don't doubt,' Murdoch replied good-humouredly. He scanned the group again. 'The rest of you will be in the chorus and required to sing, I'm afraid . . . and you have first go, since you open the proceedings with a little ditty, as you can see from your scripts . . .'

'What tune should we sing this to?' one of them asked. 'Does it say?'

'No, it doesn't. We'll have to find a tune that fits. I fancy a hymn tune myself. Using a hymn tune should be suitably irreverent.'

'And, believe it or not, I'm all for that,' Priss whispered to Kate.

The group spent a long time trying to decide on what tune to use for the first song, but didn't hit on any that fitted neatly with its metre. So they read the play through, amused by its comedy, and were confident by the end that it would be a great success. Mr Osborne had evidently chosen their material well. The rehearsal ended with everybody humming hymn tunes to themselves and each other for the opening refrain, in a desperate race to be first with a suitable one, with Murdoch asking each to come up with something in the week ahead.

As the group broke up, people were still trying various hymn tunes, including Priss and Harriet Meese who had their heads together with Kate . . . Until Harriet thought it opportune to mention a piece of very important gossip . . .

'Kate, I heard that you and Clarence Froggatt have parted.'

'Don't talk to me about him,' Kate responded acidly. 'If I ever see him again I'll spit in his eye.'

'Oh dear,' Harriet said. 'It was an acrimonious parting, was it?'

'Not particularly. But he could've chosen a better time.'

Harriet immediately wondered whether Kate might be inferring that she was pregnant from the liaison. Then it dawned on her. 'Oh, you mean it coinciding with the death of your father?'

'Course. What did you think I meant?'

'Oh, nothing at all. I was just a bit slow there, wasn't I? How stupid of me . . . Yes, I agree, it was not very considerate of him.' She was about to enquire about Algie's health and the latest on Marigold, when Murdoch Osborne sidled up to Kate.

'A moment, Kate?'

Kate withdrew from Harriet and Priss and stood before him.

'Can I give you a lift in me gig, Kate, ha?'

'What? To the Bell?'

'The Bell? What do you mean, the Bell? Are you meeting somebody at the Bell then?'

'Only me mother and our Algie. We've put up there, 'cause they turned us out of our house early.'

'They turned you out of your house and you're putting up at the Bell?' He sounded appalled.

'Only till we find a house we like. There was nowhere else to go.'

'There must be scores of houses.'

'None we like, Murdoch. None of us will put up with something we don't like.'

'Well, I don't blame you for being fussy. So how's your mother coping?'

'Not too bad. I think she's taking it all well, considering.'

'Good, good . . . Well, come on, then, ha? I'll drop you off at the Bell.'

Kate said goodnight to Harriet and Priss, who looked at each other questioningly as she followed Murdoch outside.

'She'll get her teeth into anybody,' Priss remarked. 'No wonder she always gets the plum parts and the best-looking men.'

'Oh, don't be so catty, Priss. Mr Osborne is hardly a good-looking man.'

'This new play promises to be quite funny, Murdoch,' Kate said as she stepped up onto his gig.

Murdoch Osborne had just lit the side lamps and heaved himself in beside her. 'It's why I chose it,' he said, picking up the reins. He clicked to the horse and they jerked forwards.

'I've been thinking, you know, Murdoch . . . I reckon I could do this acting lark for a living. I mean, I ain't bad-looking and all that, am I?'

'No, you're a fine-looking girl, and no two ways.'

'I can sing, as well as act, you know. Do you think I'd be good enough to do it for a living?'

He grinned amiably. 'I'd forget all about that if I were you, Kate, ha? Folk look on professional actresses in a different light to them what belong to an amateur dramatics society like ours.'

'Whether or no, it'd be better than working in a baker's shop, on me feet all day. I wonder how you go about it.'

'Forget it, I tell you. Stage actresses are regarded as no better than prostitutes, off with different chaps every night o' the week after their shows, in different towns all the while. Your mother wouldn't like it. D'you want to be regarded as a prostitute, ha?'

'No, course not,' she responded. 'But I don't see why I should be. Nobody thinks of Ellen Terry as a prostitute.'

'Aye, brought up in the theatre, she was,' he said disparagingly. 'And wed by the time she was fifteen to some painter. Had a fling with that Lewis Carroll chap, as well, by all accounts, and he's old enough to be her father. You can hardly say she's virtuous.'

'At least she got wed. I want to be like Ellen Terry. Whether or no, she's respected. I don't see why I shouldn't be. I've got the makings . . . Anyway, how do you go about it? That's all I want to know.'

'You have to be seen. You have to take the fancy of some great impresario. You'd have to share his bed first, though, and no mistake. That's the price you'd have to pay, just to be considered.'

'Is that how it's done? Is that how you get on? By going to bed with somebody?'

'Aye. In that business.'

Such a forfeit held no fear for Kate. 'D'you know any of these impresarios?'

'I do. I've been involved with the theatre – the amateur theatre – a good few years. I know one or two people, and I know how they work.'

'Would you write to one for me?' she asked earnestly. 'To introduce me.'

'Why, your mother would have a fit. I told you, it's best if you forget that nonsense. I won't have her blaming me for you going off the rails, ha?'

'But it's my life, Murdoch. I'm entitled to do with it as I please, aren't I?'

'Not till you're one-and-twenty.'

'Won't you help me, then?'

'Not till I've seen what your mother says first. Ha?'

The next day, Thursday, Murdoch Osborne closed his butcher's shop at dinnertime, a rare occurrence, and walked to the Bell Hotel at the end of High Street where it met Bell Street. There, he asked to see one of their residents, Mrs Stokes, who was occupying rooms with her daughter and son.

'Mrs Stokes is in her room, as far as I'm aware, Mr Osborne,' the landlord said, who knew him as a patron in his smoke room. 'Up the stairs out there . . .' He pointed to the door. 'And second on the right.'

'Thanks, Jacob,' Murdoch said, and went up.

He tapped gently on the second door, and waited. Within a few seconds, Clara Stokes opened it and peered around its edge.

'Murdoch!'

'How do, Clara,' he said warmly. 'I hope you don't mind me dropping in on you unannounced, ha?'

'Course not. Come in, come in . . .' She opened the door fully, stepped back and allowed him to enter.

He looked around. The bed was neatly made up, and the room tidy. 'There ain't too many men who've been in your boudoir, I suspect, Clara?' he said with a grin. 'I should count meself lucky to be among 'em, ha?'

'Only ever my husband,' she replied, feeling herself blush for the first time in years.

'Aye, and that's commendable, Clara. Very commendable.'

'Anyway, what have I done to deserve this honour?'

'D'you mind if I sit down?'

'Course not. Take the weight off your feet.'

He sat on the bed and gestured for her to sit down too.

'I was talking to your Kate last night.'

'She told me. She says you wouldn't encourage her to go on the stage. I must say, as I appreciate—'

'I ain't here to talk about your Kate, Clara. It's you I want to talk about. I didn't know till she told me, that they've turned you out of house and home, ha?'

'That's why we're here. There's nowhere else to go till we find a suitable house.'

'Well, that's a dirty trick and no two ways. And I can see your difficulty, Clara . . . I sympathise . . . The truth is, I might be able to offer a solution, if you'll only take time to think about it serious, ha?' He looked at her with an earnestness that surprised her, but she said nothing, awaiting his next words. 'You see, there's room a-plenty at my house—'

'Your house? But—'

'No buts, yet.' He raised his hands as if fending off her inevitable objections. 'Hear me out. As you know, I've been a widower these past few years, me daughters have deserted me, and I've got this big house as I share with a maid and a cook, who look after me good and proper. There's plenty room for the three of you – your Kate and your Algie – and yourself, o' course.'

Clara sat silently for some seconds. This had come as quite a shock and she was not sure of the implications. Was he doing this out of the kindness of his heart, because he felt sorry for them? Or was there another motive? Did he, for instance, intend to ask Kate to be his wife? She hoped not; he was much too old for Kate.

'That's a very generous offer, Murdoch,' she said blandly, when she had collected her thoughts. 'But we hadn't intended being anybody's lodgers. I'm not made of money, you know. I'll have to depend on Algie and Kate now.'

'Lodgers!' he exclaimed, as if the idea were ridiculous. 'No, I wasn't contemplating you as paying lodgers . . .'

Later that same evening, Reggie Hodgetts and his family moored up in the basin outside the Bottle and Glass on their way to Stourport and Kidderminster. It was dark and cold and, at his mother's behest, he shovelled a few cobs of coal into the stove of their untidy narrowboat. Smoke swirled from the soot-blackened chimney pipe in an eddying cloud and was dispersed at once by the wind, only to be subsumed into the greater volume of smoke created by the Black Country's industrial might. He unhitched the horse from its halter, divested it of its empty nose-tin, and walked it back down the series of locks to the stabling near the general stores. As he strolled past the Stokes's cottage, he saw that it was in darkness.

'What's up yon?' he asked the stableman, called Jonah, pointing to the lock-keeper's cottage. 'They'm all in darkness.'

'Ain't you heard about Will Stokes?' Jonah asked, as he took the horse and led it into an empty stable.

'Why, what's he done?' Reggie asked.

'Gone and kicked the bucket, that's what he's done.'

'What?'

'Aye, peritonitis.' He emptied a bucket of oats into a manger and the horse thrust his nose into it at once. 'Turned nasty, by all accounts. Old Doc Froggatt from Brierley Hill did all he could, but 'twas no good. 'E was a goner, mate, afore ever the doctor had been gone five minutes.'

'It was a bit sudden, eh?' said Reggie, astonished by the information. 'He wasn't a bad sort, was he, Will Stokes?'

'A good bloke.'

'So that's why the house is in darkness, eh? In mourning.'

'Oh, no, they'n flitted a'ready,' Jonah said. 'There was a new chap due to start Monday, but we ai' sid sight of 'im. We did 'ear, though, as he'd turned the job down at the last minute. We shall miss Will Stokes.'

'I was hoping I might see young Kate, the daughter.'

'Oh, well, we all want to see her, eh?' Jonah grinned waggishly. 'Fair piece that, and no two ways about it. Mind you, I don't envy the bloke as gets her in the finish – he'll have his hands full as sure as God med little apples. Her's got a roving eye, and no mistek.'

'I thought she was a-courting, Jonah. Some doctor's son.'

'Well, that's as maybe, I wouldn't know. Whether or no, there's an envelope pinned to the back door. I sid it meself when I went to see if the new lock-keeper had moved in.'

'An envelope?' Reggie queried. 'I wonder who that's for.'

'Dunno. I can't read much, me. Leastwise, I can't read fancy swirls like what's on the front of that.'

'Nor can I, but I'll go and have a peep. It's very likely for me, see. From Kate. We've been friendly, like, over the years, Kate and me. I'll get somebody to read it to me. How much do I owe you for the hoss?'

'The usual. Sixpence.'

Reggie gave him his coin and made his way back up the towpath. At the lock-keeper's cottage just before the bridge, he crept furtively across the lock gate and up the stone steps to the back gate. As he reached the back door, the sky lit up with an orange glow, as if all the fires of Hades had been thrust to the surface of the earth. By its reflected luminosity, he could see a letter pinned to the door. He snatched it, the drawing-pin that held it falling to the floor, and stuffed it in his pocket. He knew with certainty that it was not intended for him. Kate Stokes had gone up in the world, and was hardly likely to be leaving messages for him these days, especially now she had that doctor's son. It was much more likely to be for Seth Bingham's daughter, a love letter from that stupid bugger Algie. Well, he owed Algie a bad turn for setting about him that night when he was giving Kate a good seeing-to against their shed, hurting nobody. Tomorrow, when he was away from here, he would ask somebody to read it to him. It would be nice to know the sort of softness Algie Stokes was capable of; he deserved no better than having his pathetic love letter burnt. Young Marigold would never receive it; it would burn a treat in the stove. She deserved no better either. For meagre boat folk, the Binghams were way above themselves.

As Algie Stokes cycled back from work that evening, he pondered the progress of his new job and his relationship with the new draughtsman, whose job it was to translate the concept of his proposed bicycle into an engineering possibility. Algie already had the feeling that he was being used, that once his ideas had been subsumed, he would be of little further use to Benjamin Sampson. Despite Benjamin wooing him for his creativity, with that slap-up dinner to seduce him – which seemed a lifetime ago – the infatuation was evidently over already. Benjamin had got what he wanted, and now he could hardly find a civil word to say to him. If Algie had been of a more cynical nature he might have seen it coming, but he was not, and so he had not. He felt cast aside like an old shoe that has given sterling service but is of no further use, and he did not like the feeling.

Algie made up his mind finally; he did not admire Benjamin Sampson. He did not admire him at all.

He arrived back at the Bell Hotel. He left his bicycle in the passage, which he had permission to do, took off his cycle clips and went upstairs to his room. He removed his jacket, scarf and cap and tapped on the door of the room his mother and Kate were sharing.

'I thought it'd be you,' Clara said.

He thought how attractive she looked today, despite her mourning and pale complexion. A sparkle had returned to her eyes, replacing the distant look of preoccupation that had afflicted her since his father's death. It was good to see that she was getting over her grief so quickly. He didn't like to see his mother so haunted by misery, as she had been.

'Kate not back yet?'

'Not yet,' she answered, 'but I don't expect she'll be long. It's nowhere near so far to walk back here as it was to walk back home.'

'How about if we go for something to eat at Mrs Daniel's Dining Rooms in Mill Street tonight, Mother?' he suggested. 'It'd be a change for you. Let's get you out of this place and out into the big wide world.'

'I'd rather not, Algernon,' Clara replied typically. 'I'd just as soon eat here. Anyroad, there's something I want to talk to you both about, but it'll keep till our Kate gets here.'

He shrugged. It was always the same. She never wanted to go anywhere. 'What d'you want to talk to us about?'

'Oh, just an offer of cheap lodgings,' she said dismissively.

'Lodgings? I thought we wanted to rent.'

At that Kate returned. 'I got us some cakes,' she said brightly as she walked through the door. 'Mr Mills said as we could have them for nothing 'cause they're broken. They're ever so nice, though.' She placed her basket on the floor and took off her mantle and bonnet. 'Shall we have one a-piece now, or save them till later?'

'Mother's got something she wants to talk to us about,' Algie said, patently not interested in the cakes. 'Shall we talk about it over our dinners downstairs or here, before we go down?'

'Before we go down,' Clara said with a decisiveness that brooked any argument.

Kate peered in the mirror set in a wardrobe door, preened her lustrous dark hair and admired herself with a sideways look at her reflection. 'So what is it, Mother?'

'Shall we all sit down?'

'Well, let's have a cake then.'

'Never mind the cakes for now, our Kate. Having a cake will spoil your appetite for your dinner.'

Kate sat on the bed compliantly but disappointed, for she was hungry and fancied a cake. Algie sank into a wicker chair that was under the window and looked at his mother expectantly.

'I had a visitor today,' Clara began, and paused.

'Oh? Who?' Kate urged with typical impatience.

'Murdoch Osborne.'

'Murdoch?'

'Mr Osborne to you, our Kate.'

'*Mr Osborne* tittle! He's told me to call him Murdoch. He's a good friend of mine, Mother. I think I know him better than you.'

'Well, he's a good friend to me as well, our Kate. Always has been.'

'I want him to help me get on the stage,' Kate added pettishly.

'You're not going on the stage, our Kate . . .'

'Is that why he called? To talk about me?'

'Why would he want to talk about you?' Clara said, irritated by her daughter's conceit.

'Because it'll mean me going away from home if I'm going on the stage, that's why.' She shrugged nonchalantly. 'He wanted to know how you'd feel about that before he helped me.'

'He knows how I feel about it, and you're not going on the stage,' Clara replied. 'As a matter of fact, he called to see *me*. He wanted to explain that he's got a great big house with only him in it, and a maid and a cook who he kept on to look after him. What he wanted to say was that there's plenty of room for us at this house of his.'

'As lodgers, you mean?' Kate queried, a little more enthusiastically. 'That'd be handy.'

'How much would he charge us?' Algie wanted to know. 'We have to think whether we can afford it.'

'He says he doesn't want money,' Clara replied.

'So he's offering a roof over our heads out of the kindness of his heart?' Algie sounded dubious. There had to be an ulterior motive.

'There's one condition, our Algie.'

'Ah . . . I thought there might be.' He glanced at Kate who was inspecting her fingernails. 'So surprise me.'

'The condition is that I marry him.'

'You?' Algie stood up, at once perturbed, alarmed that his mother might already have accepted.

'Yes, me.'

'But my father hasn't been dead five minutes,' he protested loudly. 'He's still warm in his grave. You can't marry Murdoch Osborne, Mother. Even if I liked the idea – which I definitely do not – it's too soon. It's much too soon. Folks will talk about you scandalous.'

'It's nothing to do with anybody else, our Algie. If folk want to talk, that's up to them.'

Mental images of his spotless mother in bed with Murdoch

Osborne at once plagued him and horrified him utterly. He imagined them coupled, his mother lying submissively beneath this grunting and groaning and writhing man whom he did not particularly like, this man who gave Marigold the creeps.

'So have you accepted him, Mother?' Kate asked.

'I've been weighing it up. Murdoch isn't short of a shilling or two – a situation I've never known myself – so we wouldn't want for anything. It's a nice house he's got, he says, and in Kingswinford – a nice place. Then there's a maid and a cook. I could have a lovely easy time of it.'

'But Mother, didn't you hear me?' Algie protested. 'My father isn't cold in his grave yet. I just wish he could hear you, already planning to get wed to somebody else.'

'I haven't said that I've accepted Murdoch yet, have I?'

'I should just hope you haven't. In a couple of years you could maybe start to think about remarrying. But after three weeks . . . ?'

They fell silent for some time, long moments when they all contemplated this outrageous proposal. Was his mother about to make the worst mistake of her life, a mistake that would adversely affect Algie, and Kate as well? Was she prepared to make a bargain with Murdoch Osborne, trading the promise of a misguided and inappropriate, middle-aged romance to escape the likelihood of loneliness and insecurity in old age? Perhaps. Yet that, in itself, was excusable. What was not excusable was whether she was prepared merely to become a submissive bed partner and lose her self-respect, just to avoid the inconvenience or indignity of having to be kept by her own son.

Algie could hardly conceive of his mother actually loving Murdoch. Yet wasn't it natural enough that she should be flattered whether or no, and perhaps even a little surprised, to find herself still capable of inspiring admiration, perhaps even desire, from another man? Always assuming that middle-aged men and women still felt such things. Wasn't it natural that she should want to grasp any opportunity to scramble from the depths of misery and uncertainty into which she had been plunged? Why shouldn't she allow herself to be diverted from her grief, which might otherwise beset her for many more months yet? Indeed, was it not a recognised fact that a sure way of mending a broken heart was to expose it to new love?

It seemed likely nevertheless, that she was protecting her own future. After all, Kate might someday marry. He might himself marry one day – as soon as he found Marigold it was indeed his intention. When that happened he would not necessarily want his mother living with him, dependent upon him wholly. It could create friction in his household. Often had he heard it said that a wife and her mother-in-law are not necessarily compatible. Both believe they know the young husband best, what's best for him, and inevitably each tries to impose her conflicting will upon the other. So wouldn't it be for her own good to marry, even so soon after being widowed?

'I think I ought to tell you both,' Clara said, breaking the awkward silence, 'that afore I met your father, Murdoch and me were sweethearts.' She allowed a second or two for this revelation to be absorbed, while Kate flashed grudging glances at her. 'Oh, we were only young. I was only seventeen or eighteen, and he would have been about twenty. But when I met your father, I gave Murdoch the go-by. Whether or not it was the right thing to do I'll very likely never know, but it upset him a lot. He used to send me letters saying how heart-broken he was, begging me to go back to him. Anyway, the letters stopped after a bit and I heard as how he'd took up with another young woman called Elizabeth Caddick. Within six months he'd married her.'

'Proves he's a fast worker,' Algie remarked scornfully.

'That's as maybe, our Algie, but I've always had the feeling that he met and married Elizabeth Caddick on the rebound. I don't think as he was ever very happy with her, even though he had daughters by her. And the daughters never had much to do with him once they'd grown up, and nothing at all since Elizabeth passed away. Her influence on them, I daresay.'

'So you reckon he's always had a hankering for you, do you, Mother?' suggested Algie, scornful of the notion.

'I do.'

Algie looked intently at his mother and suddenly realised that there was an aspect of her life and her character about which he knew nothing. She was forty-three years old, had been married at about twenty, and was certainly not unattractive even now. Her face and figure were still youthful for a woman her age. He tried to imagine her at the time of her marriage; about Kate's age, lovely and alluring, stirring the hearts, the souls and indeed the loins of many young men. For all he knew she might have been of a passionate nature, too. Perhaps even wanton. Kate was wanton, after all. Perhaps Kate had inherited that from her mother, as well as her looks. It must have come from somewhere.

'So what do you intend to do?' Algie asked, emerging from his thoughts, seeing his mother in a new light. 'Are you going to accept him?'

'Well, it would solve all our problems.'

'I'd rather we solve our problems ourselves, without any help from Murdoch Osborne. I can look after you, Mother. We don't need him.'

'*You* mightn't need him, our Algie. But don't you think

that's a bit selfish? You aren't thinking about what might be best for me, are you? What about when you and our Kate meet somebody a-piece and want to get wed? You won't want me stuck with you then, nor should you.'

Algie sighed. 'It sounds as if your mind's already made up.'

'Oh, but only if I have your blessing,' Clara affirmed. 'I wouldn't do it without your blessing. You know that, don't you? Both of you?'

Kate shrugged her shoulders. 'It's up to you what you do, Mother. It ain't as if you're that well-known in Brierley Hill. Who'd care tuppence what you did? Who'd know that you'd only been a widow five minutes, apart from a few folk? Course, plenty folk know me.'

Algie rolled his eyes at his sister's vanity, while Clara looked at her son for his response.

'Well, our Algie?'

'Look, Mother,' he said earnestly, 'I've got no wish to stand in the way of your happiness, if you think it'll make you happy. You deserve to be happy. But I reckon it'd be the wrong thing to marry again so soon after my father's death. That's my position. If I said, "All right, marry Mr Osborne", I'd feel that I was betraying my father. I'm sure you must see that, Mother?'

'Course I do, our Algie.'

'But if I condemn it, Mother, I'll feel as if I'm betraying you. Because, believe me, I can see your point of view. So what am I to do? What are you to do?'

'Maybe you should let me be the judge, our Algie . . .'

He shrugged. 'You're my mother and I love you. I don't want you to make a mistake you might live to regret.'

'On the other hand, Algie, if I turn Murdoch down I might live to regret that as well.'

He nodded his acknowledgement of her dilemma. 'All I

want is for you to be content. If you feel that marrying Murdoch Osborne is the right thing to do, then so be it. Whichever way you decide to jump, I'll stand by you . . . if that makes you feel any easier.'

Chapter 19

Clara Stokes and Murdoch Osborne were married by special licence on the bitterly cold and bleak noon of Tuesday the 9th of December 1890. Murdoch stood at Clara's side in superb dignity, dominating the room in a brand new waistcoat, his shiny new hat occupying one of the vacant chairs along with his new gloves, acquired hurriedly and specially for the occasion.

Clara went through it all with surprising calm, and a ready acquiescence of this rapid marriage. She had had only a few days to think about it and all that it meant. Everything had been so sudden. A decision, so unexpectedly required of her, prompted an urgent answer and had to be made. She had been a widow for only four short weeks. Perhaps that in itself was unique. Ideally, she would have liked a longer time in mourning, if only in fairness to Will's memory, but her family needed a home, and Murdoch's was quickly offered; an opportunity too good to miss. Today, seeing all with extraordinary clarity, she was filled with an unanticipated calmness of spirit, for her son and daughter had ultimately sanctioned this union. Merely by his proposal, Murdoch had already given her so much; her sudden preoccupation with, and thoughts that they might even recapture, their youthful courting days, eclipsed almost entirely her grief over Will. Who would have thought, only four or five weeks ago, that she would be married to somebody other than Will?

It was curious how little she pondered Murdoch's first wife, but she'd never known her except by sight and what she'd heard. In all the times Clara had visited his butcher's shop she had never once knowingly caught sight of either Elizabeth or his daughters, since they obviously never contributed to his business. It was likely they'd been kept out of the way, confined to the green rurality and cleanliness of Kingswinford. Doubtless, his daughters were at some select school anyway. Clara felt no twinge of jealousy, no great desire to know more. As far as she was concerned, Elizabeth Caddick belonged to his distant past. Maybe she would happen upon a photograph or two when she was installed at Badger House, Murdoch's home in Kingswinford's tree-lined High Street. Even Will, so recently deceased, was already bewilderingly consigned to the past too, yet he was of course still vivid in her memory.

Murdoch's newly adopted family sat with him and his invited witnesses in a private room at the Bell Hotel, to which they'd been conveyed in a hired victoria. Now they were going through the motions of celebrating, with pints of best bitter for the men and whisky with orange cordial for the ladies.

'We're in good time for Christmas,' Murdoch said magnanimously to Clara. 'I'll be sure to get a decent flitchen of bacon and the plumpest goose in Staffordshire, for the best Christmas fittle we've all ever had, ha?'

Clara smiled agreeably and nodded. She was beginning to look forward to it.

'Aye, well see if you can get me a goose an' all, Murdoch,' Eli Meese responded. 'Consider this as me firm Christmas order.'

Murdoch grinned amiably. 'It's as good as in your oven,

Eli, dear friend . . . Look, the men's tankards need replenishing. Let me get 'em filled, ha?' He stood up to go to the bar.

Algie was surprised that Murdoch had asked Eli Meese to be one of the witnesses (the other was a chap Clara knew vaguely but Algie knew not at all), yet here was Eli, supping a pint with apparent contentment and joviality, unfazed by Algie's presence.

'I'll see to these,' Eli declared unstintingly, and got up from the settle, thrusting a fat hand into a pocket of his ample trousers. 'Who wants another?'

Clara and Kate decided they had had sufficient, but Murdoch definitely wanted another pint.

'Algie?' Eli prompted.

'Yes, I'll have another, thank you, Mr Meese. That's very generous.' Eli had actually spoken to him. Wonder of wonders.

When the barman had poured it, Eli first passed Murdoch his pint, then handed Algie his with a magnanimous grin, as if they had been chums since the dawn of time. He then decided to sit himself beside Algie, to Algie's consternation, and placed his own foaming pint on the table before them.

'Last time we met, young Algie, I was a bit miffed with thee, as I recall.'

Algie felt himself redden. 'Understandable to some extent, Mr Meese, in view of what happened.'

'Aye, well, I was maybe a bit hasty. All I was interested in was protecting me daughter and her good name.'

'I understand, Mr Meese.' Algie dipped into his pint self-consciously and took a swig. 'But I could've smoothed it all out proper before somebody else put their oar in, without you having to be involved and upset.'

'Aye, I realise now as you was calling to see her to explain all, which is commendable enough. You can't beat being straight, you know. Our Harriet never would have a word said again' thee anyroad. I know as you ain't a bad lad at heart, Algie.'

'That's nice to hear.' He managed a smile.

'She's a good wench, is our Harriet.' Eli gulped at his beer and wiped away the foam that clung to his top lip with the back of his hand, awaiting Algie's inevitable confirmation of his pronouncement.

'Yes, I know it as well as anybody, Mr Meese. And I was only sorry that I was the cause of her being upset. 'Specially when I think so highly of her.'

'Well, mebbe your best way round it would've been to give the wench up afore you begun messing with others. Still, it's all water under the bridge now, lad.'

Algie nodded, looking suitably remorseful, yet not quite sure why he'd been forgiven so unexpectedly.

'Anyroad,' Eli went on, 'since you'm now the stepson of my good old mate Murdoch Osborne, it puts a different slant on things altogether.'

Ah! So that was it. He'd gone up in the world. He was more acceptable now that he was Murdoch's stepson. Which actually surprised him – he would have thought that his mother's scandalously early marriage to Murdoch might have had the opposite effect. Well, indeed it might with some folk, but evidently not with Eli. He wondered what Harriet and Priss Meese thought of that aspect of the affair.

'What's more, I got no objection anymore to you being friendly with me daughter,' Eli continued. 'I just wanted you to know, that's all. Ever since you and she parted she's been mooching round our house with a face as long as a station platform. Don't know how best to cheer her up. That ain't to say as she's maudlin all the while. Sometimes she's bright enough, but the wench has got nothing to interest her much at the moment. Course, she needs another chap, somebody to perk up her interest in herself again. Young women do, you know, Algie. It's only natural, take it from me.' He took a quick slurp of his beer. 'Otherwise they go to seed. Pop round to our house sometime, young Algie, and see if you can't buck her up a bit.'

Algie smiled graciously, hiding his astonishment at receiving such an invitation. 'You never know, Mr Meese. I might just do that.'

'Any time. So how d'you reckon you'll take to living in Kingswinford?'

'It'll be further to travel to work.'

'Still got that bike?'

'Oh, yes. I've still got me bike.'

'Saves a fortune in tram fares and shoe leather, I shouldn't wonder.'

'Well, it'll be hard work pedalling all the way up to Dudley, but at least I'll be able to freewheel back.'

Eli even laughed. It was the first time Algie had ever seen the man laugh at all in his presence.

The parish of Kingswinford was somewhat different to Brierley Hill. Although only a couple of miles or so away, it was mostly green fields, small farms and big houses. One clay pit and a coal pit, the spoil of which seemed to be slowly encroaching down the hill from Pensnett, was still far enough away not to be seen. Kingswinford was devoid of the industry and its sulphurous smoke that hung over the Black Country so gruesomely. The village was where many of the successful, black-coated factory owners and merchants took up residence, a respite from the pit banks, the soot and the squalor where they spent their working hours and made their fortunes.

Badger House, Murdoch's home, promised a life of relative bucolic splendour, for he had done himself proud as a High

Street butcher. It was typical of Kingswinford's gracious style, suggesting rustic peace and quiet. This double-fronted gentleman's residence boasted a pillared porch and well-swept steps up to the glossy green-painted door. Algie saw it for the first time when the wedding party returned from the Bell Hotel. He thought how pleasant it must look in summer with its shrubbery of laurel and laburnum to the side, and a smooth lawn at the front, coated now in crunchy frost, with what looked like a pear tree set in the middle, yet sorry-looking in the grey cold of winter.

The maid, named Araminta, who opened the shining green door for them, was decidedly plain. Murdoch had previously described her as having a face like a pumpkin and figure like a bag of washing, and claimed she was engaged. The cook, Freda, was middle-aged, but could once have been a beauty and Algie assumed that she must have been married at some point. But he liked the servants, admired their conscientiousness, and was always appreciative and pleasant to them when they inevitably came into contact.

While the family's luggage was being brought in, they were shown to the sitting room at the rear, where French windows looked out onto a lawn that was host to more fruit trees; apple and damson. Beyond lay a field, lined with tall elms on one side, and a haystack in one corner, giving the distinct impression that it was closer to the countryside than to the collieries and ironworks.

Life seemed destined to settle quickly and easily into an agreeable routine at Badger House. Clara had never been used to servants, and felt no social superiority over them. Rather, she approached them with a certain deference. It was with guilt and some reticence that she began to give them their orders and they, in turn, recognised her awkwardness, which resulted in empathy between them. Kate on the other hand, immediately fell into the part into which she had been cast – the lady of the manor. She was only too eager to let them know that she considered herself way above them, and quickly established a lofty position in the domestic hierarchy.

On the evening of the second day of his marriage, Murdoch and Kate left the house together in his trap to attend the Brierley Hill Amateur Dramatics Society's rehearsal at the Drill Hall. Clara and Algie stayed at their new home, warm in front of a blazing fire, enjoying the novelty of the bright light that the gas lamps emitted. Clara was quietly planning what small changes she might make over the coming weeks to the décor, and arrangement of knick-knacks and furniture. That aspect had evidently been neglected during Murdoch's widowhood, and not since addressed with any enthusiasm by Araminta either.

Algie's bedroom overlooked the main road at the front of the house. Much as he relished the comforts of this house he dreaded bedtimes. He found himself lying in his cocoon listening for the creak of bedsprings from the room his mother now shared with Murdoch. It was torture. He hated to think of her being subjected to something that he believed she would not relish, putting up with it for the sake of gaining a roof over their heads. As far as he was concerned she had made the ultimate sacrifice, a sacrifice he would rather she had refused.

Such shenanigans would naturally occupy and preoccupy all young newly-weds, but the middle-aged . . . ? Surely not. So he tried to divert his attention with thoughts of Marigold. He wondered what she was doing, where she might be, how she felt now about their parting. Did she regret, by this time, running away? Was she as desperate to see him as he was to see her, or was he actually fading from her thoughts little by little, day by day? Come Saturday afternoon if he could, and certainly on Sunday before darkness fell, he would cycle along the likely stretches of canal to see if the Binghams were moored up anywhere, or at least ask if anybody had seen them. For his own peace of mind he had to know where he stood. Did Marigold still love him and want to be his wife, or was she so disenchanted with his antics that she would have nothing more to do with him? He had to find out. It was driving him mad.

He pondered Aurelia, too, as he lay in his new bed. And the more he pondered her, the stronger was the realisation that, against all expectations, and for some reason too obscure to fathom, she seemed to be interested in him. The way she had stood at her front door and waved him off with such apparent reluctance provided the clue, as did the way she held him so tenderly, encouraging him to share his grief over his father's death. Aurelia was no ordinary, uncaring person. She was a delightfully sensitive soul, but a soul he firmly believed was troubled, owned and overseen as she was by that over-bearing, undeserving, unsympathetic jackass who was her master. If only he had known her before the jackass. They would have been a perfect match for each other. Algie would have loved her, heart and soul, and she him. He was sure of it. But then he was deluding himself with silly, romantic daydreams, as he so often did. He could never have competed against the jackass's wealth and position . . . nor even his looks come to that; not realistically. Aurelia, therefore, was one who would have got away anyway . . . as Marigold almost certainly had.

And, in a way, so had Harriet. Yet things were different with Harriet. He had never truly desired her. He could hardly imagine her as a passionate creature, steeped as she was in the traditions of a Church that instilled into its flock that sex should be confined to the marriage bed, was primarily for the procreation of children, and discouraged as a recreational or enjoyable pastime. Harriet, however, was always good company, to her credit.

Algie made up his mind that Marigold, for all her lowly upbringing, was the ideal girl for him. If only he knew where she was. If only he could find her. When he did, he would smother her lovely face with kisses and confess how much he loved her till his tongue ached with fatigue.

But wasn't it strange how Eli Meese had invited him back into *his* home again . . . ?

Sunday came, and Algie rode his bike to the Stourbridge Canal, getting on the towpath at the Bottle and Glass, his first port of call. He asked Tom Simpson, the publican, whether he had seen anything of the Binghams.

'Aye, Seth Bingham was in here last Sunday.'

'Honest? Did you say anything to him?'

'He'd heard as your father passed away. He was sorry to learn of it, he reckoned.'

'Did he mention Marigold?'

'Not a word.'

'Did you see her?'

'Not that I know of. Ain't sure as I'd know her anyway.'

'Did Seth mention me?'

'Nothing.'

'Damn.'

'It slipped me mind altogether as you wanted to see Seth's daughter, young Algie,' Tom admitted. 'I'm real sorry. I should've said summat, but we was that busy it never crossed me mind.'

'Which way were they heading?'

'I couldn't tell yer.'

Well, if Marigold had been that way and he'd missed her,

maybe she'd called at the house and seen the note he'd left pinned to the door. He decided to go and ask the new lock-keeper if he knew anything.

So he wheeled under the bridge, dismounted, and rested his bike against the fence at the side of the towpath adjacent to the first lock. He walked across the lock gate and was surprised to see that there were no curtains up at the windows yet. Maybe the new family hadn't got round to hanging them. He clambered up the stone steps to the gate and opened it. It was a poignant moment for him. Already the garden, so diligently looked after by his father, looked dead and in want of care. He noticed a solitary rose, withering now after the early frosts had got to it. An omen, perhaps?

He looked at the back door. The letter he had left pinned to it was gone. The new lock-keeper would have removed it, of course. His heart lurched at the possibility that the man might have actually handed it to Marigold, that she might have actually called. He would enquire, just to be sure. So he knocked on the door.

No answer.

He knocked again.

Still no answer.

He stepped back and looked at the upstairs windows. They were grimy where rain had run down, leaving faint trails of soot from the atmosphere. Nobody had bothered to clean them. If his mother could see them now she would have a fit. It struck him that maybe nobody was living here yet after all, and he stepped over a flower bed to peer into a downstairs room. He wiped the window clear with his hand and peered inside.

It was just as they had left it.

Empty.

It made him angry that they had been ordered to leave this

house when it was patently not necessary, just to get rid of them. The consequences of that had been monstrous . . .

But Algie did not want to dwell on these things; what was done was done. He was heartened by the fact that his letter had gone. Maybe soon he would receive some message from Marigold through somebody. He would have to be patient; he was by no means certain from whom, or from which direction it would arrive. Nonetheless, not content just to sit and wait, he rode towards Kidderminster in an attempt to find her, before turning back and riding in the opposite direction to Dudley. As darkness fell, he made his way back tired, unsuccessful and heavy-hearted to Kingswinford.

It was Christmas Day. Marigold Bingham awoke, shivering in her bed in the freezing cabin of the *Odyssey*. The bitter cold made her realise that the stove had burnt out. She peered over the bedclothes at the cabin window to see if there was any sign of daylight yet, but it was difficult to tell how far the sombre dawn had progressed through the frosted-up window. As far as the weather went, it would be another grey day, with temperatures below freezing. In any case, there would be little to celebrate, Christmas Day or no. So she cuddled up to her younger sister for warmth and pulled the bedclothes over her head, anxious to sneak another few minutes before her mother came and roused them.

But too soon she heard her mother rapping the window. She rolled over and tried to shut out Hannah's voice by pulling her pillow over her head, but still she heard her stepping onto the gunwale and then rattling the door.

'Time to get up, you lot,' Hannah called. 'There's still work to be done even if it is Christmas Day.'

Rose, Marigold's sister, whose warmth she had been borrowing, was first to stir. She sat up in the bed, disturbing

Rachael, younger still, who complained of the biting cold, and disappeared immediately back under the bedclothes.

'Time to get up, our Marigold,' said Rose resignedly, in her croaky morning voice. 'We'll get no peace till we do.'

Marigold pushed back the bedclothes and swung her legs out of bed. At once the clinging, clammy cold stung her all over like needles, and she huddled inside her nightdress. Her teeth began to chatter. She reached for the thick dressing gown hanging on the door of the cabin, a garment which had been handed down from her mother, then opened the stove, raked out the ashes and laid a new fire. As she struck the match to light it, she shook with shivering. Her teeth were still chattering and her breath was rising up in steam. But it would be some time yet before they felt the benefit of the stove.

'I wonder what time it is,' she said. 'Oh, it's so damned cold.'

Hannah returned, opened the door and entered. She was fully dressed and had a shawl around her shoulders. 'My God, it's freezing in here. You'll catch your deaths. There's warm water to wash yourselves in the *Sultan* and the stove's hot, so get yourselves round there as soon as you can. I'm doing bacon and eggs for your breakfasts.'

The aroma of frying bacon wafted in, on the icy, foggy air.

'I can smell it, Mother,' Marigold said.

Then it hit her; the morning's first wave of nausea. Already it was agonisingly familiar to her. Suddenly she felt hot, and a white mist seemed to blur her vision. She felt the urgent need to retch, and rushed past her mother who was at once indignant at being shoved out of the way so abruptly. Marigold leaned over the stern and vomited, hardly noticing the piercing frost attacking her small bare hands as she held on to the tiller for support. Again she retched.

'Is that our Marigold being sick again?' It was Rose's voice, evidently resigned to the frequency of the occurrence.

Marigold felt instantly better, except for the bitter taste of bile that lingered in her mouth. With her head bowed she pushed past her mother. She wiped her mouth with the back of her hand and sat down on the cross-bed, her head in her hands, anticipating Hannah's torrent of insults, for she must realise, as well as Marigold herself understood from this display, just what this symptom meant. So far she had been able to hide it. Up till now her retching into the canal had been accomplished in relative privacy, save, obviously, for the ears and eyes of Rose.

'You lot,' Hannah said sternly. 'Out. Go to your father right away. I want a word with our Marigold.'

As Rose and her siblings wrapped themselves up for the icy jaunt between the two boats, Marigold concealed the tears that were now trickling down her cheeks, her face hidden in her hands. This nausea, this symptom of her pregnancy, had been plaguing her since the onset of the cold snap at the end of November. At first she'd put it down to the weather; the shivering, the hot flushes and feeling that she was going to faint, the awful vomiting that always followed. How it unsettled your system. It didn't take long for her to realise it had nothing to do with the weather.

Marigold decided to try and escape too, and she dragged herself outside, defiantly pushing past her mother again in an effort to delay the inevitable onslaught. She clambered over the gunwale onto the narrow towpath, following her younger sisters. A freezing fog had fallen and a deathly silence surrounded them. The hedge that divided the canal from the Great Central Railway line, which ran alongside, was coated in a grey-white rime, as were the rails. One thing Marigold did notice was that the *Odyssey* did not rise in the water as she stepped off it; it was trapped in a layer of ice.

Willoughby Wharf on the Oxford Canal, roughly halfway

between Rugby and Daventry, was already frozen over to at least an inch thick, and no sign of a let-up in the grisly weather. If the ice thickened much more it would be impossible to gain access to the Grand Union Canal tomorrow, let alone shoot off on the southern arm of the Oxford, where the Binghams were to offload the coal they were transporting from the Black Country's pits. Despite her preoccupation with her condition, she couldn't help wondering whether the canal company would be able to bring out the icebreakers on Christmas Day. If not, they could be held up for days at Willoughby Wharf, and even weeks if there was no let-up.

'Marigold!' Hannah called. 'Come here, I said I wanted a word with you. D'you hear?'

Marigold halted in her tracks, dithering in the cold, and looked at her mother forlornly. Resigned to receiving a lambasting, she walked slowly back to the *Odyssey* and entered the cabin.

A spare dressing gown, a child's, was hanging on the back of the door. Hannah took it and offered it to Marigold.

'Put this round you as well. You'll catch your death.'

Marigold allowed her mother to wrap it around her shoulders caringly, and shivered again, glancing at the stove. Smoke, like animated hanks of grey wool, was being drawn up the chimney pipe as the coals ignited. Pray God they would soon benefit from some warmth.

She looked at her mother with fearful eyes. This kind gesture with the old dressing gown must be the lull before the storm. The moment of retribution was finally upon her. There was no escape. Her mother knew her guilty secret.

'Well, this is a fine Christmas box and no two ways.'

Marigold nodded, just perceptibly, and shuddered with a profound sigh of apprehension.

'How long have you been getting the morning sickness, eh?'

320

'About a month,' Marigold answered, as honestly as she could.

'And you guessed right away what was causing it?'

'Nearly right away.'

'Then you must have guessed about the same time as I did.'

'You knew?'

'Course I knew. And if I knew, you must've known yourself, I kept telling myself. I was waiting for you to come and tell me. Why didn't you?'

Marigold shrugged under the two dressing gowns. ''Cause I was ashamed. 'Cause I was afeared you'd go mad.'

'Oh, our Marigold . . .' Hannah put a comforting arm around her daughter's shoulder and gave her a hug.

Marigold sniffed and wiped another tear that had run down her cheek, prompted by her mother's gentle kindness, so unexpected. She could not understand why, so far, she was getting off so lightly. 'Well, what made *you* think I might be carrying a child?' she asked, hoping to glimpse the mysterious ways mothers have of divining such things.

'We generally *see* at the same time o' the month, you and me, our Marigold – and our Rose come to that – but the last couple of times I've noticed that you ain't bled when I have. There's been nothing in your drawers, has there? I haven't seen a clout from you in weeks. I *am* your mother. I can't help but notice.' Hannah looked hard at Marigold, a look which she caught.

Marigold put her hands to her face again, in shame and embarrassment. 'Did you know all along, then, that me and Algie . . . ?'

'I mostly do your washing, our Marigold. I do see your dirty drawers . . . You only have to put two and two together. I suppose it can only be Algie Stokes's child?'

'It couldn't be nobody else's, Mother, and that's a fact.'

'Oh, our Marigold . . .' Hannah sighed profoundly, entirely sympathetic to her daughter's dilemma. 'And you've fell out with him.'

'I know.' Marigold was moved to further tears by this unanticipated commiseration. She felt so small, so pathetic, yet so guilty.

'You'll have to let him know, somehow,' Hannah said kindly.

'I know . . .' She sighed again. 'I would, if I knew where to find him. Don't forget as his father passed away and they've been kicked out of their house, by all accounts.'

'We'll find him some way or another. Let's just hope he hasn't got off with some other young woman, since you was so keen to shun him. It'd serve you right for being so pig-headed if he had. I don't believe for a minute as he was interested in anybody else when you thought he was.'

'Nor me, Mother. Not really. Not now. Not now I've had time to think about it. I thought he was seeing a girl called Harriet Meese, but now I know he couldn't have – not in the way I thought.'

'And didn't it cross your mind that you might be carrying?'

Marigold shook her head, tears falling onto Hannah's shoulder. 'I never thought it would happen to me, and he always said as how careful he was. I never expected you'd be this easy about it, neither. I always thought you'd rant and rave if I got meself in the family way afore I ever got wed.'

'Ah, well,' Hannah replied softly. 'I'll let you into a secret. I was like you once. I got into trouble as well when I was about your age – it was you I was carrying – but I wasn't as lucky as you. The chap I'd been with could never marry me, you see. My family took it out on me. They disowned me. And after what I went through, I knew I could never do that to my own daughter, no matter what.'

Marigold raised her head in wide-eyed astonishment. 'Are you telling me that me dad's not me father?'

Clara stroked Marigold's hair tenderly and nodded. 'That's right, my flower. I never imagined breaking it to you like this, but no, Seth isn't your real father. Yet he's always been a father to you. Always remember that.'

Marigold was stunned at this news, forgetting for the moment her own difficulty. She'd had no inkling ever that Seth was not her father; it was something she'd never pondered, and it came as a complete shock. She fell quiet for some seconds, pondering the fact, trying to come to terms with it. Wrapped in her mother's embrace for these epic minutes, she hardly noticed the cold and the freezing fog that was pervading all, the water that looked like lead covered in frost's coarse white powder as it froze solid in the wharf.

'Don't you want to know who your real father is?' Hannah asked eventually.

'Would I know him?'

'No.'

Marigold looked into Hannah's eyes and shook her head. 'So what does it matter?' she answered typically. 'Whoever he is, he never cared about me or you, did he, by the sound of it? Why should I care about him? As far as I'm concerned, Seth's me dad. I love him. That's enough for me.'

Hannah gave her another hug and smiled thankfully to herself. 'Yes, maybe it's better that way . . . In the meantime, what about young Algie Stokes? Do you still want him, our Marigold? D'you still love him?'

'With all my heart and soul, Mother. As long as I live there'll never be another chap for me. But he might not want me anymore now . . .'

'That's something we shan't know till we find him.' She gave her daughter another hug. 'But it's my belief as he should face up to his responsibilities once we do find him.' Hannah sighed, growing even more sympathetic to Marigold's plight. 'D'you reckon you can face some breakfast now, afore it's ruined?'

Marigold nodded and managed a smile. 'I'll try, Mother . . . Had we better tell the others yet that I'm having a baby?'

'Why not? They'll find out soon enough. Might as well be open about it. Let me tell your dad first, though, when we'm on our own.'

Flames licked around the coals in the stove, and already its precious warmth was perceptible in the intense, damp cold.

'There's still work to be done today, our Marigold,' Hannah said, as they rose from the bed on which they had been sitting. 'Your dad's already got the mangle and the dolly tub out. Providing the pump over at the Navigation ain't froze up, there's washing to be done.'

'I'll help you with it, Mother.'

'No need, if you don't feel up to it. We gotta look after you good and proper now. Our Rose and our Rachael can help instead. They'm gunna have to do more jobs now.'

'Fancy having to do your washing on Christmas Day,' Marigold sighed as they stepped off the *Odyssey* together. 'Not like some o' them swells in their nice houses with their feet up in front of a nice warm fire, I bet, with maids to do all their work.'

Hannah smiled. 'I remember days like that,' she said as they stepped side-by-side along the narrow towpath to the *Sultan*, moored fore of the *Odyssey*. 'I remember living ever so comfortable in a warm house with roaring coal fires, and Christmas dinners with all the family there . . .'

'Drying washing will be a nightmare,' said Marigold thoughtfully, unheeding her mother's reminiscences. 'Especially if we'm stuck here in the ice. I can't remember a colder winter, Mother, can you? I mean, 'specially afore Christmas.'

'Eighty-two was bad, as I recall. Don't you remember? We was froze up at Northampton for weeks. We lost a load of money . . . Seth!' she called. 'We're coming for our breakfasts now. Can you put two eggs on to fry?'

'Just afore we go in, Mother . . .' Marigold checked Hannah, holding her back gently by her arm. 'Thank you for being so good about me carrying this child . . . I'm sure I don't deserve it. I was expecting you to go mad.'

'What'd be the point of me going mad? You need our love and care at a time like this, our Marigold, not our condemnation.'

Seth appeared from the cabin of the *Sultan*, a grin on his face as he stood by the tiller. 'I should get in here quick, afore this lot o' greedy buggers scoff all the bacon . . .'

'There's plenty more,' Hannah affirmed. 'Why don't you go and see whether the pump's froze at the Navigation?'

'Aye, in a minute,' he said. 'When you'n had your bre'fasses. I'll go to the stables as well and see to Victoria. That poor hoss'll want some fresh fittles and a drink o' wairter.'

'That poor hoss'll be froze,' said Hannah. 'Throw that old rug over him, Seth. It'll help to keep him warm. In fact, I'll walk over to the pump with you. There's something I want to tell you . . .'

Chapter 20

'I still can't get over Algie Stokes's mother marrying Murdoch Osborne, you know, Harriet, so soon after poor Mr Stokes's death,' Priss said as they were walking to the Drill Hall. 'I think it's a scandal.'

Each was swathed in a scarf and a winter hat and mantle to keep out the awful cold, as well as muffs to keep their hands warm. The festive season had long since passed, but the bitter cold weather lingered on.

'Maybe she just fancied having somebody to cuddle up to in bed at night, to keep her warm,' Harriet replied dismissively, as much to defend Algie's name as his mother's. She adjusted her hat to deflect the cold wind from her face. 'Lord knows, you need some protection from this weather, and a warming pan isn't so soft and cuddly.'

'But that's the form of a girl of nineteen, not a woman of two- or three-and-forty, or however old she is.'

'Of course, you're an authority on cuddling up to a lover in bed, aren't you, Priss?' Harriet bantered with measured sarcasm.

'Oh, thank you, dear sister,' Priss responded, feigning sweetness. 'How succinctly you put things.'

'Because you're the epitome of all that's stiff-necked and straight-laced, that's why.'

'And you are not? Anyway, I still maintain that Clara Stokes should not have married Murdoch Osborne so soon after her husband's death. Why, it almost looks as if they'd been having an affair before the poor devil passed on, and she couldn't wait to get her feet up at *his* hearth.'

Harriet shook her head. 'Oh, I don't think so, Priss. I really don't. Clara would never go out at night – she was scared. When else would they have met to conduct an affair? And not only when, but where? In the back of his butcher's shop with all that raw meat? In any case, even though I felt shocked – as you do – when I first heard about it from Father, I've since altered my opinion. I think it was quite a sensible thing to do. She's had the sense to grasp an opportunity. At least the poor woman will have some security in her old age when Algie and Kate have fled the nest. Anyway, Algie and Kate couldn't have objected too strongly either, else she wouldn't have done it, I'm sure.'

'Well, I don't approve of second marriages in any case,' said Priss. 'Nothing would induce me to contract a second marriage.'

'Time enough to muse over a second marriage once you've pulled off the first,' Harriet quipped.

'All the same,' Priss went on, ignoring the sisterly taunt, 'I'd be inclined to have nothing to do with Algie ever again if I were you, even if he does come calling, as Father has so indiscreetly invited him to do. You don't want any of that embarrassment reflecting on you. There's bound to be gossip. Considerable gossip. In fact, if Father were not a friend of Murdoch Osborne, I would strongly advise Mother to avoid his shop and buy our meat elsewhere. Maybe we should avoid the amateur dramatics society, too, for fear of our own characters being tainted.'

'Oh, don't be silly, Priss. You take things too far. Talk is so cheap. It'll be just another nine-day wonder.'

'Well, I've a mind to ask the sweet and beautiful Miss Stokes what she thinks of the affair.'

'You would never.'

'Why not? I'm sure she'd love to air her views. Who else has she got to air them to now that the equally sweet and beautiful Mr Froggatt has cast her aside? By the way, have you seen Clarence Froggatt lately?'

Harriet felt herself go hot, and was glad that the darkness of the night concealed her blushes from her sister. 'As a matter of fact, I have,' she admitted, feigning nonchalance.

'You've kept that quiet. So tell me.'

'I was coming out of the circulating library as he was going in . . .'

'Go on . . . Tell me more . . . Well, why are you hesitating, Harriet?'

'Because . . . he asked to see me.'

'And you haven't mentioned it before? Harriet, fancy not telling me. You're the limit. I take it you said yes?'

'Of course I said yes.'

'So when are you seeing him?'

'Saturday. He's taking me to the Public Hall at the Mechanics' Institute in Dudley. The Netherton Amateur Dramatics Society is staging a play. And Father has given me permission to go.'

'You dark horse! I'm certain you wouldn't have said anything if I hadn't dragged it out of you.'

They reached the Drill Hall. A fire was burning in the stove, a magnet for the chilled souls who had shown up already, standing dithering under the rafters in that bare, echoing room. Murdoch Osborne followed them in with Kate Stokes; a natural arrangement, Harriet realised, since he was married to her mother now and they lived in the same house.

Kate made a beeline for the two sisters. They discussed the

bleakness of the weather, of course, and the fact that the Meeses' tap had frozen up, before Kate announced what she'd been itching to tell them.

'I've made up my mind that I want to become a professional actress on the London stage. The only problem is, my mother and my new stepfather are dead against it.'

'Your new stepfather?' Harriet glanced at Priss. 'That sounds impressive, Kate. Of course, he has your best interests at heart, I'm sure. Still, we shall miss you like the devil if you go.'

'The thing is,' Kate went on, 'I think I've got a lot to offer the acting profession. The way I go about it. I mean, considering I ain't proper trained, my stepfather says I'm a natural. If nothing else, I reckon that gives me an edge over actors and actresses what am trained. I approach a character in a different way to what they do, you see. Take this part I'm playing in *The Three Temptations* for inst—'

'I can understand your mother's, and your new stepfather's concerns, though Kate,' Harriet interrupted. 'Actresses are not considered the most reputable of women.'

'Oh, tittle to that, Harriet. I want to bring something new to acting – a new way . . . with pride . . . and honour. Why should I be looked on as a woman of disrepute when I want to invent nice new ways?'

'It's a remarkable thing when you come to think of it, Kate,' Priss interrupted, 'that it should be left to you – what ain't trained – to invent acting.'

'But other women have acted before,' argued Kate. 'So I obviously didn't invent it.'

'Oh, but you're missing the point,' retorted Priss. 'You see, inventors often take old ideas that have always been there, and apply them in ways that have never been tried before. Like you intend.'

'Quite true,' asserted Harriet, with a convincing gravitas

that spoke volumes for her own acting ability. 'I've never heard the role of an inventor more succinctly described. And you must certainly be considered one of them. Has it occurred to you that ever since the days of the enduring Polly, people have been putting the kettle on with tedious regularity, yet it was reserved for James Watt to discover the particular useful-ness of boiling water?'

'I can't say I ever thought about it.'

'Well, there you are, you see. You should consider yourself something akin to a female James Watt, since you have invented a new principle in acting, in the same way that he invented steam. Nobody really knew anything about your code of acting until you came into the business. So we're spot on when we say that you invented it.'

Kate smiled patiently. If Harriet and Priss were being sarcastic she was no judge as to their motive; if, on the other hand, they were trying to be witty, Kate felt it was far more useful to be pretty than witty, and better still to be a pretty actress. She was quite content on that score; she possessed something that patently neither of those two girls had in any measure. The Meese girls could never aspire to prettiness, or acting ability.

Harriet turned to Priss with a mischievous sparkle in her eye. 'By the way, Priss, would you rather invent a husband or discover one?'

Priss rolled her eyes dismissively. 'Women don't invent or discover husbands. They meet them out, or get introduced to them after church, or at weddings.'

'And all the better if they're a *somebody*,' Harriet remarked.

'Well, let's face it, dear Harriet, you wouldn't want to marry a nobody,' Priss replied. 'Fancy if you were really somebody and you were introduced to a nobody, and you were silly enough to marry him, and his common relatives all turned up. That's why I rather like our curate, because he has a whole cupboard full of glorious ancestors who aren't a bit common.'

'When I go in for a husband,' Harriet said, warming to the change of theme, 'I shall prove you completely wrong, Priss, and discover him, after the manner of Sir Walter Raleigh and the tobacco plant.'

'Oh, and he will trample all over you, after the manner of Sir Walter Raleigh and the cloak,' countered Priss with mocking laughter.

Kate sighed impatiently. 'I think we ought to be sitting down ready,' she said. 'My stepfather looks as if he's ready to begin.'

'By the way, Kate,' Priss said. 'How do you feel about your mother re-marrying so soon after losing your father?' She felt a nudge in the ribs from Harriet for being tactless.

'Well,' replied Kate thoughtfully, anxious to say the right thing, 'I don't think anything would ever tempt me to wed a second time . . . no matter how many husbands I lost. But it was her own decision.'

'By the way, Kate,' Priss said, smothering her amusement. 'Harriet bumped into Clarence Froggatt in the week. He's taking her to the Public Hall in Dudley on Saturday to see a play . . .'

'Harriet Meese is going to the Public Hall in Dudley on Saturday night,' Kate mentioned to Murdoch as they drove home to Kingswinford in his gig after rehearsal. 'There's a play on.'

'Who's going with her, ha?' Murdoch asked. 'Priss, or her father? He ain't mentioned nothing to me about it.'

'I don't know,' Kate lied. 'But I'd like to go as well,' she said, pulling up the collar of her mantle to keep out the bitter cold wind. 'I'd like to see some other actors and actresses at work. I think it would do me good to watch others acting.'

'Well, the experience would do you no harm,' Murdoch replied.

'Couldn't you take me, Murdoch? I mean to say, you'd enjoy it as well.'

'What's the play called?'

'I got no idea. All the same, I'd love to see it.'

'We'll ask your mother if she wants to go. If she fancies a night out, then we'll all go.'

'She won't go, Murdoch,' Kate predicted scornfully. 'Not me mother. She never wants to shift from the fire. 'Specially in this weather. But you and me could go.'

'Well, I'll ask her anyway. It's only right, ha? If she don't mind us two going off on our own, then I'll be happy to take you.'

'She won't go, I can tell you that for nothing. Didn't you know she won't go out at night for fear of being run over? She's afeared of horses taking fright. You'd never get her in this gig either, for the same reason, in case the horse took fright.'

'Well, that's daft,' Murdoch stated. 'You can't live your life in fear that summat might happen, when the odds are that it wouldn't.'

Kate smiled with self-satisfaction in the darkness. 'You try telling her that. Anyway, fancy you and my mother used to go courting together when you was young,' she said. 'You could've knocked me over when she told us.'

'It was a long time ago.'

'Was you in love with her then?'

'Me? I was mad about your mother when she was a young woman. It cut me to the quick when she broke it off with me and started seeing your father instead. I don't think I ever got over it proper.'

'Ah, well, you got her in the end.'

'Except that your father copped for the best of her . . . when she was young and beautiful. She's still a nice-looking woman, mind. You remind me of her a lot when she was your age, Kate, my flower . . . Did I tell you before, ha?'

The following evening, while Clara was waiting for her new husband to return from his butchering, she went to the kitchen to see if she could be of any help to Freda the cook. A tray of liver faggots was roasting in the oven and smelled delicious, and Freda was just about to slide in a tray of jam tarts.

'I just wondered if I could be of help?' Clara asked hesitantly.

'Oh, you needn't trouble yourself about coming to help me, ma'am,' Freda tried to assure her. ' 'Tain't your place to sully your hands in here, ma'am.'

Clara smiled patiently. Being referred to as 'ma'am' was patronising, she felt; she couldn't be sure whether the servants were being sarcastic. 'I'm sure you realise, Freda, as I've never been used to having servants, and especially a cook to do my husband's dinner. It's something that I always did myself when my Will was alive.'

Freda, fearing that her position in the household could be in jeopardy if the new Mrs Osborne insisted on cooking her husband's dinner herself, retaliated with an argument that she had already considered and rehearsed in her head in anticipation of this conversation. 'But it ain't just one person to cook for nowadays, is it, ma'am? I mean to say, there's your son and your daughter to feed besides. And not only them . . . there's young Araminta and meself to feed, an' all. We all need feeding. It's too much to expect the lady of the house to contend with . . . And besides, I've always been used to it. I'm trained in it.'

'Did Mr Osborne's first wife ever offer to help, Freda?'

'Never set foot nowhere near the kitchen, ma'am. Mind you, she was sick for years.'

'How's Araminta coping with the extra work? Does she say?'

'Why don't you ask her? She used to give me a hand when she'd got a minute. Trouble is, now she ain't got a minute. Mebbe you ought to consider setting on another maid to help her.'

'Yes, it's a thought,' Clara agreed. 'There must be a lot of extra work now with us here. I'll talk to my husband about it.' She heard the sound of horse's hoofs and the rattle of wheels outside, and knew that Murdoch had returned, conveying Kate with him, for Kate always called at the butcher's shop when she'd finished work at the bakery shop. A ride home saved her precious legs. 'He's back now. I'll go and mention it right away.'

Murdoch and Kate entered the hallway through the front door just as Clara came in from the kitchen. She smiled at him, took his hat and scarf and hung them on the hall stand.

'It's cold enough to freeze the tail off a brass monkey, ha?' he commented. 'My fingers are tingling with cold, holding them reins.'

'Come and warm yourself up by the fire, Murdoch,' Clara suggested, 'before you catch your death.'

'My poor cheeks will be all dry with this weather,' Kate complained. 'And my nose feels as if it's about to drop off.'

'Come and sit by the fire,' her mother urged.

'No, I'll get chilblains and mottled legs if I get too close to the fire. I daren't have mottled legs, Mother. You never know when I might have to show them.'

'I should hope you don't show them anybody.'

'In a play, I mean,' Kate replied impatiently.

Clara followed Murdoch and Kate into the sitting room where a coal fire burned brightly in the big marble grate. 'Murdoch, I've just been talking to Freda. She reckons Araminta's rushed off her feet with all the extra work she's got, now that me and our Kate and our Algie are living here. I was wondering if we should engage another young maid to help her out.'

'I don't see why not, Clara,' Murdoch replied generously. 'A young wench of twelve or thirteen wouldn't cost a lot, ha? No more than ten or twelve pounds a year. See to it, Clara, my love.'

Clara smiled at his amenability. 'I will. She'll be pleased at the news.'

'How long's our dinner going to be?' he asked.

'Not long. Nearly done, I think. We could sit at the table ready, if you like.'

'I'll just run up the yard afore I take me mantle off,' Kate said. 'Mind you, it's enough to freeze you in that privy. It's a pity we can't have an inside privy, you know, Murdoch. Lots of houses like this have got inside privies these days.'

'Unhygienic in the house,' Murdoch claimed. 'Not to mention the stink, ha?'

'But they have water closets now. Water closets don't stink.'

Kate made her exit and Murdoch sat in his favourite chair in front of the fire. 'There's a play on at the Public Hall in Dudley, Saturday night, Clara. I wondered if you fancy going to see it. Kate said she'd like to go, and I'd like to as well. Fancy going?'

'On Saturday?' she queried, stalling to give a positive answer.

'Yes, Saturday. We'd have to go by tram though, since there's only room for one passenger in the gig.' That should clinch it, Murdoch believed.

'No, you and our Kate go, Murdoch, and take the gig. I

wouldn't dream of going out of a night in this weather anyway. I'd rather stop warm by the fire.'

'Pity,' he said. 'Funny, but Kate reckoned as you wouldn't want to shift from the hearth. Why won't you go out at night, Clara? You always used to love it, as I recall.'

'Me? I see no pleasure in it these days, Murdoch. I'm content to stop here and enjoy this house. It's a sight more comfortable than any public hall. And I don't feel the need for company like I used to when I was young. I like me own company, and the company of me husband and family. But if you and our Kate want to go to see this play, then you go. With my blessing.'

Murdoch was inclined to reason with his new wife after what Kate had told him about her fear, but decided it was pointless yet. Some other time, perhaps.

When Algie Stokes left work that Saturday afternoon, he cycled towards the Meeses' dwelling with the intention of calling on Harriet. Well, Eli had given him permission now that he'd gone up in the world. He'd had it in mind to start seeing a bit more of Harriet himself – for a bit of female company, of course – nothing more . . .

As he rode, he pondered his dissatisfaction at the way his new job was developing. More and more, Benjamin was shutting him out of decision making, no longer seeking his opinions now that the necessary prototype Sampson bicycle was ready. He had not even invited Algie to ride it – his own creation – to evaluate it and compare it with the Swift which he knew so well. Sampson's were already training men in how to assemble them; they were making the necessary jigs and tools. They had set aside an area of the factory for production, and constructed a new loading bay to receive the incoming materials.

Should he be bold and make his feelings known, but risk appearing impertinent and perhaps ungrateful? He was, after all, earning more money as an employee than he had before. Yet where was the contentment? Benjamin Sampson had stolen his idea, used it, and was overseeing it as if it were his own brainchild. He was already spending a lot of time travelling the country, visiting wholesalers and shops to promote the product. Benjamin was reaping the glory, the recognition for being a man of vision, and ultimately the profit. Besides, it galled Algie that the swine was also married to a girl as lovely as Aurelia . . .

Algie had to pedal the last part of the journey, dodging random mounds of horse droppings and tram lines, as well as erratic pedestrians who veered unpredictably into the gutter from the pavements to avoid bumping into other shoppers and their baskets, for Brierley Hill High Street was always at its busiest on a Saturday. He stopped outside Eli Meese's drapery, mourning and mantles emporium and rested his bike against the wall in the entry. He peered inside the shop window to see if Harriet was working, but saw no sign of her, so he knocked at the side door in the entry.

Priss answered it. 'Oh, it's you.'

'Hello, Priss. Is Harriet in?'

'She is, but not looking her glamorous best at present. I'm crimping her hair ready for tonight.'

'Well, can I come in? I'm sure she won't mind seeing me, now your father has allowed it.'

'Yes, you've had a special dispensation, haven't you?' Priss called into the house and asked if she should allow Algie in. Harriet answered that she should. He followed her inside, with the feeling that Priss had no intention of making him welcome.

'Forgive me if I don't get up,' Harriet said in greeting.

'Quite all right. I can see you're a mite handicapped. How are you?'

'Very well, Algie, thank you. I thought it was nice of my father to relent and allow you to visit me again, don't you?'

'Well, it seems I've gone up in the world since my mother remarried. At least it's brought me that benefit.'

'We'd expected you sooner,' Priss commented, resuming the tending of Harriet's mousey tresses. 'Especially since your boat girl has given you up.'

'How's your work going?' Harriet enquired, frowning at Priss through the mirror placed before them. 'All this business with the new bicycles? . . . You can sit down, you know.'

Algie shrugged and sat down on the nearest chair. 'I can't say as I'm enjoying work much at the minute,' he answered glumly.

'Oh?'

'I've had my nose pushed out, to tell you the truth. But what can I do about it?'

'Nothing from your position, I suspect,' Harriet said sympathetically. 'But what a shame, after you put in all the hard work. It's a pity you couldn't have done it all off your own bat, so to speak, isn't it?'

'Yes, it's what I wanted to do, but I hadn't got the money. I still haven't.'

'Pity your new stepfather doesn't set you up, Algie,' Priss remarked experimentally, to elicit his reaction, while applying curling tongues to Harriet's hair. 'I'm sure he could afford it. D'you think he would?'

'I dunno. But I wouldn't ask him anyway.'

'Oh? Don't you like him?' she fished.

'He's all right, I suppose.'

'Quite a change of life for you, Algie,' she went on, 'your mother remarrying so soon after your poor father's death. What did you think about that?'

'I wasn't very struck on the idea, to tell you the truth. I would rather she'd waited a respectable amount of time. Folks talk, you know, Priss.'

'Oh, I know they do. Me? I can't abide gossip.'

'Sticks and stones,' Harriet piped up from behind a curtain of hair that was now covering her face. 'It had nothing to do with anybody else, so why should anybody else concern themselves? Anyway, I suspect your mother was merely trying to look after her own future, and I don't blame her one bit. After all, you and Kate are not going to be with her always, are you? I mean to say, you'll very likely wed at some time, and Kate is on about becoming an actress on the London stage, though I hope she sees sense eventually. Where would that leave your poor mother?'

'I know what you mean. I've thought about that . . . Anyway, Harriet, I came to ask if you fancied going out tonight.'

Harriet was thankful her hair was still hiding her face. 'I, er . . . That's very nice of you to ask, Algie . . .'

'But?'

'But I can't.'

'Because she's already going out,' Priss said smugly.

'Oh? Where to?'

'To, er . . . To the Public Hall in Dudley . . . to see a play.'

'Didn't you know, Algie?' Priss enquired with gleeful satisfaction. 'Clarence Froggatt's taking her.'

'Shut up, Priss, I'm well able to explain for myself.'

Priss took a comb and pulled it through her sister's hair, away from her face. Harriet looked appropriately self-conscious, and Algie saw she was blushing.

He looked at both girls with astonishment and incredulity. 'You're going out with Clarence Froggatt?'

'Yes, I am,' she said sheepishly. 'He asked me on Monday

and I said I would. I didn't see any harm in it. I didn't realise you would bother to ask me.'

'But you know his reputation . . .'

'Is it any more fearful than yours, Algie?' parried Priss. 'From what I hear of it, you're as bad as each other. People in glass houses . . . What you ought to have realised by now, Algie, is that women don't really care very much what the men they fancy have been up to previously, nor who with, as long as they're clean and particular . . . How is your sister, by the way, since she and Clarence broke up?'

Algie shrugged. 'What's that got to do with anything?'

'Just curious.'

'She seems all right. I don't think she was that bothered. She was more upset over my father's death . . . Oh, and the fact that Clarence was callous enough to give her up on the very night Father died,' he added, relishing the opportunity to get in another dig about the unworthy Clarence. 'To my mind, that's not the mark of a gentleman.'

'Kate seems to have taken well to your new stepfather anyway,' Priss suggested.

'Yes, it seems like it. They get on quite well . . . So, Harriet . . . D'you think this is likely to become a regular thing, you and Clarence Froggatt?' He pronounced the name with some disdain.

'How do I know?' Harriet responded. 'But I quite like Clarence. I always have. I might well see him again if he asks me.'

He sighed frustratedly. 'Just be careful of Clarence Froggatt, Harriet. Otherwise you might come to a sticky end.'

'A sticky end?' echoed Priss, savouring the words. She flashed a mischievous glance at her sister through the mirror facing them. 'Ooh . . . Algernon makes the prospect of a sticky end sound quite exciting, doesn't he, our Harriet?'

Chapter 21

Seeing Clarence Froggatt again at the play stirred up some unwelcome emotions in Kate Stokes, emotions which surprised and confused her. It was hard for her to acknowledge that Clarence being there was as much a trigger to attend as was the actual play. Such an admission would suggest that she still harboured feelings for him. All she would admit was that it stuck in her craw that he had had the effrontery to give her up, rather than the other way round.

Priss had not been teasing her when she announced that he had invited Harriet to go with him. Well, it was likely to end up being much more than a night at the theatre, if she knew him. Kate had lain with him, knew him better than his own mother did, and now she envied Harriet. She dearly wished she could stand beside Harriet Meese, wearing this blue dress she had on, so that he could compare them, and see who was by far the better-looking. It was the blue dress with the low décolletage, which she had worn that first night she had allowed him to seduce her in the doctor's house. She looked her best in it; she was at her most desirable. She desperately wanted to flaunt her attributes and rub Clarence's nose in it, to let him see just what he was missing, and make him suffer. If he wantonly drooled for her, so much the better. To think he had thrown her over, and was now mooning over a girl who was not in any way pretty, irked her beyond endurance. Serve Harriet right if she won him back . . .

At the interval, Kate decided she must visit the ladies' room, as much for the novelty of actually using a water closet as anything else, although nature was pressing her a little and would be even more later if she didn't go. She excused herself while Murdoch remained in his seat, and made for the rear of the auditorium. As she approached, she spotted Harriet standing at the head of a queue which had very quickly formed, and decided she would give it a miss for now. So she turned around, content that the girl had not seen her. However, just as she got back inside the auditorium, Clarence was approaching and she almost bumped into him before she saw him.

'Goodness! Clarry!' she exclaimed, feigning surprise as great as his to meet thus.

'Katie . . . Well . . . how good to see you.'

'I was just on my way to the water closet, but I ain't waiting in that queue,' she said by way of casual conversation to explain her presence on that very spot. 'You should see it. You'd think they'd put more of 'em in a public building, when there are so many women dying to go.'

He laughed at her typical forthrightness. 'Yes, you'd think so.'

'So the first public building you design, Clarry, make sure you allow for plenty of water closets for the women.'

'Oh, I will, and that's a promise.' His eyes scanned her up and down as he smiled. 'You're looking very well, Kate.'

'Thank you.' She smiled with satisfaction at his compliment. 'So are you.'

'I was so sorry to hear of your father passing away.'

'Were you?' she answered, unconvinced. She'd been waiting for this moment, to let him know how she felt about the way he'd treated her just prior to her father's death. 'The way you were that night I got the feeling you couldn't have cared less. That night of all nights.'

'I feel badly about that. I'd hoped you might have forgiven me.'

'Your timing was rotten, Clarence.'

'I know . . .' He scratched his head, embarrassed. 'You must realise, Kate, that it had not sunk in with me that your father was so ill. I was a little preoccupied that night. The possibility that you might be about to lose him just didn't register.'

'Fancy,' she said, trying hard to stifle her indignation, but to no avail. 'Well, it was nice of you to come back after and offer your condolences. It was nice of you to go to his funeral.'

'I am sorry, Kate. I would've, but I felt such a bounder. I really couldn't face you. I felt such a cad. As for the funeral . . . well, I make it a point never to attend the funerals of my father's patients. It's rather a bad advertisement for him, you see. People know me as his son, don't they? We could hardly have folk saying, "Oh, look, there's Doctor Froggatt's son again. Another of his patients has kicked the bucket. We'd better change to another doctor". It could ruin him and his reputation.'

Kate managed a smile as she accepted his logic. 'Well, I reckon you could've made an exception in my father's case. Still, it's done now. It's history, as they say . . . Harriet told me you were bringing her here tonight. I haven't seen her, though,' she said innocently. 'Are you sure she's here?'

'Oh, yes. She's here all right. I fancy she's paying a visit to the water closet, like you were.'

'Then she must've been lucky and got to the front of the queue. It's as well, if she was desperate.'

He laughed again.

'Fancy,' she remarked with all the casualness she could

muster. 'Who would've thought it, eh? You and Harriet Meese . . .'

'Harriet's a very nice girl, Kate. You know I've always admired her. She's a very homely girl.'

'Oh, I know she is . . . With a face and hairstyle like hers there's no wonder at it.' She smiled brilliantly, having scored a very telling point. 'But she's always admired you, Clarry.'

His eyes suddenly manifested a defiant twinkle. 'I'm glad to hear it.'

'Well, at least that's to her credit. You should make a very happy couple.'

He shrugged. 'Who knows? . . . So who are you with tonight, Kate?'

'Oh, my new stepfather.'

'Ah, Murdoch Osborne. Yes, I heard that he had rather rapidly wed your mother.'

'Yes, it was a bit quick.'

'And I had him marked down as rather having his eye on you . . .'

'On me?' Kate visibly wriggled at this snippet.

'Well, he does have a certain reputation . . .'

'For what?' Kate asked naïvely.

'For women, of course. Didn't you know?'

'How should I know?'

'You don't think he's in an Amateur Dramatics Society for the love of plays, do you?'

'Why else would he be in it?'

'To surround himself with likely women. Women who won't kiss and tell, lest their peers shun them for their indiscretions. You know how straight-laced some of them are.'

'Is that why you became a member, Clarence? To meet likely women?'

'Why, yes, of course. And it pays off, doesn't it?'

'Does it?' she queried. 'You wouldn't think so looking at who you're with tonight. Still . . . to think you gave up the best-looking girl in the amateur dramatics society . . .'

'There's no arguing that you are, Kate.'

'Didn't we have enough fun for your tastes, Clarry?' she asked kittenishly. 'Considering there were no strings attached, I would've thought we had lots of fun.'

'No strings attached?' he queried, feeling suddenly bothered that he had misread Kate's inclinations and deprived himself of her favours prematurely. 'But I thought you wanted to get married at sometime.'

'Me? Why would I want to get married? It was you that kept harping on about marriage.'

'Only in terms of what and what not to expect if you got pregnant.'

'I don't want marriage, nor kids, nor any of that softness, Clarry. I'll take my chances. If I fall pregnant, I'll handle it one way or the other. With no comeback on anybody.'

'I say . . . Then maybe I got you all wrong.'

'Well, maybe you did . . .'

'Maybe we should meet again and talk about it more.'

'Yes, maybe we should, Clarry . . . Why don't you write to me, eh? Suggest a time and a place. My address is Badger House, High Street, Kingswinford,' she announced proudly.

At the end of the show, Kate made sure she and Murdoch lingered, till she could be reasonably certain that Clarence and Harriet had left before them. She had no wish to see them together. She could not understand what allure Harriet Meese could possibly hold for him. All right, her figure was passable; she had a narrow waist, a pert bosom and she held herself well, but her face and her hair . . . Her hair was so old-fashioned.

'Did you enjoy that, Kate, ha?' Murdoch asked, as they stood up at last to join the rest of the stragglers making their way out onto Wolverhampton Street.

'Oh, it was all right,' she said absently. In truth she had been too preoccupied with thoughts of Clarence Froggatt to pay much attention to the play.

'I thought that girl who took the part of Lady Brighton's daughter was quite good, didn't you? Ha?'

'Not particularly. I could've done it better.'

Murdoch grinned. 'That's what I admire in you, young Kate, your confidence. I admit, you're much better-looking.'

That made her smile with gratitude. It was the sort of boost she thrived on. 'And a much better actress,' she suggested.

Out in the cold night air, they crossed Wolverhampton Street to Murdoch's gig, tethered to a gas street lamp a few yards away. Kate huddled in her cape and nestled her hands in her new muff as she took her seat. He lit the lamps, patted the horse and retrieved the travelling rug from under his seat.

'I saw Clarence Froggatt in there,' she volunteered evenly as he jumped in beside her and flicked the reins. 'He was with Harriet Meese, of all people.'

They moved off and Kate covered her skirt with the travelling rug to keep her legs warm.

'With Harriet? He gets about a bit, ha? Is that why you're so glum?'

'I ain't glum,' she protested. 'They're welcome to each other.'

'Well, she can't hold a candle to you, can she?'

'I wouldn't have thought so.' Kate puffed herself up, feeling very superior.

'Maybe he's one of them fellers what like plain women. There are some, you know, believe it or not, though the Lord knows what the hell they see in plain women. Mind you, she has got a good figure, ha? She wouldn't be so bad with a bag over her head.'

'So you fancy her as well, then?'

'Like I say, she's got a very passable figure. That's all some men are worried about. Even young Algie seemed took with her for some time.'

'Pooh! Only because nobody else would look at him,' she said disparagingly. 'Let's face it, who'd want to look at our Algie twice?'

'Oh, I don't know,' Murdoch said. 'He ain't a bad-looking lad. That young filly he used to see not long ago had got some handsome flanks on her. She must've looked at him and liked what she saw, ha?'

'Marigold,' Kate said with a shrug. 'Yes, she was quite pretty, I admit.'

'Quite? I thought she was lovely.'

'You think Marigold's lovely?' she queried.

'Aye, I do.'

'But she's got nothing about her. D'you fancy her as well?'

He chuckled like a drain. 'If I thought I'd got any chance with her . . . I'm only human, Kate. I ain't no saint.'

'D'you think I'm lovely, Murdoch?' she asked softly.

They were passing a public house in Wellington Road. A boisterous gang of youths was making its way up the hill on the other side of the road, noisy, the worse for drink. Murdoch astutely flicked the reins and the horse broke into a trot.

'Well?' Kate prompted. 'Do you think I'm lovely?'

'I do, yes. When you put a smile on it, at any rate.'

She turned, realising she must be appearing sullen after all, and gave him a dazzling smile. 'That better?'

He grinned. 'Oh, aye, that's much better. Now you're *beautiful*, ha?'

* * *

Algie returned home that night after seeing Harry Whitehouse. They had been drinking in the Four Furnaces in Pensnett, a place they had agreed was roughly halfway between Kingswinford and Brierley Hill, although Algie believed he still had the better part of the deal when it came to distance, especially as his return home was all downhill.

He went to the kitchen to find something to eat, fancying a little bread and cheese. The chink of glasses greeted him.

'You just got in then, our Kate?'

'Yes, how do you know?' She reached for a whisky bottle and unscrewed the cap.

'You and Murdoch passed me about a quarter of a mile back.'

'Didn't see you,' she said curtly. 'And even if we had, we couldn't have give you a lift . . . What're you after in here?'

'I'm hungry. I was gunna do myself a cheese sandwich.'

'Clear off and I'll do it.'

'You?'

'Yes, me. I'm quite capable, you know.'

'Just so long as you don't lace it with arsenic.'

'Don't tempt me,' she said. 'Shall I pour you a glass of whisky as well?'

He looked at her with some astonishment. Such benevolence was alien. 'No, it's all right. I've had a drink. I've been drinking since eight o' clock.'

'Go and keep Mother company, our Algie. I'll bring you your cheese sandwich.'

He did as she bid him and strolled along to the sitting room via the hallway, pondering Kate's unprecedented magnanimity. Murdoch came in. As he acknowledged Algie, the cold of outside seemed to radiate from his greatcoat as he took it off and hung it up.

'Chilly, ha?'

'Vile,' Algie replied economically.

'There seems no end to it.'

Both went into the sitting room. Murdoch greeted his wife and sat down.

'Where's Kate, ha?'

'In the scullery,' Algie informed him. 'Pouring you a whisky.'

He nodded and stood in front of the fire warming his hands.

'Was the play good?' Clara enquired, putting her knitting back into a large brown paper bag, ready for a conversation.

'All right, Clara. Not as good as our efforts, but not too bad.'

Algie watched his mother. She looked at Murdoch expectantly, but he said nothing more; he merely sat in one of the armchairs and rested his head, seeming preoccupied. He took out his pipe, inspected the bowl, changed his mind about smoking, and then returned it to his pocket without filling it. He shut his eyes again. It seemed to Algie that Murdoch hardly wished to be bothered with talking to his wife.

'What are you knitting, Mother?'

'A nice warm scarf for your stepfather. He needs it in this weather.'

'Well, there seems to be no let-up, like I say.'

Kate pushed the door open with her foot and entered carrying a tray. Four glasses of whisky adorned it, and a plate of cheese sandwiches. She offered a glass to her mother, turning the tray so that the glass she intended her to have was nearest to her.

'Ooh, I say. A tot of whisky. Well, I never. Ta, our Kate.'

Then she offered Murdoch a glass and he took the one she presented to him by turning the tray.

'Cheers!' he said.

'Our Algie . . .'

'I said I didn't want whisky,' Algie protested mildly.

'Well, I've poured you one anyway, so drink it.'

He took it, and the cheese sandwich, which he began munching. He watched his mother sip the whisky. Nobody said much; a strange atmosphere seemed suddenly to have fallen over the household.

'I saw Clarence Froggatt at the Public Hall,' Kate suddenly announced for want of something to say, as if aware of the silence and embarrassed by it. 'He wants to start seeing me again.'

Murdoch stirred in his chair and sat upright. 'Have nothing to do with him, Kate,' he said protectively. 'Once bitten, ha?'

'Oh, he's got no chance with me anymore,' she declared. 'The way he treated me.'

Murdoch seemed to relax again at Kate's assertion.

Algie finished his sandwich, swigged the last of the whisky and announced he was going to bed. He undressed, put on his nightshirt and slumped into bed. As soon as his head touched the pillow he was fast asleep, and he had the sweetest, most erotic dream of Marigold.

Chapter 22

On the 18th of January, a Sunday, Algie took an extended ride. His route was along the canals, set hard with ice, like frozen veins in the Black Country's bruised and pock-marked skin. It seemed colder than ever that day. A savage, searing chill bit into his skin and penetrated his clothing, despite the several layers he wore. The winter was already remarkable for its bleakness. Since the last week in November the temperature had been well below freezing over the whole of England and Wales, even harsher in East Anglia and the south-east Midlands. Algie had read in one of the newssheets that folk were skating regularly on the lake in Regent's Park, London, where the thickness of the ice exceeded nine inches. If it was as thick along the canals, the Binghams would of course be frozen up, unable to work, and losing money at a rapid rate. So the chances of his seeing Marigold for quite some time were exceedingly remote.

It had already been more than two months since he'd seen her, and even though she might have taken the letter he'd attached to the door of their old house, there was still no word from her, no message. The landlord of the Bottle and Glass had seen none of the Binghams since, only those boat families who were frozen up on the Stourbridge Canal and were stuck there. He suggested, logically, that wherever the

Binghams were, they were bound to remain until the thaw, for they would be frozen up as well.

Feeling miserable, Algie freewheeled down the hill from Pensnett to Kingswinford, his fingers aching with cold despite his gloves, his ears stinging from the cold. It was dusk and he must be careful not to skid on any patches of ice which, in the gloaming, were difficult to see. If only it would snow, and break this seemingly endless cycle of grey, desolate, clammy cold. If only the thaw would come so that Marigold could be on the move and the Binghams find their way to the Stourbridge Canal again, and leave a message somewhere for him as to where he could find her . . . Always presuming she still wanted him to find her.

This nagging doubt was depressing Algie. The longer they went without seeing each other, the more each would fade from the other's thoughts. He was finding this already, yet he resisted it loyally, and tried to keep focussed on Marigold. Erotic dreams helped, trying to find her regularly helped. She was right for him. He did not want to forget her. His only hope was that she felt the same and that soon he would be able to claim her. But the longer this protracted separation prevailed, the more permanent it seemed destined to be. Maybe Marigold had even met and fallen in love with somebody else by now; she would never be short of admirers, and there were plenty of randy, glib-talking young bucks working on the canals who would be easily taken with her.

As he rode, Algie realised he needed a woman's company more than anything. In Marigold's absence, Aurelia would be first choice, if only she were available. Yet he must cast Aurelia from his mind. His position with Benjamin Sampson, and thus his livelihood, seemed precarious enough already without inviting more trouble by presenting himself at his door, gracing his lovely wife with unwarranted attention.

In this crisis of tenderness even Harriet would do. Good old Harriet. At least he was easy in her company. She was, for the most part, undemanding. She understood him as well as anybody did. It might be an idea to go to church that evening and surprise her. He could sit with her and Priss, then amble home with them afterwards. It bothered him that Harriet had seen Clarence Froggatt. He did not actually dislike Clarence, but he certainly resented him paying attention to Harriet. Maybe that in itself was a selfish attitude, the dog in the manger; he did not particularly want Harriet for himself, but neither did he want Clarence to have her. Harriet was not the sort of girl Clarence wanted in any case. Clarence evidently wanted women for sexual pleasure only; he would doubtless try and have his way with Harriet.

And what if he succeeded, where Algie had failed? If Clarence seduced her he would only lose interest. Poor Harriet, though, was the sort of girl who would only commit herself like that if she was deeply in love, and she would inevitably suffer a broken heart as a consequence. She must not be so foolish as to give herself wholeheartedly, only to be cast aside as just another of his conquests.

He had tea with the family, preoccupied and contributing little in the way of conversation. Just lately they seemed to have little to say to each other anyway, apart from 'pass the jam', or 'is there any more tea in the pot?'. A strange atmosphere. He was glad to get away from it.

He took the tram to church, rather than ride there on his bicycle. In any case, it was too cold to cycle there and back. As he entered the church, he saw that Harriet and Priss were already seated in the churchwarden's pew with others of their family, and there was no room there for him. He noticed how Priss turned her head and nudged Harriet, surprised to see him as he walked down the aisle, carrying *The Book of*

Common Prayer and Hymns Ancient and Modern that was handed him at the door. He nodded and smiled a greeting at them, then sat in a pew some way towards the front, knelt and said an impromptu prayer for Marigold.

The service seemed to drag on, especially so as Algie had no interest in it, save for it coming to an early end. During the hymns and the psalms he could pick out Harriet's voice amongst the others as the congregation sang; a pleasant voice.

At last, the service was over, and Algie breathed a sigh of relief. Choir and clergy trooped out to the vestry in solemn procession and the congregation drifted into the aisles and shuffled slowly towards the main door.

Harriet, considerately, waited at the churchwarden's pew for Algie to reach her. She had an inkling as to why he might have come to church, and it was by no means to worship, for she was as aware as anybody of his lack of religious fervour. She smiled as he approached.

'What brings you here on a night like this?'

He shrugged, feigning nonchalance. 'Nothing else to do,' he said.

'Goodness, you *must* be bored. For a minute I flattered myself that you might have come to see me.'

'It crossed my mind that I might see you.'

'What's wrong? Still no sign of Marigold to keep you company?'

'She'll be iced up anyway, stuck wherever she is till the thaw.' He shrugged, to give the illusion that it was of little importance. 'Anyway, how about you?'

'Me? I'm very well.'

'Good. I've been a bit concerned about you.'

'You?' She cocked an eyebrow in amusement, able to guess why. 'Concerned about me?'

'You and Clarence Froggatt . . .'

They were speaking in low tones as they moved slowly, en masse with others of the congregation who were queuing optimistically for the obligatory handshake and benign smile from the vicar to see them through the rest of the week, before their exit for home and their warm fires.

'I'm a big girl now, Algie,' Harriet replied. 'I'm quite capable of looking after myself. As well you know.'

'Just so long as your heart doesn't rule your head.'

'Oh, you can be sure my head rules my heart, Algie.'

They were close to the vicar and the curate now and postponed their conversation. Priss blushed as the young curate bid her good evening in front of them. A few seconds later they were shaking the hands of both clergymen in turn and the vicar was expressing his appreciation for their attendance. The rest of the Meese family had already been favoured with this rigmarole and were waiting outside while the vicar asked Algie why he hadn't attended for such a long time.

In the porch there was a good-humoured donning of mantles and galoshes. Outside it was snowing. In the light of the solitary gas lamp Algie could see the snowflakes chasing each other around in the wind. The congregation were pulling up their collars in their exodus, peering up into the doubtful sky and hurriedly putting up their umbrellas, the women fastening their bonnets and toques tighter to keep out this most recent and most feared hibernal punishment.

'Are you two coming with us, Harriet?' Priss enquired when Algie finally reached them, knowing full well what the response would be.

'No, I'll walk back with Algie.' She turned to him. 'If you'll walk me back home, that is?'

Of course, there was no question of it. It was the only reason he'd gone to church. 'If you'll be nice and sensible,' he answered with sham nonchalance.

'Maybe I'm not always very nice, but I always try to be sensible,' she said.

'Funny that. You generally seem to end up being very nice, but not in the least bit sensible.'

'Well, thank you, Algie,' she replied with mock courtesy. 'I believe it's always better to be nice than to be sensible. You yourself are a shining example of the truth of it.'

The other Meese girls, with the exception of Priss, walked behind their mother, in a brisk scurry home to escape the snow as quickly as possible. Priss, however, glided alongside her, balancing that unsteady bulk lest she slip in the snow, but finding it difficult to get close due to the girth of her mother's skirts. Their father, meanwhile, entered the Bell Hotel for his customary two pints of India pale.

'So have you seen him more than the once?' Algie asked, resuming their topic as they sauntered slowly behind the family to put some space between them.

'Seen who?' Harriet queried irritatingly.

'You know who.'

'Oh, Clarence, yes.' She smiled mischievously. 'Sorry . . . I've seen him twice, as a matter of fact.'

Algie's heart sank. 'Twice? And how—? I mean, are you going to see him again?'

'Well, he's asked me . . . And I said I would.'

'So it's getting to be a regular thing then?'

'He's nice. I like him very much . . . I always have.'

'Have you . . . ? I hope you haven't . . .'

'Hope I haven't what?'

'I hope you haven't . . . well . . . allowed him any liberties.'

'And what's it to you if I have, Algie?' Harriet was enjoying this. Funny how the tables seemed to have turned so unexpectedly. Funny how the appearance of somebody else in her life could make such a difference to *him*, after all the months of self-doubt and anguish she had suffered because of him and that girl Marigold.

'I just don't want to see you hurt, that's all.'

'Clarence is a perfect gentleman . . . But it's very gallant of you to care, considering it was all right for *you* to hurt me, but not for anybody else, evidently.'

'I didn't mean to hurt you.'

'People never do, do they? But somebody always ends up getting hurt. You were hurt when Marigold gave you up. You said so yourself.'

'Well, I think Marigold is a part of the past now,' he said, beginning to believe his own words. 'Because she's out of the frame, I just thought it would be nice if we could see each other again . . . Not to start courting again, I mean. Not *that*. But just to see each other. To go out with each other from time to time.'

He wanted her friendship, her warmth, somebody to talk to. He needed her company, her understanding. A heartening cuddle every now and again would be pleasant, but with no strings attached. Serious courting was the last thing he intended. He'd allowed himself to become involved with Harriet before and had grown disenchanted, even bored. Harriet was not like Marigold. He did not feel the same things for her as he felt for Marigold. Yet how else could he protect her from Clarence Froggatt's clutches? How else could he save her from herself and Clarence's smooth but potentially devastating enticements?

'So what makes you think I want to be at your beck and call, Algie? Because that's what it would amount to. What if I say yes and I grow attached to you all over again, and Marigold shows up? Would you leave me high and dry once more, and hurry off to be at her side?'

He shrugged. Of course, that's exactly what would happen.

It was Marigold he loved, not Harriet. Harriet was more astute than he gave her credit for.

'Well?' she prompted.

'I suppose you're right, Harriet.'

'I know I'm right. The trouble with you, Algernon Stokes, is that you are suffering a broken heart, and are in mortal fear of being hurt on the rebound. Besides, I'd be no substitute for Marigold. So stop trying to be a dog in a manger over Clarence, because that's all it is . . . And, don't dawdle,' she said impatiently. 'Clarence is calling for me at half past eight.'

'In this snow?'

'Why should the snow make any difference? I'm sure it will be very romantic walking in the snow . . . with him.'

It did not snow greatly. On Monday morning there was still a covering, but it was not deep, which was just as well, since it had not thawed either. The intense cold persisted, however.

Algie cycled to work and the exertion of pedalling hard, all the way up to Dudley, warmed him. At the Sampson Fender and Bedstead Works, he made his way to the small office he'd been allotted, took off his coat and his cap, and hung them up. He reached down to remove his cycle clips, which he put in the pocket of his coat.

He picked up a bent and tapered tube that somebody had deposited on his desk and scrutinised it, wondering why he had been blessed with receiving the item. He recognised it as one side of the front forks that would hold in place the front wheel of the new Sampson 'Lion' bicycle he'd designed.

He heard footsteps in the corridor outside and turned to see who it was through his open door. Benjamin Sampson had planted himself in the door frame.

'Ah, Stokes.' He'd taken to calling him 'Stokes' lately; Algie assumed it was to put some metaphoric distance between them. 'Those front forks. They ain't strong enough to give reliable service. One has broken on the prototype already. Got any ideas how we could improve them?'

Ideas. Benjamin was after his ideas again.

'Yes, we could keep the tube diameter and section thickness constant, instead of tapering it down,' Algie replied genuinely. 'We could weld a lug to it, as well, to house the wheel.'

Benjamin nodded, serious, tight-lipped. 'Good. I'll get it drawn up and the jigs altered. I want the second prototype bike ready tomorrow with that modification on it. I shall be showing it to some wholesalers at the end of the week, and I want it fitted and tested by then.'

'I could test it, Mr Sampson,' Algie suggested. 'I'd like to try the new prototype, 'specially since I never tried the first. I could compare it with—'

'It's unlikely you'll have the time, Algie,' Benjamin interrupted. 'Harry Whitehouse hasn't shown up today. I want you to take his place for a while building bedsteads.'

'Doing my old job?' Algie looked at his employer with incredulity and bitter disappointment. 'You want me back down there?'

'You're the only man I have who knows that job as well as Whitehouse.'

'But what if he's off for some time?'

Benjamin shrugged. 'Then you'll be expected to cover his work for as long as he's off . . . Your wages will be adjusted accordingly.'

Yes, downwards, Algie thought, grossly humbled.

Harry Whitehouse, it transpired, had contracted influenza. There was another epidemic of it about, no doubt aggravated by the continuing cold weather. Algie, thankfully, had so far missed it, and hoped he would continue to remain well. He would rather be fit and healthy, working at his old bench, than be laid up in bed bored to tears in Kingswinford, suffering from influenza.

But he was deeply disillusioned, hurt even, that Benjamin Sampson should continue to treat him so shabbily, especially after it was he, Algie Stokes, who had set him on the road to greater riches with his ideas of manufacturing bicycles. As he worked constructing bedsteads, a job he thought he'd seen the last of, he silently seethed. Why should he have to suffer the ignominy of his old workmates making jibes about him falling out of favour, and being made to do this monotonous work? It was bad enough having to suffer a drop in wages without any word of regret from Mr Sampson or sign of sympathy from colleagues, let alone the stigma that went with it.

Friday came. Algie was becoming increasingly obsessed and angry. He made up his mind to go to the office and tackle Mr Sampson. He was determined to have it out with him, to try and get him to see his point of view.

'Mr Sampson is out today,' Violet, his middle-aged secretary told him. 'Would you like to make an appointment to see him next week?'

'No,' Algie replied sullenly.

If Mr Sampson was out, he was certain to be at home on a Friday evening. Algie felt so strongly that he decided he would call there when he left work and express his displeasure. Such an appearance there might make Benjamin Sampson realise just how discontented he was. He might not be made welcome, but he was determined to make his point. He was being treated unfairly, was being humiliated. He, Algie, was the man with the ideas, good ideas, but not only was he being used, but also disparaged. Benjamin Sampson had deceived him about his intentions; all Benjamin had ever wanted was to steal his ideas. Algie had been ruthlessly exploited and it was time to let Mr Benjamin Sampson know that he did not appreciate it, and was not going to take it lying down.

So, at six o'clock when he left the factory he made his way on his bike to the house of his employer.

He pulled on the bell and felt its scrape of resistance. A few seconds later the maid, who he remembered was called Mary, answered the door. She looked at him condescendingly in his working clothes, his cap, cycle clips swathing his trouser legs to his ankles.

'I'm Algie Stokes,' he said, trying to hide his impatience with her. 'I work for Mr Sampson and I want to see him.'

'Oh, hello,' Mary said, almost familiarly. 'Mr Sampson's away on business. I woulda thought you woulda knowed, seeing as how you work for him . . . same as me.'

'Oh,' he replied, suddenly deflated.

'Shall I see if Mrs Sampson will see you instead?'

He hesitated. He did not wish to burden Aurelia with his gripe. He could hardly reveal his anger and frustration to her. On the other hand, she might think it rude if he turned down the possibility of at least saying hello. She had, after all, been very kind and understanding when he was grieving over his father, and Marigold ending their love affair.

'Well?' Mary queried impatiently. 'Make your mind up, Algie Stokes, it's chilly standing here. D'you want me to ask if she'll see you, or not?'

'Yes, all right,' he answered. 'If she's not busy. If she is busy, tell her it can wait till I see Mr Sampson next week.'

Mary left him standing at the front door for some time, huddling inside his coat to keep warm. Eventually Mrs Sampson appeared.

'Algie. How lovely to see you. Won't you come inside out of the cold? I can't imagine why Mary left you standing there.'

'I didn't mean to put *you* to any trouble, Aurelia,' he said, instantly brightening up at the sight of her. She looked as lovely as ever, her eyes clear and blue, with that warm smile she always seemed to have for him, and his anger seemed to dissipate like steam in a soft, warm breeze. 'I called to see Mr Sampson, to tell you the truth,' he said as he stepped inside.

'Benjamin is away, Algie. We're not expecting him back till next Thursday. Do sit down.'

'Next Thursday?'

'You must surely have known?'

'No, I didn't know. He doesn't tell me his arrangements.'

'He left last night for Yorkshire. I understand he has appointments in Leeds, Halifax, Hull and York. He said he might be going to Lincoln as well.'

'You mean he will be away tomorrow and Sunday?' Algie was amazed at this news. Who in his right mind . . . ?

'It's the way it's worked out. Oh, I don't mind. It's not as if we are love's young dream.'

'Aren't you?' he queried, surprised she should admit as much.

'Well, hardly . . . But that's another matter. How are you, Algie? Let's see . . . How long has it been since I last saw you?'

'It's getting on for three months now. It was the time of my father's death.'

'Of course. I imagine the pain is becoming a little easier to bear . . . At least, I hope so.'

'Yes, I admit, it is,' he affirmed, with a nod.

'Would you like some tea?'

'Thanks.' He grinned affably. 'A cup of tea would go down a treat, if it's no trouble.'

Aurelia smiled, and rang for Mary. 'Would you like something warming in it? It is rather cold still, isn't it?'

'That sounds just the ticket for a cold winter's night.'

'So what about your young lady? Marigold's her name, isn't it? I suppose you've sorted out all your problems there by now.'

'I've seen nothing at all of Marigold,' he said.

'Oh, that's such a pity,' she said sincerely.

'It's a great pity,' he agreed.

'So how is your mother faring now?'

'Oh, she's got over things very well, thank you, Aurelia.' He was about to mention that his mother had remarried already, but felt ashamed of the fact. Aurelia would most likely view its incomprehensible alacrity as a scandal, and he did not want her to regard him in the same bad light as his wantonly errant mother. So he didn't mention it, and enquired about her son, little Benjamin, instead.

'He's having supper, bless him. I like to keep him to a strict routine. We all know where we are then. The problem with small children is that they can rule your life completely. The trick is to rule theirs – in a kindly way of course.'

Algie nodded and smiled.

At that, Mary answered the bell and entered the room. Aurelia ordered tea and a small measure of whisky for her visitor Mr Stokes.

'I'm so pleased to see you, Algie,' she said unaffectedly when Mary had left them. 'I often think about you. I pondered you a great deal after I saw you last. I do wish I could have helped you more to get over your grief.'

Why did he dislike Benjamin Sampson so vehemently, and yet admire his wife with an equal and opposite fervour? And because he despised Benjamin so much, so abhorred the way the man treated him, he felt all the more justified in wallowing in the warm friendship his beautiful wife offered.

'I think you did help, Aurelia,' he replied. 'But, when it comes to losing somebody, I must be the most easily hurt person in the world. Oh, I'll stand my ground gladly in a fight or an argument, but when feelings and emotions come into it, I'm as soft as tuppence.'

'I know, Algie . . .' She lowered her eyes as if reticent to look into his lest she give too much away. 'You are very sensitive, aren't you? It shines through. Too many men are not . . .' Her voice trailed away. 'But I think I've said as much before, haven't I?'

'Yes, you have,' he said softly.

'So it goes without saying how much I admire that in you, Algie . . . But not only that . . .'

He thought she was being rather forward for a woman in her position and did not know how to respond. Thus, they remained unspeaking for long seconds, silent seconds which served only one mischievous purpose; to afford both of them time to allude to the words which remained unspoken. And those undeclared words seemed to emphasise the weight of their attraction for each other, daring both to wonder whether the unthinkable might actually be possible.

Algie sighed profoundly and Aurelia looked at him expectantly with her large blue eyes.

'Oh, Aurelia,' he said at last. 'If only you knew . . . There's so much I'd like to say to you . . .'

'What?' she asked simply. 'Say it.'

He shrugged and shook his head, for he had no idea how to tell this young married woman how much he admired her, the effect she had on him, how much he wanted to protect her from her husband whom he had grown to detest so intensely. And it would be utterly stupid to tell her that he desired her, how much he desired her. She would certainly regret having heard *that* once he said it.

'If you have something to say, please say it,' she urged gently, putting a reassuring hand on his arm. 'What is it, Algie?'

He shook his head again and smiled self-consciously. 'I can't . . . I daren't . . . I don't know how anyway . . . I don't know that you'd welcome it either.'

'Go on, Algie. Please try.'

'No, Aurelia. It's best not said . . . Somethings I have no right to say . . . I esteem you far too much to presume . . . I think maybe I'd better go before I do say something, 'cause if I do I'm sure to regret it . . . And you might be angry as well.' He got up to go, unwilling, but confident it was the honourable thing to do.

'Does it have anything to do with Benjamin?' she said, rising with him.

'I can't say any more, Aurelia.'

'You're noble as well as sensitive, I see.'

'Please don't mock me.'

'Oh, no, I'm not mocking you, Algie, believe me. You *are* being noble . . . but quite unnecessarily.'

'Noble or not, I'm really only thinking of sparing my own emotions.'

'So you don't consider other people's? Mine, for instance.'

'Yours, Aurelia?' He regarded her wistfully. 'That's just the point. What have I to do with your emotions? What right do I have to even ponder them?'

'On the face of it, no right at all, I concede,' she said soulfully.

'So there's no point in me saying what was in my mind anyway, and making myself look a bigger fool than the one I've already presented to you. I'll go, Aurelia, if you don't mind.' He moved towards the door. 'Honest, it's for the best. Thank you very much for the offer of tea.'

'Algie, don't think—you mustn't think—'

He forced a smile; a smile of sadness, a smile that manifested his melancholy. 'I can let myself out.'

With deep regret she watched him go. His gloomy smile had cut her to the quick, but her inability to say what was on her mind was on a par with his. Maybe that had been the trouble with her marriage; the inability to talk things over, the tendency to let things slide without halting them by a mere discussion . . .

Mary entered carrying a tray laden with a pot of tea, two cups and saucers, a sugar bowl, a small jug of milk and a smaller jug containing whisky.

'Mr Stokes couldn't wait, Mary, unfortunately.'

'Oh, I thought I heard the front door shut, ma'am. Did I take too long over the tea?'

'No, not at all. He simply had to go . . . I'll have mine, however. That will be all, Mary, thank you.'

Chapter 23

Algie found it difficult to get to sleep that night. Over and over in his mind he relived his conversation with Aurelia. Had he done the right thing by shying away from admitting how he felt? His conscience told him he had, but he felt sorely frustrated because of it. She was sensitive, he imagined she was as sensitive as himself, easily hurt, and he hoped he had not upset her by leaving so abruptly. The last thing he wanted was to upset her.

He heard the faint creak of floorboards and the click of a door catch on the landing. Murdoch must have been mooching about downstairs, maybe to collar another slug of whisky. Funny how they had all taken to drinking whisky regularly just before bedtime, his mother among them. Funny how she was so keen to accept it these days, when she barely used to touch the stuff. Still, if it made her sleep as soundly as she said it did.

Algie rolled over onto his other side. Oh, he wanted Aurelia. The problem was he could so easily fall head over heels in love with her. In the absence of Marigold he longed for another girl who could cure his heartache, but convention decreed he would have to learn to live without that particular one.

He heard a bed creaking, the regular, rhythmic tweak of a

bedstead. Murdoch, engaged in his nightly exercise upon his mother. Algie would be glad when the novelty wore off. But it was taking time; much longer than Algie had envisaged. Just lately there seemed to be an unaccountable spurt of activity in their unsavoury nocturnal antics. And at Murdoch's and his mother's age it was nothing short of shameful. He dreaded to think to what perverse depths his previously spotless mother had sunk in her dotage, stimulated by the whisky.

A little more snow fell in the night and that Saturday morning Algie cycled gingerly to work. He went directly to his old workbench, warmed from his arduous ride, rekindled the stove, and began doing the job he had been so used to doing before. Maybe he should think about finding employment elsewhere, a place where they would appreciate him, where his talents could be used and not abused. After all, Sampson's was not the only factory in the area making bicycles. Bicycles were big business. Another manufacturer, James Parkes, conducted a business at Newhall Street in Dudley. When he finished today he would take a ride up there to see if there was a vacancy. He had experience with the manufacture of bikes; he would be an asset to any firm engaged in that business. He could learn even more about the business, which would stand him in good stead when he came to start his own firm eventually.

One o' clock arrived and Algie put down his tools and tidied the workbench. He cleaned his hands with the mixture of sawdust and powdered soap that resided in a bucket near the sink in the obnoxious, distempered latrines provided for the workers' convenience. He put on his coat, scarf and cap, went outside to where his bicycle was standing, and rode down the alley at the side of the factory to the road. There, he saw an elegant young woman evidently waiting for somebody. She was wearing a cape and bonnet and a scarf around the lower part of her face as protection from the cold, rendering it impossible to see who she was. There was something achingly familiar about the way she stood, and his heart lurched thinking it might be Marigold. As the woman became alerted by the rattle of the bicycle over the cobbles, she turned to look. At sight of Algie she stepped forward, waving her arms to gain his attention.

'Algie!' she called in a forced whisper, removing the scarf to reveal her face.

He stopped the bike, put his foot on the floor to steady himself and his heart skipped a beat. 'Aurelia! What are you doing here?'

'I came to see you.'

'Aren't you frozen? You'll catch your death hanging around here in this weather. Why didn't you wait inside?'

'Because I didn't want to be seen. Especially by Violet, my husband's secretary. But thank you for your concern . . . I wasn't even sure whether you'd be working this morning . . .'

'Yet you waited all the same . . .'

'Because I had to see you.' She looked at him forlornly. 'Is there somewhere we can talk? Away from this place? Somewhere people won't know me?'

He looked around him, feeling useless. 'I don't know. A public house maybe.'

'Isn't there a café close by?'

'There's one in Brierley Hill High Street.'

'No, not Brierley Hill,' she said quietly.

'Dudley town then. We could take a tram. It's only a few stops.'

She nodded her assent.

'I'll leave my bike here,' he said. 'I can pick it up after.'

They walked to the nearest tram stop. Almost at once they

saw and heard one rumbling towards them. Aurelia lifted the scarf to partially cover her face again as they boarded it through the smell of warm grease that emanated from the little steam engine at the front. They took a seat together, the only one that was free. The conductor touched his hat to Aurelia and her eyes, the only part of her face visible, glistened with a shy smile in response before she looked away self-consciously. Algie paid their fares, and she watched, preoccupied, as if all this was happening in somebody else's life.

As the tram began to move, the two were aware that it could be taking them towards some sort of destiny. Yet it was impossible to talk, certainly not privately, in the continuous, deafening clatter of vibrating window panes. Not that either wanted to talk then. There was evidently so much to say, so much that she wanted to say, so much that he wanted to hear, but it must wait a little longer. And he waited, with the blood coursing through his veins at what she might reveal.

Dudley was heaving with folk and the tram's passage down High Street towards the Market Place was of necessity slow, to avoid colliding with pedestrians who overflowed into the horse road from the pavements. They alighted at the Market Place and mingled, unidentified, with the town's shoppers, till Algie spotted a place called Powell's Eagle Hotel and Dining Rooms. Somewhere to sit and talk in quiet comfort.

'Are you hungry?' he enquired. 'It says they serve hot joints daily, look.'

She shook her head. 'Not a bit. But if they serve tea . . .'

He smiled affectionately. 'Let's see if they have a table free.'

It dawned on him as they entered the place so furtively, how much this meeting must mean to Aurelia, to risk being seen with not just another man, but a man who, by virtue of the clothes he was wearing, was so obviously working class and beneath her social status. Maybe it was this class difference that had prompted her to avoid recognition, but he had the impression that it had more to do with the fact that she was married to a man who was reasonably well-known as a factory owner, and for that reason did not want to be recognised.

The place was full, and noisy with conversation. As they stood looking for an available table, another couple vacated one in a far corner. Algie thanked them as they passed each other and the woman, also young and attractive, glanced at Aurelia and smiled knowingly.

They took off their topcoats and sat down, and Aurelia removed the scarf from her face. She smiled at Algie, such a beautiful yet reticent smile. Her blue eyes exuded a look of sadness – or was it apprehension? He was about to ask her why she'd taken the trouble to seek him out, but a waitress intervened, hovering, clearing the table from the previous occupants.

When she'd taken their order, Aurelia said, 'I hope you don't mind my meeting you from work, Algie.'

'Mind?' he answered. 'Course I don't mind. It was a hell of a surprise, though. But I'm mystified as to why you did. If I'd known, I'd have worn some better clothes to work.'

She smiled, evidently feeling more at ease now. 'Your clothes are fine,' she reassured him. She glanced up at the ceiling, then shuffled on her chair to make herself more comfortable. 'After what we said last night, I felt I had to come. Our conversation was unfinished, Algie. There's so much I want to say to you, so much I want you to know . . . things you didn't give me the chance to say. If I say them now, promise you won't walk out on me here . . .'

He looked steadily into her eyes, trying to read beyond those blue-tinted windows to her soul. 'I promise I won't.'

Again she smiled. 'I hardly slept last night, you know,

thinking of what you said. But more intriguing was what you wouldn't say.'

'I hardly slept either,' he admitted.

'You said you had no right to say something that was in your mind to say. I'd dearly love to know what it is. If it's what I think – what I hope – it is, then I believe I have every right to hear it.'

'So what did you think, or hope, it was, Aurelia?' His heart was beating fast. She had not come this far on a whim of triviality. There was something significant going on here.

'I hoped that it might have been a confession that you thought something of me,' she said candidly.

He put his head in his hands. She was not about to let him escape. This was evidently going to be a defining moment in his life. He either had to tell her she was wrong and put an end to it before it started, or confess that her intuition was right, that he did feel something for her; that he always had, from the moment he had first set eyes on her. One thing was certain, though; he did not have the heart to disappoint her.

Aurelia reached for his hands, withdrew them gently from his face, and they remained clasped together on the table, her eyes meeting his directly. 'I have to know, Algie,' she whispered earnestly. 'If you want me, I have something to cling to. If you don't, then I apologise for troubling you. But I see in your eyes your feelings for me. Please don't deny them . . .'

If you want me, she'd said . . . 'I do have feelings for you, Aurelia,' he uttered nervously. 'But I have no right . . .'

'I don't understand your logic, Algie,' she whispered. 'What right do you need?'

'I have no right because you're already married. You belong to somebody else. You have his child . . .'

'I am, as you rightly say, already married . . .' She paused, squeezing his hand affectionately. 'But my marriage is not a success, to put it mildly. I don't love my husband, nor does he love me. Just because I'm married to a man I have no feelings for, doesn't mean I'm incapable of feelings for any other. Oh, if only you knew . . .' She sighed profoundly. 'That evening we first met, Algie, when you came to dinner with that girl Harriet, there was something about you that intrigued me. At once I could see the kind of man you are. As the weeks and months passed I had lots of time to ponder you. That evening I sensed you were drawn to me, too . . . something you said that was meant only for me . . . "I wouldn't put you through that", you said. I remember it distinctly. Then, when you called at the house again, just as your father had passed away, I relished that unexpected opportunity to be with you once more – alone with you – even if I was only helping you over your grief. The problem is, Algie, that I *do* see in your eyes your feelings for me. It's so frustrating to behold it, and for you not to bring it into the open.'

'Into the open?' he queried.

'Just between the two of us, I mean. To declare it . . . to me. I would love us to declare what we feel for each other. You do feel this as strongly as I do, don't you, Algie?'

'Can you doubt it?' His voice was stretched tight with emotion. He held on to her hand, trying to stem the trembling in his. 'But what good can it do us? We can never belong to each other.' He shrugged despondently.

'In spirit we can, if not in fact. I am in love with you, Algie . . . There . . . I've said it . . . I've had time enough on my own to think about it. If only you will allow me to share that love with you, it would make the unhappiness and the emotional squalor I put up with at home all the more bearable. My son is the only respite I get, yet Benjamin is all too anxious to send him away to a private school as soon as he is old enough.'

'But what is it you want from me, Aurelia?'

'The same as I hope you want from me. Love . . . Affection . . . A little tenderness . . . And everything else besides . . .' Her voice tailed away as she spoke those last words, as if she was half ashamed of what she'd said.

The waitress returned bearing a tray. She set everything down on the table before them, including a hot pork sandwich which Algie had ordered for himself, and a warm pikelet with butter and strawberry jam for Aurelia.

But Algie did not feel hungry anymore. His appetite for food had mystically disappeared, so he let his sandwich lie. There was a lump in his throat that inhibited his eating anything right then. He had longed for Aurelia, fantasised about her, jeopardised his standing with Marigold because of her, and eventually lost Marigold because of her, even though Marigold wrongly believed it had been Harriet. Now, Aurelia was his for the taking . . . in spirit at least. What strange tricks life plays with us . . . and to what purpose?

'I've idolised you from a distance from the moment I set eyes on you,' he admitted softly. 'Yet it never crossed my mind that you might ever feel the same for me . . . Except when my father died – I did have an inkling then, but I told myself I was living in cloud cuckoo land for even imagining it.'

She smiled, a broad, relieved smile that revealed her lovely even teeth. 'We can meet,' she whispered enthusiastically. 'If you're prepared to take a chance . . . Just as often as we can. With Benjamin away so much on business, being together is hardly likely to be a problem.'

He returned her smile eagerly. 'Could we meet tonight?'

'Yes, yes. We could, if you want to. And tomorrow. And the evening after that. Every evening, in fact, till Benjamin comes home on Thursday.'

'But where would we go? We would have to keep our meetings secret. And it's hardly the season for strolls down country lanes.' He had visions of them cavorting in that secluded field near Dadford's Bridge.

'Where would you like to take me?' she asked, and a flicker of waywardness lit up her eyes, a look he had never witnessed in her before.

'Oh, I know where I'd like to take you, Aurelia,' he said quietly, daring to match her fleeting capriciousness.

'Do tell me,' she pleaded.

He smiled sheepishly. He was anxious not to go too far, too fast, out of respect for her. 'No, it wouldn't do.' He shook his head, embarrassed. 'You wouldn't think very highly of me at all if I told you. Besides . . .'

'Besides what?'

'Well . . . you're a lady. A cut or two above me . . .' He looked into her eyes intently, his expression serious. 'What do you see in me, Aurelia? I don't understand it. I'm nobody. Just an ordinary working chap.'

'Oh, Algie,' she sighed. 'Even if that were relevant, do you think it would make any difference? Anyway, I don't consider myself a cut above you. I'm not a cut above you at all. Our backgrounds are not so different. My father's only a tradesman—'

'But you don't even sound like me,' he interrupted. 'You sound polished.'

'Because I had a good education, which my father was prepared to pay for. I was surrounded by people who spoke well and it rubbed off. My husband's family are hardly dukes and earls either. They've been lucky or hard-working enough to make money in the past, and I happened to marry into it. But you, Algie, are more worthy than any man I've ever met. I only wish I'd met you before I met Benjamin.'

'Believe me, I've wished the same,' he said ruefully.

'Have you honestly?' She smiled, happy to hear him admit it.

'I just wish I'd met you before I met Marigold.'

'I wonder what our lives would be like now,' she mused.

'But you wouldn't have looked at me twice.'

'Oh, that's where you're wrong.' Aurelia lifted the lid of the teapot and gave the tea a stir.

'So tell me how you came to marry Benjamin.'

'Well . . . as I have already admitted, Algie,' she said quietly, 'my marriage is a sham these days, a sham that I am trapped within. We married too young, and in haste, I think, Benjamin and me. Well, *I* was too young anyway. I was barely nineteen. I was already engaged to somebody else when I met Benjamin, and it was destined to be a longish engagement, certainly not leading to marriage before I was one-and-twenty. My fiancé at the time was articled, you see, and studying to pass his examinations. One summer Sunday afternoon he took me to watch him play in a cricket match at Enville, and there I was introduced to Benjamin, who was playing in the same team. Clarence was the opening bat—'

'Clarence?' Algie's heart seemed to stop beating.

'Clarence Froggatt. Do you know him?'

'Oh, I know Clarence Froggatt.'

'Don't you like Clarence?' she asked hesitantly, picking up animosity in Algie's tone.

'It's not that . . .'

'What then?'

'Nothing really . . . Fancy you being engaged to Clarence Froggatt once . . . Go on anyway. Clarence was the opening bat . . .'

'Well, while he was out there batting away stoutly, Benjamin kept me company until Clarence was bowled out. I was flattered by his attention, of course, especially as it was a long innings. He seemed quite taken with me. Then I learned that his father was a wealthy metal master – a self-made man.

Benjamin sent me flowers – oh, quite a few times – along with invitations to meet him. In the end I did, to cut a long story short. Before very long I'd fallen in love with him, and he with me, I'm sure. Anyway, he asked me to marry him and, with the prospect of the life of Riley, I said yes.'

'You mean you were blinded by wealth and position?'

'I suppose I was.' She shrugged. 'You must appreciate, Algie, that I was a very susceptible young girl at the time . . . My mother had not long passed away . . . I was vulnerable. I was swayed by his gifts, by the trappings of wealth that surrounded him, by his loving attention. I felt like a goddess.'

'So how did Clarence take your breaking off the engagement?'

'Badly. We had been very close, Clarence and I. I still have a soft spot for him.'

'Do you regret not marrying Clarence then?'

'Oh, no. That might have never worked out either. Clarence is too self-centred, rather like Benjamin in that respect. It might have been an equal folly to have married him. He wanted an angel, and I was no such sublime entity.' She glanced at him enigmatically. 'Anyway, when we married, Benjamin and me, we rubbed along well enough at first. Yet before even our son was born we drifted apart. I had the suspicion that he might be associating with another woman . . .'

'And is he still?'

'Oh, I'm certain of it.'

'Do you know who she is?' he asked, his curiosity intensely aroused.

'Oh, yes . . . Her name is Maude Atkins. You've met her, I think. At least you've seen her.'

'Have I?'

'She is my son's nanny.'

'Her? Good God!'

Aurelia saw the look of astonishment in his eyes. 'Benjamin's real disinterest in me began almost the same day that Maude began her employment with us. Most Sundays my husband goes out under the pretence of visiting his mother. He is gone for four or five hours, time that I know full well is not entirely spent with his mother. An hour, maybe. But it coincides with Maude having her Sunday afternoon off. Of course, they don't arrive back at the same time – that would be too obvious – but I've seen the way they look at each other . . .'

'Still, you could be wrong, Aurelia.'

She shook her head. 'No. I'm not wrong, Algie. When he goes on business trips, Maude is always given time off – at his instigation – the first night he's away usually. She was away last night, under the pretext of staying with her parents. She wasn't due to return till this morning, which she did . . . looking very tired. It's easy to put two and two together. I expect he takes her to an hotel close by.'

'Maybe this one.'

'No, no, nothing like this place.' She glanced around her cursorily. 'It would have to be somewhere more plush.'

'No wonder you've been unhappy,' he said earnestly.

'But I don't care anymore, Algie. I've grown to hate him. All I know now is that I can't bear him to touch me.'

'How could he have treated you like that? He wants horse-whipping.'

'Benjamin was a spoilt child, Algie. In the beginning, I was a pretty plaything, I suppose, until he tired of me, the same way he tires of all his toys. He grew used to me, took me for granted. I suppose, when he met Maude he preferred to find his pleasure with her, once he realised she was amenable. I've asked myself since, why shouldn't I as well? What's good for the gander is good for the goose, as I see it . . .'

She paused a moment to pour the tea.

378

'This place, Algie . . .'

'Yes?' He glanced around him.

'It's an hotel, isn't it?'

'I believe so.'

'As we leave . . . if you have no objection, of course . . . why don't you ask if they have a vacant room for tonight? Nobody knows us from Adam. We could spend the night as Mr and Mrs Algernon Stokes . . . If you have no objection, of course . . .'

Chapter 24

'I'm going out tonight and I shan't be back,' Algie announced as the family were sitting down to their dinner that Saturday evening. 'So don't wait up for me.'

'Where are you going?' Clara asked. 'I don't like to think of you being out all night. I shall be worried. Make sure you've got enough warm clothes.'

'Don't worry, I will.'

'So where are you going to stay?'

'Oh . . . up at Harry Whitehouse's,' he answered, trying to sound casual.

'Then put some clean underwear on and a clean pair of socks.'

'I've got clean stuff on. And I've had a good wash down.'

'Well, don't forget to take your toothbrush.'

He rolled his eyes. 'I won't.'

'But I thought you said Harry Whitehouse had got the influenza, our Algie. You don't want to catch that, else you'll be down with it next and pass it on to the rest of us, as sure as God made little apples.'

'I called in to see him after work,' he concocted. 'It's why I was late back. He wasn't too bad at all. I don't think he's got the influenza. Just a chill. Anyway, he said he fancied a bit of company, and asked me to stay the night. He reckons they can put me up.'

'Has he got a sister?' Kate enquired mischievously.

'What's that got to do with anything?' Algie said, irritated at her inference.

Kate shrugged. 'I just wondered if a girl was the attraction, that's all.'

'So it looks like me spending a night in, by myself again,' Clara said. 'Mind you, I don't mind. Who in their right mind wants to go out this weather?'

Algie looked enquiringly at Kate. 'You off out as well, then?'

'Murdoch's taking me to a magic lantern show.'

'Your mother didn't want to come, Algie,' Murdoch felt obliged to explain. 'It's some pictures of Italy and a talk. I quite fancied it, and Kate said she wouldn't mind coming as well, ha, Kate?'

Kate nodded.

'So where's it on at?'

'Brierley Hill Town Hall,' Murdoch answered. He turned to his wife. 'Be sure to wait up for us, Clara. I don't suppose we shall be late.'

'Oh, I'll be up. I'll wait till you get back afore I have my tot of whisky. I wouldn't miss my tot of whisky for anything. I swear, as soon as my head touches that pillow of a night I'm dead to the world. Best thing ever for getting you off to sleep, eh, Murdoch?'

'Oh, I agree with you, my love.'

Algie glanced at Murdoch, then at his mother. Something did not add up. If his mother fell asleep as soon as her head touched the pillow – news which actually pleased him no end and which he had no reason to doubt – whose bed was creaking every night?

'Did you drop off to sleep as soon as your head touched the pillow last night?' he asked casually.

'Two minutes and I was fast as a rock.'

Algie glanced at Kate, but her face was inscrutable, giving nothing away as usual. He recalled the creaking floorboards on the landing, the click of a door catch, the rhythmic squeaks of the bed which he could just about detect. Maybe Kate had met up with Reggie Hodgetts again and was letting him in the house at the dead of night, for her own disgusting pleasure. The swine would have the cheek to do it as well. No, it must be Clarence Froggatt she was harbouring. Yes, she said she'd seen him again. She said he was still interested. Denying he had any chance with her was just a red herring. Nothing about Kate surprised him anymore; she was capable of anything.

Algie decided it was a pity that he would not be home tonight after all; he could have discreetly found out who the culprit was. If he knew who it was he could confront Kate about it and get her to cease the nonsense. One thing seemed certain; she was going to get into trouble one way or another. She should have more respect for Murdoch's home, for her mother's feelings if ever *she* found out.

Algie and Aurelia had arranged to try and take the same tram into Dudley. He sat next to the window peering out, as the tram drew up at the stop nearest her home, through a hole he'd made in the film of haze that misted the glass. His heart skipped a beat when he saw her, carrying a small overnight case. Her face was again half-concealed with a scarf beneath her fashionable toque, revealing just her eyes, eyes that looked tantalising as he caught a glimpse of her looking up at him. She boarded the tram and Algie felt her press her shoulder against him as she took the seat beside him. They had agreed to pay each other no heed so close to her home, so as not to arouse any suspicion – not that you could say much privately with all that clatter going on; you had to shout to be heard over the din of it. But Algie turned to look at her, as he would any stranger who took a seat beside him, and it elicited just a spark of acknowledgement. He felt the warmth of her body penetrate the layers of clothing that separated them as he sat, and he ached for her.

At the Market Place, he waited for her to stand up, ready to alight, then followed her after a second or two onto the pavement opposite the grand marble fountain that was frozen up still. He caught her up, and she casually took his arm and gave it a squeeze.

'Shall we go straight there?' he asked. 'Or do you fancy something to eat or drink elsewhere first?'

'I already ate,' she answered with a smile. 'We agreed we would, don't you remember? Not that I had much. I didn't really feel like eating, I was too churned up inside. No, let's go straight there.'

'You're sure you still want to go through with this?' He felt obliged to allow her this escape, if she needed it.

'Of course. Don't you?' She, in turn, was suddenly fearful that his heart was no longer in it.

'I wouldn't be here if I didn't,' he said.

'You're quite sure?'

'Course.' His tone convinced her.

The town was quieter now the shoppers had gone. The gas street lamps and the reflected light from shop windows lit their way. A carriage trundled past, to the rumble of wheels and the clopping of the horse's hoofs. A man who had been roasting chestnuts most of the day was gingerly loading his still hot oven onto a cart while his horse nuzzled steamily into a nosebag. A group of men wearing greatcoats, who had congregated round the door of a public house known as Lester's, after the family who owned and ran it, disappeared inside one by one.

They reached the Eagle Hotel.

'I'll go in first and get the key to the room,' Algie said, his heart thumping as the magnitude of what they were doing dawned on him.

'I'll wait here,' she agreed softly, feeling conspicuous and self-conscious.

He went in. Folk were dining as he entered, engrossed in their dinners and the company they were keeping. Nobody seemed to notice Algie. He spotted the same man they'd seen at dinnertime at the far end of the room. Algie reckoned he must be Mr Powell, the owner.

'Excuse me, my . . . er, wife and me have a room booked for tonight.'

The man looked at him enquiringly. 'Oh, yes, sir? What name?'

'Stokes.'

'Oh, yes, I remember. Room number four. Up the stairs here, and turn right at the top. Nice room. It overlooks the High Street.' He handed him the key, a smooth, well-worn article made of iron.

'I'll call the missus then,' Algie said.

'Have you got a match to light the gas mantle?'

'No, I don't carry matches. I don't smoke.'

'Never mind. There's a fire lit ready, and you'll find spills on the mantelpiece.'

He went back outside. Aurelia was standing in the shadows close to the wall, her scarf concealing her face again. He called her name softly and she turned to him.

'It's all ready. We have to go through the dining room, though.'

She kept the scarf around her face as they passed through, and they looked for all the world what they were; clandestine lovers on a secret assignation. Mr Powell smiled to himself as he watched them head for the stairs.

Algie found the room already unlocked when he tried the door handle. Inside, it was warm and welcoming, the walls alive with the light from the flames dancing over the coals in the small grate.

'Thank goodness there's a fire,' Aurelia commented.

Algie shut the door behind them, put the key in the lock and turned it. His heart was hammering hard. He was alone in a strange hotel room with Aurelia Sampson, his gaffer's wife, and it was for one reason only. He put his bag down on the floor alongside hers, and found a spill on the mantelpiece as Mr Powell had promised. He stooped down to light it in the fire.

'What are you doing?'

'I'm going to light the lamp.'

'Oh, please don't,' she whispered. 'There's enough light already from the fire and from outside. It's much cosier like this. Much more romantic.'

He put the wax spill back on the mantelshelf as Aurelia removed her hat. She stood before him, their bodies almost touching, and looked into his eyes. Never had he seen her eyes so beautiful, glistening by the fire's yellow flickering flames. His hands went to her waist; her arms went around his shoulders.

'We should take our topcoats off,' he suggested. 'It's warm in here.'

'Yes.' She let go of him and unfastened her mantle.

He gently removed her scarf. 'You won't need this in here.' He pushed her mantle from her shoulders, took it and hung it on a nail at the back of the door. Beneath the mantle she was wearing a pale chiffon blouse that fastened demurely at her throat with a cameo brooch, forming a narrow ruff. Her hair was swept up onto the top of her head, enhancing the set of her neck, which he longed to kiss. He doffed his own coat and hung it next to hers.

She turned to him, pressing herself against him once more, her arms around his neck. 'You must have thought me the most forward woman imaginable for suggesting we spend the night here,' she said softly, her forehead against his chest as if in shame. 'I hope you don't think too badly of me, Algie. I bet you think I'm a proper strumpet.' She looked up into his eyes again and smiled. 'I think I am, to tell you the truth . . . It must be in my blood.'

'If you hadn't done it, I doubt if I would've either. I wouldn't have had the nerve to suggest it.'

'That's what I thought. You're too much of a gentleman. Yet it's what I perceived we both wanted. Women are not expected to express themselves quite so liberally, nor are respectable married women expected to be quite so brazen . . . I'm sorry if I don't conform to your notions of how a woman should behave, Algie, but I thought, "What have I to lose, only him?".'

'And it's not a bad room,' he said inadequately. 'I didn't know what to expect, but it's not a bad room at all, is it?'

'As third-rate hotels go it's quite passable, I suspect.'

'You've got experience of third-rate hotels then?' he asked, and Clarence Froggatt sprang to mind.

'Me? No. Benjamin will only ever stay at somewhere swanky if we are ever away from home.'

He was watching her lips as she spoke. They were round and full, moist and naturally pouting, and extremely kissable. He focused on them longingly.

'I want to kiss you.'

'You have my full permission,' she breathed.

So their lips met, gently, tentatively, each exploring the other's softness with a suppressed enthusiasm at first.

'I like the way you kiss,' he whispered.

'Then why stop?'

He kissed her again and lingered, fuelling the mutual passion that had been pent up for so long.

Even if nothing more came of this affair, they had to experience this night. There was an intense bond of physical attraction between them which must have its head at all costs. If it all ended in disappointment, then so be it. But for each to live their lives without giving it the chance to run its course was not an option now. Each would regret having never followed their hearts to the ultimate when the chance arose, however confined they were to the rigid conventions that ruled their lives, but which especially ruled Aurelia's as a married woman.

'I want you, Aurelia.'

She smiled at him then lowered her eyes, making no reply. Of course she wanted him too. She had already made that plain.

'Shall we get into bed?'

'Yes . . .' She smiled again tenderly. 'Which side do you want?'

'The middle . . . With you . . .'

She laughed at that. 'It'd be better to get undressed first, though, I think.'

'Yes . . .' He began taking off his boots. 'Can you remember your honeymoon with Benjamin?'

'Please!' She was already removing her blouse. 'Let's not talk about that. It's such a pleasure to be away from him and his house. I don't want to be reminded of him. Not while I'm with you.'

'Nor do I, really,' Algie admitted. He loosened his necktie and pulled it through his collar.

'And especially not the honeymoon. It was a disaster . . .'

'I suppose, in a way, this is *our* honeymoon, eh, Aurelia?'

She laughed while she unfastened her skirt and allowed it

to fall to the floor around her feet. 'You are funny, Algie. It's no wonder I'm so mad about you. You're such a romantic.'

'D'you think so?'

'Only you could've translated this into a honeymoon.'

'But it is in a way. Except that we aren't wed.'

She pulled her chemise over her head, revealing her nakedness to her waist. Her breasts were full and round, yet not at all ponderous. Her waist was slender, her stomach all but flat, accentuating the delightful feminine curve of her hips.

'I wondered whether you wore a corset,' he commented conversationally, sitting on the bed to remove his trousers from round his ankles.

'Not tonight,' she answered. 'I think corsets must be the single most contributing factor to virtue in single girls and fidelity in married women. Corsets are enough to put off the most determined lover. When I was having my bath this afternoon I decided I wouldn't wear one tonight.'

'Because you didn't know how I'd measure up in the determination department?'

'Well, I didn't want you to be put off. They take an age to unlace. Not quite the thing when you're anxious to be out of them in a hurry. We women have to wear the most ridiculous clothes for the sake of fashion or convention, both of which can be stupid, to my mind.'

'Will you promise never to wear a corset when you're with me?'

'Oh, I promise,' she said. 'Unreservedly.'

'You do wear a corset sometimes, though?'

'Well, they do give a woman shape.'

'You have shape enough without,' he said. She was standing before him entirely naked now, her slender body pale but exquisitely beautiful, and perfectly proportioned in the firelight. Her shimmering skin looked as smooth as polished ivory. He sighed at the wondrous sight, a sight he had imagined he would never be privy to. 'You are beautiful, Aurelia,' he said with the utmost sincerity as he slid between the sheets.

She shot him a winsome smile, and clambered across the bed, crouching on all fours.

'I take it you haven't brought a nightgown.'

She laughed. 'I hoped I wouldn't need one.'

He chuckled conspiratorially as she crept towards him with the grace of a young lioness. He received her in his arms and they kissed passionately. He ran his hands hungrily over her body, over the bare flesh of her bottom and down the backs of her smooth thighs. She was wearing a perfume that smelt divine and he could feel her warm breasts pressed against his chest, her belly against his. His heart was pumping hot blood through his veins with a vengeance.

As she lay on him, she could feel him hard against her belly and she sighed. She slithered her naked body slowly down his, kissing him lingeringly all over, teasing him with her tongue and her soft, full lips till he was aching with desire.

'I've waited so long for you,' she sighed, moving back up again so that she could kiss his lips, her breasts lightly skimming over his belly and his chest. 'Yet I never thought that we could ever be together like this.'

'Nor did I,' he whispered. 'Not in my wildest dreams.'

A shank of her dark hair had fallen loose, hanging incongruously down one side of her angelic face. The sight appealed to him.

'Kiss me, Aurelia.'

Their lips met again for a few seconds, and then she broke off.

'Do you want to be on top of me, Algie?'

'No, I'm quite content with you on top. I like it. How about you?'

'Oh, I'm perfectly content.'

He cupped one smooth breast in his hand and felt her nipple harden, then rolled over so that her back was on the bed and he was on top of her.

'I thought you liked me on top,' he whispered.

'I do. I fancy I'll like being on top of you just as much though. I thought I'd just give it a try. Would you rather we swapped back?'

'No, I'm quite happy either way, Algie.'

He lowered his head and kissed her breasts, licking each nipple in turn to see how it hardened and extended in sensual response.

'You have lovely breasts,' he said, his voice muffled by the lovely example receiving his ardent attention.

'Oh, you're an expert on breasts, are you?'

'Not particularly. But it's hard to imagine you had a baby and suckled it, 'cause they're still so firm.'

'It's because I had my baby young, Algie,' she explained softly. 'When it comes to having babies, the younger you are the better – within reason. I believe so anyway.'

The skin of her belly was taut, smooth and supple. How on earth could her husband not want her? She was lovely, divine, sweet-natured and compliant, if this was anything to go by; all that a man could wish for in a wife. But there again, her husband was a fool . . . and in more ways than one.

He nuzzled his face in the warm tuft of dark hair that met him at the base of her belly. She parted her thighs and arched her back as his tongue probed her deliciously. Her soft vocal sighs told him she was relishing it. She clenched his hair with urgency, and gently held him into her, thrusting herself forward more.

'Oh, Algie . . .' She was sighing, wriggling shamelessly. 'God, this is beautiful . . . so beautiful . . .'

Because she seemed to be enjoying it so much, he felt it was his duty to linger there. Before long he sensed a flood of extra wetness on his tongue, a sweeter taste, and he was desperate to enter her, to plunge into her warm softness and feel her sweet flesh surrounding him. He writhed up over her, till his face was level with hers. Her head was to one side, her face contorted with the rapture of orgasm, but she looked no less beautiful because of it, and all the more desirable.

As he slid inside her, she gasped and began moving vigorously beneath him, gripping the cheeks of his backside to draw him closer, more firmly into her. Her sighs turned to cries, and he in turn was soon aware of that familiar tingling deep inside, which had eluded him for so long. Its glow intensified, and he groaned at the exquisite sensation radiating from the depths of his groin through his entire body, even to the tips of his toes. Too soon spent, he nuzzled his face into the curve of her neck with a deep sigh of contentment, while she ran her fingers lovingly through his hair.

They remained still for some minutes, resting, unspeaking, wallowing in the intimacy of the moment. Eventually, Aurelia spoke.

'Well, that confirms it.'

'What?' he muttered into the pillow.

'That I love you. Oh, I'm so happy with you, Algie.'

Reluctantly he withdrew from her and lay on his side facing her, his hand resting on her belly, which was moist with perspiration where their bodies had cleaved together.

'You don't regret it then?' he asked.

'Regret it? Oh, Algie . . .' She sounded disappointed that he should even consider such a thing.

'But I spent inside you.'

'I know you did, but I don't regret it. It was beautiful. I hope you don't regret it either.'

'Me? Why should I regret it?'

'Because of all the implications.'

'I'm aware of all that, Aurelia.'

'As long as you don't think I want it to stop here . . .'

He held her tight and kissed her. 'If I thought that, I'd also think you were a very shallow, selfish person, without any real feelings.'

'Which I am not,' she affirmed.

'But it's all happened very quickly between us, you must agree.'

'Because I need love just as much as you do, Algie. We're two of a kind, you and me, I think. I can tell you get maudlin without a bit of love and tenderness. I'm no different at all . . .' She caught his smile by the firelight and snuggled up to him. 'Anyway, I've had plenty of time to think about it.'

'So have I, my love.'

She lifted her face to him and smiled into his eyes. 'You called me "my love" . . . Do you think you might love me just a little bit, Algie?'

'I wouldn't be a bit surprised . . . Despite all my former resolve to avoid it . . .'

Chapter 25

'If you don't want to be seen leaving with me,' Algie said, sympathetic to the fears Aurelia had already expressed, 'then wait for me at the tram stop up by Top Church.'

She assented wistfully as she peered through the window onto the grey morning.

'Just while I settle the bill. And I'll find out if the room's free later. You still want to come here later if we can, don't you?'

'You know I do.' She kissed him on the cheek, put on her hat, and was ready. 'I'll leave now then. See you at the tram stop in a few minutes.'

The fire had gone out in the grate. All that remained was a pile of ashes, and it was cold in that room after the heat of the night. Algie mused over their night of love. He shook his head in disbelief that it had actually occurred at all . . . Aurelia, the most beautiful of women, had been his and would be again. She was certainly a healing salve for the heartache he'd been suffering over Marigold. He looked down on the bed they had made love in, slept in, wrapped in each other's arms, and tried to imagine her there again. But any image escaped him. Suffice it to know that she had been there, and so had he.

He went downstairs and found Mr Powell.

'The lady I was with,' Algie began in a low voice as he handed over the money to settle up. 'She, er . . . she wasn't my wife.'

Mr Powell was unmoved by this unexpected declaration. It was really none of his business, but he regarded Algie with a curious gaze. 'It didn't take much working out, lad, if I'm honest.'

'The truth is,' Algie went on, a little taken aback by Mr Powell's revelation, 'we need a place to go to do our courting. The weather being what it is, neither of us fancy walking out, and secluded spots down country lanes are just a bit too chilly. I, er . . . I wonder if I could make an arrangement with you for us to use that room again other nights. Not to stay the whole night necessarily, mind you, just to use for a couple of hours or so.'

Mr Powell offered him his change.

'No, keep the change, Mr Powell . . .' Algie believed it might curry some sympathy and understanding.

'I get respectable business folk stopping here in the week, Mr Stokes, and I don't particularly want my emporium turned into a bawdy house.'

'Oh, I appreciate that, Mr Powell . . . Look, I realise that what I'm asking might not appeal to your sense of what's right and proper, nor to any of your other guests if they knew, but if you could turn a blind eye . . .'

'Turn a blind eye?'

'I mean, me and my lady friend would be very discreet, Mr Powell. I mean, we could come and go separate, like. Nobody need ever know, barring you.'

'Oh, not to mention my missus and the chambermaid . . . They ain't daft, you know.'

'I never meant to suggest that they were. But business is business, Mr Powell, surely?'

'Oh, aye, Mr Stokes, business *is* business.'

'I could book up the room now for tonight, tomorrow, Tuesday and Wednesday, if you like.'

'But you wouldn't necessarily be stopping over them nights, if I understand you correct, eh?'

'Just a few hours. Say from seven till ten, or thereabouts. We would be out by ten if it suited you.'

Mr Powell pondered the situation. If this chap Stokes wanted to use the room every night for the next four nights he needn't have the sheets changed, so he'd save on that. If, after ten at night, on the other hand, somebody else wanted accommodation, he could oblige and make money on the room twice over, although the sheets and pillowcases would have to be changed then. But in the event he could certainly afford it.

'What you get up to in your own private lives – and in private, Mr Stokes – is up to you and none o' my business. And business *being* business, as you so astutely pointed out, I think I might be able to accommodate you. But I know nothing of your private life, nor that of your lady friend. I don't know either of you from Adam, do you understand? As far as I'm concerned you're bona fide married guests.'

Algie smiled with relief. 'Thank you, Mr Powell. It means a—'

'But I do insist that you exercise the utmost discretion, Mr Stokes. If there's so much as a whiff—'

'Course we will. You can rely on it.'

'Just so long as it's understood. I don't want my hotel getting a reputation as a bawdy house, like I say. O' course, I don't say as nobody else before you has ever done what you've done, and used the place as a love nest. Maybe they have. I don't know and neither do I want to know. But I do have a reputation to consider.'

'I'm just as mindful of our own reputations, Mr Powell,' Algie assured him. 'You can rest assured we shall do all we can to protect them, which will only help to protect yours.'

'Then we shall see you tonight?'

He nodded. 'We'll be back. If you let me keep the key to the room, you might not even see us.' Mr Powell nodded his consent. 'Thanks again, Mr Powell.'

Back at the tram stop he told Aurelia the news. She smiled contentedly when she knew they would be back again later.

'A month we bin stuck here in this ice,' Seth Bingham ruefully reminded his family as they sat huddled around the small table in the cabin of the *Sultan* that same Sunday. 'A month today. Christ in heaven knows when we shall be able to move on.'

'You'd think the icebreakers could do more,' Hannah remarked.

'They've bin doin' their best, Hannah. The canal companies am losing revenue hand over fist. It's in their interest to break up the ice, but no sooner they do and it all freezes over again. And what can yer expect? I've never knowed such an 'ard winter.'

The family were dining on rabbit stew, which had had to serve them for three days. Hannah had made it two days earlier from a rabbit another bargee had sold them for sixpence after he'd caught half a dozen. When you couldn't earn you had to do something to eke out a copper or two. Catching rabbits and selling them at least fed the family and brought in a little beer money as well. Well, Seth identified with that bargee's plight. His own family needed food and he could just about afford the sixpence, which he handed over willingly.

'If we can't work afore this week's out, then we'll be starving, 'cause there's no more money,' Seth went on. 'I'll

396

either have to look for work in Rugby or Daventry to see us through . . . or charity.'

'I can look for work, Dad,' Marigold said. 'I can earn a bit to help see us through.'

'Where'm you gunna earn money round here, eh? Willoughby Wharf is the arsehole of nowhere. Look out the window. What do you see? Nothing but flat fields for miles around, nothing but a church in sight. Where you gunna find work?'

Marigold shrugged. 'I dunno till I look. There's the Navigation Inn by the bridge. Maybe they could do with some help.'

'The Navigation depends on the cut for its livelihood. They'll be suffering like the rest of us.'

'What about the Rose in Willoughby village?'

'The Rose is bound to be suffering an' all.'

'Then I could walk to Rugby or Daventry and see what there is there.'

'D'you feel well enough?' her mother enquired. 'D'you want to be walking miles in this weather in your condition?'

'I feel well enough, Mother. I ain't feeling so queasy in a morning lately, neither. Besides, we all need to do our bit . . . and I'm used to walking a long way.'

'I could look for work as well, Seth,' Hannah said. 'And our Rose. We won't starve.'

Seth smiled sadly. 'No, I want you here, Hannah . . .'

'But it would only be till the ice melted, Seth. So what money have we got left?'

'What we had has all but gone. The poor hoss has to be fed and stabled, and that costs money an' all. I already owe money for that, and it'll have to be paid.'

'Maybe there's work for you at Braunston, Dad?' Marigold suggested.

'I already aksed,' Seth said. 'There's nothing. There's nothing anyroad while the cuts am all froze up and nobody can shift nothin'.'

'Well, at least we shall keep warm,' Hannah said, 'Even if it means burning some of this coal we're freighting.'

Algie arrived back at the Eagle Hotel shortly after seven. He and Aurelia had arranged that he would get there first and be ready to welcome her when she arrived on the next tram, it being imperative from her standpoint that they were not seen together.

When she tapped on the door of their room to announce her arrival, he opened it wearing not a stitch.

She giggled and hurriedly shut the door behind her, turning the key in the lock. 'Lord above, Algie, you're stark naked! What if somebody saw you?'

He grinned triumphantly. 'Who cares? I warmed up your side of the bed for you.'

'How do you know which side I prefer?' she teased, taking off her hat.

'I don't.' He dived back under the covers to await her. 'You spent most of last night and this morning in the middle.'

She threw her scarf at him playfully. 'Such bawdy talk, Algie Stokes. I would never have believed it of you.' She sat on the side of the bed, bent her head and kissed him.

'How's little Benjie?'

'Benjie's fine.'

'And his nanny?'

'Oh, she's being very attentive to my son.'

'Are you going to get undressed?'

'It crossed my mind.'

'But she doesn't suspect anything, you staying out all last night and leaving the house tonight?'

'What could she suspect? Anyway, who cares if she suspects anything?'

She took off her clothes with no hint of shyness and he watched her with longing, his pulse racing again. At once she slipped into bed beside him, pressed herself against him and shivered.

'Oh, you're so lovely and warm, Algie. Hold me tight.'

They kissed with passion, instantly bringing to the boil their mutual desire that had remained simmering since they parted that morning. He soon discovered that she wanted him as much as he wanted her, and rolled onto her, entering her immediately with a soft, vocal sigh. Her hands gripped his buttocks, forcing him into her and, with sobbing whimpers of pleasure, they settled into a steady rhythm. Their love-making was prolonged and ecstatic, and they were both perspiring when they later rested in each other's arms.

While they lay entwined, Algie pondered the first time he ever laid eyes on Aurelia; the impact she'd had on him. How he'd fallen head over heels for her exquisite beauty and warm, easy-going nature. Never in a month of Sundays had he believed they would become lovers. Yet here she was, lying beside him, snuggling up to him contentedly having enjoyed the ultimate intimacy two people can share.

How long could this thing go on? It could hardly last forever. She had a husband, a child, and all the domestic and moral baggage that went with them. When that wretch of a husband returned from his business trip they would be unable to meet. The thought of Benjamin Sampson lying beside her in bed, touching her, having his way, was anathema to him, even though he was aware she did not relish intimacy with him in any case.

'Do you still sleep with your husband?' he asked.

'Does it make a difference, Algie?'

'To me it does. I hate to think of you and him . . .'

'Then try not to think about it,' she said kindly, understanding his resentment.

'I can't help *but* think about it.'

She hugged him sympathetically. 'I can understand how you feel, my darling. I would feel the same about you and your wife if you were married. But remember, I don't love him. I love you . . .' She touched his lips gently with the tips of her fingers. 'Only you, Algie . . . Remember that.'

'All the same . . .'

'It really doesn't occur very often,' she said honestly. 'I don't encourage him ever, but I'm hardly in a position to shut him out altogether. I am his wife. I have a duty . . . In any case, I don't want to arouse any suspicion . . . Especially not now . . .'

'Have you ever thought about leaving him?'

'What's the point? Where would I go? It's too big a gamble . . . My son, you see . . . What would happen to him?'

'Bring him with you.'

She sighed and snuggled up to him more tightly. 'Bring?' she repeated, and the word and its meaning hung in the air. 'You're even more of a romantic than I first took you for, Algie, my love. I presume you're implying that we could set up home together and live in sin?'

'Eventually . . . If we go that far . . . If there's no other way.'

'You'd sacrifice everything for me? No, don't answer that. I wouldn't let you commit yourself to that, although it's a very appealing thought. No, Benjie and I would be too big a burden. Let's just enjoy what we have whenever we can, and not think too deeply about such things. Let time and nature take their courses. Otherwise we'll make ourselves miserable. I want to be happy when I'm with you, Algie. You're my escape, the light in my darkness.'

He smiled up at the ceiling. 'Maybe I've got a tendency to run away with myself.'

'As well as elope with me,' she said wistfully. 'Don't think I don't appreciate it.'

Outside a tram passed, its steam engine huffing busily, its iron wheels clanking over the joins in the rails. At the same time, the clock of St Thomas's church at the top of the hill struck the hour. Algie counted the strikes. Nine o' clock.

'What I want to know,' he said, shifting onto his side and propping his head up on his wrist, 'is whether you and Clarence Froggatt ever—'

'What does Clarence have to do with us?'

He kneaded one of her breasts playfully, enjoying the smooth, yielding sponginess, the sheer silkiness of her skin. 'He's seeing Harriet Meese. You know? The girl I brought to your house?'

'Fancy . . .' There was genuine surprise in her voice. 'Well, she seems a very nice, respectable girl. I'm sure she'd be very good for him.'

'He was courting my sister before that . . . He told me in confidence once the things they got up to. Nothing that surprised me, though, I can tell you, knowing my sister. He told me he'd had other girls besides.'

'How very indiscreet of him.'

'One of them at least was a virgin, he told me . . . I wondered if it was you.'

'It hardly matters anymore whether it was me or not.'

'But if it was you, and on your wedding night your brand new husband realised you were second hand goods . . .'

'Oh, Algie . . .' She chuckled at his artlessness. 'Why would he have to wait till his wedding night? If the marriage is already arranged and within comfortable striking distance . . .'

'Isn't it customary for a girl to wait till she's married?'

'Discretionary, I would've said. Although girls have much more to lose . . . You know, Algie, girls are just as anxious as boys are to taste love, however much it's forbidden before they marry.'

'That's what I mean. And if you tasted it with Clarence Froggatt you would've been only seventeen. Eighteen at most. A bit young.'

'You make it sound as if I was still in short skirts . . . Well, I wasn't . . . And in any case, Algie, I'd never admit to any such thing, even if I were guilty of it . . . Anyway, what about you and that girl Marigold you were so keen on?'

'What about her?'

'Did you and she ever . . . ? You're obviously a practised lover . . .'

'I'd never admit to any such thing, even if I were guilty of it,' he said with a grin, throwing her own words back at her, which made her laugh.

'*Touché!*' she exclaimed. 'But you loved her, didn't you?'

'Yes, I loved her.'

'And once you have loved somebody, I think you always love them. Leastwise, I think it would be awfully easy to rekindle that love in the right circumstances. Don't you?'

'I think it's very possible,' he answered truthfully. If he ever saw Marigold again, he felt sure his heart would pound fourteen to the dozen.

'So tell me about her. I've told you about Clarence.'

'You've only told me half,' he teased. 'So I'll only tell you half . . . She was a sweet girl, uneducated and as natural as sunshine. She was blessed with a lot of common sense, and she wasn't troubled by the restrictions of a religious upbringing—'

'Neither am I,' Aurelia butted in. 'Except at school where we had to worship daily. But it all passed over my head. Sorry . . . go on . . .'

402

'She was thoughtful and kind. She'd willingly hand you her last farthing if she thought you needed it more than she did. She was a devout daughter, who idolised her mother and father. She was pretty as well – *very* pretty, with wide blue eyes and a shock of very dark hair. A bit like you, to tell you the truth, but a year or two younger.'

'And did she have a good figure?'

'Oh, yes, a lovely figure,' he answered truthfully.

'I can understand why you loved her so much. You must've been desperately hurt when she said goodbye.'

'She didn't stop to say goodbye, Aurelia. She just disappeared. But yes, course I was hurt.'

'Because you had hurt her . . . That's why she acted like that.'

He sighed at the recollection of it. 'I suppose I must've done, but I did it without thinking. It wasn't intentional.'

'But that's the trouble with men. They don't think sometimes, and they leave their womenfolk to pick up the pieces.'

'Yes, I know,' he said sadly.

'Kiss me again, Algie,' she sighed. 'I feel a distinct urge to love and be loved welling up again inside me. And it would be a cardinal sin to pay no attention to it . . .'

The next day, Monday, Marigold walked into Rugby, while Hannah took it upon herself to look for work in Daventry. Then they would compare which town afforded the better prospects.

Marigold's belly was beginning to show, but in her mantle and the frocks she wore, she could hide the fact that she was pregnant from a prospective employer, especially since she wore no wedding ring. In any case, as soon as there was a let-up in the weather, they would be off to Oxford. When that happened there should be work a-plenty for the *Sultan* and the *Odyssey*, with a backlog of goods piling up in the warehouses.

While she walked along the towpath towards Rugby, through that flat and bleak landscape, she pondered her lot. Her baby would be born sometime in May, she'd worked out. It would be hard trying to wean a child and bring it up decently on a narrowboat, but the prospect did not daunt her unduly. Her mother had done it several times; most of the boatwomen had done it at some time. She was lucky as well in that she would have the help and support of her family. They had not condemned her for getting caught with a child out of wedlock. They merely hoped that once this awful winter was past they could be on the move again. If they could find Algie before she had the baby, and in time to get wed, so much the better. They would regale him with the news that he was about to become a father. Marigold just hoped she had not driven him away completely by her jealousy over Harriet Meese. She was frustrated at her inability to give him her heartfelt apologies and patch things up; she couldn't write, so was unable to send him a letter. Yet even if she could, she had no idea where to write to; he could be living anywhere since his family had left the lock-keeper's cottage at Buckpool.

She bore Algie no animosity for her condition; she was as much part as he was of the private covenant that caused it, just as keen to indulge in the delightful pastime that created this child she was carrying. She recalled with fondness and pleasure the times they had lain in the grassy hollow just off Watery Lane near Dadford's Shed, hidden by gorse bushes aflame with bright yellow flowers during that glorious summer last year. If only she could recapture those times of loving tenderness and live them again. She would do nothing different, only curb her jealousy. This absence from Algie had made her realise that jealousy was not pleasant; it made you miserable, it sowed mistrust, it had cost her her love and, in consequence, any chance she felt she had of future happiness. Even if she experienced jealousy again, she vowed to herself never to reveal it.

Naturally, she wondered how Algie was, what he was doing, how his work was faring, whether he still loved her as much as she loved him. Even if he didn't love her, how often did he think about her? She hoped against hope that she had not driven him back to the arms of Harriet. She would never forgive herself if she had.

She trudged on towards Rugby. She knew that after about half an hour's brisk walking she could leave the canal at Barby Wood Bridge and take the lane north. Otherwise the canal would take her around the east of the town and add an extra mile to her journey. Her feet were cold, her nose was cold, and her ears ached where the ice-cold studs of her dangling earrings pierced her lobes, but she pressed on, duly leaving the canal.

It was a change to walk along a lane and see the occasional horse and cart, hear the sounds of farmyards. Eventually, after walking for more than an hour, she found herself on Rugby's Lawrence Sheriff Street, and crossed it to the footpath on the opposite side. A troop of boys in a military column headed towards her, all dressed alike, evidently from the Rugby School which she was now passing. One or two of them were looking at her with interest.

Pretending she hadn't noticed them, she turned right into High Street, drawn by the shops and inns, and decided to ask in each and every one if they needed an assistant. Her inability to read would be a handicap, but she could count money and, once she knew the prices of everything, nobody would be any the wiser. The first place she tried was a drapery shop, and she got short shrift there. She didn't like the place anyway, nor the man who owned it, whom an assistant referred to as Mr Bromwich. Next was a bookshop . . . well, that would be a waste of time . . . She tried a grocer and tea dealer, a clockmaker, a tailor and woollen draper, a butcher's shop, an ironmongery, even a café, and was losing heart . . .

Then she happened upon a baker's shop, and she thought about Kate Stokes. She gazed in the window at the different loaves of bread, at the iced buns, at the fancy cakes. When she smelled the fresh-baked bread wafting deliciously into the street she realised she was hungry. She plucked up her courage and went inside. The homely warmth and divine aromas seemed to embrace her.

A man in a white apron and a straw hat was transferring egg custards from an enamelled tray onto a counter display.

'Yes, my lover?'

'Excuse me, sir, but I'm looking for work,' Marigold said hesitantly. 'I wondered if you needed anybody to help in the shop.'

'How old are you, my dear?' he enquired amenably, still transferring the egg custards.

'Nineteen, sir.'

'And what's your name?'

'Marigold Bingham.'

'Bingham?' He pondered the name for a second or two. He had finished what he was doing and looked at her with curiosity. 'Can't say as I know any Binghams . . . Rugby lass, are ye?'

She smiled apologetically. 'No, sir.'

'I thought not. Where're you from then?'

'The canal at Willoughby.' She decided it was best to be totally frank. 'Me father's a number one on the narrowboats and we'm stuck in the ice there. I needs to find work to see us over, 'cause we've run out of money.'

The man smiled kindly, moved by her candour and refreshing lack of pretence. 'By God, I bet it's cold on them narrowboats this weather, eh?'

'Well, we got stoves and all that,' she said brightly. 'We keep warm most of the time.'

He looked pensive. 'I've already got a lass who works with me in the shop,' he said. 'So I don't need anybody in here.'

Marigold's expression told of her disappointment.

'Mind you,' he went on, 'I could do with somebody in the bakehouse. Somebody hard-working who I could rely on. Have you had any experience working in a bakehouse?'

Marigold shook her head.

'It's nice and warm in the bakehouse,' the man said temptingly, 'what with the oven and that. D'you like cakes?'

'Oh, I love cakes.'

He grinned matily. 'We bake cakes after the bread. You'd love ours. Best in Rugby . . . and beyond, if you want the truth. Have you got your character?'

Marigold looked at him, puzzled.

'A letter from a previous employer saying how reliable and trustworthy you are,' he explained.

She shook her head. 'Didn't know as I'd need one. I never worked for nobody before, 'cept me dad. He'd tell you right enough that I'm reliable and trustworthy, though, and no mistake.'

The man laughed, taken with this girl's openness and lack of guile. 'I don't need your character, Marigold,' he declared. 'I know enough of human nature to know when to trust my own judgement. It'd mean starting early, you know. We have to get the bread baked in time for the shop opening. Could you get here by five in a morning if you gotta walk all the way from Willoughby?'

'Yes,' she said eagerly, her face lighting up. 'I could do that.'

She was calculating what time she'd need to get up to get there on time. It would be the middle of the night, but she would do it. Her family needed the money and they were depending on her.

'Then you've found yourself a bit o' work, miss, to tide you over. I bet there's a train you could catch at Willoughby Station, save your legs. You'd have to find out if they run that early, though.'

'Depends how much it costs, sir. Anyhow, what's the wages?'

'Two shillings a day, eh? And I'll throw in a loaf of bread every day as well for your family, eh? Can you start tomorrow?'

'Yes, if you want me to. But when would I get paid?'

'Of a Saturday. This coming Saturday, I'll pay yer what you've earned in the week out the till, eh? No working a week in hand with me, especially if you're all strapped for cash. How does that sound?'

Marigold nodded. 'Oh, thank you, Mr—'

'Fairfax, miss.'

'Thank you, Mr Fairfax. It all sounds very fair. I'll start tomorrow, then. Five in the morning.'

'Oh . . . and here's an egg custard for you to be going on with.' He picked one off his display and, with a jovial smile on his kind face, placed it carefully in a bag and handed it to her. 'You look as though you could do with feeding up a bit . . .'

Chapter 26

After those evenings Algie spent with Aurelia at the Eagle Hotel, he returned home and took himself off to bed, too tired and too contented to take much notice of what was going on around him at home. Then came the unavoidable interruption; the day that Benjamin returned from his trip to Yorkshire and Lincolnshire. Their assignations, of necessity, had to be suspended till the day he went off again somewhere else.

Algie and Aurelia had agreed a signal to let him know for certain when Benjamin was away, for he could not entirely rely on the information he picked up at work. Benjamin might be away from work at any time; it did not necessarily follow that he would be away from home. When Benjamin had gone away Aurelia would place a red vase containing yellow paper flowers in her bedroom window. Leaving a gas lamp turned up bright and the curtains open would draw his attention to it as he rode past on his way home from work. The maid would not have the temerity to alter it, so the signal could be relied on, she assured him. The plan was to meet at the Eagle Hotel about seven the same evening. If a room was available they would rent it; if not, they would seek accommodation elsewhere.

Three whole weeks passed and Algie was hungry for Aurelia.

Enquiries at work had failed to reveal any planned trips. During the third week of February, with still no hint of a departure for Benjamin, Algie went to bed dispirited. Naturally enough, he pondered on Aurelia, reliving the tender hours they'd spent together making love in that hotel room in Dudley. He tossed and turned with frustration. If only they could meet soon, so that he could tell her how he felt. There were still so many things that had to be said, so many more assurances yet to be made, so many more emotions and sensations yet to be explored.

His brooding was disturbed by the sound, coming from the landing, of a door catch, followed by the familiar creak of floorboards. He had all but forgotten about these strange nocturnal activities. Somebody was up to something nefarious, and right under their very noses. He sat up in bed, listening intently.

A door clicked shut again.

Algie slid out of bed in his nightshirt, silently opened his own bedroom door a little and harkened. He could hear nothing. The silence in the darkness was actually overwhelming. Aware that he too might cause the floorboards to creak and so alert the culprit, he crept out onto the landing gingerly. Thankfully, there was only the slightest creak, barely audible. A minute went by . . . two minutes . . . Then a stifled chuckle emanated from Kate's room.

Algie lingered, inordinately curious. Before long he was rewarded with the sound of creaking bed springs, restrained but still clear in the surrounding silence. What cheeky swine possessed the gall to enter this house at night and indulge himself with his sister?

He had an idea.

Whoever it was must have come in through the back door. To make it as easy and as quiet as possible, Kate must be deliberately leaving it unlocked. He would go down, lock it back up again and hide the key. That way, the cheeky swine would be trapped, unable to get out. He would love to see the look on the face of either Reggie Hodgetts or Clarence Froggatt, whichever it was, when he realised there was no way out except by Algie's kind permission. He particularly hoped it was Clarence Froggatt; would he have something to report to Harriet . . .

Downstairs he crept, feeling his way to the back door in the darkness. Fully expecting to open the door, he tried the handle, but the door was locked. He felt for the key and found it, gently turned it one way, then the other. It had been locked all the time.

The front door then . . . He made his way through the hall, his bare feet tingling with cold by this time on the icy tiles. The front door was locked too.

It could mean only one thing; the culprit must have been entering early and hiding in the house all the time; a highly risky pursuit. There was nothing for it but to wait.

So he waited.

He sat on the floor of his own bedroom with the door ajar so that he had a view along the landing to Kate's room. His eyes gradually grew accustomed to the darkness and he was able to see sufficiently well. An unremitting draught seared across the landing, drawn by the chimney in his own room, and Algie shivered. It was cold enough to warrant a fire in his room and it had been banked up with slack. Most of its heat was going up the chimney anyway, affording little warmth to the room, till he opened the flue in the morning and gave it a poke.

He had no idea how long he waited, but eventually he heard a muffled voice. At once he was alert, peering into the dimness, focusing on Kate's door. Before much longer it opened, and the night-shirted figure of a tall man silently appeared and immediately disappeared, like some grey, floating spectre, into the room his mother shared with . . . *Murdoch* . . .

Bloody hell!

Just what was going on?

In that split second of realisation all emotion drained from Algie. He was aware only that he was chilled, chilled to the marrow. Almost in a trance he stalked across his bedroom to the fireplace. A set of fire brasses stood on the tiled hearth and he picked out the poker. He poked the slumbering fire and opened the flue. The coals guttered into life. The smouldering slack, wetted and patted down on top of the coals to make it last the night – but dry now – ignited into a fluster of sparks and half-hearted blue flames. Algie sat cross-legged before this display of hampered pyrotechnics and stretched out his hands to warm them, hardly able to come to terms with this devastating discovery. He rubbed his feet to restore some semblance of warmth to them, and realised he might be warmer in bed.

But bed, for once, offered no enticement.

As the fire's flames spread and its warmth increased he went across to the window and parted the curtains. The frosted trees on the opposite side of the road were silhouetted against the lighter clouds of night. A barn owl, like some airborne ghoul, flitted silently past the window looking for prey.

He wished he'd had a drink or two, that he'd gone to bed drunk and slept undisturbed in a stupor all night. Better to be ignorant of this abominable liaison than to be aware of it, and not know what to do for the best. He wished, too, that his feet were not still so cold as he stood on the oilcloth under the window. He wished he could stop this shivering. Maybe it was nerves. Yet no wonder.

Slowly, the first coherent thoughts of exactly what was

412

going on began to infiltrate his mind; his sister and his step-father! Murdoch Osborne was committing adultery with his own stepdaughter. The picture invading his mind was suddenly extraordinarily vivid, almost as if it were a photograph and hanging, lit up, on his bedroom wall. And what a picture it was! Did they understand just what they were doing, those two? His sister and his stepfather? Did they comprehend the implications, the likely consequences? And not necessarily the consequences of Kate conceiving a bastard child from this ill-matched and stupid liaison. The consequences would affect each of them, and in different ways.

Algie had half a mind to go to Kate's room. He felt like giving her a thorough shaking and a good slap across her stupid face. How could anybody be so half-witted as to take her mother's husband for her lover? Had she no respect, no feelings for her poor mother? Come to that, what respect did she have for herself? None, obviously. She deserved to be on the receiving end of some avenging justice. But what? Plain, down-to-earth adultery was one thing, but this . . . His sister and his stepfather! This whole thing was bizarre, scandalous. It was so loathsome and unspeakable that it was not something you could broach with the perpetrators without creating monstrous upheaval. It would be like stirring up a wasps' nest. Worse. Most likely, what they were doing was illegal.

If his mother found out, that would be the end of her marriage. In a way, that might not be a bad thing. With this madness going on she was living in cloud cuckoo land anyway. She could kiss goodbye to the comfortable existence she'd begun to enjoy, the security she'd expected to benefit from for the rest of her days. She would be a laughing stock besides, for folk would wag their fingers and say, 'I told you that nothing but bad would come of marrying in such haste'.

Everything must surely collapse around them. Those two

stupid people. His sister and his stepfather. Kate, he knew, was hopelessly wanton. But Murdoch . . . Well, he thought that Murdoch might have a bit more sense at his age.

Algie's faith in human nature was in utter crisis. He had lived in the same house as Kate too long not to know her faults and her weaknesses. His happening upon her and Reggie Hodgetts as they copulated against the shed that spring night last year manifested a monumental clue as to her lack of virtue, and Clarence's comments merely confirmed it. But here, at the heart of this reprehensible business was not merely the simple principle of trust, but that of basic decency. A young woman simply did not sleep with her stepfather.

He began to wonder what had really possessed his mother to marry Murdoch in the first place. All right, they had been a courting couple when they were younger, no different perhaps to himself and Marigold . . . Then a thought struck him. A vile, monstrous thought. What if he, Algie, was the son of Murdoch Osborne? He hoped to God it was not true. He loved his mother, admired everything about her. There was little about Murdoch that he admired, however, and he hated to think she might have been tainted by him all those years ago. If only it was daylight and he could study himself in the mirror, try and discern any facial similarities between him and his wayward stepfather.

Up until the time his mother had expressed a wish to marry Murdoch he had believed her to be spotless. But that very eagerness, which she had tried to conceal, had made him question her virtue. Now he questioned it more. Just what had gone on in the past between her and Murdoch? Just how deeply had they gotten involved all those years ago? Had they been as deeply, as intimately involved as he had been with Marigold?

* * *

414

That illicit, inglorious affair, unwittingly discovered by Algie, had begun when Murdoch and Kate had left the Public Hall in Dudley, where the Netherton Amateur Dramatics Society had staged a play. They'd been discussing Harriet Meese and Algie. Marigold's name had cropped up, and Murdoch had said he thought the girl was quite lovely, prompting Kate to ask him if he thought she, Kate, was lovely too. He replied that he did.

'So do you *fancy* me, Murdoch?' she asked, keen to wring as much out of his admission as she could.

'Oh, aye. No question.' He turned to look at her. 'Especially when you smile at me like that. But I'm married to your mother, ha? For better or worse. That puts a different slant on it altogether.'

'Do you fancy my mother?' Kate's large eyes were clear and challenging, even by the sparse light the street lamps and carriage lamps afforded.

'Now what sort of question is that for her own daughter to ask, ha?'

'It's a question what needs answering, Murdoch. I mean, has she lived up to what you would've expected when you were both young?'

The horse was going at a steady trot. Murdoch had privately decided that the poor animal needed the exercise to warm him through after standing tethered to that lamp post for nigh on two hours in the freezing cold.

'Your mother's in her forties, Kate,' he replied with seriousness over the rattle of the wheels and the horse's hoofs on the cobbles. 'And she's bore two children between times. She ain't quite how I imagined her to be when she was eighteen. How could she be?'

'So you don't fancy her now? You're disappointed in her?'

'Well, I'll tell you straight, just between we two, ha? Any

man, 'specially one of my age if he's still got any spark o' life left in him, would rather his bed partner was a bit younger with fresh, smooth skin, ha?'

'So you'd rather have somebody young . . . like me . . . ?'

'Bugger me, Kate . . .' His pulse was suddenly racing. 'Are you suggesting something, by any chance?'

His astonishment amused Kate. 'It's a serious question, Murdoch. Favour me with a serious answer.'

He paused, wishing to choose the right words, dangerously anxious not to put a damper on what could be a very interesting development. 'Well . . .' he began carefully, 'from the point of view of having a bit of fun between the sheets, I can see the advantage in having somebody like you there. What man wouldn't, ha?' He grinned self-consciously as he spoke. 'I bet *you'd* be a heap o' fun in bed, ha? Your mother ain't that much fun at all, is she, let's face it? It didn't take me long to find that out. Won't go out at night, don't want to do anything other than sit in front o' the fire with her knitting or sewing . . .'

'I know . . .'

They remained silent for a few long minutes, each digesting and analysing what the other had said, and the tantalising suggestions each had implied. Before they knew it they had reached Badger House. The horse, out of habit, turned into the driveway and headed straight for its stable.

'You know, Murdoch, you married the wrong woman,' Kate declared with a finality that defied argument.

He looked at her with utter astonishment. 'Oh, aye? Would you have had me then, if I'd asked you instead?'

She smiled at him coquettishly. 'Oh, you wouldn't have needed to marry me, Murdoch . . .'

The horse, its breath rising in clouds of steam, scraped its hoofs in the gravel impatiently, waiting to be unharnessed.

Murdoch, meanwhile, looked at Kate with a perilous mixture of disbelief and longing.

'I take it you've got bags of experience already of what goes on in bed between a man and a woman?' he whispered.

'Yes, and without all the baggage of marriage.'

'Clarence Froggatt, ha?'

Kate shrugged, and an unfathomable smile flickered across her lovely face. Already she knew she had Murdoch on the hook like some great slobbering fish. She also knew she was playing a very dangerous game, but its very danger was exhilarating. Dangerous games were not alien to her. She thrived on them. They stimulated her. And Murdoch, for all the difference in their years, was not unattractive. He bore his years well, he was clean, presentable, and personable, not marred by an unsightly beer belly. He must have enjoyed a decent measure of success with women over the years if Clarence's comments about him joining the amateur dramatics society, just to meet available young women, were true. Besides, and just as relevantly, she would be getting one over on Clarence, wouldn't she?

'If you fancy trying me for size, come to my room tonight while my mother's asleep.'

Neither Kate nor Murdoch moved, for her challenge was not yet accepted, no arrangement yet ratified. She might yet be winding him up.

'Bugger me, Kate . . .' Murdoch gulped. 'Are you serious, ha?'

'I've never been more serious.' She looked provocatively into his eyes by the light of the gig's flickering lamps. 'It's all yours, Murdoch.'

'Then let's get to it,' he said eagerly, ready to jump down from the gig.

'Hang on, hang on . . . I ain't doing it for nothing, you know. You have to earn it.'

'Earn it?' he queried. 'So there's a catch . . .'

'You know I intend to be a professional actress no matter what anybody thinks. Well, you have to promise me that you'll write to one of them great impresarios you know in London and help to get me on the stage there.'

He sighed ruefully. This glorious chance was slipping through his fingers. 'But you know very well that your mother wouldn't like it.'

'Who cares about my mother anyway? You don't.'

'That ain't quite true, Kate. Whether or no . . . I don't approve of you becoming an actress either.'

She cuddled up to him. 'It's worth it, ain't it, Murdoch? . . . Ain't it? A night or two between the sheets with me instead of her? Just for writing to one of them great London impresarios? Promise me you'll do it, Murdoch, and I promise you your reward.'

He'd sighed longingly and decided, in a flash, to take her at her word, weighing up the pros and cons, the odds of being found out, and considered that it was too good an offer to turn down.

'Aye. All right. I promise.'

Kate grinned, flushed with self-satisfaction at negotiating what she deemed a fair trade, and left him with the horse.

Murdoch fumbled like a novice groom as he unharnessed the horse and tacked down. He was charged with exhilaration, coupled with a strange sense of foreboding, the likes of which he had not experienced before. As he settled the horse into the stable with some fresh straw and a bucket of grain, he pondered the enormity of what he was getting drawn into. It was madness, total madness. He could jeopardise everything he'd ever had, all he'd worked for during his entire life. But he had neither the willpower nor the desire to turn his back on this unbelievable offer. Of course they would get away with it if they were careful and discreet.

Ever since that night when she presented herself to him after the Amateur Dramatics Society's efforts last spring, he had wanted her. Never in the world of pigs' pudding, though, did he ever think it likely he would have her. Never would he have believed that a man of his age would have any chance at all with Clara Stokes's nineteen-year-old daughter, whose desirability made him ache with longing. She reminded him so much of Clara at the same age, and his sentimentality for Clara in those bygone days had driven him, too recklessly it now appeared, to seek her hand in marriage as soon as she became available. It was strange, he thought, how the prize he would have considered so marvellous then could turn out to be hardly worth the having now. He could never have believed he could ever suffer such a disappointment.

Kate, however, was about to redeem him, was about to make it all worthwhile. Fair enough, if she wanted to go on the stage and make a strumpet of herself, he could go along with it. But he would dilly-dally, string her along. Why rush to make any arrangement with any impresario who would end up having all the fun? He would tell Kate he'd written, and keep her believing it until such time as he had to make a move, or she forgot all about it.

He entered the house, took off his cape and his tall hat, and hung them on the stand in the hallway. As he went into the sitting room, Clara greeted him with a smile. She was sitting with Algie. Soon, they were clutching a glass of whisky each. Neither Algie nor his mother, however, had the least notion that Kate, who had poured it, had laced both measures with laudanum to ensure they slept very soundly.

Algie cycled to work tired, dispirited and feeling completely useless. His head was muzzy, but his mind was nevertheless full of what he had discovered during the night. The trouble was, he had no idea what he should or could do with the knowledge. Maybe nothing. Perhaps it would be better for everybody if he were to say nothing, but simply leave it be. He wished he could make a decision. He wished there was somebody he could turn to for guidance, but what he had discovered was too shocking a thing to discuss with anybody.

'What's up wi' you?' Harry Whitehouse asked when they had been at work for half an hour, unspeaking.

'Nothing,' Algie said morosely.

'You look as if you've lost a sovereign and found a three-penny bit. Cheer up, man. Have you heard from that Marigold saying as she don't want yer after all, or summat?'

Algie shook his head and forced a smile.

'Well, summat's upset yer.'

'I just got a funny head, Harry,' he lied. 'It'll go off soon.'

'Then why don't you go up the office and ask Violet if she's got summat as you can take for it?'

'I'll be all right, Harry. Don't fuss.'

'Strikes me you got that influenza coming. It took me like that at first. Headaches, and feeling miserable. D'you feel miserable, Algie?'

'I do, to tell you the truth.'

'You look as miserable as sin. I'd go and ask Violet for summat if I was you, if it was only summat as would put a smile of your face . . . Go on . . .'

'Mr Sampson will only want to know why I ain't at my station,' Algie said.

'D'you reckon? I know he thinks he's clever, but he ain't that clever.'

'What d'you mean?'

'Well, he ain't here today, by all accounts. And while the cat's away . . .'

Algie instantly perked up at this news. If he went to the office he could find out for certain. He left Harry, and rushed to the office to verify the claim. He tapped on Violet's door and entered.

'Hello, Algie. What can I do for you?'

'I've got a vile head, Miss Pugh. Have you got something I could take for it?'

Violet Pugh, stout and in her mid-fifties, had been a faithful employee and dogsbody since the days of Benjamin Sampson Senior. The poor, overworked woman was often asked for remedies to common ailments, and kept a stock of pills, ointments, powders and syrups at hand for such emergencies. She got up from her chair and rummaged in a wall cupboard above an antiquated and dusty bookcase that contained rows of business directories and files. She pulled out a bottle of Dr Collis Browne's Chlorodyne, and a spoon.

'Best thing for headaches, this,' she proclaimed. 'I swear by it.' She uncorked the bottle and poured the liquid into the spoon. 'Open up.'

Algie stood there with his mouth open while Miss Pugh stood on tiptoe and poured it into his mouth. He screwed up his face as he tasted it.

'Best thing for anything, Dr Collis Browne's,' she said. 'Diarrhoea, rheumatics, lumbago, ague . . . even childbirth, I shouldn't wonder. Give it half an hour and you'll feel a new man.'

'Where's Mr Sampson?'

'Bristol today and Taunton tomorrow. He's a busy man these days, what with this new bike to sell and everything. It's given him a new lease of life.'

Algie couldn't help but smile at hearing it confirmed, despite all his worries.

'There, you got a smile back on your face already, young Algie. See? I told you it'd work in no time.'

* * *

As Algie passed the house of Benjamin Sampson on his way home, he peered intently towards it to see if there was a signal. His heart leapt when he saw the light spilling through Aurelia's bedroom window, and the red vase with the yellow paper flowers as bright as a beacon, announcing just what he longed to know. If nothing else, it gave him a reason to be out of the house and so not have to put up with the company of his perverse family.

When he arrived home he could not look his mother in the eye lest she could read in them the truth about Murdoch, and if he never saw Kate again in his whole life it would not bother him.

But he had to see his mother. He had to tell her he would not be staying to dinner.

'Where are you going?' she asked.

'Out.'

'Oh? Are you going on your bike?'

'No, the tram,' he answered impatiently. 'I shall eat while I'm out. I might not be back tonight either, so you needn't wait up for me. If I do come back I've got my key.'

She regarded him with suspicion in her expression 'You're doing this regular. Is it a woman?'

'Don't be daft,' he answered, failing to look at her. 'I'm done with women.'

It was partly true in any case. He was done with his sister anyway, he was done with Marigold – or, rather, she was done with him, which amounted to the same thing – he was done with Harriet Meese now that she and Clarence Froggatt were courting.

'So I'll be on my own again tonight,' Clara said, with self-pity evident in her tone. 'Murdoch and our Kate will be going to the Drill Hall later for rehearsal.'

'Then it's your own fault, Mother,' he said harshly. He had

no sympathy with her illogical phobia about runaway horses. She'd brought on this looming crisis, of which she knew nothing as yet, by her own reticence to accompany her new husband anywhere. 'You have the chances to go out, why don't you take them? Your husband has offered to take you out more than once to my knowledge, yet you never go because of your stupid fears. I bet he thinks you're a real stick-in-the-mud. You could even join the amateur dramatics group, if only to help with the costumes, but you won't. You'd rather stay here and rot.'

He wanted to say more. He could say more. He felt like telling her that her attitude made her marriage extremely vulnerable. He felt like saying that her refusal to accompany Murdoch had even stimulated his interest in other women, or had at least given him the opportunity. But he could not bring himself to do so. It would be too cruel, especially since it was the truth.

Clara sighed and nodded. 'Don't be so hard on me, our Algie,' she called after him. 'I always thought it was our Kate who was the hard one, not you.'

He turned his back on her. Of course, he blamed her for what had happened. It was entirely her own fault.

'I'm going up to have a good wash and to change into some clean clothes,' he said over his shoulder as he headed for the stairs. 'I'll be gone as soon as I'm ready.'

Chapter 27

Aurelia was already awaiting Algie when he arrived at Dudley Market Place. The elaborate marble fountain which stood majestically before it was a rendezvous point for many of the town's citizens. So as not to look as though she was waiting for somebody and so allay any suspicion, Aurelia browsed in the shop windows nearby, affecting a distinct air of interest in the merchandise on display. When the tram arrived, Algie saw her, her back towards him, looking deliciously elegant in her long dark skirt, her mantle and fashionable hat. There was something enigmatic about her demeanour; part the little-girl-lost, part the unhappily married woman who had no chance of permanent escape, but was partly resigned to her lot so long as she could steal a couple of illicit hours in the arms of the man she loved. Algie wanted to take her in his arms there and then, and hug her protectively. Instead, he tapped her gently on the shoulder.

'Oh, it's you,' she said, turning round with a smile of relief.

'Were you expecting somebody else?'

'Don't be silly.' She took his arm with warm affection and they began walking in the direction of the Eagle Hotel. 'I saw you ride past the house on your way home from the factory. You slowed down and looked straight up at my bedroom window, then sped off. I knew you'd seen the vase. Didn't you see me?'

'No, I didn't. Anyway, the plan works.'

'This time at any rate.' She gave his arm a squeeze. 'Oh, I'm so thrilled to see you again, Algie. It seems ages.'

'You look lovely, Aurelia.' He looked into her clear eyes and grinned. It seemed the first time in ages he'd had occasion to be happy.

'Thank you. Do I really?'

'I don't know how I keep my hands off you. I'd give anything to throw my arms around you now, in full view of everybody in Dudley, and give you a great big lingering kiss on the lips.'

That made her laugh. 'You've no idea how much it means to hear you say that, how much I've been looking forward to tonight.'

'How d'you think I've felt?'

'The same, I hope.'

'Course I have . . . Are you hungry?'

'Yes . . . but not for food particularly,' she added coyly.

He chuckled at the incongruity of her words and her manner of speaking them. 'Well, I'm starving,' he replied. 'For food and for you. I bet that Mr Powell will look at us sideways when he sees us again.'

'He should be glad of the business.'

'I reckon he is . . . By the way, have you taken your wedding ring off?'

'Of course,' she said. 'We're a courting couple, aren't we? I'm not a married woman engaging in a scandalous affair, as far as Mr Powell is concerned.'

Snow was falling, swirling round in the wind, flakes swarming around the street lamps like white moths. Aurelia looked up into the slate-grey sky and blinked as the snowflakes skimmed her long eyelashes.

'Don't you mean to stay out all night?' he asked, fearing a

heavier fall and a problem returning home. 'You haven't got your overnight case.'

'I have to get back,' she replied apologetically. 'Maude isn't there to look after Benjie if he wakes – only Mary. She was granted the evening off by Benjamin. I can't think why, can you?' She looked into his eyes and smiled, as if to say that it didn't matter anyway so long as she had him to love instead. 'Besides,' she went on, 'it will look awfully odd to Mary if I too decide to spend the night away every time Benjamin does. Don't you think? I get funny looks from both Maude and Mary as it is, when I tell them I'm going out. I only ever go out alone when he's away. Lord knows what they must think.'

'Then for the sake of their easy minds let's hope the snow keeps off and doesn't detain you.'

'Well, that might not be so bad anyway,' she answered with an angelic smile. 'It's not out of choice that I go back home.'

They reached the Eagle Hotel and entered. Mr Powell spotted them and approached at once while they scanned the room for a free table.

'Mr Stokes,' he greeted. 'Miss, er . . . Dinner for two?'

'Yes,' Algie replied, then added in a low voice, 'and afters please, if you can accommodate us,'

'Of course,' Mr Powell said quietly, smirking to himself. 'I'll arrange for a fire to be lit at once. Your usual room?'

Algie nodded and allowed Mr Powell to lead them to a vacant table.

Aurelia ate little, but talked brightly while he listened and ate heartily. Her lively chatter pushed to the back of his mind for a while the unresolved problems he'd left at home. She gossiped about everyday things, told Algie how she'd been filling her days, all the time thinking about him, longing to be with him. 'It's torture,' she said, 'when I know you are there and I'm not able to see you, just because I'm married to *him*, and I have to sit in *his* house and pretend to everybody that I'm *his* devoted wife. I sit downstairs, or in my bedroom, in the dark and wait just to see you ride past our house. I feel such a hypocrite.'

'If you won't leave him, what can you expect?'

'A little sympathy might not come amiss, Algie,' she pouted. 'I can't leave him, can I? You know I can't leave him.'

'I don't reckon I'm capable of giving much sympathy at the moment. You'll have to forgive me, Aurelia. I'm afraid I've got troubles enough of my own to worry about.'

'Why? What's wrong?'

'Oh, nothing to do with you and me.' He smiled reassuringly, and reached for her hand across the table.

'What then? Do you want to tell me?'

'Not really.'

'But it doesn't concern us?'

'No, no. It concerns my sister.'

'Is she in trouble?'

'She's ever likely to be. . .'

'Does Clarence Froggatt have anything to do with it?'

He shook his head, his expression grim. 'No, it's nothing to do with Clarence . . . I don't want to talk about it, Aurelia. I want to forget all about it while I'm with you. Only because I have no desire to trouble you with it.'

She smiled sympathetically. 'Then let's be happy that we *are* together, if only for a few hours.'

He nodded and smiled, gladdened by her tenderness. 'If you're ready, I'll get the room key off Mr Powell.'

By the time they entered the room the fire was blazing gloriously. Algie parted the curtains and looked out onto the street below. It was still snowing, but not heavily, and there was a mere suggestion of a covering on the ground. He undressed quickly and dived into bed naked.

'God, it's cold in this bed.'

'Warm my side up please, Algie,' she pleaded as she doffed her chemise. 'Maybe we should've asked for a warming pan.'

'No need,' he said, shivering. 'Quick, get in here. We can warm each other.'

She slid in beside him and laughed, then shivered too as the cold of the sheets enveloped her. She snuggled up to him, and he luxuriated in the warmth and smoothness of her skin against him. He held her tight, their lips met and they kissed passionately. Her leg came across his and they were instantly entwined in a fervour of mutual desire. There was barely any time for foreplay, barely any need. He rolled onto her, pressed himself urgently against her for entry. She gripped his buttocks and, with an ecstatic vocal gasp, felt him slide easily into her with such sweet, sweet intensity.

'Oh, Algie,' she sighed. 'I've wanted you so much . . .' She relished the pleasure that was flowing through her and out of her.

This must be how it is for a husband come home from the seas or from the wars, Algie thought as he wallowed in the sumptuous sensations she eagerly bestowed on him. The feel of her as he moved inside her was delightfully familiar by now, of course, and yet somehow new, fresh and unexplored. It was a sheer, sensual joy to be here, and the comparison crossed his mind, not for the first time, between Aurelia and Marigold. For a few seconds he imagined it was Marigold beneath him, moving in pleasurable concert and emitting little vocal sighs, just like she used to do. Oh, where was Marigold now?

They lay silent in each other's arms for some time afterwards, content and perspiring in the heat of that room with its blazing fire. The ceiling was alive with the swirling glimmer of the fire's flames, which cast a jigging shadow of the unlit

428

gaslight hanging down. Algie absently watched this frolicking display for some time, while Aurelia lay with her eyes closed, a look of serenity on her beautiful face.

Thank God he had Aurelia. She was a sort of touchstone, as she had been in the past. She was easy to talk to, easy to pour out your troubles to, as well as being an enthusiastic lover. And he had troubles enough looming. Troubles galore. Troubles on which he would dearly love some sound advice.

'Aurelia, are you awake?'

'Yes, I'm awake, my love,' she answered softly. 'I was just resting my eyes, thinking how lovely it would be to wake up next to you each morning.'

'Yes, wouldn't that be grand? But even that would become commonplace after a while.'

'Of course it would,' she sighed. 'But at least we'd be happy, wouldn't we? You can put up with the commonplace easily enough if you're happy. I know we would be happy, you and me. I sense it. We're like souls, Algie, don't you think?'

'Yes, I do,' he said sincerely. 'I don't feel as if I have to put on airs and graces for you.'

'Nor should you. I don't put on airs and graces for you. I am as I am. But we understand each other, don't we? We have a rapport.'

'Yes, a rapport,' he repeated with a smile. 'That's a good word.'

'It is. It describes us perfectly.' She turned towards him and fingered the patch of sparse hairs that were sprouting on his chest. 'The only insurmountable problem is the fact that I can never be yours. Oh, I'm yours in spirit – you know I am – but I can never be yours in reality. The fact that you understand it so readily makes it easier for us in a way. At least I'm glad of that.'

'How does it make it easier for me?' he asked. 'I hate the

thought of you and your husband . . . It's just something else to myther about . . . I wish you'd leave him.'

'It's a tempting thought, believe me.'

He turned onto his side to face her. Up till now she'd said it was impossible, unthinkable. 'Then do it.'

'But where would I go?'

'We could live in glorious sin together.' He grinned boyishly. 'Just think – we'd be the talk of the place.'

'Where would we live?'

'I'd rent a house . . . A long way from here, where nobody knows us.'

'Your romantic streak is getting the better of you again, Algie.' She planted a kiss on his lips. 'But I love you the more because of it.'

'Just think,' he said again, his enthusiasm for the idea increasing. 'We could live as Mr and Mrs Stokes, and nobody need be any the wiser. Benjamin would be my son as far as anybody else was concerned. I'd find work wherever we went . . .'

'But you wouldn't be able to afford to send him to a public – or even a private – school.'

That unanticipated comment highlighted his own limitations, and he felt suddenly inadequate. 'But you'd have him with you all the time,' he countered. 'He needn't leave home, I mean. There are other schools.'

'Yes, that's true . . .'

'And, who knows? We might have children of our own.'

'Yes,' she answered dreamily. 'Of course we might. Who knows?'

'But I couldn't afford to keep you in the way you've been used to,' he admitted, expanding on the theme of his financial constraints to see how she would react. 'There'd be no servants.'

'Do servants make you happy, Algie? If I was happy I wouldn't give a fig whether I had servants or not. They can be a bit intrusive, if you want to know the truth. They can steal your husband . . . Anyway, if I had no servants I would find things to occupy me all the time. Looking after my new family . . .'

'Then will you think about it? Will you think seriously about leaving Benjamin and everything it involves?'

'I will. It all sounds delicious. I'll think about how many illegitimate children we might foist on the world in our life of relative poverty.'

'Oh, we won't be that poor,' he said with a smile. 'I intend to do well in life. But things might be hard at first.'

'I wish you'd tell me what it is that's troubling you about your sister,' she said, changing tack completely. 'It can't be any worse than the usual scandal of being in the family way. There's nothing fresh in that. It afflicts a lot of families.'

He sighed heavily. 'I feel too ashamed to tell you,' he replied. 'Lord knows what you would think of me and my family if I did. It's dreadful, Aurelia. It really is.'

'So you don't want to tell me?'

'Oh, I would tell you, if only to get it off my chest. But I'm fearful of what you might think of us afterwards.'

'If it's something your sister's done, why should I think any the less of you?'

'Because it's bound to involve my mother and me at some time. Especially my mother.' Suddenly his notions of eloping with Aurelia looked somewhat remote. 'Sometime soon there's going to be a massive eruption in our house, like some bloody great volcano going off.'

'Do *tell* me, Algie,' she begged. 'It sounds such a juicy scandal. And I do love a juicy scandal.'

'If I tell you, I don't think you'll want to risk being seen with me again. I doubt if you'd want to elope with me anymore. You'll run a mile in the opposite direction.'

'Oh, Algie,' she sighed. 'Nothing could ever be that bad. I love you, my darling. I'm hardly likely to turn against you. Especially about something over which you have no control, something that's not your fault. You have to trust me more than that . . .'

At the word 'trust' he felt more inclined to reveal the torrid secret. Of course he could trust her.

'Well, all right . . . I suppose I'd better start at the beginning . . . It began just after my father died. The house we lived in was owned by the Stourbridge Canal Company and therefore tied to my father's job as lock-keeper. So we had to move out of it to make way for a new chap who was due to take over. We had nowhere to go, of course. We knew we would have to rent a house, but there just hadn't been the time to look, what with the upset, making funeral arrangements and everything else. So we rented two rooms at the Bell Hotel in Brierley Hill to tide us over. When along came this chap who, it turns out, used to be my mother's sweetheart when she was about eighteen. He came to see her while me and our Kate were at work, and he suggested we all go and live with him. The only stipulation was that my mother should marry him – he was a widower, you see.

'Well, to tell you the truth, Aurelia, I wasn't very keen on the idea. My father was still warm in his grave, and I thought it was much too soon for her to think about marrying again. But she convinced herself that it was the right thing to do, and so I went along with it, thinking it might bring her some companionship and security in her later years. After all, I thought, I would most likely leave and get married at some time, and so would our Kate. So, from that point of view it seemed sensible.'

'And did she?' Aurelia asked. 'Did your mother marry this man?'

'By special licence within a couple of days. Then we all moved to his house in Kingswinford.'

'And yet you've never told me any of this, Algie. Why?'

'Because I was ashamed. I was ashamed of my mother marrying again so soon after my father's death. And folk talked when news got out. I know how they talked.'

'Folk do,' she said. 'Imagine what folk would say about us. They'd talk about me especially, a married woman having what they would regard as a sordid affair, especially if we go off and live in sin. Lord, they'd talk the clack off a church bell. But I don't care. Our affair isn't sordid, Algie. It's beautiful. So they can say what they like. Words never hurt anyone . . . Anyway, we digress. How does your dear sister fit into all this?'

'My dear sister already knew this chap . . . And I sort of knew him a bit, though I never really liked him. I don't know, for the life of me, whether anything was going on between this chap and our Kate before, but—'

'My God . . . Oh, Algie . . .' Her face was an icon of sympathy and shock. 'Are you saying something's going on now?'

'No question of it.'

'But your poor mother . . . Are you absolutely certain of this?'

'Oh, yes.'

'How can you be so certain?'

'Because I've heard him go to her room at night. I've heard them at it – the bed springs creaking. I've seen him coming out of her bedroom afterwards and go back into my mother's.'

Aurelia gasped. 'Oh, but that's just dreadful, Algie. No wonder you didn't want to tell me . . . But what a risk they're taking. Have they no sense, no respect? I mean, they've already been found out, haven't they, if you've witnessed their comings and goings.'

'But I've said nothing to anybody. Only you. I don't know what I should do about it . . . If anything . . .'

'Can't you confront your sister?'

'She'd only deny it.'

'So how did she know this chap previously?'

'Because she's a member of the Brierley Hill Amateur Dramatics Society. She met him there.'

'Oh?' Aurelia looked suddenly alarmed. 'You've already said it's not Clarence Froggatt.'

'Clarence is hardly likely to have wanted to marry my mother,' he answered flippantly, belying his concern.

'So who is it?'

'His name's Murdoch Osborne.'

'Oh, my God!' She sat up, immediately erect, and held her head in her hands as if suddenly stricken with a severe pain.

'What's the matter, Aurelia? Do you know him or something?'

'Do I know Murdoch Osborne? Oh, yes, I know him all right . . .

'How?'

'He is my father . . .'

Chapter 28

'You know what this means, Algie?' Aurelia said, after the initial shock had worn off.

That you might be my sister, he was half inclined to remark. The horrible possibility had been gnawing at him corrosively ever since his first doubts about his mother's propriety, or lack of it, in her younger days; whether or not she'd had an illicit affair with Murdoch.

'What?' he uttered miserably instead. 'What does it mean?'

'It means that you are living in the house I used to live in. Which bedroom do you sleep in?'

'One on the front. At the end of the landing on the right.'

'That was mine! Oh, fancy, Algie, you're sleeping in the same room I used to sleep in. Such a bizarre coincidence, don't you think?'

'Pity you still don't,' he said, trying to sound cheerful. 'I wouldn't be so cold and lonely at night.'

'Just think. If things hadn't happened the way they did, I might still be living there. You and I would have met anyway. That proves we were destined to meet. Just imagine if you had been slipping into my room in the dead of night,' she chuckled artfully. 'Because there's no doubt in my mind that we would have become lovers sooner or later. Don't you think so, Algie?'

'The fact that your father married my mother wouldn't have stopped me fancying you, Aurelia.'

'Nor me you. That much I know.'

'But I'm not even sure it's legal,' he remarked. 'Stepbrother and stepsister.'

'If they are of different blood, then there's nothing to stop them. And we are of different blood, Algie. We could have married.'

I wish I had your confidence, he thought. 'Your mother died a couple of years ago, didn't she?'

'Three and a half years ago. She died in the July. Her death was one of the reasons I was in such a rush to leave and get married . . .'

'Oh? Why?'

'Because I had to get away from my father,' she explained. 'I only stayed at home for the sake of my mother. When she died, the offer of marriage from Benjamin was an escape for me. My father assented to it because I believe he was just as glad to be rid of me.'

'You seem to spend your life trying to escape one master for another,' he commented.

She laughed. 'Yes, I suppose it must seem that way.'

'So why did you want to escape from your father?'

'Because of what he did to my mother. He ruined her. I loathe and detest him for it, Algie. I couldn't have stayed with him after my mother died if they'd crowned me with gold.'

'So what did he do?'

'The same as he's done to your mother . . .'

'Had an affair, you mean?'

Aurelia nodded. 'It came to light, some years ago – I forget how exactly – that he'd had an affair with my mother's youngest sister. It caused ructions in the family.'

'Struth! I don't suppose your mother was very impressed with this revelation.'

'Well, you can just imagine, can't you? . . . She never got over it. From that moment her health declined. She shut herself off from my father and from the rest of the world. I wanted to finish my schooling to be with her and to look after her, and so did my sister who is younger than me, but Mother wouldn't hear of it. I dreaded school holidays, but I knew I had to go home to look after my mother and offer her my support, but I had nothing to do with my father ever again. In the house I avoided him like the plague. In the end I think my mother died of shame. In her day she was a beautiful woman, you know. From a respectable family. All the women on her side were beauties, though I say so myself.'

'That's who you get your looks from, eh? Your mother.'

'Well, if I have decent looks at all, they're certainly not from my father,' she said scornfully.

'So what happened to your sister?'

'Rosalind? Oh, she seized her chance and eloped with a young soldier, a captain. She, at least, is very content with her lot.'

'Her eloping raised a few eyebrows, I bet.'

'Not half as many as my father's affair with his sister-in-law would've raised, had that become common knowledge. Can you imagine?'

'Just think,' he said. 'If you had married Clarence, he would have been Murdoch's son-in-law. I presume Clarence knows all about Murdoch and your aunt.'

'Oh, I doubt it very much. He knew I was not very friendly with my father, but he didn't know the reason, I'm sure. Consequently, Clarence sided with me and didn't admire my father for the simple reason that I didn't.'

'And yet he still joined the amateur dramatics society, and performed in their plays under his direction.'

'Not till after I broke off our engagement. Maybe he felt peeved and thought he might get some sympathy from my father. They had women of the same family in common after all.'

'I can't get over you being Murdoch's daughter,' Algie said after a brief silence. 'Where does that put us now, I wonder?'

'Why should it make any difference?'

He sighed heavily. 'It shouldn't,' he replied, giving the answer that would provoke no alarm or heart searching.

Of course it would not be expedient to reveal his suspicions. He had no proof that he was Murdoch's son. He might yet be wrong. But if he suggested that they might be closely related, Aurelia might well find their affair an abomination and end it when, in the long run, there might be no need. He enjoyed the intimate stolen hours he spent with Aurelia. Being suddenly faced with the possibility that he was her half-brother could hardly alter the way he felt, nor could it obliterate the intimacy they'd already shared. What was done was done, whether she turned out to be his half-sister or no. Only convention could have any material effect at all.

'I wonder what time it is,' he said. 'If the snow's coming down heavy maybe we'd best leave while the trams are still running.' His inbred regard for the morals of convention and decency were surfacing within him; his suggestion would give her the opportunity to take advantage of the offer of escape under the pretext of the foul weather, and yet be a salve to his own probity.

'So soon?' she protested.

He clambered out of bed and peered through the curtains. Snow was still falling, but it was certainly no blizzard. He watched a tram chug past from the direction of Top Church.

'The trams are still running,' he reported.

'I can hear.'

'It's not too bad out there. In any case, we could walk it if need be.'

'So come back to bed, Algie.'

He looked at her, her head just visible over the sheets, her hair awry, her eyes wide with expectation.

'Come back to bed and let me try and take your mind off things.'

He grinned. Of course he was going back to bed. How could he resist? She was so beautiful, so desirable, and so appreciative. Odds were that she was not his half-sister anyway . . .

Aurelia stepped off the tram into the flurrying snow. As she crossed the street, Algie caught sight of her and waved. She blew him a kiss in return, and disappeared into the darkness. Pondering their night of love and the things they had spoken of, she sauntered the short distance home. Yes, it was very tempting to leave Benjamin, and elope with Algie, to dwell in some strange town where nobody knew them, where they could live happily as man and wife and bring up Benjie as their own. It certainly appealed to her romantic instincts. But she could not pin her hopes on that just yet; she was conscious that the uncertainties raised by Algie's sister's affair with Murdoch Osborne, damn him, were too real and must affect everything at some time or other. Time alone would determine their fate, and it would be foolhardy to rush into anything now.

She walked at a leisurely pace up the drive to the house, the gravel and the fresh snow crisp beneath her feet. It must be about half past ten, she reckoned. Not too late; not extravagantly late at any rate. Mary might still be up awaiting her return. Lamps from a couple of the front downstairs rooms shone out welcomingly onto the snow through the windows, suggesting that the girl was still up.

She opened the front door and entered. The drawing room was lit up. Strange. Mary would not presume to sit in there to wait. Then she smelled tobacco smoke, heard the rustle of a newspaper. Her heart, all of a sudden, seemed to have stopped beating.

'Is that you, Aurelia?'

Benjamin.

'Yes, it's me, Benjamin. You're home a day early.'

'To be sure. Where the hell have you been?'

She presented herself at the door in her snow-flecked mantle and bonnet.

'Oh, I, er . . .' She scoured her mind for a plausible excuse. 'I only popped out to see Mrs Holden, my dressmaker.'

He looked at her in patent disbelief. 'On a night like this?'

'I had . . . a note in the post this morning. There was a query on a new dress I ordered.'

'Take your hat off.'

Biddably, she doffed her hat and melting snowflakes dripped onto the carpet at her feet.

'Are you sure that pulling a dress over your head at the dressmaker's has made your hair so unkempt?' He got up from his chair, putting the newspaper down and approached her, his eyes steady upon her. 'You look as if you've just got out of bed. Are you sure you've not taken to becoming a dolly-mop to earn some pin money on my nights away?'

Maybe he knew.

Good God, what if he knew?

Aurelia feared that he might have guessed, just from the lingering, tell-tale signs of passion enjoyed; her rounded cheeks still glowing from recent exertion, her eyes, still soft and dreamy and full of the loving tenderness she'd shared with Algie Stokes. Aurelia felt naked under her husband's scrutiny, as if he could even perceive her wetness from ardent and prolonged lovemaking, could see the sensual skin of her pleasured body glowing like a lamp through the fabric of

440

her clothes where Algie had caressed and savoured her. The intense tingling she'd felt deep in her groin that still lingered, seemed to be radiating its message. In a brief exchange of wordless looks, he seemed to know.

'Go and tidy yourself up, Aurelia.'

'I'm going to bed anyway.'

She could not shift from her mind, however, the sheer joy and pleasure of feasting on Algie's torrential desire. It was going to be hard to contain her emotions; it was going to be even harder to maintain her equilibrium in her increasingly mundane marriage. But did Benjamin really know anything? He had not accused her directly. Maybe he was just testing, to see her reactions. Well, she would test him. She turned back to her husband.

'Are you suggesting I've been with another man? Or even men?'

'How the hell would I know whether you have or no, without having you followed? But your leaving the house while I'm away, and coming back at this hour looks mighty suspicious.'

'And what if I told you I had been with another man?' she asked airily. 'What would you do?'

'Have you been with another man?'

'As I told you, Benjamin, I've been to see my dressmaker. But you haven't answered my question. What would you do if I had been with another man?'

'I'd whip you. I'd thrash you good and hard.'

'Which would endear you to me no end . . . Wouldn't it occur to you that maybe I have reason enough to be unfaithful, Benjamin? You don't care for me anyway. You treat me like a servant. In fact, you are more polite, more considerate to our servants than you are to me. Never have you shown me any tenderness, any consideration. At the first opportunity it's your intention to rob me of my son by packing him off to some distant boarding school. You have no interest in what happens to me or to him. Yet you were quick enough to steal me from under the nose of Clarence Froggatt, wooing me with fine words and promises of enduring happiness, none of which have ever materialised. Oh, you flaunted me in front of your friends and your family, putting on a show of attention, so that they could envy you and compliment you on your choice of fiancée. But all it tells me is that you are only interested in yourself. It tells me that all I ever was to you was an ornament, a fashion accessory that enhanced your own standing in the eyes of others. Once you married me – once you owned me – once I was out of everybody else's reach – it seemed that you wished you hadn't bothered. Looking back at the frequency of our intimacy, it amazes me that Benjie was ever conceived.'

'Since you mention it, I've harboured the same doubts.'

Aurelia looked at him scornfully. 'Oh, you can be sure he's your child . . . Our marriage doesn't work,' she went on after a pause. 'Oh, it might work for you. I'm sure it works very well for you. But it certainly doesn't work for me. Marriage is not merely a convenience for men to be waited on hand and foot, to bed their wives for a bit of selfish sexual indulgence whenever the fancy takes them. It is a partnership – or it should be. Two people striving together, in harmony, with love and visible affection between them, sharing the responsibility of raising the children they have made. I don't see our marriage in that light, Benjamin. Nor can you.'

'So, as far as you're concerned it's failed.'

'Yes. To be frank.'

'I had no idea you felt that way, Aurelia,' he said limply.

'Because you don't look. I've felt it since Benjie was a tiny baby. I should have spoken of it sooner, perhaps. It's as if you think I should be grateful to you for you deigning to marry me.'

'You were grateful, at the time, I seem to remember.'

'I would have survived. Possibly better if I'd stuck it out.'

'Then see if you can still survive, my dear,' he said ominously. 'Maybe we should consider a separation. A temporary one at any rate, to see whether we're as incompatible as you make out.'

'Yes, perhaps we should,' she replied, prepared to call his bluff, and left him to go to bed.

While they waited for the tram back home, Algie and Aurelia had talked about ways he could approach the problem of his sister and his stepfather, but reached no conclusion. She'd suggested that if his mother's marriage had not been consummated, then it was likely it could be annulled. Algie, however, considered such a circumstance unlikely, given Murdoch's past record.

Despite his evening of stolen love, Algie was depressed. Doubts about his parentage rendered the prospect of any elopement with Aurelia abhorrent. He would carry the burden of this secret fear alone, however, until such time as it was resolved. Its outcome would determine any future they might have together but, if it turned out that he was Murdoch's son, telling her would be the hardest thing he'd ever have to face.

Anger and concern about Kate's perilously illicit affair with Murdoch, and not least his worries for his mother, were piling up on him as well. His mother did not deserve this degeneracy going on behind her back, whatever she might or might not have been capable of in the past. She had only recently buried Will, her first husband. Now her second marriage was in turmoil, although she was not aware of it yet. Algie just did not know what to do with the devastating knowledge he possessed, and it was driving him mad, tearing at his emotions.

Algie arrived back home shortly after Kate and Murdoch

443

returned from the Drill Hall and their rehearsal. Murdoch walked in the house noisily stamping the snow off his boots, after tacking down the horse. He greeted Clara cursorily.

'Where's Kate?' Algie asked.

'In the scullery getting me my tot of whisky,' his mother replied. 'Can't do without my tot of whisky these days.'

Murdoch smiled patronisingly. 'Yes, get it down you, my flower. It does you the world of good.'

Algie looked at him with loathing for being so two-faced. How he hated this man. 'I think I'll have one as well, Mother,' he said. 'I'll go and do it and take it up to bed with me.' It would get him out of the way. Besides, he needed a drink after what he'd learned tonight; that Murdoch was Aurelia's father.

Kate had taken the bottle of whisky to the scullery and, as he entered, he witnessed her pouring a few drops of something from a tiny bottle, patently not whisky, into the glass.

'What's that you've got there?' he queried, alarmed at what it might be.

'Oh, it's you, Algie.' She smiled innocently, sweetly, and quickly turned her back on him to put the cork back in the tiny bottle and slip it into the pocket of her skirt without him seeing. 'I didn't hear you come in.'

'Answer my question,' he rasped, his patience in tatters. 'What have you just put into Mother's glass of whisky?'

'Nothing,' she protested.

'You liar. I just saw you.'

'Don't you dare call me a liar, Algie Stokes,' she answered with indignation. 'You've got a nerve.'

'Give me that bottle you had in your hand a second ago.'

'What bottle? You're seeing things. Look . . .' She raised the empty palms of her hands to show him.

'I know what I saw, Kate. What have you done with it?' He glanced around him rapidly but there was no sign of it.

'You're going mad, our Algie,' she said, laughing scornfully. 'I've thought it for some time now. You're going soft in the head.'

'Soft in the head I might be and no wonder at it, but my eyes have never deceived me yet. What have you done with it? Is it in the pocket of your skirt?'

'Don't be daft. There is no bottle.'

He grabbed hold of her, surprising her, and felt around her skirt deftly where he knew her pockets to be. There was something hard there, something that could well have been a small bottle. But Kate soon recovered her equilibrium and struggled frantically, releasing herself from his grip.

'How dare you assault me,' she hissed, trying to maintain some semblance of quietness, to keep this matter private, and not to alert the rest of the household.

'I swear I just felt it in your pocket. Give it me.'

'Go and jump in the cut.'

Algie grabbed her again, twisting her round so that her back was towards him. He thrust one arm around her neck and pinned both her arms together tight behind her with his superior strength, so that she could not strike out at him.

'You're hurting me, you swine,' she shrieked.

She wriggled like a snake in her effort to break free, calling him all the names she could lay her tongue to, but his greater force ensured he held her fast. She kicked out at him with her heels and hurt his shins. He winced with the pain, but would not let go. Eventually, accepting that she was trapped, she ceased her struggling. When he sensed that he could let go of his arm from around her neck he fished in her skirt pocket. As he withdrew the bottle, he shoved her away and scrutinised it.

'Laudanum!' he pronounced, and looked at her aghast. 'You're lacing mother's whisky with laudanum?' At once he understood her motive. 'And I know why, you dirty little whore!'

'Don't call me a dirty little whore,' she screeched, half in anger at his resentment, half in frustration for getting caught.

'But that's just what you are, Kate, a dirty little whore. I know exactly what you're up to.'

Hearing the commotion, his mother and Murdoch stood together at the doorway looking perplexed.

'What's going on in here, ha?' Murdoch enquired sternly.

'D'you really want me to say, with my mother standing behind you?'

'Has he hurt you, Kate?'

'Hurt her? I ought to bloody-well kill her.'

'Don't swear like that, our Algie,' his mother interjected, her delicacy offended, but also trying to remain calm under these disagreeable circumstances.

Algie sighed in frustration. He could contain his pent-up emotions no longer; he was at bursting point. 'Never mind my swearing, Mother. That's just a bit petty compared to what your daughter does. Isn't that right, *sweet* Kate?'

Kate made no reply, merely glowering at him from under a furrowed brow and rolling her big brown eyes resentfully.

'See this, Mother?' He held up the small green bottle. 'It's laudanum. Well, your delightful, precious daughter has just put a few drops of it in your whisky. Something she's been doing every night to make you sleep.'

'Laudanum? Lord, I thought it was knocking me out,' Clara admitted, still not aware of the greater relevance.

'And you know why?'

'Why?' Clara enquired, obviously puzzled.

'Tell her, Kate. Tell your mother why you want her knocked out every night.'

'I don't know what you're talking about,' Kate scoffed. 'You're losing your wool.'

446

'Shall I tell her, Kate? . . . But it'd be better coming straight from the horse's mouth.'

'You're mad, Algie Stokes,' Kate cried haughtily. 'You've lost your mind.'

'I know I lost it the night you spiked *my* whisky with laudanum, but since then I've woken up . . .'

'I think you ought to apologise to your sister for making such stupid accusations, Algie,' Murdoch said vehemently, with a threat unmistakable in his tone. 'Say you're sorry, lad, and we'll all get to bed and forget about it, ha?'

'Oh, you'd like that, wouldn't you, Murdoch? It'd conveniently take the heat off you, *ha*?' said Algie, disdainfully mimicking Murdoch's tedious habit of speech. 'You think *I* should apologise, do you? That's rich coming from you.'

'Who d'you think you're talking to, ha? You cheeky young whelp. Hold your tongue, lad, else I'll beat the living daylights out of yer.'

'Oh, I'd love you to try, *Step*father. I really would.'

'Stop this senseless arguing at once, both of you,' Clara butted in, staring in wide-eyed disbelief and shame at this unanticipated flare-up in her family. 'I never heard anything like it in my life. Have you been drinking, Algie? Are you drunk?'

'He must be drunk,' Murdoch agreed.

'No, I'm not drunk. I haven't touched a drop all night. I'm stone cold sober as a matter of fact, and I want you to hear why Kate's been spiking your whisky . . . Go on, Kate, tell her . . .'

Kate remained sullenly silent.

The new maid appeared and hovered, to all intents and purposes on her way up to bed. Murdoch spotted her out of the corner of his eye and shooed her away impatiently. Algie didn't care whether the maid heard what the argument was all about or not.

'Right. Then I'll tell you, Mother,' he went on regardless,

unable to keep quiet about the scandalous shenanigans any longer. 'It's to knock you out so that you sleep all night, while Murdoch visits her room and gets into *her* bed . . . You can imagine the goings-on.'

Clara looked at her son with wide-eyed incredulity, then at Murdoch, then at Kate.

'I never heard anything so damned preposterous in my life,' Murdoch protested fervently, looking with apprehension at his wife. 'This is slander. Out and out slander, ha?'

'I've *seen* you, Murdoch,' Algie countered. 'I've stood outside Kate's room and listened. I've heard her giggling and you grunting, and I've heard the bloody bed springs creaking as well. Then I've watched you stagger back to my mother's room, she none the wiser for having been knocked out by the laudanum in her whisky.' He turned to his mother, an agonised look on his face. 'Mother, I'm so sorry I have to put you through this,' he said earnestly, tears in his eyes at this shameful revelation. 'But it's the truth, I swear it. I didn't want to have to tell you, but I'd have been betraying you as well if I hadn't.'

His shoulders seemed to slump, and he shook his head as if he was drained of all strength and emotion; the effects of enduring this heavy burden, coupled with the absolute necessity of having to release it.

'Is this true, Murdoch?' Clara asked simply.

'Course not. It's a ridiculous lie from start to finish. It's nothing less than slander, I tell you.'

'Our Kate? . . . Is it true?'

Kate turned away from her mother guiltily. That simple movement spoke louder than any words could have done. Then her inborn defiance bubbled to the fore, overriding any feelings of shame, guilt or blame. She would not go down without a word of justification for her deeds.

'All right, it's true, Mother,' she cried. 'But I don't regret it. Not one bit. And you know something? Murdoch was easy to pinch from you, and you know why? Because you're a dreary old stick-in-the-mud. You bore him to tears already. You won't go out, you won't do anything. All you're interested in is stopping in the house with your feet up, sewing and mending. What company is that for a man? You don't deserve to keep him.'

Clara felt as if she'd been punched in the stomach, a horrible, sickly, gut-churning feeling, and her legs suddenly felt weak beneath her. She looked at her daughter with an expression of incredulity that the girl could stoop so low and yet show no inclination to repent. She then looked at Murdoch with utter contempt, before turning to Algie.

'I don't think I want him, if all this is true,' she said quietly, finding her voice at last. To Kate, she said coldly, 'Keep him, Kate, and welcome.' Her heart was by now thumping with the unbearable pain that accompanied the awful realisation of how callously she had been betrayed by those who professed to love her. Again she looked at her daughter, with a deeply hurt expression. 'I pray to God that I never see either you or *him* again, so long as I live.' She turned to Murdoch. 'Now, you rat, will you please afford me the courtesy of being alone while I gather my belongings together?' Then to Algie. 'Algie, you and me have got some packing to do. We're leaving this house tonight.'

He heard his mother's shuddering sigh at the same time that he heard the stairs creak, as the new young maid crept up them.

Chapter 29

A tear ran down Clara's cheek which she stemmed with her tiny handkerchief. How could she continue to live in this house now under the crushing pressure of this disastrous knowledge? How could either Murdoch or Kate ever summon the gall to face her again, even if she wanted to stay? Such carryings on as she had been told of were utterly alien, bizarre, depraved. It was impossible, after such an outlandish union, that either of them could ever be a part of her life again. They could tread their own path from now on. She had neither lain with, nor known her new husband long enough to be aware of his weaknesses and his faults, but the trust was gone anyway. Her own limited experience, her innate naïvety, made it impossible to understand why or how this despicable perversity had happened. She could not excuse it, she could not countenance it, nor could she forgive it.

She blamed herself. She had managed to drag everybody into this quagmire of sin by marrying Murdoch. Because of it Algie's life was in turmoil, and through no fault of his own. Her own life was also in shreds, and all because of the promise of care and affection, which she had desperately needed to allay her grief over Will.

Dear, dear Will . . .

Clara sighed at the recollection of him. What would he say

if he could see her now? How utterly foolish she had been for a grown woman.

Kate, on the other hand ... What demon had they spawned, she and Will? She had no sympathy with Kate; the girl had engineered her own disgrace, bolstered only by Murdoch. It was the ultimate betrayal. What they had done was unthinkable and unforgivable. She meant it when she'd said that she never wanted to see either of them again.

As far as Clara was concerned there was only one thing for it; to leave at once, and Algie must leave with her. Not that she thought for a minute that Algie would want to stay. Not in Murdoch's house. Despite his immaturity in so many things, Algie was constant. He was, not least, her son. Without doubt, she could depend on him.

Without further ado, she pulled a large canvas bag from inside the wardrobe. They would find a room at an inn for the night. There was one up the road, the Old Court House. She could not stay here in this house of sin and condone her daughter's and her husband's reckless, wanton behaviour. Whatever had Murdoch been thinking, to imagine for a moment that he could get away with something as abhorrent as this, under his own roof with his own wife just across the landing, his stepson just along it, and two maids and a cook sleeping in the bedrooms above him?

She rummaged through the drawers of her dressing table and through her wardrobe, and hurriedly threw as many things as she could into her bag. Anything she had forgotten or could not carry would have to remain where she had left it. Awkwardly, she lugged the bag downstairs and placed it in the hall by the front door. There she waited for Algie. She was aware of Murdoch and Kate in the sitting room, talking in hushed tones, discussing, no doubt, the best way for them to redeem themselves, to lessen or mitigate their sin in the eyes of the society in which they existed, for this sin would doubtless destroy the reputations of both.

Algie emerged from upstairs carrying another canvas bag containing all his worldly goods. He saw his mother looking forlorn and agitated in the hall, and went to her. Smiling sympathetically he put his arm around her and gave her a hug.

'Are you ready then?'

'I am,' she answered solemnly.

'Are you sure this is what you want to do?'

'It's not what I would've chosen, Algie, but there's nothing else for it.'

'Are you sure you want to leave tonight? Wouldn't you rather leave in the morning?'

'No, I'm not staying in this house another minute.'

He nodded. 'I agree. Come on then.'

He opened the front door, and the howling wind blew in a rain of snowflakes. They turned their backs on the house and walked away without a word to the remaining occupants. Even a goodbye would have been more than they deserved.

'Let me carry your bag and you can have mine,' he said considerately. 'Mine's lighter for you . . . Hang on, though. I'm not leaving my bike here, just to have to come back and fetch it tomorrow. I don't want to see that pair ever again. I'll get it now.'

He put down the bag and rushed round to the rear of the house to retrieve his bicycle from the outbuilding where he kept it. Clara waited, huddled under her mantle, shivering from shock and the bitter cold. She was not used to going out at night, especially a night like this. When Algie returned, wheeling his bike alongside him, he picked up the larger bag and lugged it into the night, not knowing where they would end up.

'Maybe we'll get rooms at the Old Court House,' he suggested.

'I thought that,' Clara said.

'At least we can try. If they've got nothing we'll go to the Bell, like we did before.'

'No, not the Bell, Algie. They'll think it's proper queer if me and you show up there. We had the wedding party there only a few weeks ago.'

'I hadn't thought of that.'

'And tomorrow we'll find a house to rent somewhere.'

'I have to work tomorrow, Mother.'

'It won't hurt either you or Mr Sampson if you take a day off to find us a house,' Clara responded matter-of-factly. 'It's a question of getting your priorities right.'

'All right,' he agreed. He had no wish to gainsay her. She had put up with enough lately. Algie accepted that he must humour her.

'How long have you known about the two of them?' she asked outright.

'Not long, Mother. Not to be certain at any rate. I knew something was going on a week or two back, but it was only the other night that I watched and listened, and I saw *him* coming out of *her* room. She's always been wayward. You might not have realised it, but I know it for a fact. She's a trollop. I could make your hair curl with stories about her and her antics.'

'I don't think I want to hear them. But fancy her lacing my drink with laudanum, that's what I can't get over. Mind you, it worked wonders. It was like being in heaven.' Clara even managed a smile.

'It's habit-forming, they say. You're getting none off me, whether or no.'

'No, not if you don't know what day it is once you've had it.'

She asked nothing more, seeming to accept the situation

for what it was with a resignation that took Algie by surprise. She seemed calm; as if she was glad the whole episode of her second marriage was at an end.

And at least it had got her out of the house at night . . .

They were successful in renting rooms at the Old Court House and, as planned, they sought somewhere permanent to live the next day. An advertisement in the *Brierley Hill Advertiser* led them to a lettings agent in Dudley who had on his books a furnished house in Abberley Street, near Top Church. They inspected the property, were satisfied, accepted it and paid a deposit. The following day, Friday, they moved in.

On Saturday morning, Algie rode to work. His journey there from Dudley did not take him past the house of Benjamin and Aurelia Sampson, which was in the opposite direction, but that was hardly a worry yet. The problem was that neither Marigold nor Aurelia would have a clue as to his whereabouts any longer. Not that Marigold was such a concern anymore. Somehow, though, he must let Aurelia know; a letter, if all else failed.

He arrived on time and went to his workbench. He raked out the stove, laid a fire and was lighting it when Harry Whitehouse arrived, puffing and panting.

'How come you ain't been at work the last couple o' days?' Harry enquired as he hung his coat up on a hand-made brass hook they'd fixed to the whitewashed wall.

'It's a long story, Harry,' he answered evasively.

'Well, let me warn you that Mr Sampson's hopping mad 'cause you ain't been here.'

'He can go and play with himself for all I care,' Algie replied. 'I'm just about ready for *him*. If he thinks he can upset me he's got another think coming. Anyway, I'll have the last laugh on him and no mistake.'

'The last laugh? How d'you mean?' Harry was intrigued.

'Never mind.' Algie had no wish to compromise Aurelia by gloating.

Before long, Benjamin Sampson was doing his rounds of the factory. He spotted Algie and beckoned him, looking fittingly grim. Algie approached resignedly.

'Where the hell d'you think you've been the last two days, Stokes, without so much as a by-your-leave?' he asked, well away from Algie's workbench.

'My mother and me suddenly found ourselves in a bit of a pickle, Mr Sampson,' he said evenly, controlling his resentment, and wishing to give away as little as possible. 'We had to find new rented accommodation as a matter of urgency. I couldn't leave her to her own devices – she's recently widowed, you may remember. We moved to another house and we're settled now. It shouldn't be necessary for me to have any more time off, Mr Sampson.'

'Necessary or not, Stokes, your personal life is your own affair, not mine,' Benjamin said, lacking any sympathy whatsoever. 'So I see no reason to either subsidise it or put up with it. I've had enough of your having time off, your unreliability. You're sacked. Collect your belongings and go.'

Algie shrugged nonchalantly, which Mr Sampson interpreted as impertinence.

'When I speak to you, Stokes, do me the courtesy of a verbal reply and not an insolent shrug.'

'Do *me* the courtesy of not speaking to me in such a tone, Mr Sampson,' Algie replied calmly. 'I'm not your lackey. And what makes you think you're a better man than me anyway? What makes you think you have the right to talk down to me?'

'Because I employ you,' he sneered. 'I pay your damned wages. Therefore, by definition you are my servant.'

'You did employ me till two minutes ago, but by your own announcement you don't anymore, so I'm no longer your servant. But whether or no,' he went on coolly, 'you still owe me my wages.'

'Which you'll have in full come payday.'

'I'm sorry, Mr Sampson. I can't wait till payday, nor do I intend to. You have a legal obligation, I believe, to pay me now. I'll take my wages before I leave.'

'I want you off the premises right away.'

'And I want my wages . . .'

'They will have to be worked out and put up.'

'Then work them out and put them up. I'll wait.' Then he had an idea, an idea that could serve two purposes. 'I'll compromise, Mr Sampson. As a favour. I'll leave the premises now, as you wish, and I'll collect my wages from your house this afternoon.'

Benjamin pondered the proposition momentarily. Such an arrangement would give him time to work out what he owed and get rid of the impudent scallywag at once. Even if Stokes called at the house, he needn't see him; he would instruct the maid to hand him his wages, and good riddance.

'Very well,' he conceded. 'Collect them from my house. But I do it for my own convenience, Stokes, not yours. And please don't expect to see me.'

'You flatter yourself, Mr Sampson, if you imagine that I'd want to. I've seen enough of you to last me a lifetime. You pinched my ideas, my design and my method of building bikes, then pretended it was all your own work and treated me as if I never existed. Well, let me assure you, Mr bloody Sampson, that I do exist, and I wouldn't be a bit surprised if one of these days you'll begin to believe it.' He turned his back on Benjamin in resentment and returned to his work-bench to pick up his things. As he made his way out, past his

456

old gaffer who was watching incensed, Algie added, 'My wages, Mr Sampson.' He wagged his forefinger goadingly. 'I'll collect them this afternoon, as arranged. Be sure they're ready and waiting . . . in full.'

'Be sure,' Mr Sampson retorted angrily, 'that if need be – if you create a fuss – I shall report you to the police.'

Aurelia had overheard her husband's instructions to the maid to hand over an envelope to Mr Stokes, who was expected to collect it later.

As soon as Benjamin was out of the way she sought the maid. 'I'll hand that packet to Mr Stokes when he comes, Mary,' she said. 'There's also a message I have to give him.'

'Very well, ma'am,' said Mary. 'But Mr Sampson said I wasn't to let him come in the house.'

Aurelia smiled. 'That's all right. I shall abide by Mr Sampson's wishes.'

Shortly after half past three Algie rode up the drive on his bicycle and rang the bell. He was surprised, but gratified to see Aurelia answer the door. At once she stepped outside, away from the house.

'I'm to give you this,' she whispered, showing him the envelope, 'but I'm not to let you in the house. What on earth has happened?'

'I've been sacked,' he replied with a shrug.

'Sacked?' Her face bore a look of alarm. 'Does he know anything?'

He shook his head to reassure her. 'No, but a lot has happened, Aurelia. I need time to explain.'

She took his arm and, glancing behind her, urged him to the side of the house where they could not be overlooked or overheard. 'What's happened?' she asked, speaking low.

He explained briefly about exposing Murdoch and his sister

and how he and his mother had subsequently left the house and since found rented accommodation.

'Which puts our escaping to another town together in a totally different light,' she whispered, with disappointment manifest in her eyes.

'I suppose so,' he admitted.

'Oh, Algie, I just long to get away now we've talked about it,' she sighed, shivering in the cold air. 'And I've almost got him to agree to a separation. We are so close to being able to fulfil our dream. But your mother would not welcome me into the same house, married to another man as I am.'

'To say the least of it,' he agreed sadly. 'She's seen enough of infidelity to last her a lifetime. And I couldn't leave her. Not yet at any rate. Not until she's had time to get over everything that's happened. I couldn't desert her yet, Aurelia. You do understand, don't you?'

'Of course, I understand,' she said, full of sympathy for him.

'Well, don't do anything rash in the meantime that might jeopardise your situation here,' he advised. 'You and Benjie still need a roof over your heads.'

'If the worst comes to the worst we should be able to take refuge elsewhere.'

'It'd be as well if you did. Do you have relatives?'

'Of course.'

'Good. Because this setback might plague us for some time yet. You do see, don't you, Aurelia, that I can't forsake my mother?'

'Of course,' she said again, and touched his hand briefly in reassurance. 'I understand perfectly. The poor woman. My heart bleeds for her.'

'And I have to find work. In the meantime, you can write to me if you want, at number twelve, Abberley Street, Dudley.

If ever *he's* going to be away, write and let me know and we can meet at the usual place.'

She smiled, all her affection oozing from her eyes. 'Let's hope and pray it can be soon.'

'Yes, let's.' His hand lingered on hers as she handed him the envelope containing his wages.

'You'd better go now, my love. If Benjamin knows you have arrived he'll be watching for you. I don't wish to compromise myself quite yet, do I?'

'No, we're not ready for that. But don't forget to write.'

'Oh, be sure that I shall write, Algie,' she answered tenderly. 'Twelve, Abberley Street.'

Towards the end of February there was a let-up in the weather and the temperature rose a little. The ice began to lose its formidable grip, freeing up at last the lakes, the ponds and the canals, to the relief of all. The Binghams, along with all the other trapped boat people, were able to continue their journeys and recommence working. Marigold had enjoyed her temporary employment in the warmth of the bakehouse in Rugby, where Mr Fairfax, the owner, had been extraordinarily kind. Every day he handed her not only the promised loaf of bread, but a bagful of fancy cakes and egg custards as well, most of which were broken and unsaleable, but eminently edible, and it was the thought that counted. The little she earned was a significant help to the rest of her family, and lessened the hardship of those bitterly cold, frustrating days and nights trapped in the ice at Willoughby Wharf. Marigold was not sorry, though, to be giving up her early morning walk into Rugby in the frost and darkness of that cruel winter. Returning to the narrowboats late afternoon wasn't so bad though; she could take the train, which stopped at Willoughby Station, close to where the *Sultan* and the *Odyssey* were stuck fast.

Her belly was growing inexorably by this time and there was no hiding her pregnancy. Mr Fairfax could hardly fail to notice, and was concerned that a girl so vulnerable might have fallen victim to male abuse. He questioned her about it one day just before she left.

'Do my eyes deceive me, young Marigold, or are you carrying a child?' he said with no hint of condemnation in his voice. 'I've been wondering for some time now, and meaning to ask you. I hope you don't mind me being so blunt.'

'Course not, Mr Fairfax. It shows too much to deny it anymore, don't it?' she answered with a grin, and felt herself blush. 'Course I'm a-carrying, Mr Fairfax.'

'Yet you're not married either? What happened to the fellow who got you in that pickle?'

'Oh, he'll be waiting for me, I hope, Mr Fairfax. Because we've been stuck in the ice with no hope o' getting out, I ain't been able to see him and get wed yet. He lives at Brierley Hill, see. I ain't seen him since November, and he don't even know as I'm in the family way. He'll have such a shock . . .' she chuckled as she imagined Algie's surprise. 'But we intended to get wed anyroad, Mr Fairfax, sooner or later. I reckon it'll just be sooner. As soon as I can get back to him.'

'Then let's hope you manage it before the little blighter's born, eh?'

'Well,' she replied brightly, 'now the weather's letting up a bit, we should be on the move any day. Who knows, we might be heading Brierley Hill way afore too long. In any case, me mother says I'm to go away for me confinement. She says a narrowboat's no place for a laying-in, and she should know, having had a few herself. In any case, we couldn't afford to stop, even if I was in labour, so it's best that I goes away for a bit.'

Mr Fairfax smiled sympathetically. 'So when's the baby due?'

Marigold shrugged. 'I ain't really sure, to tell you the truth. I thought it might be sometime in May, but I ain't really sure. It might even be sooner.'

'A spring baby anyway, eh?'

She nodded and smiled. 'With the summer to look forward to. I hope we have a summer like last summer,' she said dreamily. 'Last summer was lovely . . .'

Algie Stokes was out looking for work in Brierley Hill when he happened upon Harriet Meese and her sister Priss walking along High Street in the direction of their father's drapery and mourning wear emporium. He was glad to see them and stopped to pass the time of day.

'Algie,' Harriet greeted. 'What a lovely surprise. Seems like a century at least since I've seen you. Are you well?'

'Pretty well, thanks. And yourselves?' He looked from one to the other of the sisters.

'It's so long since you've been to see us after my father forgave you for jilting me, that I meant to send you a map with our house marked on it in red ink.'

'I haven't felt much like paying social calls, Harriet,' he replied glumly. 'I'm sorry. I've been a bit otherwise occupied, as you might say.'

'For goodness sake, don't make excuses,' Priss said, opening her mouth for the first time. 'If you wanted to come and see our Harriet you'd come, and if you didn't you wouldn't. You don't have to make bland excuses. It's hardly one of the seven deadly sins. Merely a matter of preference.'

'Preference has nothing to do with it, Priss,' Algie countered. 'It's always a pleasure to see Harriet. But in any case, I hear she's still stepping out with Clarence Froggatt.'

'I know. Still. It's amazing, isn't it? I do believe Mr Froggatt's quite taken with our Harriet.'

'I still say Harriet's too good for him. Anyway, what about you, Priss? Have you been proposed to yet?' Algie enquired flippantly.

'She's gone off the curate,' Harriet said, with a mischievous glance at her older sister. 'I believe she's taken with that young Mr Tapper, who's taken over the apothecary's shop.'

'Oh?'

'Yes, he raised his hat to her the other Saturday and she blushed to her roots.'

'It was nothing to do with Mr Tapper raising his hat, Harriet,' Priss objected indignantly. 'I was hot from walking. It heightened my colour.'

'But she wasn't walking, Algie. We were standing looking in his window talking about the parish flower rota and, only a minute before, I'd remarked on how pale she looked. I was about to suggest that maybe Mr Tapper could recommend something for her when he passed through the door and raised his hat. Suddenly she was the colour of a beetroot.'

'Thank you, dear sister, but "rose" would have been a much preferred expression to describe my delicate colouring.'

'So what of you, Algie?' Harriet enquired. 'Have you heard from your little rose of the waterways yet?'

'Not a word. I've really given up all hope. She's forgotten all about me by now. I've moved on. Between me, you and the gatepost, we've all moved on. Literally . . . The whole family.'

'Do tell us,' Harriet said.

'Well, you know my mother married Murdoch Osborne . . .'

At once their ears pricked up, and Algie duly related the scurrilous events that had led up to him and his mother leaving Murdoch's house to find accommodation elsewhere. As the story unfolded, Harriet and Priss stood listening with open-mouthed incredulity, their faces like two gargoyles hanging off the side of an ancient church.

'There's been a desperate shortage lately of good quality gossip,' Priss replied crisply. 'But that rather takes the biscuit. A little more to it than the usual nonsense that we have to embellish to make more interesting.'

'But that's dreadful,' Harriet commented, with perfect understatement. 'Mind you, Algie, I always imagined there was something rebellious about your sister Kate.'

'And that horrible Murdoch Osborne,' Priss scoffed. 'You know, Algie, I'm not a bit surprised that he lost his silly head to your sister. The way he looked at her was always very suspicious to my mind.'

'He'd lose his head to anything in a skirt,' Harriet replied scornfully. 'According to Clarence anyway. Did you know Clarence used to be engaged to Murdoch's elder daughter?'

'Yes, I know.'

'And you know who that daughter is, Algie?'

'Who?' he asked, feigning ignorance.

'Why, no less a person than Aurelia Sampson. That girl you fell in love with on sight so irrevocably. The wife of—'

'Yes, I know whose wife she is, Harriet. I happen to remember her very well.'

'And very fondly, no doubt.'

'Yes,' he admitted. 'Very fondly.'

'But how futile to fall in love with a married woman,' Priss suggested with ample disdain. 'I mean, dancing a *Roger de Coverley* with a married woman at a party is one thing, especially if you secretly fancy her, but allowing yourself to fall in love with her is quite another. Only heartache can come of that.'

'Is Mr Tapper the apothecary married?' Algie fenced.

'I hope not,' Priss replied. 'Else I should be as guilty as you of fancying a married person.'

'So you admit you fancy him,' Harriet declared with glee. 'Oh, our Priss! How sweet.'

'For all the good it will do me, I suppose. Men just don't fancy me.'

'Oh, Priss,' Harriet said, full of sisterly sympathy. 'Lots of men fancy you.'

'Yes, in the same way that they fancy olives. I appreciate I'm an acquired taste.'

'Well, you have a spicy outside and a heart of stone – not relished by every male.'

'I don't like olives,' Algie said. 'Not that I've ever had many.'

'So where are you living now, Algie?' Harriet enquired, reverting to the subject that had been suspended meanwhile.

He told her.

'Please give your mother my very best wishes, Algie. And I do believe she is well out of it.'

'So do I, Harriet. Thanks. I'll tell her. So shall you be going to the next rehearsal?'

'Oh, yes . . . I wonder if they'll be there, Algie? Mr Osborne and your Kate?

Algie shrugged indifferently. 'Whether or no, folk will find out soon enough about them . . .'

Chapter 30

March arrived and the days passed in a swirl of blustery winds, which complemented perfectly the savage winter. Algie sought the kind of work which he felt was to his liking, and approached the small bicycle manufacturer in Dudley, James Parkes, but there were no vacancies. That is not to say there was no other employment available; there was in fact plenty, but nothing that took his fancy. So he bided his time, sure that the right job for him would come along sooner or later. Rather sooner than later, though, he would have to plump for something. He had some money put by, enough to keep him and his mother for the time being, but it would not last forever, especially if he had to pay for more erotic evenings at the Eagle Hotel with Aurelia.

It was evident that Benjamin Sampson had not been on his business travels up and down the country, for no letter had arrived from Aurelia. She had his address; he would have thought that she might have written. Aurelia, he felt, had been ominously silent. Perhaps something had happened. Algie grew anxious, worrying that something was wrong. Several times he had ridden past the house on the off-chance that he might see her, but there had been no sign.

He was beginning to question both the wisdom and the futility of this affair, spurred by the comments Priss Meese had made when he stopped to talk to her and Harriet. It made him think, for the first time seriously, about whether he wished to have a broken marriage on his conscience. He wasn't sure that he wished to be vilified either, which he certainly would be. There was little doubt that he would be regarded as the villain, however noble his intentions towards Aurelia. He would be seen as the one breaking up a family, but she too would be branded a loose woman for being unfaithful to her husband. The gossiping public could not see into the homes in which these unhappy marriages abounded, so they were not privy to the unsavoury truth. They were ignorant of the ignominy that one or other partner sometimes had to suffer, in particular Aurelia. For Algie, it would also mean taking on the extra burden of another man's child, and he did not honestly know whether he would even take to that child. If little Benjie were his own, it would be a different matter.

At the end of the first week in March, the longed-for letter arrived. Algie opened it eagerly and read:

My own darling Algie,

I do hope that you and your poor mother have settled into your new home, and that she has come to terms with those awful, unspeakable events. I have been quite unable to get her off my mind for some time, and I am convinced she should never have married that horribly irresponsible man. I know the worry it caused you, my love, before ever it all blew up, and be assured that my thoughts are with you constantly. My dearest wish is that I could be with you, especially at times like this when I know I could be of comfort to you.

Still Benjamin shows no sign yet of going away on another business trip, which is awfully inconsiderate of him, considering that I long to be in your arms again in our love nest. Something I did not have the chance to tell you, which is entirely relevant, is that when I returned home that snowy night the last time we went there, Benjamin had already arrived home quite unexpectedly, a day early. Naturally, he questioned me as to where I'd been and actually insinuated that I might have been with another man. The very cheek of it! Can you imagine? So I concocted some excuse about having to call on my dress-maker with regard to a query, and as far as I could tell I think he accepted it. However, I think it has planted some seeds of doubt in his mind as to the prudence of leaving me for days and nights on end, just in case I am prone to straying. Prone! I should say I'm prone. If only he knew how much I love you.

His insinuations meant that I had to go on the attack, and I asked him what he would do if I said I had been with another man. He responded that he would strike me. He is such a gentleman, my husband. Straight out of the blue he suggested we separate and naturally enough I was secretly elated, although I tried to appear indifferent. That was just before I saw you all too briefly at our house. I can't remember whether I told you that, although I do remember telling you that I believed our dream of a life together was now almost entirely tangible. Well, that is the reason why, my love. But ever since then he has been most attentive. Most attentive, I may say! I have not known him like it since the days when he was trying to woo me. Thinking he might have a rival has definitely rekindled his interest in me. I suspect he believes I'm worth nurturing after all, the poor devil.

But I won't be swayed, Algie, trust and believe me. I am resolved to resist this new crop of promises and this new show of overdone affection. What does melt me, *though, is his softened attitude to our son. Whether it is just a ploy to win back my affection I do not know.*

But there is another tactic he is using. Yesterday he suggested that we ought to be looking at a bigger and better house, that if we were to enlarge our family (some chance), the extra space and a larger garden would be a boon. For obvious reasons I didn't show much enthusiasm for the idea. If, ultimately, it is my intention to leave him, as it certainly is, then why should I wish to be troubled by looking at new houses and have all his extra expense on my conscience if he decides to plump for one? I am sure it is just a ploy, however, to divert me.

But don't worry about me, Algie, my love. If we do decide suddenly on a separation, I have relatives who would doubtless be prepared to take Benjie and me in. I would have to confide to them the state of my marriage, of course, how desperately unhappy I am, and how I fear that my son will be dragged away from me just so that he can attend boarding school. They would be sympathetic, I'm sure.

Please write to me with news of yourself, my darling, for which I wait in earnest. Be assured that it is quite safe to write, since I always get to the post before Benjamin comes down.

I love you always,
Aurelia

If the letter had been written to arouse his jealousy, it had succeeded. He read it again, feeling intensely agitated. What did she mean by '*ever since then he has been most attentive. Most attentive, I may say!*'? Did it mean they had been intimate again? Did it mean Benjamin had forced himself upon her? Or did it mean that he had merely tried? It would be very interesting to know, yet how could he ask her outright? In any case, did he really want to know if the worst had happened? And yet, she had followed it with, *'But I won't be swayed, Algie, trust and believe me. I am resolved to resist this new crop of promises and this new show of overdone affection.'* Her reassurance to him. Her reassurance that whatever happened, her love would remain steadfast. The key was in the word *resist*. If only he could be that certain. Benjamin Sampson was a bully. To outface a bully you had to stand up to him, be stronger than him, morally at least. He prayed Aurelia possessed that strength of will.

And yet . . . And yet if he turned out to be Aurelia's half-brother, all this worrying, all this fretting over whether she and her despicable husband were engaging in bedtime activities would be for nothing. Someday soon he must tackle his mother on the question of his parentage. It was essential that he should. But how could he now? The time was not yet ripe. His mother was still too raw for such probing questions into her erstwhile propriety, or lack of it.

Anyway, he replied to Aurelia's letter. It was a bland missive, deliberately so, if only for fear that Benjamin got to it before she did. Despite her assurances that she always picked up the post before him, he realised the merit in being uncontroversial, and not declaring outright his love. He merely stated that he looked forward to hearing from her again soon. Nor did he sign it with his name; just the letter *A*.

During the extra time he had on his hands, Algie began to ponder Marigold more. Dear, sweet, unschooled, unpretentious Marigold. How much simpler his life would have been if Marigold had not made herself scarce that fateful night of his father's death. Although he had admired Aurelia so immensely, he would have been perfectly content with

Marigold. Now his life was complicated by this emotional involvement with Aurelia who, to confuse things even more, just happened to be married already, with a small child. Well, he might eventually be content with Aurelia, if she left Benjamin and it could all be done with the minimum of chaos. But he foresaw problems ahead with his mother.

Algie fancied a ride out along the canals to clear his head. He might just be lucky enough to catch sight of the Binghams, now that the ice on the canals was all but gone. If he did not actually see them, somebody might have news of them. So he got on his bike and rode to the canal, getting on the towpath near the Parkhead Viaduct. He passed the pits, the brickworks and the ironworks, wishing that round the next bend he could happen upon them. He imagined Seth Bingham leading their strong little horse, Victoria, as the animal hauled their pair of narrowboats. He imagined Marigold running before them to open the locks early to expedite their passage, Hannah at the tiller on the stern, the smaller children bobbing about on one or both boats, and the lark hopping about in its cage placed near the smoking stovepipe to keep it warm. It was a hard life on the canals, devoid of life's little luxuries. Yet he had never met a boat family who would order their lives any other way. How wonderful it must be to live a life so uncomplicated, so unfettered. All you had to worry about was what load you would be able to pick up when you had offloaded the one you were carrying now.

He passed plenty of narrowboats on the move, but nobody he knew well enough to enquire about the Binghams. He reached the Bottle and Glass. Time for some refreshment anyway. He went round to the front, leant his bike against the wall and entered the taproom on the left.

'Good God above!' Tom Simpson, the landlord, exclaimed at sight of him. 'Look what the cat's brought in.'

'Just passing, Tom, so I thought I'd call in and pay my respects.'

'Pale ale, is it?'

'Please.'

Tom Simpson reached for a tankard and began pulling a pint into it. 'No work today?' he asked.

'No job, Tom. I got sacked.'

'Sacked?'

'For having too much time off.'

'Lucky as you can afford it, eh?' Tom handed Algie his tankard. 'I heard as your mother got wed again already.'

'Yes, and separated already. That's why I had to have the time off, to resettle us.'

'Separated already?' Tom blew his lips in shock. 'How come?'

'Didn't work out. Too soon after my father's death.' He did not want to say how or why, so took a quaff of beer.

'I ain't surprised.' Tom shook his head. 'Takes months, if not years, to get over somebody you've bin close to most of your life.'

'Seen anything of the Binghams?' Algie enquired, setting his tankard down again.

Tom shook his head. 'A bit soon, maybe. Traffic ain't long bin on the move. We've had one or two up from Coventry and Brum, some from Stourport, and some from beyond Wolverhampton an' all, but I've seen nothing of the Binghams. Lord knows where they might be.'

'Might still be miles away,' Algie said with a sigh. 'So what's the new lock-keeper like?'

'What new lock-keeper? There ain't no new lock-keeper. The cottage as you used to live in is still empty.'

'There's still no lock-keeper? After all this time?'

'Not on this stretch. I wonder you don't apply for the job

yourself, Algie, since you're out of work. You know the ropes, you know the canal folks. The company would be glad of a strapping young chap like you. Why don't you apply?'

'It's a thought, Tom . . .' Algie quaffed his beer thoughtfully, then instantly brightened up. 'You know, it's a thought. I'll see what my mother says. It could be the answer to a good many of our problems.'

News of the indiscretion between Murdoch Osborne and his stepdaughter, a female member of the Brierley Hill Amateur Dramatics Society called Kate Stokes, soon reached the gossip-hungry ears of the general population of Brierley Hill, with devastating consequences. Nobody from within the society's ranks wished to be associated with him once they knew the depths of his immorality, and they left en masse. The forth-coming play had to be abandoned, and the use of the town hall, where it was being staged, was subsequently cancelled. The very name *Murdoch Osborne* was anathema.

Few people, except those connected with the amateur dramatics society and those who had seen her act in the previous production, knew very much about Kate Stokes, which would have surprised and disappointed her immensely. However, news of the monstrous deeds against her mother of which she stood accused quickly reached the owner of the baker's shop where she worked, and she was asked to leave forthwith.

'What shall we do?' Kate asked Murdoch when she went to tell him at his empty butcher's shop immediately after she had left. 'Nobody wants to know us anymore.'

'That's plain enough,' he replied, standing forlornly behind the counter in his striped apron. 'There's been ne'er a soul in here for days.'

'Why don't we just go to London till it's all died down?' she suggested. 'It'll serve two purposes. First, it'll get us out of the way of the vicious wagging tongues, and second, you can introduce me to those important impresarios you promised to write to for me.'

'You're still keen to be a professional actress, ha?'

'Course. Nothing's changed. I'm even more determined now. What have I got to lose?'

'Aye, well you've got talent, Kate, and no two ways. It'd be a shame to let it go to waste.'

'So you agree then, Murdoch?'

'What have *I* got to lose, ha? All else is in ruins. I got no business worth having anymore, everybody's left the society, and folk I always thought of as my friends treat me like a pariah. At least if I go, the society might all get back together again under somebody else's leadership. We'll get rid of the servants, shut the house up and go, ha?'

Momentarily, he imagined the nights they would have in London, living together, unashamedly sharing the same bed. He was besotted. She was the most sensuous creature, the most fun he'd ever had in bed with anybody in his whole life. No woman, married, single, divorced or widowed had ever given him pleasure like she did. In London he could manage her stage career, guide her, make sure she met only the best people, the right people, and protect her from randy and unscrupulous impresarios who merely wanted her body.

Kate smiled with satisfaction meanwhile. She was going to get her way at last. To her it did not matter the cost. She would become a famous actress, admired and desired by the wealthy. The world was about to become her oyster. She would be besieged by stage-door Johnnies, able to take her pick of the handsomest, the richest, the most generous. What need would she have then of paltry Murdoch Osborne? He was but a stepping stone.

* * *

473

On the Monday morning – it was the 9th of March – Algie cycled to the offices of the Stourbridge Canal Company and leant his bike against the front wall of the building. He recalled the last time he had been there, to report the death of his father, and it amazed him how much had happened in the short time since then. The same woman who had greeted him last time greeted him condescendingly once more, showing no sign of recognition.

'Is Mr Munslow in?'

'Mr Munslow? I think so. Who are you?'

'Algernon Stokes, son of the late Will Stokes, who used to be one of the company's lock-keepers,' he explained.

'Oh, yes. What is it in connection with?' the woman enquired.

He didn't like her tone. Besides it had nothing to do with her. 'I'd rather discuss that with Mr Munslow.'

She looked at him with indignation at his impertinent answer and slid off her high perch haughtily. In a minute Mr Munslow presented himself, but seemed aloof, hardly pleased to see him.

'Mr Stokes. What can I do for you?'

Algie glanced at the woman at the desk. He did not wish to discuss his purpose in front of her, after what he had said. 'Can we talk somewhere private?'

'If you insist.'

Mr Munslow led him to the grubby office he'd been in before, cramped and overbearing, with flaking cream paint and yellowed, frosted glass. The man sat down and gestured for Algie to do the same.

'So what can I do for you, Mr Stokes?'

'I understand the position of lock-keeper, made vacant by the death of my father, is still available. I would like to be considered for the job, Mr Munslow.'

'Hmmm.'

'I've got plenty of experience,' Algie went on enthusiastically. 'I used to help my father when I was a lad. I know what's involved. I also know the canal folk. I reckon I could do the job as well as anybody, and as conscientiously. Besides, my mother would love to be living back in that house. It'd mean so much to her.'

'Your mother?' Mr Munslow uttered with a look of scorn. 'I'm afraid the vacancy is not open to you, Mr Stokes. Of course, I can't stop you making a formal application, if you so wish, but I can assure you it would be futile.'

'Futile? On what grounds would it be futile?'

'I would rather not discuss it.'

'Does it have anything to do with my mother?'

Mr Munslow fixed his eyes on a paper on his desk, avoiding Algie's. 'To be frank, Mr Stokes, news – and gossip, I'm afraid – both travel fast in a small community like ours, especially when one's sister's daughter was recently taken on as a maid in the house you and your mother recently occupied on her remarriage, and almost as quickly dismissed. I have to be candid, Mr Stokes. We, as a company, could not be seen to condone what has gone on by affording you employment and your mother shelter.'

'But my mother is the injured party. She's done nothing wrong.'

'I understand your desire to protect her, Mr Stokes. Your loyalty is commendable. But merely by association—'

'Oh, I see.' Algie stood up, seething with anger, and went to the door, desperately trying to control his emotions and retain some dignity. But the man's attitude warranted some appropriate response. 'I'm sorry to have troubled you, Mr Munslow, and to have embarrassed you with my earnest approach for work,' he said with composure. 'Be assured I shan't trouble you again. You can stick the job up your jacksie. Good day to you.'

Algie left, reeling with indignation at his treatment at the hands of Mr Munslow. All the man was worried about was how the company would be perceived in the light of accepting him as an employee after the scandal surrounding his mother's second marriage. How shallow and insensitive these people were. Well, if they didn't need him, he certainly didn't need them. He would find other work. He would still look after his mother come what may, whatever people might say.

He rode back towards Dudley along the canal network. The weather seemed to have turned cold again; there was a biting wind from the east that foretold of snow. He sniffed the wind like a hound and smelled its promise. Would this winter never end? He stopped at the Bottle and Glass for a pint, and for a warm in front of the welcoming fire.

'Any luck with the lock-keeper's job?' Tom Simpson asked as he pulled the beer.

Algie gave a rueful little laugh. 'I've just come from there, Tom. They reckon I'm unsuitable. But I shall have to find work soon.'

'You'm best off doing what you know,' Tom said, and handed him a foaming tankard.

'Well, I know about making beds and bikes, if that's any use to anybody.' He took a swig, which left white froth on his top lip. He wiped it off with the back of his hand.

'Make 'em for theeself then, lad.'

'Bikes? I wish I could afford to set up in business, Tom. I'd welcome the chance.'

'How much money can you muster?'

'About twenty pounds as yet, but that'll soon go if I don't find work soon.'

'Does your mother have any money?'

'A bit. What my father managed to save.'

'Would she lend it you?'

Algie smiled. 'She might. If I asked her nice.'

'Would you have enough to start a workshop if she did?'

'I don't know. Maybe not.'

'Do it anyroad,' Tom advised. 'And if you find you'm still a bit short of spondulicks let me know. I might be able to help you out with a small loan.'

'Honest?'

'I don't see why not, young Algie. You're a trustworthy lad, hard-working, bright. I tell you what, an' all – I'll give you your first order if you can build a bike as good and as strong as the one you ride yourself.'

'I know I can, Tom.'

'Then make me a good strong bike and I'll pay you the proper price for it . . . But while you're at it, make two. You'll be bound to sell the other at a profit.'

Algie beamed. 'D'you think I should? It's a big step, you know.'

'And not beyond you, lad. Do it. I got faith in you. Why work for somebody else when you can work for yourself? The rewards are much greater.'

'You know, Tom, I think I will. I'll take you up on it . . . By the way, have you seen anything of the Binghams yet?'

'Nothing at all, lad. Nothing at all.'

That same night the snow came down with a vengeance – heavy, powdery snow. Strong easterly winds raged across the south and west of England and Wales for the rest of the week. More than four days of the bitterest weather many folk had seen in their lifetime battered much of the country. Gales wreaked their havoc. More than half a million trees were blown down; telegraph poles did not escape the onslaught either. Trains were buried for days in the drifts; fourteen were stranded in Devon alone. It was reported that 220 people died and 6,000 sheep perished in the storms, while sixty-five ships foundered in the English Channel. Although the West Country was the worst affected, southern England, the Midlands, and South Wales also suffered badly. Twelve-foot snowdrifts were recorded at Dulwich in London, and even at Dartmouth in Devon.

Once again the Binghams were thwarted in their efforts to travel, and to work. Having taken advantage of February's thaw they had managed to move on from Oxford, their cargo of coal delivered, and were headed towards London. The blizzard caught them in Hemel Hempstead, where they were once more trapped, again for as long as the weather might determine.

'I'm worried about our Marigold, Seth,' Hannah said, when their family were out of earshot. 'I need to get her to our Edith's to have this bab, but the weather's against us as usual.'

'What's the rush?' Seth queried. 'It ain't due till May.'

'That's if she's worked it out properly. If you ask me, she's a bit on the big side to be carrying a seventh month child. I wouldn't be surprised if it came afore that.'

'Well, when we've got shut of this gravel we'm a-carrying, I'll see if we can't get a load to the Black Country.'

'But it could take weeks to get up to the Black Country, Seth, especially if this weather holds out. I don't want her having this bab on the narrowboats, and especially not in this weather. If anything happened to her or the bab we'd never forgive ourselves.'

'So what alternative is there?'

'The train. I could take her to our Edith's by train. If we could go tomorrow I'd be back the day after. The way the weather's looking you'd still be here anyway.'

'That's if the trains am a-running,' Seth reasoned. 'How do we know the trains am a-running?'

'The railway runs close by. I heard a train this morning. Some lines must be open at any rate. If not all. The railway companies will soon open them now the thaw's set in.'

'How much does it cost?'

'Does it matter?' Hannah asked. 'My peace of mind is worth any price. I want her at our Edith's.'

'And what if your Edith don't want *her*? You ain't seen Edith for donkey's years.'

'Me and our Edith was always all right, you know we were. She'll do it for me.'

Chapter 31

Algie rose from his bed and peered out of the window at the bleakness of this prolonged and unhappy winter. Abberley Street, where he and his mother now lived, was perched on a shelf high on one of Dudley's many hills, but thankfully sheltered from the bitter east wind. The landscape about him wore a heavy shroud of white that seemed to muffle all sounds, rendering everything eerily tranquil. Sleepily, he shivered. The shock of the ice-cold air in his room exorcised the phantoms of sleep and jolted him into the full awareness of day. He pulled on his long johns, doffed his nightshirt, and went downstairs. His mother was already up and about, and had made a fire which was burning bright. A steaming kettle sat on the hob, and he poured some of the hot water into his shaving mug, which he'd retrieved from the cupboard next to the grate.

He shaved and his thoughts turned, like pages in a book. Marigold, Aurelia, Harriet, Kate, Murdoch Osborne. So many unresolved questions did those pages pose, questions for which he had no answer. He pondered his unemployment; yet another problem to beset him, for it went against the grain of his nature to be idle . . . Tom Simpson's idea of setting up on his own demanded some serious consideration. If only he could raise a hundred pounds . . .

He rinsed off the residue of shaving soap, washed and dried his face and neck, then returned upstairs to finish dressing himself and comb his hair. Meanwhile, his mother was standing in front of the fire preparing his breakfast of bacon, eggs and fried bread. It smelt divine. When he came down again she set it before him, then sat opposite him at the scrubbed table in the tiny scullery of that rented house to enjoy her own breakfast with him.

'It seems funny you not having to rush out to go to work, our Algie.'

'I know it does, Mother, but it's a novelty that'll soon wear off. I need to get my teeth into something.'

'Well, something will turn up soon enough.' She hedged her chair a little nearer the table. 'Maybe you're just being a bit too fussy.'

'How much money did my father leave?' he asked outright, and forked a piece of crisp bacon into his mouth.

'Just over a hundred pounds,' Clara replied candidly. 'Why?'

'Have you still got it?'

'Best part of it. I wasn't about to leave it for Murdoch Osborne. Why?'

'Would you lend it me? The biggest part of it?'

'If you tell me why you want it, I might.'

He smiled his appreciation and regarded her intently. 'I'm going to set up my own business, building bikes. If I can do it for Benjamin Sampson with all the constraints he put on me, I can do it even better for myself. I need to rent a workshop first, though, and buy some second hand machinery and stuff.'

'Don't you think you're being over-ambitious, our Algie?' Clara suggested, putting down her knife and fork momentarily.

'Course not,' he replied dismissively. 'And if everybody

481

thought like that nothing in this country would ever get started. I know I can do it, Mother. I did it all before, but for the wrong reasons and the wrong man. He pinched all my ideas and designs. Those bikes – my bikes – are starting to sell like hot cakes from what I can gather. I intend to show him what a fool he was, treating me like he did . . . And I will . . . In more ways than one.'

Clara looked pensive as she resumed eating. 'Are you sure that's a good enough reason?' she said after a brief pause. 'Just to get back at Benjamin Sampson?'

'I have good reason to want to get back at him anyway, Mother. By fair means or foul. He's despicable.'

'But can you make a go of it, such a business?'

'I've already got my first order. I'm going to make two bikes to start with, and the money I make from them I'll put back into the business. In two or three years we could be well-off, living in our own smart house.'

Clara smiled with admiration for her son. 'We?' she queried. 'Are you sure you want *me* around you all the time? One day you're likely to get wed. You won't want me around you then.'

'Then I'll be rich enough to buy you your own house and pay for servants. Till then, I shall look after you, come what may. Have no fear.'

His reassurance touched Clara. 'You've been a good and dutiful son, our Algie, through all our troubles. No mother could have wished for better. Different to your sister. Course you can have the money, for as long as you need it. Pay me back, if you feel you must, when you can afford it. It's hardly a fortune.'

'Thanks, Mother . . .' He smiled appreciatively. 'No, it's hardly a fortune, but I intend to turn it into one . . . Oh . . . and there's something else I've been meaning to tell you . . .' Now seemed as good a time as any.

Clara regarded him apprehensively.

'I fell in with another girl . . . A lovely girl . . .'

'Ah . . . I wondered . . . You've given up on Marigold, then?'

'She's given up on me, more to the point. Nobody's seen or heard of the Binghams since November. Not since my father died. It's March now. Why should I wait any longer for her to show up, just to be snubbed again if she does?'

'So who is this new girl? Are you going to tell me?'

'You're not going to like it . . .'

'I won't know till you tell me.'

'Her name's Aurelia . . .' He studied his mother's face to try and perceive whether the name meant anything.

'Aurelia?' A look of alarm clouded Clara's face. 'I only ever heard of one Aurelia, our Algie. Murdoch's estranged daughter . . . You don't mean her, do you?'

He nodded solemnly.

'But isn't she wed?'

'Wed, yes, and she has a child. But she's miserably unhappy with her husband. She's thinking about leaving him.'

'Leaving him? For you, you mean?'

'For me or not, she's been thinking about leaving him anyway. I wondered whether you would be prepared to countenance her and her child staying here.'

'No, I would not,' Clara declared stoutly. 'After all we've been through, Algie, you ask me to find succour for a fallen woman in this house? Not just a fallen woman, but the daughter of that rogue of a second husband I was misguided enough to marry? It would look well, wouldn't it? Lord, we'd be a laughing stock.'

The thing that really struck Algie was that his mother had obviously not connected Aurelia with Benjamin Sampson. During their short marriage, Murdoch had obviously never discussed his son-in-law.

'I didn't think you would agree,' he said dispiritedly, and put down his knife and fork.

'I don't even know why you bothered to ask, our Algie.'

'Aurelia hates Murdoch as much as you do, Mother. With good reason. You have that in common.'

'It makes no difference, our Algie. She's a married woman. Another man's property, so never likely to be yours. It's the road to nowhere thinking otherwise. In any case,' Clara went on, 'if she did come here, don't think for a minute that I'd condone you and her sharing a bed, 'specially while she was still wed to somebody else. I don't believe in that sort of thing between married and unmarried folk. I'm not so daft as to think such things don't go on, though, you know. If you've committed adultery with her already, our Algie, well, it's your business, but you should be ashamed of yourself all the same, and I urge you to give her up. I don't know what the world's coming to.'

'You're not trying to put me off her for another reason, are you?' he asked suspiciously.

'What other reason?' Clara enquired, looking mystified. 'What other reason could there be?'

'Well . . . what if I was Murdoch's son, for instance?'

'What d'you mean, Murdoch's son?' The notion elicited a look of disdain on Clara's face, a response which gave Algie hope.

'I get the feeling you might have had a fling with him after you married my dad.'

Clara gasped with indignation. 'I most certainly did not. I don't know where you—'

'Sorry, sorry.' He held his hands up in a defensive gesture. 'It's just that . . . if I thought I was Aurelia's half-brother, course I would have to give her up.'

'I can assure you, our Algie, if I thought it would make

you give her up I would say you were Murdoch's son, if it was the truth. But you're not, and I won't lie, not even to achieve that. I never heard such a thing in all my life. Rest easy, Algie, you're not his son!'

'Well, that's a relief at any rate.' He smiled his apology that he could think such impropriety of his mother. At the very least, it freed him to pursue Aurelia with a greater conviction. He'd held back because of his doubts. Now he could encourage her wholeheartedly to leave Benjamin, with marriage to her his own ultimate goal. 'I admit it was a stupid notion, but one that kept gnawing at me. I just wanted to be sure.'

'Have you been worrying yourself over that?'

'A bit.'

'Silly boy . . . So what do you intend to do about this Aurelia?'

'I intend to have her, by hook or by crook. She's such a lovely girl . . . More like her mother, I suspect, than her father. I know you'd love her.'

Marigold and Hannah arrived at Stourbridge Junction in the late afternoon of the 18th of March, a Wednesday. They stepped from the train, carrying a large canvas bag containing Marigold's things, and began their walk through snow-lined streets to Rectory Road in Oldswinford, where Hannah's sister Edith lived. The sun, having finally broken through the dismal winter earlier in the day, hung low, a red lantern in the western sky.

'I haven't been around here for years,' Hannah remarked with a sigh of nostalgia. They turned into Church Road, which in turn dog-legged onto Rectory Road, just a short walk from the station. 'Why, it's just as pretty as ever it was.'

Church Road was overhung with tall trees, their branches burdened with the weight of snow that lingered upon them in the shimmering rosy glow of the setting sun.

485

'It's like a grotto,' Marigold said. 'And that's a lovely little church ahead. Does my Aunt Edith live close by?'

'Just around the bend by the church, past the big house. Course, this is Oldswinford, our Marigold,' she said approvingly. 'Not really Stourbridge at all.'

The house they were seeking overlooked the walled churchyard. It was a beautiful setting, typical of the loveliest of English villages, surrounded by fields blanketed in deep snow. As Marigold opened the wrought iron gate and walked up the path she felt pangs of apprehension. What if Aunt Edith refused to take her?

Hannah rapped the polished brass knocker, and waited.

The woman who opened the door bore a distinct resemblance to Hannah, except that she was older. Her greying hair was swept up on her head and topped off by a white mobcap. She wore wire-rimmed spectacles that seemed to enlarge her kind blue eyes, which creased appealingly with a smile of delighted astonishment as she recognised her caller. 'Why, it's our Hannah, or I'll eat coke.'

Hannah grinned affably. 'Hello, our Edith.'

'What brings you here after all these years?'

'I brought me daughter, Marigold, to see you.'

'Marigold?' She looked Marigold up and down. 'Well, I never. Why, Marigold, you're quite the young lady now. You were little more than a babe in arms last time I saw you. Come on inside, both, out the cold. How have you got here?'

'By train. We just arrived.'

'I bet you're clammed in this weather. Let me put the kettle on and I'll get you something to eat. You must be frozen to death.'

Hannah smiled at Marigold reassuringly as they followed Edith. Inside, their boots echoed off the tiled floor of the hallway on their way to a neat little parlour at the rear. A coal fire was burning cheerfully in a low grate and, on the mantel-piece, a shelf clock in a wooden case whirred, about to chime the half hour. Marigold noticed the floral curtains and the sofa that looked so comfortable and inviting, the rugs on the floor that would protect your bare feet from the cold tiles. This all looked very cosy, very accommodating. She could be comfortable here . . . if only Aunt Edith would allow her to stay . . .

Marigold realised that her mantle concealed her belly, so that Aunt Edith had most likely not yet ascertained that her young guest was pregnant. When she did, that would be the critical moment, the moment that might well decide whether or not she would be allowed to stay, for it would then be obvious why she had been brought here.

'I've already got some hot water on the hob in the scullery,' Aunt Edith declared as the clock struck the half hour. 'I'll make a pot of tea. What can I get you to eat? Fancy some bread and jam to keep you going till later? I'll cook later if you're stopping. I got a rabbit from the butcher's only yesterday.'

'Let me come and help you, our Edith,' Hannah suggested. 'We can talk while we work. I'll just get me mantle and bonnet off.'

Hannah duly divested herself of her mantle and bonnet, winked at Marigold and followed Edith into the scullery.

'Still living on them barges, our Hannah?' Edith said, lifting the kettle onto a gale hook over the fire.

'Narrowboats,' Hannah corrected with a smile. 'Yes. Same as ever.'

'No regrets, I take it?'

'Regrets? We're poor as church mice, our Edith, but I've got no regrets.'

'So how's Seth?'

'Seth's golden. I love him, and I'm proud of my children. I got five now, you know. No, I've got no regrets. I take it as you've never been interested in remarrying, our Edith?'

'Me, remarry? Well . . . you never know who might be round the next corner, eh? But being a widow has its compensations. What little bit Harold left me sees me through.'

'The reason I've come, our Edith, is to bring our Marigold to stay with you for a few weeks. If you'll have her, o' course. I take nothing for granted.'

Edith took a loaf from a wooden bread bin. 'Ah . . . Is she in trouble?'

'In the family way, yes, but I couldn't let her go through the misery of childbirth on a narrowboat, like I've had to do, especially the weather being so bad . . . Here, let me slice the loaf . . . I wondered if you'd look after her till she finds her chap again. She lost contact with him, see.'

'Lost contact?' Edith looked at her sister cynically, passing her the loaf. 'You mean he hopped it as soon as he knew she was carrying?'

'No, no, it wasn't like that at all,' Hannah asserted. 'He's a good lad, is Algie . . . Where d'you keep the butter, our Edith? . . . Oh, ta . . . We've been froze up for weeks near Rugby. The poor chap has no idea she's carrying, and she couldn't let him know either. Well, none of us can write that well for a start, but then neither did we know where to write to, 'cause we heard that his father had died, so Algie and his poor mother had to move house. We don't know where he lives now, but it ain't because he tried to give our Marigold the slip. They was in love, and no two ways. It was beautiful to see. I'm sure that as soon as she finds him they'll get wed.'

' 'Tis to be hoped, if she's having his child. Does she know where to start looking?'

'Oh, yes. Folks he knows, places he goes to. I'm sure she'll find him.'

'Then let's hope he still wants her.'

'Oh, I agree, our Edith. You can't take anything for granted. Let's hope and pray he does. But he thought the world of her, like I say.'

'A child puts a different complexion on young love, our Hannah. It takes the shine off romance, as you know to your cost. I wish I'd got two foot of lead piping in me hand and that swine that put you in the family way standing next to me. Would I give him what for!'

'It takes two, our Edith,' Hannah said philosophically. 'I was as much a party to what went on as he was, so I was as much to blame. It ain't as if I didn't know what was what. I should've had more sense, I'm the first to admit. I'm only thankful that you and Harold took me in when our mother and father disowned me . . . And that's why I thought of you when our Marigold told me she was in the family way. I thought you'd take kindly to her and help her through her trouble.'

'Takes after her mother, don't she?' Edith said, tongue-in-cheek.

'And for that reason, I can't be angry with her. Apart from everything, she's a golden wench. She needs my support now more than ever.'

'Family's family, eh, Hannah? We have to watch out for one another, don't we? Nobody else will. She seems a lovely girl anyroad, like you say – quiet and reserved considering she's been brought up in one of them narrowboats, as you like to call 'em. And ever so pretty. Now that you've come all this way I can hardly turn her away, can I? . . . Nor would I. To stop tongues a-wagging we can always say as her husband's a soldier, and he's in Africa or India.'

Hannah smiled gratefully. 'Thanks, Edith. I knew as you'd be all right about it. I *will* pay you for her keep, though. I don't expect you to look after her out of the kindness of your heart. She'll be an extra mouth to feed, an extra expense. Then there's the baby as well to take into account when it arrives . . .'

'Save your money, our Hannah. From what you've told me I think you need it. I can manage. I'm careful – I have to be – but I'm no skinflint.'

The next day, after ensuring that Marigold was content and comfortable in her new lodgings with her aunt, Hannah left, making the return train journey to Hemel Hempstead. She promised to make certain that, as soon as they could, the family would try and secure work that took them to the Black Country so that they could all be reunited, if only temporarily, until Marigold and her baby could eventually rejoin them, or get wed to Algie.

The thaw had set in, the middle of March ushering in milder weather. After just a day of cosseted apathy, Marigold became restless and decided that it was time she actively tried to find Algie Stokes. She told her aunt what she intended to do and asked her the best way to get to Brierley Hill. Aunt Edith advised her to take the tram and handed her a shilling for her fares.

With difficulty, she tried to recall the name of the firm where Algie worked. She had heard him say it was at Queen's Cross in Dudley, so she stood at a tramcar stop and waited for a tram going to the town. One soon arrived.

'D'you go anywhere near Queen's Cross?' she asked the conductor as she stepped tentatively aboard his vehicle.

'We pass it on the way, miss,' the conductor answered. 'That'll be thre'pence.'

She handed him the shilling. 'Can you tell me when we get

there, please? I'm after a factory there, where they make bedsteads.'

'That'll be Sampson's or I'm never here. I'll gi' thee the nod, my wench, when we get there.'

She thanked him, and carefully counted the change he gave her before she sat down. When the tram began to move she was enthralled with the feeling of speed as the buildings flashed past in a blur. It seemed only a few minutes before the conductor drew her attention to tell her she needed the next stop. Apprehensively, she rose from her seat and made her way to the exit, clutching at the poles to steady her as the tram slowed to a halt.

'That's the place, there, miss,' the conductor said, pointing.

She smiled and thanked him, then alighted. Nervously she walked towards Sampson's. Within a few minutes she would be reunited with Algie, her dream fulfilled, and her heart was pounding hard with expectation.

A red-brick building, which she presumed must be the office, stood in front of the factory. There was an open door, which she entered, and looked around her. The door had opened onto a sort of hallway. A staircase ascended on her left, and two closed doors faced her, one directly in front of her, one to her right. She tried the first, and at once the crash and bang of industry assailed her ears, since it opened directly onto the factory floor. She shut it immediately and tried the door on her right, which opened up onto a storeroom of sorts, but devoid of personnel.

The stairs . . . She ascended them and on a landing at the top was a hatch. She tapped on it and waited. A plump woman in late middle-age opened it.

'Can I help you, miss?' She smiled patronisingly.

'Yes, I'd like to see Algie Stokes, please. It's important that I see him.'

491

'Algie Stokes?' the woman – who was, of course, Violet – queried. 'I'm afraid he don't work here any longer, miss.'

'He don't?'

'No. He left a week or two ago.'

'D'you know where I could find him? It is important.'

Violet turned down the corners of her mouth and shook her head ominously. 'I wouldn't have a clue, miss. He left under a bit of a cloud, as far as I can make out. Something to do with having time off to move house again.'

'Again?' Marigold said, with a profound sigh. 'I wonder where he's gone to now?'

'Dunno,' said Violet, not without some sympathy in her voice. 'I don't think Mr Sampson knows either, else he would've let me know.'

'He didn't leave an address then?'

Violet shook her head.

Marigold smiled, but with bitter disappointment. 'All right . . . Thank you . . . Sorry to have troubled you.'

'It's no trouble, miss.' Violet couldn't help but notice that the visitor was heavily pregnant. 'I do hope you find him.'

'Oh, one way or another . . . Cheerio . . .'

Marigold's second plan, if the first yielded no results, was to locate Algie's sister. She was aware that Kate worked in a cake shop in Brierley Hill town, so she took another tram directly, back to Brierley Hill. Having been shown it before by Algie she quickly located it. But when she enquired within she met with the icy response that Kate Stokes no longer worked there and nobody knew where she had gone. She sensed some haughty disapproval of Kate, manifested by scornful facial expressions rather than actual words. Then she recalled the butcher who had given her the creeps, and decided to call there for information; Algie and his mother, she remembered, were well-known to him. He might well be able to shed some light on his whereabouts. But the butcher's shop, which she recognised, was shut up. The window bore no display, save for a painted plaster model of a pig's head set in the middle. There was certainly no sign of activity there. It looked as if it had been unattended for ages. It seemed as if Algie, and everybody connected with him, had disappeared off the face of the earth.

That girl Harriet could have been an option, but Marigold had taken it into her head to avoid Harriet at all costs. She'd only ever seen Harriet once, and could not be certain she would recognise her again anyway, even if she knew which shop housed their family business.

Then she remembered the Bottle and Glass. She was sure she could remember how to get there. She'd found her way in the dark, that fateful night she left Algie helping the poor injured folks in that dreadful tram accident. Surely she could find it in daylight.

As she walked towards Buckpool, she relived in her mind the events of that evening last November. How pathetically foolish she had been to allow herself to get worked up about that girl. She had failed to heed Algie's earnest assurances that he was having nothing else to do with Harriet. And no wonder at it, since the girl was not the good-looking type she felt Algie liked. He was a well-set-up lad, and could take his pick of the best-looking girls. They must surely be queuing up to be noticed.

Why had she been so pig-headed as to let him go? Why had she asked her father to leave their mooring early next morning – a whole day early – when, had they remained, she and Algie would have patched up their differences beautifully. Her unborn child would have a father, by now she would be married to him, cared for and adored. Instead, she had nothing, save the prospect of being an object of scorn and derision for allowing herself to get pregnant out of wedlock. She would be tied forever to a life on the narrowboats where the stigma of illegitimacy existed as fiercely as it did anywhere else. Gone were all hopes of ever living a life of relative contentment in her own little house, made homely and comfortable, like that of Aunt Edith, unless she could find Algie and win him back . . .

She reached the Bottle and Glass, aware that women and girls were hardly likely to venture into such a public house alone. Filled with trepidation, she hesitated. It was approaching dinnertime and plenty of men would be in there, forcing as many pints into their bellies as time would allow. They would gawp at her, make unkind and lurid comments. But she was here, standing in front of the public house. Because she had come this far there was no sense in foregoing the opportunity to ask the landlord if he had heard anything of Algie Stokes. So, in she went.

She stood at the bar of the taproom forlornly, shrinking away, self-conscious, wishing that she could look entirely inconspicuous. Tom Simpson regarded her with some surprise when he saw her.

'Yes, my dear? What can I do for you?'

'I . . . I need some help, if you please, Mr Simpson.'

'You know my name.' He looked at her with concern, and Marigold could not discern whether he had noticed her large belly under her mantle. If so, maybe he thought she was about to give birth there and then. 'If I can be of help, miss . . .'

'I think you know my dad . . . Seth Bingham . . .'

'Seth Bingham! Course.' Tom smiled amenably when he realised it was Seth's daughter standing before him. 'How is he, the old sod? We ain't seen him round here for a while. Is he about?'

'He's at Hemel Hempstead, Mr Simpson. Or he was the

day before yesterday. We've been stuck in the ice and snow nearly all winter.'

'I ain't surprised. Young Algie Stokes is forever asking if I've heard from you.'

'Is he? Honest?' Marigold smiled, much heartened by the news.

'I keep telling him, I ain't seen aught of you in months. Wait till he knows you've been here.'

'I came up here by train. I need to know where I can find Algie, Mr Simpson.'

'Ah . . . That might be a bit ockerd. I ain't got no address, you see, my flower. He was in here not long ago, but he's never left his address. He was living in Kingswinford after they left the lock-keeper's cottage, but I think him and his mother have flitted again. I think he might be living somewhere in Dudley now.'

'Dudley?' Her bitter disappointment was manifest in her eyes.

'I know,' he said sympathetically. 'It's a big town if you'm looking for somebody.'

'If I tell you where I'm living, can you pass it on to him next time he calls?'

'Course I will, my flower,' Tom said kindly. 'He'd kill me if I didn't. So where are you living and I'll write it down for him?'

'Rectory Street in Oldswinford. At Mrs Archer's house.' Tom Simpson picked up a blacklead and wrote it down on a piece of paper. 'When d'you think he'll be in here again?' she asked.

'That I couldn't say, my flower. Could be tomorrow, could be next month. He's out o' work at the present, so I reckon he's got time on his hands. But once he starts working again, who knows when he'll find the time?'

'How is he?' Marigold asked earnestly. 'Is he well?'

'He don't seem too bad, considering. Anyroad, don't fret theeself. I'll tell him as you've been looking for him.'

Marigold nodded. 'Thank you, Mr Simpson. Thank you ever so much.'

She left, no further forward in her search, but happier in the knowledge that Algie had been asking Mr Simpson if he'd heard anything of them.

The following Tuesday, Algie received a letter. It read:

> *My own darling Algie,*
>
> *At last Benjamin is going away for a couple of nights. I write this on Monday morning to reach you Tuesday, his first night away in ages. Meet me at our usual place, seven o' clock.*
>
> *My love forever,*
> *Aurelia*

Chapter 32

It seemed an age since Algie and Aurelia had last lain together in that bed at the Eagle Hotel which they called their love nest. Aurelia gave herself with an intensity and reckless abandon that told of her hunger for him, while his response was moderated by guilt because of his mother's disapproval of the affair. They lay in each other's arms afterwards, quiet, as usual, Aurelia reliving in her mind the tenderness and the simple pleasure of being together, while he was mentally struggling to find a way to please both women. Aurelia had sensed Algie's reserve, however, and it worried her. She turned her head to look at him. His eyes were closed, but he was not asleep.

'A penny for your thoughts,' she whispered into his ear.

He turned to look at her. Her eyes, reflecting the flickering firelight, were wide and beautiful. Her skin, taking on the monochromatic gold of the fire's flames, glistened smooth and silky as the dancing shadows gave emphasis to the gentle curves of her body.

'I was thinking about all sorts of things,' he replied softly.

'Were you thinking about us?'

'I hardly ever stop.'

She smiled at his reassurance. 'It's just that you seem preoccupied. Don't you want to go on seeing me?'

'Course I do,' he said, alarmed that she should think otherwise. 'It's just that . . .'

'What?'

'Well . . . I made the daft mistake of telling my mother about you.'

'Oh, you didn't.'

He sighed. 'I did.'

'I can imagine she was suitably unimpressed. Did you tell her I was Murdoch's daughter, and married?'

'As soon as I mentioned your name she knew.'

'I'm surprised she hasn't forbidden you to see me.'

Algie uttered a little laugh. 'I'm a grown man, Aurelia. I make my own decisions who I see and don't see. My mother doesn't make them for me.'

'Anyway, I can only imagine her disapproval.'

'Let's just say that she doesn't *approve*. But only because you're married with a child. Not because of who you are. Your husband would disapprove of me, if he knew what we were up to.'

'From his past actions, it's obvious he takes a dim view of you anyway,' she responded, a reply which amused Algie. 'But who cares? Did your mother approve of Marigold?'

'Yes, she did. But then Marigold wasn't married to somebody else.'

'It's just possible she might be married to somebody else by now, though.'

The thought pained him, when he had believed he was beyond pain now where Marigold was concerned. 'I daresay it's possible,' he reluctantly admitted. 'But whether it's likely or not is another matter. I haven't seen her or heard anything of her for months.'

'But you were in love with her.'

'Course I was,' he admitted without hesitation. 'You know I was.'

'I presume she was very pretty.'

'Very.'

'Did you love her more than you love me?'

He gazed at the ceiling, hoping its whitewashed, cracked surface would supply an inspirational response. He could not gainsay what he'd felt for Marigold. He still felt it, though less intensely these days. 'How the devil can I compare?' he answered plausibly. 'How do you measure the strength of your feelings, so that you can compare them one with another? There isn't any such device that I know of. You and Marigold are totally different to each other, in outlook, class, upbringing, education . . . everything.'

'Did you lie with her?'

'As we do, you mean?'

'Yes, that's what I mean. I shan't mind if you say you did, Algie. I mean, what's good for the goose is good for the gander, after all.'

'Yes, we did,' he admitted. 'But fancy you asking. I don't ask you if you still lie like that with Benjamin.'

'You did once. Whether I do or not, I'm still inclined to leave him, Algie.'

'Then leave him. I wish you would. It's no more than he deserves.'

'Except that I have no money of my own.'

'I would look after you. You know I would.'

Aurelia sighed. 'But with your mother disapproving of me there's no prospect of us starting a life together, is there? Especially as you are committed to looking after her. If we could start a life together, of course I'd leave him tomorrow.'

'I suppose my mother could hardly complain if you were divorced. That would enable us to marry.'

'You know, I never really thought seriously about a divorce before. Not really seriously. It's such a rarity. I mean, a divorce is so difficult to get. But yes, that could be the answer. We must marry. The only problem is, you need grounds for divorce. Adultery is one, cruelty is another.'

'He's not cruel, though, is he?' Algie remarked.

'Not physically, but he is committing adultery, I'm sure . . . Then again, so am I . . . Algie . . .' She sat up in bed excitedly as an idea quickly developed. 'If I admitted as much and you confirmed you were the co-respondent, I daresay he would be quick enough to start proceedings . . . It's a thought, you know.'

'But if your adultery became common knowledge, you would be treated like an outcast wherever you went. What you should also consider is that a judge would certainly declare that you weren't fit to bring up your own child if you admitted adultery. Anyway, how long would it take, I wonder, till you were free of him, even if all went well?'

'Months, I suppose. Years, maybe . . . I'll have to think about it a little more.' She lay down again, deflated, and snuggled up to him. 'It's a way, though, you know, Algie.'

'Well, we'd better think of other grounds for divorce that won't involve me being saddled with the legal costs, because I would be if I was named as co-respondent.'

'Would you really?'

'Course I would.'

'Sorry. I hadn't thought about that.'

'Don't you recall Charles Stewart Parnell, and that Mrs O'Shea?'

'Oh, yes, of course,' Aurelia said. 'I'd forgotten about that. Goodness, I don't want you to be saddled with legal costs, Algie. They could be enormous.'

'Yes,' he said. 'And that would really take the shine off things . . . So, you admitting adultery is out of the question. In the meantime, I can be concentrating on my bike building business. I found a workshop, by the way. I'm looking for some second hand machinery now.'

'That will really stump Benjamin, you know, Algie, you competing in the bicycles market. That will hurt him more than if he found out I've been unfaithful with you.'

A month passed, a month in which Algie and Aurelia met four more times at the Eagle Hotel, a month in which he was too engrossed in his new bike building enterprise to go anywhere near the Bottle and Glass to collect his message from Marigold. It was a month in which Marigold sought him regularly, but without success. Living in Dudley, he might as well have been living on the moon.

On the 22nd of April, a Wednesday, Aurelia packed a trunk with things for herself and little Benjie. She had finally made the decision to leave her husband. The possibility of a happier, more fulfilled life with Algie Stokes at some time in the future beckoned like a beacon in her darkness. It was hypocritical in the extreme to stay with Benjamin when she loved another man so dearly. She waited for him to return from his factory so that she could announce her intention.

Benjamin arrived home at half past six in the evening, and saw the trunk standing in the hall as he entered.

'What's this? Are we taking a holiday all of a sudden?'

'It's mine and Benjie's things, Benjamin.'

'Oh?' He regarded her apprehensively.

'I'm leaving you.'

'Leaving me?' he said, indignant and incredulous. 'Tonight?'

'Tonight's as good a time as any. I've ordered a cab for seven o' clock.'

'A cab? So where d'you think you're going?'

'To an hotel. For tonight at any rate. I'll write and let you know where I end up eventually, if you're interested in knowing.'

'Of course I'm interested in knowing. I have my son to consider. You won't be allowed custody of him, you do realise that, don't you, Aurelia?'

'I understand that will be for a judge to decide. It's a risk I have to take, Benjamin. I believe any judge with one iota of sensitivity would grant custody to a mother who can give her child constant love and attention, as opposed to handing him over to a father who is always at work, and disinterested in his child anyway.'

'To say that I'm disinterested in Benjie is a blatant lie, Aurelia. Besides, he's got a nanny to look after him who is just as competent as you are. What's more, you need grounds for a divorce.'

'I'm giving you grounds . . . Desertion.'

'Desertion? Not adultery?'

She gave a laugh of scorn. 'You seem preoccupied with the idea of me committing adultery, Benjamin. Are you quite sure you are not judging me by your own standards? In any case, if I had been committing adultery, I don't suppose I would be granted custody of Benjie anyway.'

'But have you been committing adultery?'

'Certainly not,' she lied with monumental conviction, driven by the fervent wish not to lose her child, nor cost Algie money.

'Then I don't see why you have to go, Aurelia. I've got no desire to see you leave this house.'

'I have no reason to stay. I don't love you anymore. Nor do you love me.'

'I've feared this moment for some weeks now,' he said morosely. 'Don't go, Aurelia. Stay. We can work things out. Marriage has to be worked at.'

'Then why did you not think to work at it when you had the chance, instead of treating me as if I didn't exist? A woman can only stand so much indifference, Benjamin.'

'Stay,' he entreated earnestly, 'and I'll try to change. I promise . . . I promise to be a good and devoted husband.'

'It's too late, Benjamin.'

'Leave for a trial period, then, eh, if you're so determined to go? Have a few weeks away from me, by all means – a rest from each other. That might be all we need to rekindle our marriage. Then let's see how we feel after that.'

She sighed. It might be expedient to agree to such terms and be allowed to make a quick exit. Once he had allowed her to go, it would be a simple enough matter to say she was never coming back. 'If you think it's more sensible, Benjamin.'

'Course I do. Divorce is a massive step. One not to take lightly. And it's expensive. There's so many things to consider.'

'I'm well aware of it.'

'Do you need money?'

'I have money, Benjamin. Enough for the moment at any rate.'

There was a knock at the door. Aurelia rushed to answer it. The driver of a growler declared that he was at the service of Mrs Sampson.

'Can you take the trunk, please?' she asked him. 'I'll be just a minute.' The driver entered, picked up the trunk and took it outside. She closed the door behind him and hurried past Benjamin to fetch her son. 'Benjie, we are going now.'

Maude, the nanny, looked suitably distressed at having to bid farewell to her charge, to whom she had inevitably grown attached. She gave the boy a kiss and stroked his hair cursorily. 'Goodbye, Benjie.'

'Goodbye, Nanny,' the boy replied confused, aware that something significant was happening from the behaviour of the hovering grown-ups around him, but not sure what.

Aurelia lifted the child, and he sat in her arms, his arms

around her neck. She turned to her husband. 'Goodbye, Benjamin. I'll write.'

Benjamin leaned towards the child to say goodbye and to give him a kiss. 'You'll come and see me soon, won't you, Benjie?'

The boy nodded his solemn promise.

Benjamin watched the driver strap the trunk onto the back of the cab, while Aurelia and little Benjie settled themselves in. When they had departed, Maude stepped into the hall from the room where she and little Benjie had been playing. She stood by Benjamin proprietorially, as if she were the lady of the house, immediately shedding the pose of a servant.

'I'm certain it's another man,' she said quietly. 'Every time she thought you were away on business, Mary says she was off like a shot from a gun, not returning till late at night. Occasionally, she wouldn't come back till the next morning.'

Benjamin looked astonished. 'Maude, why did you not tell me of this before?'

The girl shrugged. 'Because there's no proof of it. Anyway, I didn't want you to think I was trying to oust her by telling tales. I didn't want you to think I was being too pushy. I'm only a nanny, after all.'

'You are only a nanny when my wife's here . . . And a very lovely one at that.' He took her hand and stroked it. 'Is Mary back?'

'No, it's her day off, isn't it? She goes to her mother's on her day off. She won't be back till the morning.'

His eyes lit up. 'Good. Then there's another whole night ahead of us, my angel . . . I'll get a bottle of brandy. See you in your room.'

'We could use yours for a change, Benjamin . . .'

Rather than spend a night at the Eagle, where she was well-known to Mr Powell, the proprietor, Aurelia had already determined that she would stay with her son at the Dudley Arms Hotel, where they alighted from the four-wheeled growler. She had written to Algie warning him of her intention and suggesting that he call there after about half past eight, by which time she hoped to have Benjie settled and asleep.

He arrived at twenty minutes to nine, asked what room she was in and made his way upstairs. He tapped lightly on the bedroom door.

She answered it, putting her forefinger to her lips as a signal to be quiet, and let him in. Little Benjie was asleep in the big bed he would share with his mother that night.

'He's not long gone to sleep,' she said quietly.

Algie peered at the child who might one day be his charge, snuggled up under the bedclothes. 'He looks content anyway.'

'Yes, so far, so good.'

'So . . . you've finally left Benjamin?' He resigned himself to a whispered conversation. 'Was he shocked?'

'He had been half expecting it, I think. But he still claimed he didn't want me to go. At least he'll have his grounds for divorce – desertion.'

'Then let's hope he acts on it. And he let you go without a struggle, without an argument, or threats?'

'With hardly a word of opposition. He very quickly made a concession. He considers it a trial separation. He did ask me, though, if I had money enough, as if he might even hand me some if I hadn't . . . no doubt to hasten my departure.'

'So you are going to throw yourself on the mercy of some relative meanwhile?'

She nodded. 'I said I would. I shall write to let you know where I am. I hope we can see a lot more of each other. Oh, already I feel free, Algie. It's a new beginning . . .'

* * *

Early the following morning, Marigold, looking pale and anxious in her dressing gown, sought her Aunt Edith, who was preparing breakfast in the scullery.

'Aunt Edith,' she said, smiling a pallid apology. 'I think maybe the baby's coming. I've been getting some pains in me belly.'

At once Aunt Edith threw her arms up in a panic. 'How long, Marigold? How long have you been having the pains?'

'A couple of hours now. They woke me. I was having a lovely sleep an' all.'

'And how often are they coming?'

'Dunno. Regular, though.'

She really did not know, not having thought to time them. But the news was sufficient to send Aunt Edith into a tizz of some vigour. She scurried to her pantry, collared a bottle of brandy and poured some into a glass.

'Drink this, my angel, and I'll get dressed. I'll have to run and fetch the midwife.'

'What about our breakfasts?'

'Oh, I couldn't face breakfast now, young Marigold. Nor could you, I shouldn't think, if you got the pains a-coming.'

'You ain't sending for a doctor as well, are you, Aunt Edith?' Marigold sounded concerned.

'Not unless it's necessary, my flower. Why?'

' 'Cause me mom told me once that you have to act genteel in front of a doctor. I don't see how I can act genteel while I'm showing everything I've got, a-grunting and a-shoving. If it's gonna hurt as much as me mother said it would, I can see meself using some hefty swear words an' all.'

'It's up to the midwife to decide about a doctor. If all goes well we shan't need one, so you can swear as much as you like. But I think this child is a mite early, from what your mother told me.'

'Not that early,' Marigold said, and took a slurp of the brandy. 'Besides, I might easy have miscounted the weeks.'

'I shall have to teach you to add up and subtract properly as well as your letters,' Aunt Edith said. 'You can't go through life not knowing where you are.'

'Oh, I know where I am all right, Aunt Edith. I'm well organised. I got me some towels ready, and the baby's new gown put out ready, all nice and white . . . I wish Algie was here, though,' she sighed. 'I do wish he could be with me. I miss him ever so much . . . 'specially now . . .'

'Algie!' Aunt Edith repeated disdainfully. 'The damned elusive Algie. The child's father and still you haven't found him. Lord have mercy on us. I'm going upstairs to get dressed, Marigold. I think you should get back to bed. Your waters could break any time.'

'I don't think I'll go to bed just yet, Aunt. I daresay I'll spend long enough there soon enough. Besides, there's things what I can do. I can get me breakfast for a start.'

Aurelia awoke that morning in that strange bedroom at the Dudley Arms Hotel. At once she realised that she did not feel well. She turned to look at Benjie, angelically asleep still, his hair a riot of dark, wayward curls, his eyelashes long and dense as they seemed to rest on the infant curve of his cheek. She sighed, rapidly becoming aware that this was her first morning of freedom. If only she did not feel quite so queasy. She tried to recall what she had eaten last night that might have upset her.

She sat up in bed, slowly so as not to disturb her sleeping son, and was overwhelmed by a wave of nausea. She realised she was not going to be able to hold back from vomiting. At once she swung her legs out of bed and reached for her dressing gown. There was a water closet at the end of the landing, and she hoped and prayed nobody was occupying it yet. When she reached it, still fastening her dressing gown, she saw that the door was ajar. She burst in, spewing immediately into the pan.

She was on her knees panting, trying to catch her breath between bouts of convulsive retching. Tears squeezed from her swollen eyelids and she felt them running hot down her cheeks. Her mouth tasted foul and she spat the residue of her vomiting into the pan and breathed deeply. At least now she felt better. What could she have eaten that had upset her like this? She wiped her eyes on the handkerchief she took from her pocket, and the awful truth dawned on her, like a sudden thunderstorm blighting a bright summer's day. How stupid of her not to have realised at once. She was with child.

Every morning lately, although feeling not quite right, she had not considered that *that* was the reason, never thought for a moment that she might be carrying a child. When she had failed to bleed at the usual time she had dismissed it as merely the excitement at the prospect of meeting Algie, the sheer thrill of sharing forbidden pleasures, the exhilaration of stolen love. Anyway, why should she have worried? She had been meticulously careful, had applied a douche after every evening with Algie as soon as she got back home. She had missed her monthly bleeding before, caused only, of course, by the excitement of planning her wedding. Perversely, that curse of many a bride had started on her wedding day, delaying consummation by some five days, to Benjamin's abject frustration.

Aurelia was afraid. She felt alone, daring not to think what the future might hold. She was adrift in a sort of no man's land, having just left her husband, without yet having secured the man she really loved. Had she been too impulsive? What if Algie changed his mind? What if he decided to take heed of his mother's disapproval and refused to have anything else to do with her?

This sickliness was how it had been with Benjie, except that with Benjie it was not nearly as violent. Perhaps after this first time it would become less fierce. She wiped her mouth and hurried back to her room. Benjie was still asleep; he had not missed her. She caught a glimpse of herself in the long mirror on the wardrobe door and was glad that Algie could not see her like this – yet at any rate. She drank water from the glass that stood on the bedside table and rinsed her mouth. It was time to get dressed, time to compose herself, time to face the world, time she took Benjie away until she and Algie could commence their life together – with Benjie . . . Oh, and their own child now, the fruits of their union, already rooted in her belly.

She got herself ready then woke Benjie. He was generally boisterous when he awoke, and always boisterous just before he was put to bed at night. Maude was not here now to manage him, a job she always did so effectively. But Aurelia was easily able to get him washed and dressed, and she took him downstairs for breakfast, which she could not face herself. That done, she asked the porter to bring down her trunk and get her a cab, then paid her bill and left the hotel.

As Benjie sat beside her, avidly peering out of the cab's window to the clip-clop of the horse's hoofs, Aurelia nibbled the end of her glove deep in thought, seeing but not noticing the Black Country's grimy streets being washed with soft April rain. The harshness of that bitter winter was gone. The first buds were greening up the trees, and birds were flitting about in a frenzy of nest building. The colourless industrial land-scape began to change the further they travelled, and they were soon approaching lush green fields and bluebell woods. The gardens of bigger houses were coming alive after their winter rest, playing host to clusters of spring flowers, all in a rush to bloom.

Eventually, Aurelia reached the home of her mother's sister, with whom she had always enjoyed a rapport. She paid the cab driver, who dropped off her trunk at the front door, and she led Benjie by the hand up the front path. She composed herself, forced a smile, and rapped on the shining brass door knocker.

'Aurelia!' her aunt said when she opened the door and saw her. 'What a time to come visiting. We're up to our necks—'

'We haven't come visiting,' Aurelia replied. 'We've come to stay.'

'Come to stay?' The woman put her head in her hands as if all the troubles of the world had come to roost on her shoulders. 'You young women! I don't know when you'll be able to get comfortable then. There's a bit of a flap on. But come in out the wet.' She stood aside to let them enter.

At once, Aurelia could hear the screams of a woman emanating from upstairs. She turned to her aunt. 'What's going on?'

'You remember your Aunt Hannah?'

'Of course I remember my Aunt Hannah. I'm hardly likely to forget her. She had an affair with my father.'

'The girl you can hear is her eldest daughter in the throes of childbirth.'

'Childbirth?' Aurelia regarded her aunt with unease. 'Is the poor thing all right? Is there anybody with her?'

'Oh, yes, I engaged a midwife. She's up there with her.'

'Maybe I can help, Aunt.'

'Yes, maybe you can. Perhaps you ought to make yourself useful anyway, if you want to stop here a bit.'

'I'll settle Benjie down first, and find him some toys out of my trunk.'

Another series of heart-rending shrieks came from upstairs as Aurelia lugged in her trunk and opened it. She took out a rag doll and sat Benjie on her knee with it, ready to humour the child in this strange and raucous environment of shrieking and energetic women that he found himself thrust into. Then a thought struck her.

'Aunt, how old is this daughter of Aunt Hannah's?'

'Not yet twenty.'

'Only nineteen? . . . Is she . . . by any chance . . . ?'

'Your father's bastard child?'

'I wasn't aware there was a child from that affair . . . but is she?'

'I'm afraid she is, Aurelia.'

'But . . . why was I never told that poor Aunt Hannah had had a child by my father? . . . And yet, the way she disappeared and was hardly ever spoken of, I should've realised . . . Good God! You know what this means, Aunt? She's my sister . . .' Aurelia's eyes lit up. 'I have another sister . . . Oh, Aunt, I really must go and meet her . . . I really must try to be of some help, some comfort to her. Will you keep Benjie entertained while I go up?'

Chapter 33

Two days after Aurelia had left Benjamin, Algie received a brief note. It said simply:

> Dearest Algie,
>   Just a line to let you know that I am staying for the time being with an aunt at the address written above, and having a very interesting and busy time of it. So busy and so interesting, in fact, that I've hardly had time to consider what I've done. However, I have found time to sneak to my room to scribble this note.
>   Please do not write to me here under any circumstances. I shall write again in a few days' time, once things have settled down, when I hope we shall be able to meet.
>   Love always,
>   Aurelia.

Although Algie waited patiently for his promised next letter, it did not arrive until the 1st of May, a Friday. Nearly two weeks had elapsed since Aurelia had left her husband. Again, the note was brief, requesting him to meet her on the Saturday at noon, not at the Eagle Hotel, but at the entrance to Stourbridge Junction Railway Station. At once he was concerned that she might be unwelcome where she was, and going away to stay with some other relative, more remote, hence the station. Saturday came and noon approached. He cleaned himself up, left his new workshop where he had been installing a hand press, and rode to the station to meet her. There had been no time to change, so he still wore his working clothes. When he arrived Aurelia was already waiting, looking as straight-backed and elegant as ever, but a little pale and unwell, he thought. He rested his bike against the wall and greeted her with a kiss and an anxious smile.

'I thought you were never going to write.'

'I found it quite difficult, Algie,' she replied ambiguously. 'I see you've come straight from work. How is your new venture going?'

'Very well, to tell you the truth. I've been able to pick up some machinery ever so cheap. A small steam engine, a lathe, a tube-bender—'

'I asked you to meet me here,' she said, interrupting him, 'because I have something very important to tell you.'

'What?' he said, uneasy at what it might be.

'Shall we go up to the station platform and find a bench to sit on? I think it will be better if we sit down.'

'If you like.' She took his arm as they entered the station, ascending the flight of steps to the nearest platform. 'When I read your letter and you asked to meet me here at the station, my first thought was that you wanted to say goodbye. I thought you were going away. Are you?'

She smiled enigmatically. 'No, I'm not, Algie. Some things you cannot run away from. A difficulty has arisen which affects us radically. I have to talk to you.'

A score or more folk were milling about. The rasping huffs of a departing train punctuated the atmosphere.

'You look pale,' he said. 'Are you unwell?'

'Oh, I'll survive.'

He regarded her anxiously. It was unlike her to be so

513

morose. She was normally so cheerful, with a natural, ready smile and sparkling eyes. 'Has leaving Benjamin been a big cause of worry for you?'

'Of course,' she replied candidly. 'Of course it has.'

'And how's little Benjie?'

'He's well, thank you.' She smiled in acknowledgement of Algie's thoughtfulness in asking.

'Is he missing his father?'

'More likely missing Maude. After all, he spent a lot of time with her.'

They reached the platform and stepped out, squinting against the brightness of the springtime sky. Shafts of sunlight were penetrating obliquely through the swirling smoke and steam exhaled by the departing locomotive. It had rained overnight and the new leaves on the tall trees around the station were glistening with moisture. Stourbridge Junction was set in a shallow valley, and to one side the hills reared up higher than the other, up to the pale sky. In the rising distance the hedges were tinted with greening shoots, and looked for all the world as if somebody had thrown a gauze veil over their dark undergrowth.

They headed towards a vacant bench and sat on it, Aurelia primly erect, Algie leaning back, his arm stretched across the backrest behind her.

'So, what do you want to tell me that affects us so radically?'

She turned towards him so that her knees were touching his, and took his hand in hers. He thought how serious, how sad she looked.

'I am going back to Benjamin,' she announced softly. 'It will be for the best.'

'You're going back?' he queried incredulously. 'You've hardly given it a chance, Aurelia.'

'It will be for the best, Algie.' Tears welled up in her eyes.

Seeing she was troubled far more than she was claiming, he put his arm around her, and she rested her head against his shoulder. 'Best for who? Best for you? Best for me? Best for your son?'

'Best for everybody.'

'Forgive me, Aurelia, but I can't agree with you. You've been miserable with Benjamin – by your own admission – and yet you want to go back to him?'

'Please don't be angry with me, Algie. It's more than I can stand.' Her bottom lip trembled and she began to weep. 'It's not because I don't love you,' she sobbed. 'My dear, sweet Algie . . . I love you more than you'll ever know . . . now and always . . . Always remember that . . . But not going back to Benjamin would be unforgivably selfish of me. I should never be able to live with my conscience.'

'To hell with your conscience, Aurelia. I never heard of anybody who had a conscience over wanting to be happy. I'll make you happy, believe me.'

'You would,' she said, with a great shuddering sob. 'I know you would . . . But I know myself better than you do, my love, and I know it would not be fair.'

'Is it because of Benjie, this change of heart? Is it because you think I wouldn't be a good father to him?'

She shook her head and pulled a small handkerchief from the reticule on her lap with which to dab her eyes. 'No, I'm sure you would be an excellent father.' She looked into his eyes evocatively. 'A better father than Benjamin.'

'Then I honestly don't understand. I honestly don't know what's got into you. You'll regret it, you know, going back to him.'

'Perhaps . . . It's a cross I'll have to bear.'

'Have you already discussed it with him? Is it already arranged?'

She shook her head again. 'No . . . I haven't seen him. I've written to let him know where I am, how Benjie is, but I've heard nothing from him in return.'

'So you don't even know that he'll have you back?'

'Oh, I agree. It's by no means certain.' She sniffed, and wiped her nose.

'Then let's hope he turns you away . . . If he does, you and I have a chance together. So when do you intend to go back?'

'This afternoon. I have ordered a cab for three o' clock.'

He had a thought, and his face brightened up. 'I presume, then, that we shall go on seeing each other as before, once you're back there? When Benjamin goes on his business trips.'

'No, Algie,' she sniffed, and another flood of tears wet her pale cheeks. 'I shan't be able to do that.'

'Then it's all over between us? Is that what you're saying?'

'It has to be, my love.'

Algie shrugged, frustrated by her illogical decision. It made no sense at all. He sighed deeply. 'Only a minute or two ago you said you love me and always would.'

'Yes, it's true,' she protested, as if it could never be otherwise. 'I do love you. More than I can say . . .' A renewed and reinvigorated bout of weeping assailed her.

He held her tight, tenderly. 'So what you are doing makes no *sense*.'

She wiped her eyes again, which were becoming red with her tears, then blew her nose delicately.

'It will all make sense soon, Algie.'

'Oh?' he uttered. 'D'you honestly think so?'

'I want you to promise me one thing.'

He nodded his agreement.

'And you must promise it on your mother's life.'

He looked at her with a puzzled frown. 'I promise you

anything, Aurelia, if it's within the bounds of possibility to do it.'

'Promise me you will call on my Aunt Edith.'

He laughed. 'Why? Are you trying to fix me up with her?'

'Don't be absurd.'

'Well, she is a widow, you said.'

'I'm being very serious, Algie.' Her expression left him in no doubt as to how serious she was. 'Promise me you will call on her tomorrow . . . when I'm gone. She holds the key to all this.'

'Where does she live?' he asked resignedly. 'I've forgotten her address, since you told me I was not to write to you there.'

'Number eighteen, Rectory Road, Oldswinford.'

He repeated the address, memorising it. 'All right,' he said. 'I'll visit her tomorrow. I'd better wear my Sunday best.'

'Of course, you must. Her name is Mrs Archer. I'll tell her to expect you at three.'

'I promise I'll be there.'

'I'd better go, Algie, else I shan't be ready when the cab calls to collect us. Will you walk back down to the street with me?'

'Course I will.'

They rose from the bench together, and Aurelia took his arm again as they walked sombrely along the platform to the steps. Out in the street, near to where he had left his bicycle, they turned to each other.

'So this is goodbye?' he said quietly.

She nodded, looking at the folds of her skirt, as if she could not bear to look at him. 'I'm afraid so.'

Their eyes met again. Hers, normally so bright and animated, made it obvious how much emotional pain she was suffering. Her lids were red and swollen from her weeping, and tears still clung to her beautiful, long lashes. It occurred to him that maybe she'd been weeping long before she'd met him today.

He threw his arms around her in a poignant embrace. Tears stung his own eyes and he blinked long and hard in an effort to stem them. 'What am I to do if ever I see you out and about?' he muttered, his voice wracked with emotion. 'I shall want to hold you tight, like this.'

'I know,' she whispered. 'And I'll want to hold you. It will be so difficult . . .' She sighed profoundly. 'I must go now, Algie . . .'

He unhanded her and gave her a brief goodbye kiss on the lips. To have given her a long, lingering kiss, which he really felt inclined to do, would have served only to prolong the agony.

'I thought at one point that you were going to tell me you were carrying our child,' he said. 'I only wish you had.'

She smiled, all her love exuding from her streaming eyes. 'Yes, I know. If only . . .'

'It's goodbye then, Aurelia? So soon.'

'Yes . . . So soon . . . Goodbye, Algie.'

She touched his hand, turned away from him and, as tears rolled down his cheeks in profusion, he watched her walk elegantly out of his life.

Aurelia left the tender care of her Aunt Edith that afternoon, together with little Benjie, as she had said she would. The hansom turned onto the drive of the house that had been home since her marriage, the house she believed she had left for good, only two weeks earlier. It came to a halt at the front door with a scrape of shifting gravel under its wheels. She paid the driver and asked him to leave her trunk at the door.

She sighed with apprehension as she tried the door. It was locked. She pulled out her key and unlocked it, then opened it gingerly. 'Come on, Benjie,' she said gently to the child, taking his hand.

All was quiet. The house seemed dead, save for the slow, heavy pulse of the grandfather clock in the hall, a sound so excruciatingly familiar. She called Benjamin, but there was no reply. She called Mary, the maid. Still no reply. She called Maude, just in case she was still there.

The house was clearly devoid of any living soul.

She decided to pull the trunk inside, so propped the front door open with an umbrella stand and lugged it in, allowing it to rest behind the front door so as not to cause an obstruction when Benjamin returned.

'Let's see if Daddy's gig is in the stable,' she suggested to her son. 'Shall we?'

The child nodded, and took her hand as they made their way to the back of the house and the outbuildings. She pulled open the wide stable door. The carriage remained, but neither the horse nor the gig was there.

'You see, Daddy's gone out in the gig,' she cooed. 'Perhaps he's gone to see Grandmamma.' Perhaps he'd gone to break the news that his wife had left him, if he hadn't already done so. 'Let's go back inside and wait. We can play with some of your toys. Shall we?'

The child nodded his head enthusiastically and grinned, and Aurelia led him back into the house to his playroom. Nothing there had changed. His toys remained, returned tidily to the box in which they were always kept.

They played together for more than an hour, with building bricks, with a selection of rag dolls, with a wooden railway engine painted dark green. The grandfather clock in the hall struck five o' clock. Surely Benjamin would be back soon. She wanted the ordeal of her return to be over as quickly as possible, to feel something approaching normality so that she could get on with her life, so that she could try to forget Algie Stokes. Her amorous adventure with Algie, though gloriously inspiring, had been costly in so many ways. Not that she would have changed anything. Love, the love she felt for him, had been so fulfilling. It had enriched her life. She had experienced emotions she never would have believed possible otherwise. But all things must pass, and her affair was one such beautiful thing. It had been too beautiful to last, like some delicate flower, but at least she was having Algie's child.

At ten past five, she heard the sound of wheels and horse's hoofs on the gravel outside, and she stood up in readiness to meet Benjamin, her heart beating fast. From Benjie's playroom, with the door ajar, she would see him enter the front door.

Two minutes later it opened, and she heard Benjamin say, 'You know, I could swear I locked the door when we went out.'

We . . . When *we* went out.

Aurelia lessened the gap between door and doorframe so as not to be seen, and turned to look anxiously at her son, hoping he would make no sound. The child was engrossed in his wooden railway engine, trying diligently to pull the funnel off. Then there was the trunk . . . If only she had moved the trunk out of sight . . .

Through the narrowed opening she peered again towards the front door. A woman was following Benjamin inside, a slender woman with a well-proportioned and youthful figure. Aurelia knew the hat she wore, recognised the gait, the stance, the set of her head, her delicate mannerisms. She watched, as Benjamin took the woman in his arms and kissed her hungrily.

Time to announce she had returned.

She opened the door and stepped into the hall.

'Good afternoon, Benjamin . . . Maude . . .'

Instantly, the couple unhanded one another, decorously allowing a few feet of space between themselves. In so doing, Maude immediately stumbled backwards over Aurelia's trunk and let out a scream. She ended up on her back, with her legs propped up in the air against the trunk.

'How very inelegant you look with your garters showing, Maude,' Aurelia declared, amused by the fall. 'Please do cover yourself up.'

'What brings *you* back?' Benjamin exclaimed huffily.

'My two weeks away, Benjamin – our trial separation – has made me realise the relevance of our marriage.'

'The relevance of our marriage? Well, that's a new one. What do you mean – *relevance*?'

Maude struggled to her feet and straightened her hat, which had been knocked askew.

'I mean that I am carrying a child, Benjamin. Therefore, our marriage has more relevance than it did when I went away. I did not realise when I left that I was pregnant.'

'A child?' Benjamin queried, with some suspicion. 'Are you sure?'

'Oh, I'm quite sure. Do you require a note from the doctor confirming it?'

'But what if it's not your child, Benjamin?' Maude hissed. 'What if it's out of wedlock?'

'You impertinent hussy!' Aurelia scolded haughtily, before Benjamin could utter a word in response. 'So tell me, is it such an impossibility that you might have a child out of wedlock yourself, after you have doubtless been sharing my bed with my husband? People in glass houses, Maude . . .'

Maude's face was a burning peony. She looked at Benjamin, hoping he would reply for her. But he said nothing, at this stage not wishing to incriminate himself more.

'If you are without sin, Maude,' Aurelia went on, 'I might tolerate your insinuations, but since clearly you are not, I shall afford them the contempt that they deserve . . .'

Benjamin stood there, looking cravenly sheepish. If Aurelia had been unfaithful, so had he. Thus, they were on level terms, he quickly decided. He might well yet have to answer for it if Maude did happen to be carrying his child. To accept Aurelia's now would mollify any possible trouble later.

'We've got some talking to do in private, Aurelia,' Benjamin said, asserting himself and glancing guiltily at Maude. 'Maude will leave us while we speak privately in the drawing room.'

'Maude will leave us, most certainly,' Aurelia conceded, with a coolness she did not feel. 'Permanently . . . But while we have this discussion, Benjamin, she will remain, so that she is under no misapprehension. I have returned to this house – my home – after giving due and careful consideration to the entire position. I cannot deprive the child I am expecting of a father, and nor can you, Benjamin. It is up to us to make a fresh start. With this new baby comes a new commitment. We have every chance of making our marriage work. But we shall not need a nanny. I shall attend to my children myself from now on. Now . . . if you would like a minute to say goodbye to Maude privately, Benjamin, I shall happily grant it . . . As long as it is no more than a minute . . . Oh, and by the way . . . where is Mary?'

'I dismissed Mary,' Benjamin responded. 'Should we get her back, d'you think?'

'I think not, Benjamin. Let us start afresh, with a new, more mature servant.'

Algie was mystified by Aurelia's unanticipated change of heart. The sudden about-turn in her intentions left him frustrated, disappointed and sad. There was also some misgiving in his heart, that she could change her mind with such apparent ease, especially after her very plausible commitment to a future life with him. It posed the question of trust. However, it resolved one problem. He did not have to juggle her life with that of his mother. It is doubtful whether his mother would ever have come to terms with him settling down with a woman who had been married and divorced. There was such a stigma attached to divorce; divorced women were further stigmatised as being either mentally retarded or whores.

For the rest of Saturday he contemplated Aurelia's unfathomable decision, without coming to any conclusion that made any sense, save that she was inclined to be impulsive; she could just as soon change her mind again and come running back, if her husband refused to take her back. It was with this possibility firmly planted in his mind that he left his workshop on Sunday, to go home for his dinner and to change his clothes before he embarked on the visit to Aurelia's Aunt Edith, which he'd promised faithfully to fulfil. But Algie was baffled. What could Aurelia have possibly meant when she told him that her aunt held the key to it all? Why her aunt?

As he rode to Oldswinford, he was glad it was another fine sunny day for the ride out. The weather reminded him of how it had been last spring, especially that fateful Sunday when he had forced himself to approach Marigold, and actually struck up a conversation with her. So much had happened since then, so many unexpected twists and turns in his life and in the lives of his family. But none as strange or as mysterious as the quest in hand today. He wondered again what had become of Marigold. If only she had not taken umbrage with him so pointlessly. Nothing would have come of his exposure to Aurelia. He would have had good reason to side-step her irresistibility, and would not now be smarting over *her*. But he would get over it. It had been an exciting and intensely emotional adventure; planning their lives ahead, discussing their hopes, their dreams of a life together, lying with her, one of the most scintillating women he'd ever had the privilege to cast eyes on, during those stolen, illicit hours. But, yes, he would get over it.

He found Rectory Road and rode along it slowly, peering at the numbers trying to locate Aunt Edith's.

Then he found it. A small cottage in its own neat garden. It faced the church and the old brick wall surrounding the graveyard. A pretty spot. He leaned his bike against the garden wall of the cottage, took off his cycle clips and checked his fob watch. It said two minutes to three. Perfect timing. He walked up the path, rapped on the shining brass door knocker. The door opened, and a pleasant-looking woman wearing spectacles answered it, middle-aged, veering towards fifty, he reckoned; certainly older than his mother.

'Good afternoon, Mrs Archer,' he said with one of his winning smiles. 'I'm Algernon Stokes. I've been told by your niece Aurelia to pay you a visit. She said you would be expecting me.'

'So you're Algie,' the woman said, apparently unmoved by his amiability, when she'd finished eyeing him up and down. 'You'd better come in.'

She stepped aside to let him pass and closed the door behind him. 'This way, if you please, young Algie . . . You don't mind if I call you Algie, do you? I feel I know you well enough.'

'No, I don't mind, Mrs Archer,' he said as she led him into the room and gestured for him to sit down.

'Never mind the "Mrs Archer" bit. You'd best start calling me "Aunt Edith".'

He grinned inanely. 'Why? What's this all about? Your niece obviously told you about me. She said you hold the key to something or other . . .'

'What key? I don't know about no key, Algie, but I know there's somebody spent a lot of time and effort looking for you, but in vain . . . Till our Aurelia said as she knew you and knew where to find you.'

'Somebody's been looking for me?' he questioned, with a puzzled frown. 'My sister, do you mean?'

'Lord, let's hope she ain't your sister, else there'll be hell to pay.' She gave a wry laugh and stood up, went to the door and called, 'Marigold! He's here.'

At once Algie's face bore a look of utter astonishment, of incredulity. 'Marigold's here? Marigold Bingham?'

'She's coming,' Aunt Edith said, and there was a hint of devilment in her eyes, that said she was really enjoying this. She sat down again.

Algie heard hurried footsteps on the hard tiles of the hallway and looked at the door expectantly. He could scarcely believe his eyes when, standing in the doorframe, was none other than Marigold. She looked radiantly lovely and refined, wearing a bright blue dress with bodice buttoned to the throat, and obviously new. Her face was just as beautiful, yet there was such a change in her. He was at once reminded of Aurelia. She looked so much like her that he was astounded by their similarity. The same shaped face and nose, the wide, sparkling blue eyes, and the same rich, dark hair. Why had he not considered it before?

'Marigold,' he exclaimed with a smile of delighted bewilderment. 'Is it really you?'

She ran to him unhesitatingly, and threw her arms around his neck. 'Oh, Algie, Algie . . . Is it really *you*, after all this time? Where've you been hiding? I've hunted high and low.'

'I've hunted high and low for *you* . . . I'd given you up for lost . . . Let me look at you . . .' He held her at arm's length and gasped. 'God . . . You look . . . well, Marigold, you look beautiful. There's no other word. You've put a pound or two on, I see, but it suits you well. You look really beautiful.'

She laughed with joy at his reaction, blushing, self-conscious at his compliment. 'I'm ever so glad you think so, Algie,' she said. 'You as well . . . You look more handsomer than ever.'

'Would you like a cup of tea, Algie?' Aunt Edith interrupted. 'And a piece of my cake, which I've made 'specially?'

'Thank you. That would be very nice. Special cake for a special occasion, eh?'

Aunt Edith nodded and smiled. 'Just for the occasion, as you rightly say. Well, I'll leave you two to get reacquainted. Marigold's got such a lot to tell you.'

'I don't know where to begin, Algie,' Marigold said, as her aunt left them. 'Maybe first I should say sorry for running away from you that night after the concert. I know now how daft I was. Can you ever forgive me?'

'Come and sit by me,' he said warmly, and she did as she was bid, smiling happily. 'I think I can forgive you anything. I still can't believe you're here, in the same room as me. I spent hours searching the canals and basins for you, hoping you'd come back.'

'Did you, Algie? Honest?'

'I did. I rode for miles, day in, day out.'

'I heard about your dad dying,' she said, suddenly looking solemn. 'I was that sorry, Algie. It must have been heart-breaking for you. I know you thought a lot of your dad.'

'He died the same night you left me. I felt pretty rotten at the time, as you can imagine. Everything bad seemed to happen at once.'

'I'm really sorry about that . . . Are you sure you can forgive me for causing you so much upset?'

'Course I can . . . now.' He regarded her admiringly. 'But

what I don't understand, Marigold, is how you come to be here? I mean here, of all places, at the same time as Aurelia.'

'Oh, Aurelia's lovely, ain't she? And I just love her little lad. She was such a help, such a friend to me. More than a friend, to tell you the truth.'

'So what happened? How did it all come about?'

'Well, for a start, Algie, I have to tell you, my dad ain't my dad . . .' She paused for this information to sink in. 'What I mean is, I'm illi—illiterate.'

'Do you mean illegitimate?'

'Yes, that's what I mean, but I can never remember how to say the word. My mom had me before she met Seth, see, but I always believed he was me dad. I didn't know any different. Then me mom brought me here to stay for a while with Aunt Edith. Aurelia arrived a few days after with her little lad, and it turns out that her mother, and my mother, *and* Aunt Edith am all sisters – *was* sisters, 'cause Aurelia's mom's dead now. Then, as we got talking more and more, it came out that her dad is my real dad as well. Somebody called Murdoch Osborne . . . That name's familiar, you know, Algie,' she said pensively. 'Anyway, he had it off with my mom, the dirty devil, when he was already married to my poor Aunt Elizabeth. So we'm sisters, see? Half-sisters anyway.'

Algie was further astonished by this news. 'She's also your cousin,' he suggested intently, at once caught up in the thread and seeing the relationship from another angle.

'Cousin – sister – half-sister. What difference does it make? We'm close relations anyway.'

Somehow it seemed to Algie that he could not get away from the influence and questionable deeds of Murdoch Osborne. But it was not Marigold's fault. She could not help who her father was. Then he recalled how he'd taken her once to Murdoch's butcher's shop.

'You met him once, your father.'

'Did I?'

'Remember I took you to that butcher's shop and you wanted some meat but refused to buy it off him. Because you said he gave you the creeps?'

'Yes . . .' She regarded Algie with open-mouthed incredulity. 'Was that him?'

'That was him.'

'Oh, Lord! I hated him. I thought he was horrible. Then we saw him after at that concert, didn't we?'

'Well, I doubt if you'll see him again. But that's another story . . . Anyway, why did your mother bring you here?' he asked, changing the subject, not wishing to get bogged down with the tale of Murdoch and his mother just yet.

'Because of the dreadful winter, all that snow,' she replied. She looked at him uncertainly, and he caught her look. 'I got something else to tell you, Algie . . .'

'Go on . . .'

'I got a baby.'

'You've got a *baby*?' he spluttered, incredulous. 'My God.'

'That's why my mom brought me here. So as I could have it away from the canals, and so as Aunt Edith could look after me.'

'Whose baby is it?' he asked, half choking with confused emotions.

'Mine, you daft thing.'

'No, I mean who is the father?'

'You am, you daft ha'peth.' She rolled her eyes, feigning impatience. 'Who d'you think?'

'Me?'

'Course, you.' She smiled, amused by his obvious surprise.

'Where is it? The baby, I mean.'

'Upstairs, in her little crib. It's a girl. And she's so beautiful, Algie. Just like you.'

'I would've hoped she looked more like you,' he said flippantly, rapidly warming to the situation. 'Can I see her?'

'She's asleep. But I'll fetch her down if you like. Shall I?'

'I'd love to see her. My own daughter. Blimey!'

Marigold was on her feet in a swirl and a swish of blue skirt, and raced daintily up the stairs. His eyes followed her. She was all slender, the only way he'd ever known her, her neat figure showing no signs of coarseness after giving birth. Within a minute she descended, slowly this time, with the child securely, lovingly in her arms. Algie stood up, the better to see his daughter, while Marigold proudly tilted her in his direction, so he could see her more easily.

He gently shifted the white blanket away from the child's face with his forefinger and peered at her. 'She *is* beautiful.' His voice was quiet, taut with emotion, his look intense. His eyes welled up with tears, which ran down his cheeks unchecked. Then his face brightened into a tearful smile. 'She's the spitting image of you, Marigold, thank the Lord. Please let me hold her?'

'Course.' She carefully handed the little bundle over and they sat down again.

He was overcome. Tears flooded down his cheeks. All the time they were apart, Marigold had been carrying his child, and he had known nothing about it. He could have lost her, he could have lost his daughter, never been aware of her. Through his tears he looked at this helpless child with absolute tenderness. He had not known she existed until those amazing moments. He wiped the tears away with the back of his hand and grinned excitedly. 'What are you calling her?'

'Rose,' she answered without hesitation. 'I hope you like it. All the first-born girls on the canals are called Rose. It's a sort of tradition.'

'I know it is.' He looked down at the child sleeping in his

arms, with a natural, intense affection and rapidly growing pride. 'Rose,' he said quietly. 'I should have guessed you'd call her Rose . . . I wish she'd open her eyes, so I can see them.'

'Oh, she will soon enough. She's due a feed in half an hour. She feeds ever so well, you know, Algie. You'll see.'

'Are you taking her back to the narrowboat?' he asked, not without some angst. He did not know for certain yet how he stood, if at all, in Marigold's plans for the future.

'Well . . . that really depends on you, Algie . . .'

'On me?'

'Course.'

'Then I'll ask you now what I intended to ask you the morning you rushed away from the basin by our house, the morning my dad died . . . Will you marry me?'

'Oh, Algie . . .' It was Marigold's turn to shed tears of joy. 'Course I will . . .'

Chapter 34

Algie cycled back home elated, scarcely able to believe he'd just spent two hours with Marigold and his very own daughter, who had captivated him instantly. It was blindingly obvious to him by this time what Aurelia had meant when she said that Aunt Edith held the key to her actions. Aurelia, he quickly realised, had nobly sacrificed herself for the benefit of her new-found sister. Marigold, she evidently believed, had a greater claim on him than she herself. Nor did he harbour any doubts as to how difficult such a sacrifice must have been to make; the heart-rending decision to return, humbled, to that disagreeable louse Benjamin Sampson. Algie, of course, had no notion of the circumstances of her return.

Algie learnt from Marigold that Aurelia had arrived at Aunt Edith's house with her little son while Marigold was in the throes of childbirth. Acknowledging from the outset that the stranger was her own half-sister, Aurelia had insisted on helping, and making herself known. During her labour, Marigold was prone to regularly shrieking Algie's name in her agonies, which in turn had prompted Aurelia to seek confirmation of this particular Algie's identity. The revelation must have afforded her plenty of scope for some serious heart-searching.

Algie was amazed at how the sight of Marigold and his own child had put everything into perspective. He had a responsibility to them both, a responsibility he would not shirk. He was delighted with his daughter, he was delighted with Marigold. His prior feelings, emotions which he thought had faded, came flooding back with a vengeance. He loved her. He had never stopped loving her. He wanted to take her in his arms and never let go. Maybe his feelings for Aurelia had been intensified simply for want of love and affection, that same love and affection that Marigold had blessed him with, which he had been sorely missing. Maybe he had become involved and enchanted with Aurelia on the rebound, subconsciously responding to her sisterly likeness to Marigold.

Now, it just remained to tell his mother everything, although he dreaded the inevitable confession that he had put Marigold in the family way.

He reached home and put away his bike in the brewhouse, then went in the house.

'Ah, you're back.'

He grinned massively.

'You look like the cat that got the cream, our Algie. Yesterday you were like a dying duck, your face as long as a wet weekend. Now look at you. How you do change in a day. Whatever have you been up to?'

'I'm getting wed, Mother,' he answered proudly, and allowed her a second to inwardly digest this titillating morsel.

'Not to that Aurelia?'

'Course not, she's already wed, I told you. Anyway, it's all over with Aurelia.'

'Good. I can't say as I'm sorry. Who are you getting wed to then? Isn't that a bit sudden as well?'

'I'm marrying Marigold.'

Clara gasped with relief, and clasped her hands to her face in astonishment. 'Marigold? You found her then?'

'Aurelia found her, to be more precise.'

He told his mother the whole story, embellishing it not one bit, but omitting nothing either.

'It means that Murdoch Osborne is Marigold's father,' he said hesitantly. 'You do see that, don't you, Mother?'

'I'm not altogether stupid, our Algie. I can work that out for myself. He's been a bugger-up-the-back in his time, has Murdoch, and no two ways. I knew Hannah had a child before she went on the narrowboats, but they certainly kept it quiet that her sister's husband was the culprit. I had misgivings when you first started courting Marigold. But then, I thought, what does it matter? As long as you love the wench it doesn't matter a bit. But that rogue I married is capable of anything. The more I hear about him, the less I'm surprised.'

'When you see Marigold, please don't mention that you married the blighter. I've said nothing yet.'

'But somebody will blurt it out, as sure as sparks fly upwards, so you might as well tell her as not. The sooner the better, I reckon. So when d'you intend to get wed? That little child of yours needs a father.'

'I know, and it'll be as soon as we can arrange it. Marigold isn't one-and-twenty yet, so we need her mother's or Seth's consent. It depends how soon they pass this way. But you'll be kind to her, won't you, Mother, when she comes to live here?'

'I bet her Aunt Edith could sign for her, as her guardian, Algie.'

'D'you think so?' he asked excitedly.

'It's worth finding out. Anyway, as regards Marigold, I'll help her all I can, course I will, without trying to interfere.' Clara clapped her hands together and beamed. 'Well, what news this is, Algie. I'm getting a new daughter to take the place of the one as turned out to be no good, and I get a granddaughter as well. Oh, I long to see the little mite.'

'You don't mind that little Rose was born out of wedlock, do you, Mother?'

'Oh, our Algie, it makes no odds to me, so long as you wed the dear girl and love her, and take care of her. You're Rose's father, and you'll be Rose's mother's husband. Sounds like a perfect arrangement.'

Sunday the 31st of May 1891 saw Algie Stokes and Marigold Bingham made man and wife. Clara had delved deeper into the small inheritance her late husband Will had bequeathed her, and found another fifty pounds. Some of it would pay for the wedding, she said, for it was certain the Binghams could not afford the expense. It would also pay for a new suit and shoes for Algie, a new dress for Marigold, a new outfit for herself, and a small party at the Bell Hotel afterwards.

The knot was tied at the Church of St Michael in Brierley Hill by the young curate of the parish. He delivered a nicely worded but predictable homily, felicitating the happy couple on the excellent judgement each had displayed in selecting the other as a life partner, and gently hinting at the advisability of cultivating mutual adaptability.

It was a pretty wedding, but couldn't fail to be with such a beautiful bride, dressed as she was in blue, matching exquisitely the colour of her eyes, which was manifestly noticeable when she lifted her veil. Both Clara and Aunt Edith felt that white would have been inappropriate in the circumstances.

Those attending included the whole tribe of Binghams who had contrived that work brought them to Brierley Hill at the proper time. Aunt Edith was there, as were Clara's sisters and others of the Bunn family, various Stokes, as well as friends of the bride and groom, in particular Harriet and Priss Meese, Clarence Froggatt and, not least, Aurelia and Benjamin Sampson. Algie realised it would be an interesting mix, and queried with Marigold, for obvious reasons, whether Aurelia warranted an invitation.

'She's my sister,' Marigold had replied doughtily. 'And my cousin as well, you said. So she's got two claims. I can't not invite her, can I? 'Specially when she was so kind to me.'

'Do we need to invite her husband?'

'You can't invite one and not the other, Algie,' she reasoned. 'It wouldn't be right or proper. Aunt Edith says so, and she knows about these things. Anyway, you want to invite that Harriet and her sister.'

'Only because Harriet's always been a good friend.'

'Yes, and I shan't get the huff about her no more,' she said with a grin. 'I promise.'

'Good, I should hope not,' he answered good-humouredly, 'especially now she and Clarence Froggatt are courting strong. I told you in the first place you'd got nothing to fear from her. Anyway, she might well turn out to be a good friend to you as well. She's like that.'

The ceremony progressed. In due time they signed the register and stepped back down the aisle, nodding to the guests with smiling faces, first to one side then the other. Algie was relieved to see Aurelia smile at him with apparent good-will as he and Marigold passed the pew she and Benjamin occupied. She looked delicious in a cream outfit and fetching toque with a projecting front brim, a feature Algie considered would render her very kissable lips difficult to access, a challenge which he immediately dismissed now that he was a married man with responsibilities. Benjamin, however, avoided his eyes, though he did glance assessingly at the bride.

Outside in the warm afternoon sunshine the newly married couple and their guests mingled. Aunt Edith and Clara Stokes had held little Rose by turns throughout the ceremony. Once they were outside it was the turn of Hannah Bingham, the child's maternal grandmother. She was in a rapture of pure joy as she became better acquainted with her delightful granddaughter.

The three women eventually vied for possession of the child throughout the rest of the celebrations, as envious as schoolgirls of whoever was holding her, though always evincing smiles of approval. Rose's parents were now married, and sentimentality nullified any remaining stigma over the child's illegitimacy.

Waiting till last, Aurelia and Benjamin Sampson stepped forward to offer their congratulations. Till then, she and Benjamin had dallied in conversation with Aunt Edith and Clara, who was the soul of discretion. Algie, for once, felt decidedly uncomfortable in Aurelia's presence.

Aurelia planted a kiss on her new sister's cheek. 'Congratulations, Mrs Stokes,' she said cheerfully, emphasising her new name, and anxious to keep the envy out of her voice. 'Congratulations to you, too, Mr Stokes, for picking such a beautiful bride.'

The said Mr Stokes felt his colour rise as she allowed him to kiss her on the cheek. Her perfume was so poignantly familiar. 'Thank you, Aurelia. But you *can* call me Algie, you know, especially now that you're my sister-in-law . . .' His smile lingered fondly for a second, as he tried to read her eyes. He turned to her husband, aware that he must acknowledge him sooner or later. 'Which also means, Benjamin, that you and I are brothers-in-law.'

'So it would seem,' Benjamin replied evenly.

'Then shall we make the best of it, and shake on it?'

Benjamin managed a smile, and nodded. 'All right, Algie,' he said with resignation. 'Let's agree to let bygones be bygones.'

They shook hands. *Some bygones*, Algie thought.

Murdoch Osborne crossed Aldwych in London to reach the restaurant at the Gaiety Theatre. Kate Stokes skipped along beside him, hurrying to avoid a hansom cab which threatened to collide with her. Dusk was falling on the busy streets and a lamplighter, stepping off his ladder, touched his cap and nodded as they stepped onto the pavement.

They reached the restaurant and Kate passed regally into its glowing yellow interior, with Murdoch tagging behind in her wake. He looked hardly the man of the world he used to be, but rather a lapdog anxious for a kind word, or even some acknowledgement from Kate that he still existed.

At once the head waiter made a great fuss of Kate, and she revelled in his admiration. 'Miss Stokes,' he cried in his fawning French accent. 'You are very beautiful tonight, and we are pleased to welcome you and your farzer in dining wiz us again zis efening. I 'af a splendid table for two all ready for you, if you will follow me.'

'We shall be three,' Kate, the light of the London stage, informed him impatiently, taking on a very superior English accent, which she had been typically quick to learn and to adopt after her early success in London. 'We are expecting Sir Lionel Chesterton to join us very shortly.'

'Ah, Sir Lionel . . .' The head waiter sounded surprised, and bowed deferentially. 'So, you are ze guests of Sir Lionel zis efening. He already reserved a table . . . Please, come zis way . . .'

'Has he arrived yet?' Kate asked.

'Not yet, ma'mselle.'

As he led them away, Kate caught sight of herself in a gilt mirror and loved what she saw. Her eyes gleamed. She was an icon of youthful feminine sophistication. She nodded and smiled imperially to two men she recognised, one with a waxed moustache, one clean-shaven, who were already seated with a pretty girl, painted and overdressed but flaunting an overabundance of alluring cleavage.

They arrived at a table discreetly situated in a velvet-draped and velvet-upholstered alcove, well away from sight and sound of the street.

The head waiter smiled obsequiously. 'What would you like to drink?'

'Champagne,' Kate was quick to reply with a charming smile. She loved the expensiveness of it, especially as she could afford it, but even more especially since Sir Lionel would be paying, and he could afford it even more easily. 'Piper-Heidsieck, if you please.' Piper-hide-seek was thankfully easy to remember, reminding her of her childhood by its reference to the childhood game she used to play. She sat back on her seat in a delicious fever of anticipation . . .

However, amid the hushed conversations and tinkling, chinking restaurant sounds, Murdoch looked around him in a fever of foreboding, fidgeting, tremulous. He had felt this way for some weeks now, ever since Sir Lionel Chesterton had appeared on the scene. Murdoch sensed from the outset that Sir Lionel was trouble, that he was about to lose the love of his life to him. But Murdoch had no defence, no protection from what must surely befall him, sooner if not later.

He had noticed Kate's instinctive reactions to the man with increasing trepidation. Every time Sir Lionel entered a room where she was sitting she would wriggle with anticipation, until he acknowledged her. And when he did so, she would blush deliciously and cast her eyes down virginally. Murdoch saw too that Kate had a similar effect on Sir Lionel. It was obvious that here was a love match in the making.

So Murdoch resigned himself to losing Kate. Naturally, he did not relish the prospect, rather he absolutely dreaded it, since he had renounced all for her. He had been a fool, an utter fool, and he recognised the truth in the old adage that there's no fool like an old fool. Quite possibly, there had never been such a fool as himself in the whole of history.

Within a few days of her arrival in London, Kate had badgered Murdoch to present her to the great and influential impresario he knew, Zadok Lipman. So he dutifully wrote, extolling the virtues of his daughter without exaggerating either her wonderful looks, her fine acting, or her propensity for the stage where, Murdoch assured Zadok, she had a scintillating presence. He enclosed a photograph taken of her, dazzlingly wearing the costume she'd worn in *The Forest Princess*. If Zadok would agree to see Miss Kate Stokes – her stage name – he, Murdoch, would be only too happy to accompany her for an introduction and an audition.

Murdoch received a reply later that week. Zadok Lipman presented his best wishes. He must have been impressed by the photograph and Murdoch's glowing reference, for he said that he would be happy to receive Miss Stokes on Monday of the following week, at ten o'clock in the morning at his office in Leicester Square.

Mr Lipman liked Kate even more when he saw her in the flesh, and recommended her for a part in a burlesque show, *Carmen up to Data*, being staged at the Gaiety Theatre. She shone brightly in one of the minor roles, got to know by heart every other part, every song. She practised those songs in the privacy of their rented apartment till she was perfect. She had a wonderful singing voice, too. It soon became obvious that she had the potential for greater things and, when Miss Florence St John was indisposed, Kate was a brilliant stand-in for the leading role of Carmen. She received ecstatic reviews and several offers of marriage from the young mashers she charmed. When that show closed after two hundred and forty-eight performances, she was chosen to play the lead in another burlesque, *Cinder-Ellen, Up Too Late*, again at the Gaiety. Now, in April 1892, she was already an established young star of the London stage, fulfilling her dream that everybody back home had tried to talk her out of. Well, what did they know?

Her freshness, her looks and her performing ability had also ignited a flame somewhere in Sir Lionel Chesterton, a young baronet who, still unmarried, had recently inherited his father's title and estate near Cromer in Norfolk. He followed Kate Stokes's career with an early avid interest. Whenever he was in London he never failed to see her shows, and was quick to send bouquets of flowers to the stage door and eventually to request a private audience. Kate, after playing hard-to-get for a decorously lengthy period, eventually acceded, and received him in her dressing room one evening after her show in February. He was the very essence of aristocratic charm and politeness, which quite took Kate unawares. But he left without any reference to another meeting, which intrigued her. It never occurred to her that he was also playing hard-to-get. She later saw him a few times at receptions and in this very restaurant, when they would exchange a few polite words and agonised glances. It was at these haphazard meetings that Murdoch feared there might be something untoward afoot. What he did not know was that romance had already blossomed, romance which Kate had managed to conceal from Murdoch at first.

But Murdoch, wily old Murdoch, had got a whiff of what was in the air. Ostensibly, he and Kate were father and daughter. The world did not know how they lived and slept together as lovers in their apartment at Lincoln's Inn Fields. Kate's declining interest in Murdoch only signalled her burgeoning interest elsewhere – in Sir Lionel especially – and he perceived that the end of his own romantic interlude with her was in sight. The prospect made him miserable. He worshipped Kate, idolised her. He had given up everything for her; his home, his wife, his business, his leadership of the Brierley Hill Amateur Dramatics Society – his pride. And for what? To be ditched in favour of some young upstart?

'He's here,' Kate said.

Murdoch was about to light his pipe.

'No, don't set that thing a-going, it'll stink us out,' she said, reverting to the Black Country girl.

A tall, handsome man, wearing tails and a white muffler approached, beaming. He carried his top hat and white gloves in his hand and looked every inch the aristocrat. When he reached the table he bent down to kiss Kate on the cheek and, in so doing, knocked her hat a little askew. He apologised profusely, and she set it right again with a practised hand, and smiled graciously with instant forgiveness. That over, he offered his hand to Murdoch.

Murdoch stood up and they shook. 'Good evening, Sir Lionel.'

'And a very good evening to you, Mr Osborne.'

'Glass of champagne?' Kate enquired.

'Oh, yes, capital.'

'Father will pour it, won't you, Father?'

Murdoch poured carefully, and topped up his own flute. Kate's was still decorously untouched.

'What time does the show start, darling?' Sir Lionel asked.

'Eight-twenty-five.'

He pulled out his watch, glanced at it, and returned it to his waistcoat pocket. 'Seven-fifteen already. Sorry I'm a little late. Have you ordered yet?'

'We wanted to wait for you, Lionel.' It was a voluptuously sweet, seductive voice that spoke.

Sir Lionel smiled in appreciation of it. 'Then let's order. It's on me, of course, since I asked you to meet me here.' He picked up a menu, opened it and glanced down it.

'That's very kind,' said Murdoch.

'Not at all.' He raised a hand to the head waiter who came running. 'I take it we all know what we want?'

They ordered their food and the head waiter moved away content.

'Time is rather short before Kate's show starts,' Sir Lionel began. 'So I'd like to get right to the point . . .' He fixed his eyes on Murdoch as if seeking permission to continue. 'I've asked you to meet me here for one reason. I am here to ask, most humbly, sir, for your permission to marry your daughter.'

Murdoch had expected this request, of course, but still it came like a kick in the stomach, and he winced. He understood, naturally, how Kate might benefit from bettering herself as the bride of a baronet, but it rankled nonetheless. He had hoped that he could have retained her as his exclusive lover, but he knew well enough the fickleness, the emotional ruthlessness of which she was capable, especially when a better offer came along. Murdoch was no match for Sir Lionel, could hardly begin to give her what she needed. Sir Lionel offered wealth, security, youth – above all, youth. As his wife, Kate would gain privilege, esteem, position – and a title. What woman would not yield to all that, especially as Sir Lionel was so obviously a decent and honourable chap? Murdoch might be an old fool, but he was not such a fool that he didn't understand all that.

Despite his years and all his experience with women, Murdoch was no match for Kate, either. He had no protection from her wiles, or from what was about to befall him. London believed she was his devoted daughter, the fruit of his loins, and what caring father could have any feasible reason to deny her marriage to a wealthy baronet, a very personable and proper baronet at that? Such was the exalted fate of many a showgirl, but he had hoped, wished, prayed even, that such a fate might pass Kate by and spare him the agony he must otherwise endure.

'I've got one or two observations to make afore I say yea

or nay,' Murdoch replied, trying to convince himself more than Kate, or the young man sitting opposite, that he wielded the power to stall the liaison. 'I imagine the two of you must've talked about marriage between your two selves already, ha?'

'Of course,' replied Sir Lionel.

'So I'm just a little upset that Kate has made no mention of it, ha, Kate?'

It was a pointed question, and Kate avoided his eyes guiltily, acutely aware of his intense feelings for her. She stared into her glass of untouched champagne, saying nothing, then took a sip to try and hide her reddening face.

'Also, Kate, you know you earn enough money to keep yourself in the lap of luxury if you prefer to remain single. There's no financial reason for you to scoot off with this gentleman and marry him.'

'I know that, Father,' she said quietly.

'Also, young man,' he added, discarding all etiquette of address, 'would it be your intention to allow her to keep on with her work, or would you rob the London stage of one of its brightest stars?'

'If Kate desires to continue working after we are married, then she will be free to do so . . . at least until her wifely duties render it unwise or impossible.'

'You mean if she gets pregnant, ha?'

'You have to admit, Mr Osborne, that such an occurrence is not beyond the realms of possibility once she is married, even for the brightest star of the London stage.' Sir Lionel smiled charmingly.

'I only mention it because she has talent, ha? It would be a sin to waste it.'

'I agree,' said Sir Lionel smoothly, 'which is why I stress that such a decision must be Kate's own. I shall not try to influence her one way or the other.'

'Well, Kate?'

Kate's eyes met Murdoch's at last. 'Yes, I'd like to carry on working . . . for the time being . . . It's what I enjoy. I don't have to give it up just because I get married. Lionel knows that.'

'And you're sure you want to marry him? You're in love with him?'

Such a stupid, stupid question. Kate sighed with exasperation. 'Yes, on both counts. Else we wouldn't be here having this conversation.'

The old fool could not win. The old fool had no protection. The old fool had no valid reason which would satisfy the world as to why he should deny them his blessing.

'It sounds like she's yours, young man. She's of age now anyroad, so she can do as she likes.' He got up from his chair. 'I'll leave the pair of you alone together to celebrate in private. Just how soon is this here marriage going to take place?'

'Next week. By special licence . . . Look, you don't have to go, Mr Osborne. Please.'

'Yes, I do, lad . . . Yes, I do . . .' He glanced desolately at Kate, and picked up his hat. 'I'll see you when you get back home, ha?'

Kate nodded, without looking at him. Of course, she would be in for a verbal lashing, but she would deal with that when it came.

'I'll cancel me dinner on me way out . . .' Murdoch said, as his parting shot.

It was June of the same year. The new Stokes family had had time to settle down to a normal and exceedingly happy life. On Marigold's arrival, Clara had relinquished any sovereignty over the household, of which she had once been queen. She was now entirely dependent on her son, and content to give way to Marigold on matters of looking after Algie, and even on raising Algie's delightful little daughter.

As for Marigold, she had arrived at the house unsure of herself at first. She could not at first believe that she was the wife of Algie Stokes but, as the weeks and months passed, she became aware of her new importance. Nobody in Dudley, where they continued to live, was aware that she had had Algie's child out of wedlock and only later married. Everybody assumed she had married first; thus she was treated with utmost civility and respect from those with whom she came into contact. She brimmed with hope for the future, filled with ideas that could only enhance their lives. She felt she had a real purpose in life, something she could never have imagined living a nomadic life on the canals in a narrowboat. Her daughter was the epicentre of her world, and she idolised the child. Nor was Algie ever far from this epicentre. She made sure his meals were ready on time and sufficient in quantity, that his clothes were clean, that he always made the best of himself, for she was inordinately proud of him and what he had so far achieved. She established a good accord with her mother-in-law, and many tasks they shared; Monday was washing day, and they maided and rinsed and mangled and pegged out together, contentedly sharing jokes. They became close, sharing secrets and exchanging gossip.

Marigold made the best of herself, too. Her weeks living with her Aunt Edith had changed her for the better; Aunt Edith had tutored her, not in the academic sense particularly, but in the ways of the world; what it was acceptable to wear, how to wear it – everyday things that had escaped her on the canals despite her mother's example. Aunt Edith also taught Marigold her letters, for Aunt Edith had enjoyed some schooling, and Marigold's ability to read was thus all the while improving. Her confidence increased accordingly, as did her self-esteem, and her natural loveliness was enhanced because of it. Even now, despite the hard work and relatively new responsibility of running a home, she remained radiant. Algie was inordinately proud of his wife in return.

As to the matter of Aurelia, Algie suspected that the second child she had had in the late summer of the previous year could well be his. He now understood and appreciated even more fully, that if so, the sacrifice she had made in returning to Benjamin just so that Marigold, who was after all her half-sister, could be redeemed and reunited with the man they both loved. Whilst Marigold regularly saw Aurelia – they had established a sisterly loyalty and affection laced with mutual admiration and respect – Algie tended to remain in the background as far as that relationship was concerned. However, he was aware from the gossip that Marigold brought back home, that all was not well between Aurelia and Benjamin, and Algie felt responsible. Benjamin had, apparently, got wind that she'd had an affair and was doubting the parentage of his second child, although he had no idea with whom she had conducted this 'alleged' affair. On the other hand, Benjamin did not have much of a leg to stand on, since their former nanny, Maude, had also had a child which was patently his. Thus they faced each other like two enemies, each with the power to destroy the other. And because each had that power they did nothing, coexisting, just in case the one who began an offensive ultimately lost the battle. Algie was prepared, however, to assist his sister-in-law and erstwhile lover if the need arose, for he felt his responsibility acutely, but never would he allow any assistance to adversely affect his own marriage. His marriage was sacrosanct, his wife and child were absolute priorities.

The only thing that materially blighted their days was the shortage of money. Algie was trying manfully to make a success of his bicycle manufacturing business, and to a large extent he had succeeded beyond his wildest dreams. He had customers galore and it was a struggle to produce his bicycles fast enough to render the exercise profitable. He could sell every bike he made, and more besides, but slow payment and the lack of capital was impeding him. He needed money to invest in more modern equipment; he needed to employ men who were reliable and skilled in what they were doing. And to get the best you had to pay the best wages. There was vast potential to make a fortune but, unless he could raise investment money somehow, he lived in fear and dread that he would have to fold the business and return to working for somebody else. It would be a monstrous pity, but his family came first. They were paramount. They had to be fed and clothed.

Two items of mail had arrived in the post one day. Clara handed them to Algie unopened when he returned from his workshop on a bicycle of his own manufacture.

'One's addressed to you, Mother. *Mrs Clara Osborne.* It looks very official . . .'

'Read it to me, our Algie.'

He opened the envelope and unfolded the letter with due ceremony.

'It's from somebody called Stothert, French and Stothert, Solicitors and Commissioners for Oaths,' he said, reading the heading on the notepaper and raising his eyebrows with instant curiosity. 'It says, "*Dear Mrs Osborne, It is with deep regret that I am obliged to notify you of the death by suicide of your estranged husband, Mr Murdoch Jeroboam Osborne, on the 14th of May 1892. I apologise for the delay in advising you of these very unfortunate tidings, but our efforts to trace you only bore fruit when we lodged enquiries with the Parish Church of St Michael in Brierley Hill which, we understand from your esteemed daughter, Lady Chesterton, is the parish in which you dwelt until recently. The fact that your son was recently married there afforded us the connection which enabled us to trace you.*

'*Your late husband made his last will and testament in May of this year just prior to his death, which document was deposited with us for safe keeping. It nominates yourself as the sole beneficiary to his entire estate. In order that we can complete our legal administration and assess the total value of the said estate please forward any documents which you feel are relevant to our enquiries, such as bank books, deeds of the properties he owned in the parishes of Kingswinford and Brierley Hill, any share certificates, et cetera. Your marriage certificate is also required to confirm your marital status. Once I have received these documents I shall be in touch with you again shortly thereafter. I remain,*' blah, blah, blah . . .'

'Murdoch's dead,' Clara said, quietly astonished at the news. 'The poor devil killed himself. I wonder why he did that. I wonder who told them he had a wife.'

'Kate, I imagine,' Algie responded pensively, folding the letter up. 'Her conscience getting the better of her for once in her life. It sounds as if she's done well for herself – Lady Chesterton, by God. I pity Sir Chesterton, though, whoever he is, the poor devil.' There was no doubt in Algie's mind that Kate had done all right for herself, that she would have latched on to somebody daft enough to be beguiled by her big brown eyes and exquisite looks . . . 'I never told you, Mother, but I saw her name in the *News of the World* a month or two back. It was an advertisement. She was the star of some burlesque show at a theatre in London – her name was in big letters. She's done well for herself all right.'

'At Murdoch's expense, by the sounds of it.'

'He knew what he was taking on, Mother,' Algie said without sympathy for the man. 'It's my guess that he bit off more than he could chew with our Kate. I bet she led him a merry dance.'

Marigold looked from one to the other apprehensively, while Rose sat on her lap gurgling with contentment. This was obviously significant news. 'I wonder why he killed himself,' she said.

'Because he'd ruined his life and any chance of happiness by running off with our Kate,' replied Algie, correctly divining the situation. 'I imagine he couldn't face the shame of coming back here once she'd found and married somebody else. In any case, it's my guess he got so engrossed in Kate that his heart was broken . . .' A broken heart was something with which Algie had had some experience, and therefore some sympathy. But feelings of sympathy for Murdoch did not dwell long in him, for the silly old fool knew what he was doing when he plunged headlong into his highly illicit affair with Kate, devastating everybody's lives. 'I reckon this is his comeuppance, Mother. You can't say he didn't deserve it.'

Clara shrugged and sighed, a look of sadness clouding her face. She would not have put it as strongly as Algie had done. She had married the man, she once had feelings for him, she'd lain with him. Suicide was the way of desperate men. She hated to think of him being in such straits. It was also obvious that he had not forgotten her. He must have been planning his own death to have made a will in her favour just days prior to killing himself. For that reason she could not condemn him. In any case, she hated to think of him suffering to such an extent that he was driven to it.

'D'you reckon he was worth much?' Marigold asked.

Algie shrugged. 'It depends how much he owes, and how much he squandered when he and our Kate ran off together.'

'I wonder how our Kate is,' Clara mused. 'I wonder if she's content now she's evidently married so well. I often think about her, despite what she did.'

'Oh, I daresay she's got quite a story to tell, Mother. But

never mind her. Just think . . . you might be rich. Murdoch can't be short of a shilling or two. That house of his in Kingswinford must be worth something. You could sell it. Better still, rent it, and get some income from it.'

'I want none of his money, our Algie,' Clara declared resolutely. 'However much, or however little he leaves, his daughters should have it. None of them have ever had any life with him, no love, no attention. I think they deserve it between them . . . All three of them.'

The 'three of them', of course, included Marigold.

'That's a noble gesture,' Algie remarked, putting the folded letter carefully back in its envelope. 'And I can understand how you feel. But I reckon you deserve a share as well, the trouble he brought you. None of his daughters would begrudge you a quarter share, if you really want to share it out. Would they, Marigold?'

'No, not a bit,' Marigold agreed. 'I daresay Aurelia could do with a bit of extra money to fall back on, what with her new baby and everything, and the way Benjamin's behaving . . . And heaven knows we could use the money in the business, couldn't we, Algie?'

He smiled lovingly at her. 'That, we could, my flower. We need to build a secure future for our little Rosie, eh? . . . And for any others that might come along after her,' he added as an afterthought.

'But none of us would begrudge you any of it, Clara,' Marigold added. 'Anyway, Algie, what about that other envelope?' she asked, nodding in the direction of where he'd left it lying on the table, evidently forgotten in the agitation caused by the first letter. 'Aren't you going to open it? It's addressed to you.'

'So you were able to read the address?' he said, delighted that his wife had made such remarkable progress in her reading.

'Yes, I could read it,' she replied with a proud smile.

'Then why don't you open it, and read it out to us? Let me have Rosie while you do.'

He took his daughter in his arms and murmured baby talk while Marigold opened the envelope. She looked at it, studying it with an intense expression, while Algie and Clara watched her expectantly.

'It's a wedding invitation,' she said at last. 'It says, *"Mr and Mrs Eli Meese request the pleasure of the company of Mr and Mrs Algernon Stokes and Rose, and Mrs Clara Osborne, at the wedding of their daughter, Harriet, to Mr Clarence Froggatt on Sunday 4th September at 2.00 p.m. at St Michael's Church, Brierley Hill"*.' She looked up with a broad smile, proud of her reading, but also delighted by the news.

'Well, I'm blowed,' said Algie. 'Yet I can't say I'm surprised. But I don't remember hearing that they'd got engaged.'

'Getting engaged don't mean much, Algie,' Marigold said. 'We never got engaged. Anyway, are you pleased for her?'

'I'm pleased as Punch. I had the feeling it was on the cards from the outset.'

Marigold looked at the invitation again. 'What does *RSVP* mean, Algie? It says that here.'

'It means you have to reply to let them know whether we shall go or not.'

'We shall, shan't we?'

He grinned. 'Course we shall. You and Mother will have to have a new outfit each as well. And Rose. I won't have you seen in anything inferior to theirs.'

Marigold smiled happily.

Author's Note

The Bottle and Glass public house featured in this story was built around 1780. In 1976 it was carefully dismantled, each brick and timber numbered, and was transported from its original location in Moor Lane, Buckpool in Brierley Hill, to be reconstructed at the Black Country Living Museum in Dudley. It now operates there as it always has done, as a focal point for companionship and refreshment. The museum setting is 1910, and the Bottle and Glass is virtually unchanged from the 1890s, in which this novel is set. I acknowledge the assistance given to me in my researches there by Deborah Boddison, the publican of the Bottle and Glass at the BCLM.

In my efforts to make my novels as historically accurate as possible, I discovered that there was an incident at 10.10 p.m. on the night of Saturday the 1st of November 1890 in Brierley Hill's High Street, involving a steam tram, when the car decided to take a different line to that of its engine. The incident was reported in the *Brierley Hill Advertiser* dated the 8th of November. It fitted perfectly in time and place with the story.

The winter of 1890/91 was also the worst in contemporary living memory and I have not exaggerated its harshness nor its effects for the sake of the story.

Whisked from the industrial Black Country to the dazzling clubs of New York City . . . 1936 will be Maxine Kite's year!

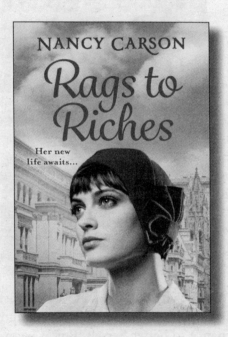

But a girl's good name can be all she has in the world . . . and once lost, is almost impossible to reclaim . . .

Rescued from destitution and poverty . . . but at what price?

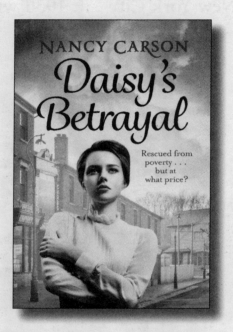

When charming Lawson Maddox asks Daisy Drake to become his wife, she jumps at the chance to better herself. But as soon as the honeymoon's over he shows his true colours, and Daisy's life descends into chaos.